SECRETS OF A GOOL

Katie Jane Newman

Dedicated to dreamers everywhere

Dream: Noun
Aspiration; goal; aim

Copyright © Katie Jane Newman 2014

JUNE

FRIDAY

The whirring of the sewing machine is strangely hypnotic this evening. Yards and yards of red fabric flow through the machine and fall silkily onto the floor as I follow the line of the white chalk. On the easel in front of me is the my design, a short, fitted cocktail dress that I have spent the last month perfecting and tonight, finally, making. In the background the sounds of the eighties fill the silence between bouts of stitching and I pause to drink the now warm white wine in the glass beside me.

Evenings like this are at the top of the list of my favourite things to do. It's so rare that I get to indulge in my love of dressmaking that I grasp every moment as it comes my way. William is working late again and with no commitments of my own this evening I revel in the luxury of time alone.

Tying my hair up tightly again I return to the final seam of the dress and watch the needle bobbing up and down. When the needle completes its task, I tie off the thread and with flourish I scoop the dress up and dance it around the kitchen, hips swaying in time to the music, before crashing painfully into William who chooses that moment to come home.

"Hi!" I wince rubbing my shin. "Look…all finished."

"Nice." William replies giving me a perfunctory kiss on the cheek. I reach my arms around his neck, pulling him to me but he feels rigid against me and the strange smell of shower gel and sweet perfume stings my nose. He sighs and puts his arms about me, briefly and without affection, before dropping them and moving from me to get a bottle of lager from the fridge.

"Have you been to the gym?" I ask moving up behind him to refill my wine glass from the opened bottle in the fridge. The bottle drips condensation onto the floor that I rub with my toe to remove.

"No why?" Is it my imagination or is William looking shifty?

"You smell of shower gel."

"Oh." He pauses. "I went at lunchtime." I suspect William's gym attempt is half hearted given that he looks pudgier these days and his once boyishly handsome face seems rounder.

"I am going to have a bath," I twinkle at him, "fancy joining me?"

"I've showered." He opens the lager, leaving the lid on the work top. Automatically I pick it up and put it in the bin. William looks at me strangely as though he has something to say.

"You don't have to join me to get clean..." I giggle trailing my fingertips up his arm, "you could just get dirty."

"I'm tired Freya."

"You're always tired," I grumble.

William shrugs and leaves the room. I hear the sofa creak under his weight as he sits down and momentarily I feel rejected and almost invisible. I can't shake the little voice that whispers the very things I just don't want to hear. I leave the kitchen and pass William, sprawled on the couch leaving no space for me, and go into the bathroom to run myself a deep, hot, bubble bath.

The water is soothing, calming and I close my eyes allowing the scent of the bubble and the music, coming through the ceiling speakers, to float over me. William must just be stressed, I tell myself, excusing his distance from me these past few months. He has been promoted to partner at the law firm where he works in Canary Wharf and with the responsibility so has come the longer hours. I am proud of him, deeply proud, but wish it didn't spill so much into our private life. I can't remember how long it's been since we made love and I miss him physically. The days of William slamming the front door in his haste to get to me have gone and recently, it seems, so has his sex drive.

I hear William's mobile ring and strain to listen to the conversation but he speaks with muted tones.

"Who was that?" I call when the conversation has ended.

"Work." He calls back.

"Will?"

"Yes?"

"Come and wash my back." I giggle to myself as I position myself seductively in the bath, the bubbles floating around my body.

The door opens. "I need to go back to the office," he says. "A report wasn't filed."

"Can't it wait?"

"No, it needs to be in New York."

"New York? Since when do you deal with New York?"

"Since recently."

"It's nine thirty at night!"

"I'll try not to be long."

"Will?"

"What?"

"Is everything alright?"

He shrugs again and leaves the room.

***

I can't shake the feeling that something is very badly wrong and when William eventually gets home, he smells of beer and that strange perfume again. He doesn't even meet my eye as I uncurl, yawning, from the sofa to greet him.

"Have you been for a drink?" I ask squinting at the clock on the mantelpiece.

"Only for one." His reply is short, dismissive. It unnerves me, bringing an almost painful squirming in my belly. I lick my lips, suddenly dry, with an equally dry tongue that seems to have swelled to twice its normal size in my mouth.

"Is something going on Will?" I ask pulling my fleece tightly around me.

A look so raw, so broken flits across his face and it's an age before he speaks in a tone that sends shards of ice through my soul.

"Freya, I'm leaving." He doesn't look at me.

"You're what?" I whisper too shocked to move, too shocked to breath. "What?" I shake my head from side to side as though trying to clear my ears. A sudden trembling in my hands distracts me from his words momentarily but I am aware of an acute pain as my insides begin to shatter.

"Leaving."

"Why?" My blood thumps in my ears, painful and deafening, a fast drum beat that brings with it a shock so agonising that I feel my legs give way beneath me. I sit down on the sofa, noticing for the first time that the padding has flattened in places. *We need to replace the sofa.*

"I just don't feel the same way about you anymore Freya, I never thought I would be saying this to you … I am so sorry, so sorry." William stammers his voice cracking.

"Sorry?" I repeat in desolate tones. "Sorry. How can you say sorry for this? Sorry is for forgetting to pick up the dry cleaning or for inviting your parents over last minute. Sorry is not for when you tell me you're leaving me!" The silence hangs heavy in the air until an emotion so dark rises through me and I begin to screech. "Who is she William? Who the fuck are you leaving me for?" The rage is so black that I want to kill him, to rip his limbs off one by one and then shove his heart down his throat.

"I'm not leaving you for anyone." I don't believe him. William gets a twitch in his eye when he lies and it's on full power.

"Liar!" I yell throwing a magazine at him. The magazine travels in slow motion until it hits him on the head and he grimaces in pain. I look around for something else to throw and leap off the sofa to grab the nearest thing - a pot plant.

"Stop Freya you are acting insane." William holds his arms up to his head as he moves across the room away from me.

"Insane? Can you blame me?" I throw the plant across the room where it shatters against the wall. "WHO IS SHE?" I shriek. "And don't tell me there isn't anyone William, don't you lie to me."

"There isn't anyone else. I just don't want this. We aren't the same couple we were, too much has changed. It's not working for me anymore and I can't live a lie. I am so, so sorry Freya."

"A lie?" I can't breathe. My hands instinctively go to my stomach holding tight, keeping me together. "How long have you been living a lie?" I crumple at the weight of his words a chill spreading out from my stomach until every organ, every nerve, and every fibre is frozen in time.

"Too long. I didn't want to hurt you." William kneels in front of me, taking my hands in his. His hands burn against my ice cold fingers and it hurts, really hurts. I want to pull my hands from his but I can't make myself move. "I never wanted to hurt you Freya, not after all these years and everything we've been through. I truly did think that we'd be forever but as time ticked by it all stopped feeling right. You must have noticed." He moves a lock of hair from my face and tucks it behind my ears but I hardly notice the action.

"A lie." I repeat desolately. "After all this time? After everything we've been through? I gave up my dreams for you. I booked a holiday." I mumble staring unseeingly at the wedding photo on the mantle. "I booked a holiday to fix it, sort it, to save it. I knew things weren't going very well but I never imagined you'd leave me…" I can't go on. A sob, a raw, animal sound escapes me and I wrap my arms around myself to prevent my chest breaking open. "Why are you leaving me?" The tears fight each other to roll in a torrent down my face where they pool in my collar bone. William reaches for a tissue and wipes my face. "Who are you leaving me for? I know you! You'd never just walk away like this. Just have the decency to tell me the truth." I beg.

"There isn't anyone else, it's just over for me." He walks away from me and into our bedroom. Numbly I follow concentrating on putting one foot in front of the other, feeling so dizzy I don't know if I am remembering to breathe.

"What did I do?"

"Nothing Freya, you didn't do anything, this is all down to me."

"Where are you going to?"

"My parents for tonight."

"Then?"

He doesn't answer me.

"Don't you think we should talk? Don't you think we're worth saving? I do. We should talk." Any minute now I am going to wake from a bad dream.

"There isn't anything to say Freya, I've made my decision." William's voice cracks.

"William, you can't leave me. You can't. We had plans…we had a future." I clasp his hand tightly in mine. "It's always been you and me. We can make it better…"

"I'm sorry Freya," he whispers wrenching his hand from mine. "I'm sorry I don't want to make it better I just want to go…"

"You want to go?" I repeat in disbelief sitting heavily on the bed. "What happened to forever?" The tears begin to roll down my face again and I bury my head in my hands. "What happened to I will love you forever?"

"Forever? Not everything lasts forever Freya and I should never have promised it would." He kneels in front of me and brushes my hair from my face. "I will always love you and I will always be sorry that it didn't work out. Always."

William kisses me on the cheek and picks up a bag I didn't even see him pack. "I'll be back for the rest of my things soon." He turns to go. "I am really sorry Freya I never meant to hurt you it was never part of the plan."

"Your leaving me was never part of the plan." I can't control the shaking in my voice and as I watch him go the sobs begin to choke me.

JULY

THURSDAY

"Still moping?" Henry breezes into my office in a haze of aftershave and hairspray.

"No!" I retort coughing and rapidly waving my hand in front of my face. "Did you bath in cologne today?"

Henry gives me a sharp look. "Sweetie, I know you are moping and do you know how I know?" He perches on the edge of my desk and picks up the photo of William and me.

"How?" I ask leaning back in my chair.

"Firstly, you have no makeup on and your hair is a mess, secondly you still have a photo of the rat on your desk and thirdly, which is the most important, you haven't left to get ready for the Graduates of London Fashion Event and you absolutely have to go."

"Why do I have to go? I don't want to go!"

"You don't want…" Henry fans his face. "Of course you want to go! It's *the* fashion event of the year! Everyone who is anyone will be there and most importantly of all the Good Time Boys are going to be entertaining you all and I very much want Fred Lynch to entertain me!"

I roll my eyes. "Henry…"

"Don't roll your eyes at me and don't 'Henry' me! You know how I feel about him, he is a God amongst men and here is where you come in, I have it all planned." Henry looks at me with his eyebrow raises as though daring me to comment. I hold up my hands and wait. "Fred Lynch looks incredible, which even you have to admit, he has the perfect model look and he would look divine in a moody, designer jeans bare torso advert. " Henry fans his face and I shake my head at him. "I digress…Fred's look, the James Dean angst model look makes it well within your remit to invite him here to do a modelling shoot, I can be the photographer, our eyes meet and we live happily ever after. You cannot let me down on this otherwise I will just have to banish you to social leper hell." Henry pouts.

"I am a social leper and how do you even know he's gay?"

"Oh please, there is no way an Adonis like that is straight. Now go. Please. Please. Please!"

I laugh. "Ok, Henry, I will go for you as long as you organise for Kirsty to come and make me look amazing."

"You always look amazing!" Henry files his nails while looking at me critically. "Well maybe not today! What is going on with your hair?"

"I look like a woman dumped." I smile wryly, "I am a woman dumped!"

"Well Kirsty will make you look like a glorious ripe goddess. I'll go speak to her now."

"Wouldn't it have been easier to get an invite yourself?"

"Sweetie do you think I've not tried? No one wants the photographer they want the award winning fashionista that is you."

I groan. "I did ask Carrie to send someone else. It will be full of Z List celebrities I've never heard of…"

"Carrie knows full well if anyone else went there would be no article."

"And she really thinks she'll get one from me? Everything I've written recently has been shit."

"It doesn't matter! All that matters to Carrie is that you don't get swept away by the celebrity razzmatazz like the rest of us…"

"Yes I do…"

"No you don't! You don't ever know who anyone is and before you say anything designers and models don't count. Sweetie, light of my life, you need to go out and have some fun, drink some fizz and let your hair down, get laid, you're dying here, go out, be you, be fabulous and get me a date!"

I sink my head into my hands.

"If you loved me you'd be enthusiastic." Henry huffs pouting.

I click open my email. "It's because I love you that I am going to go! Now buzz off so I can get some work done."

Henry hops off my desk, loudly kisses my cheek and sashays to the door. "You're the best friend Freya. Now smile, you can mope tomorrow."

"I'm done with moping!"

"Thank God." Henry disappears out of the door.

I grin to myself.

***

"So do you look spectacularly glamorous?" Imogen asks down the phone line.

I peer critically in the mirror. Kirsty, the magazine makeup artist, has just left on a sea of the champagne that she stole from the boardroom fridge that we shared during the two hour makeover and despite the fizz she has performed miracles.

"The girl is a genius," I reply. "I am also feeling slightly under the influence of bubbles so I may not look as good as I think I do!"

Imogen laughs. "I bet you look a million dollars."

The face that looks back at me has glowing porcelain skin, bright eyes and the redness of my hair has been set off by bright red lips and dramatic dark eyes. "I look better than I have done recently!" I giggle. "I feel ready to face the world."

"Excellent news! I will buy Henry a Malibu for making you go. Are you doing ok today?"

"Don't say a word to Henry but I am really looking forward to this evening. I didn't want to go and if Henry hadn't come in my office when he did I would have cancelled..."

"Really? You would have really cancelled the biggest event this year?"

"It's not the biggest, not far off, but yes I would have. I was overcome by fear this morning, I've not been out since William left and I guess he took all my confidence with him. Although," I say putting on a final slick of lipstick, "I have to admit that Kirsty has done an amazing job..."

"Have you seen him?"

"Nope, not a peep. It's almost like he never existed, except in a really bad dream. If he hadn't left most of his things here you'd think there'd never been a William."

"It's a shame there is!"

"Imogen!"

"Have you seen Lexi?"

"No! Apart from when she came around with you and Erin, after Will left, and that one other time I told you about, it seems she's always manically busy. I can just about reach her by phone and even then, she's quick to get the conversation over. I guess her work load is insane."

There is a beep beep from outside. "My taxi is here, I must go. Let's meet next week?"

"Yes definitely, have a lovely evening and if there is any gossip ring immediately!"

"What kind of gossip are you expecting?"

"Oh, I don't know, something along the lines of you meeting the man of your dreams!" Imogen chuckles, "and his best friend will just happen to be the man of mine!"

"That's highly unlikely! I work in fashion, all the men are gay!"

"There is always the exception to the rule!"

"My heart is broken, I'm not ready to give it away again!" I say sadly.

Imogen says something that I can barely hear. "I didn't hear you." I tell her.

"I said, and don't hate me for saying it," she says hesitantly. "I think you'll find your heart was never made for Will."

There is a long pause.

The taxi beeps again. "I must go Im, I'll see you in the week."

"Love you." Imogen says, "have a lovely time."

"Love you." I reply hanging up the phone.

I have one final twirl in the mirror, the radiant face looking back at me gives me hope. Hope that I am now on my way out of the big black hole William left me in and hope that life will show me the way forward. Imogen's comment repeats in my head *I think you'll find your heart was never made for Will* but after a fifteen year relationship who else would own it? Can I let go of the hope that this is a temporary separation or do I just take a deep breath and let go of the past?

I watch the boroughs from the taxi window for once paying attention to the architecture of the London landscape. The golden sunlight captures the ever-changing stone work and for the first time since William left I feel a flicker of vivacity.

Tonight's event is huge. All of the top international fashion houses, journalists and celebrities converge as the most talented of the fashion graduates showcase their designs hoping for an internship with a leading designer and for a moment I have an intense feeling of jealousy. Once upon a time it could have been me.

I select a number on my mobile and press 'call'

"Hello."

"Hi Lexi it's me."

"Freya!"

"Long time, no speak! Are you ok?"

"Yes yes fine thank you. I'm really sorry Freya this is a bad time. Can I call you back later?" The normally impeccable Alexa sounds flustered.

"I'm on my way to the London Graduate event, I'll ring you tomorrow."

"Uh, ok, bye Freya." Before I can reply the line goes dead. I sigh and put my phone away.

Eventually the taxi arrives in Mayfair and slowly rolls to a stop outside the St Fredericks's Club bringing a fresh set of nerves. Normally my work takes me out to events two or three times a week, there are always drinks with the girls and dinner with Will. Over the past month I have declined everything and it has just added to my melancholy. To be here, at one of the biggest fashion events in London is a good thing I surmise and I take a deep breath to calm my racing heart. The taxi door is opened by a suited security man to whom I show my invitation and he stands back for me to exit the car. The noise outside is at fever pitch with the shouts and hollers of overexcited teenage girls that are restrained behind barriers hoping to catch a glimpse of their idols.

"Good evening Miss," the security guard says smiling.

"Good evening," I reply grinning. "You have quite a crowd here!"

"Some of them have been here for two days."

"Two days? That's dedication!"

He laughs. "I'm glad they're not my kids!"

I give the teenagers a quick glance, flash backs to chasing Take That around the country hit my mind and I grin as I walk into the venue. It's beautifully decorated in cream and gold with polished wooden floors and the light scent of citrus filters through the air. Everywhere I look glamorous people jostle for space. The atmosphere is charged and the hairs on my neck prickle. I accept a glass of champagne and a canapé from a waiter and move further into the crowd.

"Freya darling," I hear the throaty voice of Darcy Danes the Editor of Teen Times behind me so turn to greet her.

"Hello Darcy." I smile as she gives me two loud air kisses.

"Darling you look radiant. I was expecting a total mess. What a fucker about your husband, still plenty more fish in the sea and there are lots of glorious young things here this evening you'll be snapped up in a nano second."

"I don't think I want to be snapped up just yet Darcy." I laugh nervously.

"Freya, gorgeous Freya, of course you do. You just need to see the goodies in here. Go and fish. We must do lunch it's been too long. Ciao darling." Darcy blows me a kiss and swivels on her heels to greet her assistant editor. I grin to myself. If I had a pound every time Darcy suggested lunch I'd be a multi-millionaire. Darcy exists on coffee and cigarettes, maintaining a size zero by avoiding anything that resembles food. She looks like a bird, beaky and sharp eyed, is fabulous at her job and can recognise new talent in her sleep. I admire her and when I was starting out she was my editor and a wonderful mentor. I watch her work the room marvelling at her ability to make everyone feel as though they are the centre of the universe.

"Hello Freya," a twenty year old dazzling blonde says in greeting.

"Hello Lacey, how are you?" I turn and give her a warm kiss on the cheek. Lacey Lucas hit the dizzy heights of supermodel status aged fifteen but within three years became so disillusioned with the industry that she turned her hand to designing and has excelled at it. Her debut collection sold out within minutes of hitting the London stores and critics have hailed her a genius.

"Very well thank you Freya. I'm looking forward to seeing you next week."

"Likewise Lacey. Who are you here with?"

"Just some friends. I love evenings like this, don't you?"

"Yes I do, very much." I smile at her.

"Are you sure you're ok Freya?" Lacey looks at me with ill-disguised concern and I realise with a sinking heart that I've been the subject of gossip across London.

"Yes absolutely fine. Don't worry!" I give her hand a squeeze and move in to say in a conspiratorial whisper. "Don't tell anyone but I'm more excited about the Good Time Boys than the collections!"

"Freya you are too cool." She smiles.

I laugh. "Thanks Lacey. Come and find me for a drink later!"

"Absolutely!" Gracefully Lacey walks away from me to a group of people stood by the stairs. Her companions are all in their twenties, impossibly beautiful and self-assured. I recognise the women, all models that I have done various shoots with, who wave and smile across to me. I wave back and nod to the males within the group who stand flexing their muscles, brimming with testosterone, like peacocks with their plumes on show.

The group appears to be centred round one man who seems unaware of the flirtatious actions of the girls. He laughs at something someone says and looking up he catches my eye. His eyes are the coolest mixture of blue and green and bore into mine with the arrogance of a spectacular looking twenty-something. I want to tear my eyes away from his but he has caught me like a rabbit in headlights. A smile forms on his full, sensual mouth and he raises his glass in a 'cheers' gesture. From nowhere a thunderbolt hits me, an unexpected and powerful jolt of electricity that flickers across my skin and sends my heart racing uncontrollably. For a moment it's just him and I in the room, two figures bathed in a heavenly light with sparks that crackle between us.

Two waiters momentarily distract me and I pull my gaze away. I hold my glass out for one to fill up my champagne and from the other I take a chocolate dipped strawberry. I take a bite, sucking on the ripe strawberry to prevent the juices running down my chin, and, although I tell myself not to, I am unable to refrain from looking back over at him. He cocks his head to the side eyebrows raised as deliberately, with my eyes focused on his, I slowly lick the berry juice from my lips, my tongue following the line of my mouth. It's been a long time since I flirted with anyone but there is something about him that makes me forget my usual caution. His aura is arrogant, controlled, sexy and dangerous, I can feel it radiating across the room. He is obviously a player used to his own way and I need to walk away from his gaze now. I am too fragile for someone like him.

Except I can't stop looking.

The girls appear to vie for his attention flirting, giggling and pouting to which he appears to take no notice. He leans casually against the sweeping staircase in the centre of the hallway and makes conversation with his party without taking his eyes from mine. He appraises me, his eyes scanning every inch of me and I feel my body respond to his composed regard. I suddenly become very aware of myself and the soft gentle throbbing that begins to beat deep within me. I break eye contact and hurry away to the ladies room to compose myself.

I feel self-conscious walking across the hallway, my back to him. I can't remember how I usually walk or hold myself...but I hope I look normal. I don't feel normal. I can't quite put my finger on what it is about that man that has affected me so much. It's not just his looks or his poise or the way he acts so causally separate from all around him - there is more, its charisma and sexual energy along with the arrogant air of self-importance that is like a giant magnet to everyone around him.

I look at my reflection in the mirror with critical eyes. I look fevered – gone is the broken person that William left behind. Instead there is a glowing woman with a spark in her eye and a flush on her cheeks ready to embrace whatever life throws at her so it's a crushing disappointment that I return to an empty hallway. One of the waiters directs me into the banqueting room and I take my seat in the dim light. I try to refrain from looking out for him but I can't help but wonder where he is.

The expansive banqueting room has been laid out with row upon row of circular tables each with ten places laid with cream napkins and gold cutlery. Candles burn in the polished golden holders and the shiny wine buckets hold bottles of champagne.

At the front is a stage spanning the width of the room upon which are propped guitars against microphone stands, drum and percussion kits and a piano. Beautiful clothes modelled by beautiful people and the album launch of one of the world's biggest boy bands, how does it get much better?

The stage lights up and the graduates show begins. All around me flashing lights from cameras aluminate the room and my fellow journalists and I scribble notes, names and take endless pictures. There is some real talent here and for a moment the man from the hallway is forgotten. The hour speeds by and at the end the graduates take their place for the final bow.

"What did you think to that?" Darcy asks in her scratchy voice taking the vacant chair beside me.

"I saw some real talent there."

"We'll see you up there next year. Now that little shit isn't putting you down…"

"Darcy…!"

"You shouldn't be writing about fashion Freya, you are fashion. What you design is beyond what some of the leading houses come up with. Find your confidence dear girl. Consider this your time, now that frightful little arse is no longer dismissing everything you can take a chance. Think about it." In a blink of an eye Darcy moves away to her own seat. I sigh and fill up my champagne. *Think about it.*

I can't think about anything because I can't stop wondering where he is, his face keeps coming to the front of my mind and distracting me from my work. Who is he? I try to focus my mind, concentrate on making sense of my notes but his cool allure, the intense beauty and the casual aloofness of someone who knows he looks good dominates. Where is he? *Stop it Freya*, I tell myself, which works until he walks past me with the slow prowling movements of a cheetah with its prey in sight. I don't look up but I feel his eyes on me and I stop breathing, the hairs on my arm raising and the thumping of the carnal drum loud in my ears. Trembling I pour more champagne and will him to keep walking past.

"Enjoying yourself?" Asks the middle aged man who has appeared in the seat to my right.

"Oh yes I am thank you," I reply, slightly too enthusiastically.

"I can tell." He gives me a wink that is a little unsettling and I look to escape just as the waiters bring round the starter thus trapping me in my seat for three courses. Julian, an overweight, fusty smelling record company executive from LA, is the most boring man the gods could have sat me next to and the more he talks, the more I drink until I am close to becoming a dribbling mess. He has a one sided conversation, obviously loving the sound of his own voice and, thinking himself a comic, has me reaching endlessly for the bottles of champagne. Occasionally his pudgy hand strokes my thigh which sends shivers of revolt through me. He leans closer and I get the whiff of sweat, coffee and cigarettes mixed with a strong aftershave - a stomach churning mix.

I try to speak to the others on the table but find that Julian dominates all the conversations. One by one my fellow diners turn back to their partners until the compere takes to the microphone.

"Ladies and gentlemen," the compere announces and I breathe a sigh of relief. "I hope you have your dancing shoes on…because with no further delay…it is time" he pauses then roars, "it is time for the Good Time Boys." The room erupts as the band come on stage. Four handsome, talented, world famous young men set the room alight. Their new material is nothing short of outstanding and I can quite understand why Henry feels the way he does about Fred, the bass player who has so much stage presence the others pale beside him. I dance along with the other guests to song after song until the final song, a slow number, telling the tale of heartbreak and sadness. The soft vocals of the lead singer, Seamus, the single spotlight, the gentle guitar has the room entranced, and the story, so desperate, could have been written for me.

"Just believe, just believe…" Seamus sings. "Just believe that true love will find its way to you."

"Nice song." A lilting Irish accent says quietly in my ear.

"Yes it is," I reply. I am aware of a golden light flickering out of the corner of my eye and it fills me with the confidence to turn round and face him. His intense looks are breath-taking up close. The slight imperfections in his face add character and his blue/green eyes, old in such a young face, are glittering.

"Your dinner partner is on his way over!" There is humour in his tone but his eyes flash.

"Oh crap, really?" I duck down in front of him, my five feet five height easily blocked by his six feet. "Can you see him?" He wraps his arms around me and swivels. I can see Julian through the gap in between the man's arm and his torso looking about and then lumbering off towards the bar. "Thank god!"

"I presume he didn't excite you then?" He laughs, letting me go.

"No. Far from it!"

"You should have been seated next to me."

"Should I?"

"Yes."

"And why is that?"

He moves in close enough for me to feel his warm breath on my cheek. "Because I would have excited you" and without warning he lightly drops a kiss on my neck. I reach out to steady myself, gripping the muscles in his arms as my body reacts to his words. I am aware of a heat rising, reddening my skin and my hands trembling as I hold tight. His smile is in the air and I long to tell him that he in no way excites me but my treacherous body has given me away.

I take a deep breath and let go of him, speaking as calmly as possible. "Would you?"

He smiles a satisfied smile. "I think you know I would."

"You're very sure of yourself aren't you?" I reply with a coolness I don't feel.

"Yes." He trails a finger down my forearm and smirks as goose bumps appear. I am shocked at the effect he has on me. "But you know I am right."

"Do I?" I breathe. He is right, I do want him, this too beautiful, too cocky, too arrogant man with the angelic face and the body of a god. I should say no, I should remember who I am, how I behave and what has recently happened instead I say. "So what are you going to do about it?"

"I'll show you." He guides me from the dance floor, his hand on the small of my back. I stop at the table to collect my bag and allow myself to be led from the room.

"Oh shit!" I suddenly remember my promise to Henry. "I have something I need to do."

"Can't it wait?"

"No, it can't." I bite my lip to prevent myself from screaming and cursing Henry.

"I am leaving now. I am staying at The Stark Hotel in suite four. I'll see you there." He leans in closer and I stop breathing. He whispers, "don't keep me waiting."

I watch him walk away. Without the closeness of him the conflict in me rages. There is a longing so powerful that it takes my breath away, a longing for him, for the nameless man who has made me come alive with one brief exchange, then there is the Freya who follows the rules, never steps out of line and may still want her marriage to work. With a big sigh I seek out the band's manager who agrees to contact me regarding an article for our publication. The band, euphoric after an exceptional night are enthusiastic about my invitation. I take a picture of Fred on my phone and send it to Henry with a 'thumbs up' icon and walk out of the room towards the unknown.

The doorman hails me a taxi.

"Where to Miss?"

Where to indeed? Home?

"The Stark Hotel please." I hear a voice that sounds like mine give the opposite instructions to the one it should be giving. I should be going home but instead I tingle from head to toe with anticipation and the delicate heartbeat in my centre increases its pulse.

I sink into the seat and wonder what I have just let myself in for.

***

The bell boy escorts me to the penthouse suite. "Have you had an enjoyable evening madam?" He makes polite small talk as the lift takes its time rising up the towering hotel.

"Pardon?" I am only vaguely aware of him. I know I should just turn around and go home, have a smattering of self-preservation but I feel as though the decision was made long before this night even happened.

"Have you had an enjoyable evening?" He repeats.

"Yes thank you." My voice sounds different, higher pitched, quieter.

He smiles, understanding that conversation is pointless. He must see hundreds of women like me. Faceless, nameless women, in and out, only to be forgotten when the sun comes up.

I thank him as the lift doors open and with as much confidence as I can muster find the suite and knock on the door. He takes an age to answer and briefly I wonder if he leaves me there on purpose. I hear the lock turn and he opens the door bare chested only wearing a pair of jogging bottoms that hang low showing off his muscular chest and the delicious v of his abs.

He was expecting me. He is not the sort of man that women say no to, and he knew I would not be any different. It's written on his face, in the self-satisfied glint in his eye, in the confident way he stands before me, his torso displayed, he knows how good he looks and it's the power he has to wield.

"You took too long." He says.

"I had work to do." I retort. "We can't all stand around looking pretty."

"I don't like to be kept waiting."

"I'm sure you don't. If you wanted me here sooner perhaps you should have had a taxi waiting for me."

"Yes," he says, "yes I should have. I won't make the same mistake again."

As he looks at me there is a crackle in the air, static, electricity, something that moves us together and I find myself wrapped in his arms, my hands caressing over the skin of his back, his hands moving to grip my hair and we kiss each other with ferocity. I feel alive, that something has awakened - a part of me that has been dormant for too long. This nameless encounter, the champagne and the evening, has all culminated in making me feel ready to begin again.

A discreet cough behind us brings our attention to the surroundings. The night porter is assisting two elegant, elderly guests along the corridor, all looking embarrassed to be witnessing such a display. He pulls me inside as he bids the three good evening. I feel flushed, on fire, something inside burning out of control. To hell with sensible, cautious Freya, I think and I throw myself wholeheartedly to the lions.

"You knew I'd come didn't you?" I say as he closes the door. My nerves have dissipated and in their place is a woman who sparkles.

"Yes."

"So now I'm here?" I walk into the suite and turn to study him. His face is oval, his nose straight and his lips, so full and enhanced by the day old stubble that I long to run my fingers across his jaw, to feel the roughness under my skin. His eyes are a mix of blues and greens, the colour I imagine tropical waters to be and his long eyelashes, dark like his hair, look so soft I want to dust my fingers over them to see if they're real. His face is perfect, manly and masculine and he smells so divine that I become very aware of the drum beating deep within my belly. I shift uncomfortably as my body arouses and I am sure that my desire for him is written all over my face.

"Now you're here…" he leans into me and wraps his hand around my wrist. Thunderbolts explode in my head and I have to lick my suddenly dry lips. I want him. I want him so much it's painful, a heavy weight that sits in my belly pulling down towards my dampened groin. He wets his finger and rubs it across my lips. I gasp and he smiles. "…I am going to give you what you came for."

"Which is…?" I ask in a whisper.

He tangles his hand in my hair and when he speaks his lilting Irish accent is husky and deep. "I am going to fuck you."

"Oh..." I gasp, swaying dizzily. I close my eyes as his breath caresses my cheek and his lips, warm and soft, begin a slow, mind-blowing caress of my neck. His hand moves from my waist, cupping my breast, rubbing his thumb across my nipple back and forth until it stiffens and swells under his touch. The loud gasp is mine and I lean into him.

"You want me, don't you?" He asks quietly.

"Yes," I groan as he nips my earlobe with his teeth.

"I like it that you do." He kisses me, his mouth firm against mine. My lips feel bruised under the power of his kiss but it sends lava racing through me. I return his embrace, holding him tightly to me, running my hands across his strong back, the skin smooth and tight against my hands. He is unleashing something in me, something raw and animalistic. It's powerful and unnerving but I lose myself in him and give into the moment, the risk free, no chance of being hurt, moment. I writhe under his touch, my body rising and swelling to meet his hands, his body reacting to my touch. He's hard, huge and hard, against my stomach and my insides melt as he begins to moan against my mouth.

The desire floods my senses, the desire for him. His lips, hot against my neck, leave imprints on my skin, imprints that no one else will see apart from me and his hands, the hands that explore my body over and over smooth their way down to my burning groin, raising my dress then stroking me, intimately, firm strokes with digits wet with the silkiness of my excitement.

"So wet," he says appreciatively.

I can't control my groans until he unzips my dress and I shrug it off.

"You are very beautiful." He comments stroking my skin. "Very beautiful," his mouth is on mine. His kisses become forceful, owning and controlling. I give into them and his tongue probes my mouth. I rake my hands through his hair and down his hard body to his joggers, pushing them down his strong thighs and releasing his glorious cock. So impressive and sizeable I grip it firmly and move my hand up and down, slowly, revelling in his groans.

"Harder, Red, I like it hard." I do as he asks and he sighs appreciatively, saying, "yes, Red, yes…just like that…"

Slowly I sink to my knees and gently run my tongue up the underside of his erection before taking him into my mouth. He tastes of shower gel and of sexy man, this intimate of acts increasing the tempo of my internal drum. He says "Red," over and over again as I increase the pressure with the soul aim of pleasuring him. Roughly he pulls me to my feet. "I don't want to come yet." He says and walks me over to the bed, his mouth never once leaving mine. He kisses me like I've never been kissed before, with urgency and a need so desperate that fleetingly I wonder if he has had his heart broken too. I barely breathe as he lies me down upon the biggest bed I've ever seen which could easily fit ten people. It wouldn't surprise me if it has. The bedding is soft, pale blue and cream and cool under my burning skin.

I wonder what I look like, to him, now. Is my skin, normally pale and creamy, flushed? Are my green eyes hidden by the black of my pupils, widened with desire? I look up at him. Simply he is the most beautiful man I've ever seen. He stands before me, my face tilted so I meet his gaze. His probing eyes are bright and hooded. He wants me. He rubs his thumb over my lips and my mouth falls open. He slips his thumb into my mouth then rips down my dress, freeing my breasts and rubbing his wet thumb across my nipples. They harden to his touch and he lowers his head, taking my nipples, one then the other, into his mouth. He sucks firmly using his hands to support the weight of my breasts then his teeth nip me, sending waves of painful pleasure through my nerves. I cry out and arch my back pushing myself further towards him. "Oh you like this do you?" he whispers huskily.

"Yes." I groan.

My body is agonisingly sensitive. Everything I touch feels white hot and scalding and the heat of his hands and mouth on me burns to the point of exquisite torture. The sounds of London have faded and the universe is wholly centred round this room and us. Only us. As he kisses my stomach and trails his tongue down to my throbbing clitoris I cry out, gripping his hair in my hands, tugging at it, grasping the bedding as he licks me slowly, painfully slowly, until my mind is going to explode.

"You taste divine," he murmurs. "And so wet, I can see it on your thighs."

His touch is firm and controlling, experienced and knowing. He knows how to please a woman, to please me. And he is pleasing me. I am so high on lust I don't ever want to come down. His tongue is sending intense feelings through me, my legs shake as he continues to lick my silken wetness from them, my stomach is flipping with the intensity of his fingers on and in me…then I hear myself crying out, my body shuddering and he holds me down, his tongue back on my clitoris stroking pleasurably as I scream out in orgasm. He flips me over, lifting my hips and slides his huge hard cock into me thrusting and thrusting, holding me still as he takes me hard, firm, powerfully filling me and I am crying now as the intensity blows my mind and I come again with an explosion, collapsing under him. Moments later he comes powerfully into me.

***

He sleeps with his face turned to mine. Bathed in the moonlight that streams in through the windows high up above London he looks like an angel. Never have I seen a man more perfect. Slowly, lightly, I trace my fingers across his face, feeling the smooth skin, the rough stubble, the bow of his mouth and down to his throat, the hollow at the base of his neck and down over his muscles, the V of his abs and as I do I feel tears begin to fall, my tears, Real life beckons and there is no escape from it, no matter how long I lie here next to this beautiful man, it still waits and when the sun rises this illicit night will be gone.

 I close my eyes knowing I need to leave but unable to move. I feel a gentle touch and my tears are wiped away before soft lips are on mine, kissing me, strong arms holding me safely, tightly and as the first light nudges the deep blue of the night, so we make love, both knowing that when the new day dawns so this will be over.

***

FRIDAY

"I must go." I tell him tying up my hair. He comes up behind me.

"I don't want you to go."

I look at him in the mirror. "I need to." I turn around. "This has all been amazing but now I have to go back to real life."

"Husband?" He turns from me.

"Not exactly. My life is pretty complicated right now." I sigh. "And I have to go to work." I glace at the clock. "In thirty minutes!"

"That sounds like a bullshit excuse to me."

"Bullshit or not it's the facts."

There is a long uncomfortable pause. I don't know what to do or say now.

"Well beautiful Red it's been a pleasure."

"Yes," I grin, "it really has." I cross the room picking up my bag. "Just one thing..."

"Yes?"

"What's your name?"

He looks surprised. "You don't know?"

"No! You haven't told me."

He laughs. "My name is Connor."

"Connor...I've had fun."

"Me too Red. And I will see you again."

***

I crawl into the office with the bags of clothes I bought on my way into work and head straight for the shower in the ladies room. I bundle last night's outfit into a bag and stepping into the shower I turn the heat up until is scorching and stand underneath letting the water wash over me. My body is covered with Connor's fingerprints, invisible evidence of the night. What happened? Did he put a spell on me? I didn't even know his name but he drew me to him like a light does to a moth. The guilt is unexpected and with it comes the fear that someone will find out, that William will find out, yet I know that I would, without hesitation seek Connor out again. I scrub my body, cleansing it of the excess champagne and too much sex. Try as I might, I cannot wash away the intimate ache, the final evidence that Connor was real.

I cross the magazine floor, head down, sunglasses on, avoiding eye contact with anyone lest they see the sign above me declaring *"Ask Freya what she did last night!"* entering my office closing the door behind me.

I log onto my computer as Henry skips in. "You look like shit."

"It's your fault." I mutter, "it's all your fault."

"Why?"

"For making me go."

"Did you enjoy it?"

"Yes but that's not the point. You owe me coffee all day for this."

"And mission was definitely accomplished?" Henry perches on my desk and flips over the photo of William putting it face down.

"Yes mission was accomplished. Their manager is going to ring me next week to arrange an interview and photo shoot."

"I love you!" Henry looks delighted.

"I should think so."

"Were you fabulous? Did you sparkle? Did you get laid?"

"Henry!" I splutter.

"It's been a month since the rat left, you need to get back in the saddle otherwise it'll heal over!" He grins. "Who did they seat you next too? Anyone famous?" Henry looks poised for gossip.

"They sat me next to a vile smelling, boring, revolting man who groped my thigh as often as he could."

"Eeugh really? How vile are we talking?"

"Jabba vile!"

"Yuk!" Henry shudders.

"Quite! So as a result I drank far too much and I really am paying the price. If you really loved me, you'd get me coffee. Strong coffee. And a bacon roll." I remove my sunglasses and look beseechingly at Henry.

"Freya, I'm a vegetarian!" Henry looks offended.

"I don't care, you owe me big time!"

"Yes," he concedes, "I do. Alright cupcake I'll get you your pig in a roll but this is the only time I do it and angel, it would be better if you put the glasses back on!"

"I'm not ever drinking again so there are no worries on that score!" I grimace putting the shades on.

"I've heard that before!" Henry skips off.

I dial Lexi's number. As proud of her as I am for reaching partner in a company that deals in international markets I wish that I had more time with her. Twice I've seen her since Will left and can count on one hand the amount of time we have spoken. I miss her.

"Hi Lexi it's me. I hope you're ok? I feel like I've not seen you for a hundred years! The event last night was fabulous, lots to tell you. Ring me. Lots of love." I sigh and hang up. Henry comes in with my coffee.

"Double shot," he says bowing theatrically. "Dead pig roll on order."

"Thanks." I grimace. "There is no need to be so descriptive Henry. Karma has already bitten me on the bum, the pig won't have died in vain and if you keep this up it's going to be a long day!"

"Drinking on a school night, tut tut."

"You can stick the tut tuts where the sun doesn't shine Henry, this is down to you. Now leave me to wallow in hangover hell will you?"

Henry grins and breezes out.

***

I'm the last to leave the office. My work remains untouched because I have spent the day going over over last night. I have never been the kind of girl who views recklessness as a good thing. I've always been more sensible, thoughtful, always considered the outcome before I did anything. Somehow that got lost and there was no consideration for anything other than what I knew would happen when I went to Connor. His face flits by my mind's eye - his beautiful, open face with its rugged contours – and the memory of it and the soft lilt of his accent sets my heart racing. It's unlikely that I will ever see Connor again yet the brief interlude he provided to my misery somehow felt real. Too real. Truthful. It was just sex, nothing more than a carnal act yet the lack of promises, lack of conversation, lack of knowledge somehow made it all the more sincere.

"Goodnight," I say to the security guard as I cross the foyer.

"Good night Freya." He replies. The air outside is warm, dry and heavy with smog, car horns toot impatiently at each other and the bars that line the street are already full, chic office workers spilling out onto the pavements looking for a relief to the stresses of the working week. The light filters down between the buildings, casting shadows upon the dirty pavements. Suddenly I long for the sea, a sunny beach, clean air and the colours of nature.

"Red?" I turn abruptly to the sound of my nickname.

"Connor?" He is standing in front of me wearing a baseball cap and dark glasses, a tee-shirt clings to his body and a low slung pair of jeans, tight on his thighs, are long enough to cover his trainers. "What are you doing here? How did you know where I worked?" I look around me frantic that someone should see.

"Nervous?"

"A little."

"I have an hour free, wondered what you were up to. But you look like a cat on a hot tin roof so I'll let you get on."

"No…I'm…sorry…it's ok, I wasn't expecting to see you again and…"

"And you haven't told anyone?"

"No." I look down at the pavement. "No, I haven't. It was out of character for me."

"It was fun though."

I grin. "Yes, it was definitely that!"

"So are you busy?"

"When?"

"Now! I just said I have an hour!" He grins. "There's a lot than can be done in an hour!"

I giggle and flush. "I'm sure there is!"

"Come on Red, don't you want to find out what it's like sober?"

I laugh. "Sober? I'm so hungover I can barely see straight!"

His face falls. "I'll see you around then Red." As quick as a flash he gets into a black car idling by the kerb and is gone, out in the stream of traffic heading out of the city.

I remain standing like a statue, watching the car fade into the distance playing the scene over and over.

***

The heat of the bubble bath eases my head, taking away the pounding. I take a long drink of the ice cold water beside me and close my eyes, listening to the music coming in through the speakers. In my mind's eye I see colours, swirls of rich hues, cascading down the body, accentuating curves, enhancing features and I have to draw what I see, now, before it fades with the day.

Quickly I finish my bath, wrapping my hair up in a towel and pulling on my pyjamas. The kitchen is bathed in the evening light so I open the patio door and after pouring a glass of orange juice I sit down at the kitchen table with my A3 pad. The gentle summer breeze drifts in and with it the scent of pollen, perfuming the room. I take a deep breath and begin to sketch. The images in my mind fight for space as I discard one then the other, drawing and rubbing out design after design, line after line, whiling away the hours until, with final shading, it's finished.

It's perfect.

The colours I have blended for the floor length evening gown with its deep plunging neckline and ruched skirt, are exactly right. It's a dress for that one special night, a dress that would stand out from the crowd and wow everyone. I want to make it but even with all the hope in the world there will be no fabric shops open at this time of night. I clip the drawing to the noticeboard and stand back looking at it with admiration. In my head I hear Darcy's smokey tones. *You shouldn't be writing about fashion Freya, you are fashion.* Is she right?

With a big sigh I push the idea from my mind. Designing requires a confidence to put your soul out for judgement. Every time I discussed it with William he made it clear that I wasn't quite good enough, that writing about fashion was where my talents lay. I pour another glass of juice and sit, for an unknown length of time looking at my design and knowing it is fabulous. I pull a face when I begin imagining wearing the dress, but wearing it with Connor. *Honestly Freya, it was one night* I tell myself. My gaze falls to the photo of William and me on our wedding day, a snatched moment where the sunlight bathed us in gold. We looked so happy. A solitary tear falls down my cheeks.

A knock at the door makes my jump and I slosh my juice down my front. "Bugger." I grab a tea-towel on my way to the door and swing it open.

"It's you!" I say with surprise ringing in my voice.

"Who were you expecting?"

I feel strangely disheartened seeing my husband stood at the door. "No one I guess. What do you want?"

"I need to collect my clothes." He says coming into the house.

"And you had to get them tonight?" I follow him to the kitchen. "Could you not have come when I was out?"

"It's still my house and I'm busy this weekend. I'm going away on Monday."

"Away?" I sit down and reach awkwardly for my drink. It tastes disgustingly acidic, curdling in my stomach despite being deliciously fruity just moments ago.

"Yes." William takes a beer out of the fridge.

"Who with?"

"Why do you assume it's with someone?" He asks.

"You're not the kind of person who goes away alone." I mutter.

"Things change." He waves my comment away.

"Yeah they do, don't they?" I snap.

I watch William drain his beer and wipe away a dribble of froth. "There is no need to be shitty Freya, it's a work thing."

"Shitty? Shitty? I think I have every right to be shitty don't you?"

"Look Freya, there is only so many times I can say sorry."

"I don't want you to say sorry," I shout, "I want the truth. This has been eating me up inside since you left…" I crumple and choke on a sob. "I just want the truth Will. Because I feel that it's my fault, that it's something I did wrong and I don't want to feel like this. Please..." I whisper so quietly I think he strains to hear me. "Please tell me the truth."

"There is nothing to say, Freya, I've told you it all." He looks at my drawing on the notice board. "The colours don't go."

"Like us then." I refuse to cry in front of him but I can feel the tears burning behind my eyes. William looks at me strangely as I contort my face into all sorts of grimaces fighting the tears back. "Can you hurry up please William, this is just too hard."

He mutters something under his breath which I ignore and turn from him back to the drawing. The colours do go, whatever he may say, and it just becomes more apparent how very different we are. I just want the truth, the truth I know he is hiding from me.

I can hear him banging the wardrobe doors and slamming shut the drawers and each sound is a fresh stab to my chest. I don't believe that he is going away alone and I don't believe anything he has to say. In short, I wonder who he is.

"I'll have to come back for the rest."

"Please make sure it's when I'm out." I say sharply. "I can't keep going through this." I swirl the juice around my glass.

"Freya?"

"Yes?" I look up. His blue eyes are bright with unshed tears.

"Never mind." William gives me a short smile and with a pat on my shoulder he leaves the room. The front door slams and I give into my tears.

***

An hour later my taxi pulls up outside of the Stark Hotel and I pay the taxi driver. "Thank you." I say handing over my money.

"Have a good evening Miss." He replies. I gesture to say keep the change and climb out the car to be greeted by doorman, smart in his top hat and tails.

"Good evening." He says.

"Good evening." I reply smiling as I walk through the door he is holding open for me. What am I doing here? What possessed me to come? I don't even know if Connor is here and perhaps some things should just be left as one night only. I detour to the ladies room and stare critically at myself in the ornate mirror. I look pale and no amount of blush I've added to my cheeks can give my face a glow. For a moment I think about going home but when I close my eyes all I see is the broken shards of my life and I want to forget for just one more time.

I leave the room in search of oblivion.

Connor is sitting in the far corner of the bar. He is an exceptional looking man, broad and defined with the halo of thick chestnut hair and the sensual mouth that is transfixing. I shouldn't be here. Life is too much of a mess for flirtations, but I cannot turn back, my need for this beautiful man is too consuming. It feels like I'm in a film, being directed, moved forward as the plot twists and changes, the outcome as yet unknown and the reason for the meeting not yet clear. I falter, watching him. He is swirling amber liquid around a glass, reading a document with a frown furring his brow. He looks perturbed, his face closed, his lips forming into a tight line. This is not a good time. I must go. I swivel on my heel and, acutely aware of the painful disappointment massing in my belly, I begin to walk across the bar.

"Red?" Connor is beside me.

"Hello." I say with more confidence than I feel.

We stand facing each other, his eyes boring into the side of my face as I look away.

"I'm surprised to see you."

"I'm surprised to be here." I say and take a deep breath. "Are you busy?"

He shrugs, "not anymore."

"Am I interrupting?"

"Not really. It can wait. There is a brief pause and he says. "So why did you come? I thought life was complicated"

To escape. "It is complicated I just wanted…I don't know really, an escape, a drink…something other than real life"

"Oh," he nods slowly as though realising the obvious. "And the complication?"

"Let's just say, I want to forget about all that."

"So you plan on using me?"

"Is that a problem?"

"Not for me but I wonder…"

"Wonder what?"

"If it's a problem for you."

"I wouldn't be here if it was." The truth is that I can lose myself in him, in the blue of his eyes and the confident curl of his smile. He can take away real life and replace it with something exciting, dreamlike and secretive, a whisper of the mysterious and mask reality with a kiss. The gaze is intense. His eyes burn into mine and I feel the fire, the intensity and I know he feels it too, I can see it in his face. There is something in the air. It pings and zips between us. The other people in the bar look across at us and I know they see it too. It shimmers and glistens around us like an impenetrable force field and there is a strange silence for a brief moment. Just now I see him as an angel sent to take my troubles away, a temporary reprieve from real life. How much of life is predetermined? I was never one for fate and god and the influence of the universe but something or someone guided me here. There is no obvious planned out reason, there is only this moment and only us.

"Who are you?" I whisper.

"I'm Connor." He replies, his tone low and gruff. The crackle of sparks as he touches my hand is audible and I know that he has heard it too. With his hand on the small of my back, he guides me across the bar and towards the lift. My skin blisters and with each step I feel heavier, full up with a dangerous and ill-advised need for this enigmatic man. The effect he has on me is like being possessed by something that I can't fight against it, it brought me here. His scent seems to infuse everything, little bubbles of raw man that dust over my skin. His is the musky, masculine, natural scent that I draw down into me with each breath.

The lift doors ping open and we step inside. The minute the doors close I move toward him and reach my hand up to the back of his head pulling him down and kissing his lips pushing my body up against his. It is not a soft kiss, more the urgent, determined kiss of a woman needing to be healed. He matches the force of my kiss as we bruise each other's lips with the sheer power of the embrace. My centre stirs releasing wetness and I press my groin against the firmness of Connor's thigh.

"I can feel you." He whispers tugging at my earlobe with his teeth, "wet and hot…"

I groan as his stubble grazes my neck. "I can feel you too." I whisper reaching for the fly of his jeans. "You want me…" It is not a question but I need to hear a reply.

"Yes," he murmurs moving his thigh against me. My ache intensifies and the throb within me takes on the beat of a bass drum. "I do." Connor wraps his hands in my hair and tips back my head. I look up at him, sliding my hand into his jeans as I do. I watch his eyes widen as I caress my hand over his cock, hard and smooth, before freeing it from the constraints of his jeans. Connor groans and I tighten my grip on him, his cock hardening further under the pressure. Abruptly the doors open and Connor makes himself presentable before pulling me from the lift and walking quickly down the hall to his room.

Inside the suite we fly at each other, tearing off clothes and discarding them on the floor. I stroke his skin, lightly scratching my nails across his muscular chest and down to the soft hair that trails from his belly button to his groin. His groans are like my own personal symphony, an arousing sound that is in time with my own desire and I sink to my knees to take him into my mouth. The taste of him is delicious and the pleasure I get from the act I perform is immeasurable. Each moan from him turns me on further until my body glistens.

"Red!" Connor gasps, tightening his hands in my hair.

I ease my mouth from him and murmur "Connor, I want you..." Taking his hands I move slowly across the room to the bed. "Lie down." I command. He does as I ask, never taking his eyes from mine. I sit astride him my eyes and hands exploring every inch of him until he begins to beg for more. My need for release becomes all-consuming and slowly I guide him into me, gasping as he stretches me, the sweet pleasure of the entry unleashing the wild longing. I move my hips and wrap my hands up in my hair, closing my eyes, giving into my feelings and my needs.

Never once do I touch him as I move for my pleasure, accepting him deeply and feeling the short hair on his groin caressing my clitoris. My cries of joy echo around the room and losing all sense of inhibition I begin to stroke my breasts as I move, feeling them swell in my hands, my nipples hardening like bullets that I pinch and roll in my fingers. I am aware of Connor's moans and murmurs of delight at my pleasure I find in my own body. He grips my thighs tightly and we move together, the intensity increasing, the touches becoming more rough as the delicious heat begins to flicker in my centre and rises as my orgasm takes effect, a powerful, breath taking explosion that shoots through me, my cries mingling with Connor's and we collapse together satiated.

***

I leave the room while Connor sleeps soundly, not really wanting to go but suddenly unable to stay. Lying in his arms, as I was, the weight of the muscular biceps holding me tight, hands crossed over my body made me feel so safe – too safe – that it suddenly felt more real than the dream I am hoping it is. Bathed in moonlight he looked so young, so handsome and so completely perfect but tired, purple shadows under his eyes that I hadn't noticed before. He stays asleep as I dress, his breathing is deep and contented, and soft smile crosses his lips.

"What's your story?" I whisper. "Who are you really?" I blow a kiss and quietly leave. The hotel driver brings the car around to the front of the hotel to take me home. I get an almost sympathetic look from the doorman as I leave with my coat and shoes bundled in my hands. What kind of woman leaves in the middle of the night? I can hear the word, buzzing in my head, like a persistent fly and sinking into the leather upholstery and the harsh reality is nothing like the momentary analgesia that Connor brings, there is no escape from the voice in my head, telling me everything I don't want to hear.

I thank the driver as we pull up outside my house. I tip him and exit the car, rushing into the house before anyone sees. Not that anyone would see. It's four am and the sky is beginning to change colour, the midnight blue is turning red at the edges, but the world sleeps as the new day slowly begins to emerge. The colours are rich and vibrant and hold tightly to my secret. It may be the dawn, the natural cycle of the earth as it turns, but to me it is the conception of another design, a dress for that secret moment where a woman feels wanted and desired and instead of going to bed I embrace the silence of the house and sketch.

SATURDAY

I wake with a stiffness in my shoulders and realise that I have spent what remained of the night asleep with my head on the kitchen table. Underneath me is the finished dress the paper crumpled from being my pillow. I don't know when I fell asleep but I saw six am come as I was shading the design. A simple dress of midnight blue shading into the pale blues, oranges, pinks and reds of a summer morning. Tiny stars are dotted across the neckline and down over the bust. It looks like the dawn. I grin, thinking that it is the dawn of my new life. Everything I want and everything I am has been embodied in the dress, the colours capturing the moment that the new day peeps below the glittering stars, the kind of dress that gives hope to women that there is more to come, that they will survive and like me, move into a new tomorrow.

I pin the dress to the notice board and look at it with a self-satisfied grin. No more wondering about William's reasons for leaving, no more hoping that he'll come back. I can wither and emotionally die or I can take a positive from all this. I may never know the real reason that William left me but it can stop defining my existence. I stretch deeply grimacing as my limbs protest from the uncomfortable position in which I slept. It doesn't escape me, as I make a pot of strong coffee, that in the couple of days I've known Connor I have been more inspired to design than in the past fifteen years with William.

I potter around the kitchen, clearing away dishes and mugs before deciding on pancakes for breakfast. I give Gloria, William's mother, the imaginary finger as I mix the batter until it's thick, gloopy and bubbling merrily in the butter. Gloria couldn't be any more different to me – whippet thin, coiffed, immaculately made up with an appetite like a sparrow. I've never understood the need to be skinny and even though I work in fashion I've never wanted a model figure, never felt the need to attempt to attain the unattainable.

Pancakes made I sit at the kitchen table and look out over the courtyard garden. "Silly cow." I mutter to the memory of Gloria's face as she sniffed with disagreement. Her disapproving look was quite common particularly when it came to me. Gloria has never taken to me, never really approved of my relationship with her beloved first born. I add a generous squirt of maple syrup to my pancakes and feel almost rebellious. It's another warm day, somewhere someone is mowing their grass and beyond that are the sounds of Camden Town on a Saturday. Busy, vibrant, exciting and welcoming - an entire universe in one town. William just liked the kudos of living here but to me this is home. The smells and the chaos and the tourists and the market…I couldn't imagine living in another part of London, somewhere lacking the soul and the uniqueness of this wonderful borough.

I drop some pancake and syrup down my pyjamas. "Crap!" I huff wiping it and causing a sticky mess.

The doorbell rings and I swing open the door expecting William. Instead I find Connor standing on the doorstep, hair wet from the shower, wearing jeans and a t-shirt with Guns n Roses emblazoned on the front. "Oh my God." I say without thinking my heart thumping wildly.

"No, not God, just me." Connor says. He takes in my appearance with a raised eyebrow and I give him a shrug.

"How did you find me?" I stammer.

"The hotel driver brought you home, remember? Nice place." He comments.

He came looking for me.

"Thanks." There is a long pause. "Do you want to come in?"

"Yes, I didn't come here to stand on the doorstep." I move aside to let him in. "You just left. Why do you keep leaving?"

For a moment there is an awkward silence. "I told you before, my life is complicated and I don't need any more complication."

"Complicated how?" He asks picking up the photo of William and me. "I guess this is the complication? Where does he think you were then?"

"My husband and I are estranged." I pick up my coffee. "Only recently."

"You want him back?" It's more of a statement than a question.

"It's hard to walk away from. We were together for a long time."

"Did he leave or did you?"

"He did. He said we weren't what he wanted anymore." I take the photo from him and put it face down on the window sill.

"So you're separated?"

"Estranged."

"Estranged is the same as separated, separated means free to have fun. Don't you want to have fun with me? I want to have fun with you."

"Fun?"

"Yes Red, fun. The sort of fun married people don't have."

"You presume to know a lot about married people…"

"I've known a lot of married people, ladies…" He grins.

"I bet you have!" I retort feeling more jealous than I care to. "Coffee?"

"Please. What's for breakfast?"

"Pancakes."

"Any left?"

"Sure."

I pour a coffee with trembling hands.

"I make you nervous." It's a comment not a question.

"Yes you do." I reply honestly turning to face him. "I don't know where you've come from. I don't know who you are, sometimes it matters…"

"Do you want me to go?"

"I should but no, I don't. Sugar and milk?"

"No thank you."

I busy myself with the pancakes, melting the butter in the pan and mixing up the batter – eggs, flour, and milk – and add it when the butter begins to sizzle. He leans against the worktop, drinking his coffee, never taking his eyes off me. I'm not sure if I'm breathing and the flow of blood past my ears is deafening. He's definitely put a spell on me, it's the smell of him, manly and raw, sexual and charged. There is something in the air, something between us and I can't relax. I try to control the trembling in my hands but the smile on his face suggests I'm failing.

"Did you do that?" Connor asks looking at the evening dress design that is still hanging on the notice board.

"Yes."

"It's really good. You'd look nice in it."

"Thank you." The pause is awkward.

Connor smiles. "And this one?" He asks lifting the crumpled summer dress from the worktop.

"Yes, that one too."

"Did you sleep on it?"

"Why?"

"You have pencil on your cheek."

I rush over the mirror. "Oh bloody hell."

"You know," he comments, "if you only had paper for a pillow you could have just stayed in my bed."

I'd like to be there now. "I must have fallen asleep drawing."

"You are good. Have you ever thought about doing it professionally?"

"Sometimes. It didn't really fit in with what was going on."

"Your husband?"

I nod.

"And now you're separated…"

"Now I still don't know if it's a risk worth taking."

"All risks are worth taking."

"Are they?"

"Sure otherwise how would life move forward?"

"Very wise for one so young!" I grin.

Connor laughs. "I'm not that young and besides, I've lived a lot of life, so being street wise adds years!" He comes to stand close behind me. I can feel his breath on the back of my neck and I tremble he slides his hands around my waist. "I was a risk…don't you think it was a risk worth taking?"

"You still are a risk." I whisper, barely audibly, visibly quivering as his arms tighten around me. Connor lets me go and with all the nonchalance I can muster I flip his pancake. "Syrup?"

"Yes please."

He sits down at the kitchen table and I hand him the plate and a fork. He takes the carton of syrup from me and adds a generous amount. I try to flatten my hair, running my fingers through it.

"You look fine."

"Fine?" I turn away and look out of the kitchen window to the small garden.

"Yes, fine."

"Thanks!" I giggle.

"Good pancakes."

"I'm glad you think so."

"Do you miss him?"

"William?" I ask watching a bird peck at the seed on the bird table.

"Yes."

"I don't really want to talk about it, if you don't mind." I say looking down at the white ring marks on my wedding finger. Talking about my husband to a man I barely know doesn't feel right somehow.

"Why not? It's just a conversation and I'm very discreet." He smiles.

"Are you?" I ask, not looking at him. "I suppose you must be, you don't give much away."

"You don't ask me anything." He replies and I turn to look at him. He has a dribble of syrup on the corner of his mouth and I long to lick it off.

"You have syrup…" I brush my finger along my lower lip.

He darts out his tongue and licks the drip. I am transfixed. A rush of heat swells through me as I watch his tongue on its journey across his plump lower lip until his mouth curls into a smile. "You're staring."

"Sorry." I flush crimson and busy myself clearing the worktop.

"What do you want to know then Red? Ask me anything." Connor pops a cube of pancake in his mouth.

"What brings you to London? I know that you know Lacey, are you a model or something?" I ask.

"I'm here for work, no I'm not a model but I have modelled…"

"So what do you do then?"

"I'm in…uh…sales I suppose." He says and grins. "Occasionally a spy, sometimes a car thief, whatever takes my fancy. I wear a lot of hats!"

"You're taking the piss." I huff.

"No I'm not!" He says offended. I pour out more coffee and sit down at the table. "My turn."

"Ok." I brace myself for his line of questioning.

"Do you want your husband back?" He stares intently at me.

"Sometimes." I say quietly and take a deep breath. Looking up at Connor I continue. "It's hard to let go of something that has guided my life and my choices for fifteen years. It's always been Freya and William that just being Freya is a strange concept." I smile. "I probably sound really old fashioned and I don't mean to, I'm actually a very strong person but there are times when I just want my marriage to work. This morning I decided that I needed to move on, take a few risks and say 'to hell with it.'"

"Risks are good. They keep the world turning." I can't read his expression but something flickers in his eyes.

"Risks require a certain confidence though. I think it's the confidence that I need to work on." I reply. "I suppose being an international jewel thief requires a certain confidence!" I cock my head and laugh. "I am sure you look very fetching in a black balaclava and ski suit."

"I'll show you later!"

"Later?" I ask.

"Yeah, I'm anticipating seeing you. A hot single woman…a hot single man…imagine the fun,"

"I am!" I reply huskily. Connor puts his fork down with a clatter and pushing his chair backwards he stands up and walks round to me. I look up at him, his eyes brimming with intent and I feel my body respond, opening up and swelling for him. "Connor…"

"Yes?" He says gruffly pulling me to my feet.

"I want…"

I can't finish the rest of the sentence. His lips find mine and he kisses me ferociously. The sparks light the room, the crackles loud like the popping of a machine gun. Life fades around us as I give into his kiss, the powerful, commanding kiss. Whatever he is doing to me I am doing to him, we have the same need, the same unexplainable compulsion that brings us back together. I've not experienced a desire like this before, something so strong that I can almost taste it on my tongue. I melt against Connor, his strong arms holding me so tight that I gasp to breathe, his muscles rigid against my flesh.

"Do you want to know something Red?" he murmurs pulling away from me and sweeping my hair over my shoulder. "I am going to…" He sucks on my earlobe. I close my eyes and my body wakes up. "…fuck your husband right out of you."

"Oh." The voice that comes from me is breathy and excited.

"I need to go." Connor announces. Does he realise how aroused I am? Is he doing this as a power trip, to leave me wanting? "I'll see you later, come to Cullen's at eight."

I don't turn around even when I hear him leave the room. The front door slams shut but I remain holding onto the worktop, hot and more confused than ever.

***

I lie in the bath until the water goes cold thinking over and over how unexpected the past month has been. How can life change so quickly, almost in the blink of an eye? One moment married, the next finding myself in the midst of an affair with a man who I know nothing about. Things like this don't ordinarily happen to me yet I find myself living for the moment, enjoying the sexy secret that he brings to my life.

No longer able to tolerate a cold bath I get out and dress myself in my favourite La Perla underwear and my t-shirt. It smells faintly of Connor and it's an arousing scent, manly, masculine and full of promise. I laugh until my belly hurts. It's all so crazy. I select the David Guetta cd and dance around the living room, no cares, no worries, no embarrassment at my uncle-at-a-wedding dancing just giving myself to the moment and the natural high that comes with the excitement of the evening ahead.

Mid hip swing the door opens and William comes in with Gloria. Gloria purses her lips at my exuberance William just looks confused.

"Hello." I stop dancing. "I wasn't expecting to see either of you." I reach for the blanket lying on the sofa and wrap it around myself.

"Clearly," Gloria bristles. "We're here to discuss the house."

"On a Saturday evening? It's not convenient, I am going out shortly."

"Then you will have to delay Freya."

"I can't delay Gloria, I have somewhere to be. Now what is it you want to discuss, I can give you twenty minutes."

William looks between his mother and me. I realise in that instance how weak he is, how easily he gives in to her. How have I not noticed this before?

William clears his throat. "I want to talk to you about selling the house." He has the good grace to look uncomfortable. "If you want to buy it. I will sell to you for what we paid for it."

I reel. "You want to sell? For what we…William how do you suppose I can find one hundred thousand pounds to give you your deposit back?"

"Freya, that is not for William to concern himself with. The apartment needs to be sold. William wants to move on with his life and you must do the same." Gloria is firm to the point of sharpness. She doesn't care about me. She has never cared about me.

For a moment a look of sadness flits across William's face. I wonder how much of this is Gloria's doing. His lovely, animated face is ashen and drawn. I feel heart wrenching sadness. It's a stabbing pain in my stomach and I close my eyes to regain some control and stop the tears from falling. I want to reach for him, comfort him and have him comfort me as the foundations of our marriage crumble around us.

"Mum, can you give us a minute please?" William asks.

Gloria leaves the room muttering something under her breath. I stare at her retreating back hoping desperately that this will be the last time I ever have to see her. "I bet she's loving this." I whisper, the pain I feel ringing in my voice.

The front door slams. "I am so sorry Freya sorry for everything, for all the hurt and pain I've caused you, for breaking all my promises. You deserve more than this, you are a wonderful loving person and I will love you forever. I am sorry mum is being such a bitch and I am sorry for the way she has always treated you."

"Why did you bring her William? You know she has always hated me and this is yet another kick in the teeth. Don't you think you have done enough?" I whisper, my voice cracking.

"Oh Freya she doesn't hate you. No one could hate you."

Tears fall and I am powerless to stop them. "You know she does Will and she always has. I've never been good enough. No matter how many promotions or how well I did it was never ever enough for her. What did I do wrong Will? What on earth did I do wrong?"

William holds me tightly in his arms. The familiar arms that have held me so many thousands of times before are wrapped around my back. I rest my head on his chest, soft and so very different to the Connor's strong, muscular chest. "You didn't do anything wrong Freya, nothing." Williams tone is low. He strokes my hair. "I did wrong. I am so sorry darling girl, so sorry for making you cry."

"Why did you leave me?" I ask, shivering in his arms.

"Oh Freya, don't do this." William begs.

"Can't we try again?" I sob.

The front of his pale blue shirt is drenched in my tears and blackened by mascara. "I don't think we can Freya."

"Why?"

"Because it's not what I want."

He holds me while I cry clasping onto his body with its now unfamiliar smell. I feel drops of water fall and realise that he is crying too and that this is the last time I will ever be held by my husband.

***

Why am I looking at my wedding photos? Why am I not getting ready to meet Connor? Daylight is fading and dusk rises but still I sit here, my wine glass untouched, surrounded by crumpled wet tissues from my tears. I am stronger than this. So why am still sitting here? It's just before eight o'clock. I need to move now. The floor is becoming uncomfortable and I am stiff from being sat in the same position for an hour. The enthusiasm for Connor has dimmed with the day and I just want to be alone.

***

At nine thirty I walk through the door of Cullen's, a private members club in the heart of Mayfair. I have made an extra effort with my appearance in a pale pink silk dress that fits my curves and the daring V neck gives more than a hint décolletage. My hair is piled up on top of my head and I have pale makeup, just a dusting to bring out the green of my eyes.

Connor is sitting alone with a glass of whiskey on the rocks. He looks thunderous and tension radiates from him. I falter for a moment then head high walk as confidently as I can manage across the bar to him.

"Hello Connor."

"You're late." He doesn't look at me.

"I know. Sorry. I would have called but I don't have your number."

"I am never kept waiting."

"Well this is the real world and shit happens."

He shrugs.

"Look, Connor, I have had a pretty crappy afternoon and I am not staying here for you to be incommunicative. I've said sorry, I was late for personal reasons, ones that I shan't bore you with but quite honestly I've had enough man-shit to last me a lifetime so I'll be going now. Enjoy your evening." I spin sharply on my heel and hurry across the bar.

A hand reaches out to grasp my arm and Connor pulls me across the foyer to the door. The doorman opens it and with no words Connor leads me outside to where a black Mercedes is parked. A suited man opens the rear door and I am steered into it.

The car pulls away. We sit in an angry, awkward silence and although I stare out of the window I don't focus on the city outside. The heat from Connor's rigid body drifts across me, bringing with it his scent, the masculine, musky sexual scent that overpowers my senses.

"Where are we going?" I ask eventually. Connor's furious silence is strangely erotic and being in such close proximity to him makes me want to reach for him, to touch him, to run my fingers around his frown line, to dust my tongue across his firmly set lips. It doesn't seem to matter that he has taken over the situation nor that I willingly allow it. All that matters is my desire to forget and for Connor to be the one to make that happen.

"Red, I am too pissed off to speak to you right now." He says angrily. "You kept me waiting like a dick for an hour and a half. No one has ever kept me waiting." For a moment he sounds like a petulant child.

"Oh dear, poor you. Did you have to sit by yourself? Did no one want to play?" I retort sarcastically before I lose my temper. "Have you heard yourself? You utter brat. What's the matter? Do women usually swoon at your feet, desperate for even a glance from the mighty Connor? Who do you think you are? Superman? I am very sorry that my insignificant life got in the way of what you wanted, we can't always have what we want Connor, or perhaps you do? Perhaps you are one of the lucky ones for whom life is full of sunbeams and rainbows. Well life is very different for the rest of us, and right now my life teeters on being a total shambles so fuck off with your whiny attitude and go find someone else who will jump when you click your fingers, I'm sure there have been plenty."

We have stopped outside my house. I look out of the window. Night has fallen and the streets have the orange glow from the lights. Two feline eyes are reflected in the headlights, briefly before the cat is distracted and leaps off into a bush in pursuit of something edible.

"You are so quick to judge aren't you Red?" I glance at Connor but he's looking out the window on his side. He continues in a low tone. "How would you feel if I judged you? You slept with me before we'd even had a conversation, before you even knew my name." He turns to glare at me. "You talk about real life but you seem intent on avoiding it."

"You know nothing about me or my life." I spit incensed.

"I know enough and you know what? I'm not your fucking punch bag. I've known you three days..." He clenches his hands into fists. "three days. What do you know about me? Nothing. Because you've not asked. Yes there have been other women, lots of other women, and not one of them have ever been as wrapped up in themselves as you."

"Then go and find one of them to spend the evening with." I wrench the door open and once out of the car I slam it with as much force as I can manage and run up the path. My hands are trembling with angry, unhappy tremors that prevent me from opening my front door on the first attempt. Connor's car speeds away. I watch the taillights to the end of the street and finally manage to open the door. The silence inside my apartment is deafening. I pour a glass of wine from the opened bottle in the fridge, turning on the radio before sitting down heavily at the kitchen table. What a mess. What a total fucking mess. I feel a rage spreading out from my stomach, a rage at myself, William, Connor and everyone else. I drink down the wine trying to quell the flames of fury but it doesn't help so I pour another glass and down that too. It doesn't take long for the bottle to be empty. Then I cry.

***

There is a hammering that rouses me. At first I think it's in my head but as I come too, stiff from falling asleep on the sofa I realise it's the door. It's 2am. Blearily I stumble towards the door, tripping over the discarded wine bottle and open it on the catch. Connor is glowering at me through the gap.
"What?" I snap.
"Open the door Red."
"Why?"
"For fucks sake open the goddamn door."
"Go away Connor." I move to push the door closed but he jams his foot in the gap.
"Open the door."
"No."
Time seems to speed up. Connor pushes the door with such force that the chain breaks and I stagger backwards suddenly sober. He looks furious as he comes towards me and for a fleeting moment I am fearful.

His hands move to my face and he kisses me with such intensity that it almost hurts. "You've really pissed me off, Red, and I don't like it." He murmurs against my neck.

I tip my head back. "So why are you here?" I whisper.

"I still wanted to fuck you."

I grasp his head, pulling down until his face is level with mine. His eyes flash navy, dark and hooded, his intent fully readable within their depths. "Good." I say. "So fuck me then."

I walk backwards and he follows me into the lounge. I sit down on the sofa and lean backwards. "I'm all yours Connor, what are you going to do." He leans over me and twists my hair tugging my face closer to his.

"I am going to make you scream." He replies.

"Promises, promises." I murmur, his statement going straight to my groin. I feel myself dampen, the longing for him heavy and pulsating. When he touches me the rest of the world disappears, he is a magician, casting his spell, a spell I am powerless and unwilling to fight against.

His hand rubs against my hot, wet centre. "Oh, look how wet you are and I haven't even touched you yet." He comments running his index finger up the inside of my thigh then puts it in his mouth. "You taste good." He says and spreading my legs he moves my panties to the side and inhales. "You smell good."

Connor kneels beside the sofa and slowly, mind-blowingly slowly, licks up the inside of one thigh then just as painstakingly slowly up the other side. I arch my back lifting my hips from the sofa but he continues his slow journey up my leg. Then nothing.

"Connor please." I beg.

"Connor please what?" His breath is cool against my hot centre.

"Please touch me." I whisper dizzy with desire.

"Touch you how?" He asks. "Like this..." and rubs his thumb over my engorged sex. "or like this..." and his tongue brushes softly over me.

"Yes your tongue, please Connor." I can hear my blood pumping loudly in my ears and my body is one complete erogenous zone aching for his touch.

"Or maybe I won't..." He says huskily. "Maybe I'll just leave you waiting like you left me waiting. How would you like that?"

"Don't play games."

"Games? I would have thought you'd like playing games."

"Don't Connor..." I beg weakly, hating myself for playing along with his power trip.

"Don't Connor what?"

"Don't play with me like this."

"But isn't this what you want?" He asks.

"I want you." My confession rings loudly in the air. Connor crushes my lips under his and ripping off my panties he enters me, moving hard and fast. I rise to him, my body wrapped around his, holding him tightly as our lips meet, perspiration glistening in the light, our cries of pleasure filling the room and I come, loudly, explosively, my body trembling uncontrollably as he finds his own release burying his face in my neck while his orgasm courses through him.

Connor stands up. He has the look of satisfaction on his face as though he is the winner. "Don't leave me waiting again," he says. Then he is gone.

SUNDAY

I wake up with a glorious ache and a smile that pains my swollen and bruised lips. My body complains loudly as I try to move from the curled up positive I've been sleeping in so I give up and pull the covers tightly around my body. What has happened to me? What am I doing giving something of myself to a man who I know nothing about? I would battle Satan just for the chance of Connor touching me, yet for all I know he could be the worst type of person for me. But then, what kind of person am I? After fifteen years with the same man is this just the actions of a woman who didn't want to admit she was bored? Or is it that buried somewhere deep down inside of me is a sexual side of me that William didn't ever look to find? Is this all just a dream?

The cosy cocoon of my bed releases me to the chill of the morning and wrapping myself up in my robe I walk through to the kitchen in search of coffee. I feel sleep deprived. The events of the past few days have been exhausting and I make the coffee extra strong for a much needed hit. The photo of Will and I looks down on me from the windowsill. Were we every truly happy? I'd like to think so, fifteen years is a lot of life to waste but knowing that he is lying to me over the reasons for leaving puts the past firmly in the shade. Despite what I said yesterday I have no intention of ever again asking, or hoping, for him to come back. It's over.

The coffee is too hot so I leave it to cool while I take a shower, singing loudly as I wash away Connor's scent from my skin. The smell of him, even hours later, is still able to produce intense feelings in me, it's like a drug, a strange, sexual craving that my body yearns for and the mere whisper of the scent hits me deep inside. I want to seek him out, to experience more of what he can get my body to do but work looms and I finish my shower resignedly and dress for the meeting with Lacey.

I rush down two cups of coffee, my head spinning as the caffeine takes effect and suitably attired I leave the house just as the taxi pulls up. The street is quiet, the residents clearly still sleeping off a Saturday night out and I feel somewhat envious that they can remain in bed, except I'm wishing I was in bed with Connor.

***

"Here you are miss," the cabbie says as he pulls up outside of the converted warehouse pulling me from my thoughts.

"Thank you." I reply handing him the fare and climbing out of the car. I rearrange my features into a composed mask and walk towards Henry.

"Hey cupcake!" he says giving me a loud kiss. "What's the matter?"

Everything. "Oh, nothing beyond Will wanting to sell the house." I lie. "Are you all set up?"

"Yes, George and I have been here for hours. I can't believe you didn't bring coffee. Freeeeeeeya!" He whines.

I ignore the moan. "Is Lacey here?"

"Not yet." Henry groans. "Bloody designers! Such prima-sodding-donnas…"

"In that case I'll go and get some coffee." I look at Henry over the top of my glasses. "I hope you're not hungover?"

"Not really." Henry doesn't look me in the eye.

"Henry!" I admonish.

"Don't give me a hard time! You don't exactly look radiant!"

"I don't feel it. Jeez, so much for being a professional, work focused team!"

"Of course we are." Henry pouts. "When has my work been anything but? Feel free to trade me in for a younger model Freya, I'll happily sod off back to bed."

I give him a kiss on the cheek. "You know I can't live without you Henry!" I take my purse from the bag and hand it to Henry. "Keep an eye on my worldly possessions while I get coffee."

Henry begs. "Large and strong please…it's my new motto for life, men and gin!"

I laugh.

***

"These designs are stunning Lacey," I tell her as we pour over the proofs. Around the room on mannequins are the dresses each one tailored to perfection. "You really have surpassed any other collection I have seen recently."

"Thank you Freya," Lacey replies lighting another cigarette and blowing out smoke through plum coloured lips. "This is the collection I've been most nervous about. You're the first magazine to see them. Do you really think they're good?"

"Lacey, this collection needs more than a magazine to show it off, you need a launch party and to get a catwalk organised! Maybe even model them yourself. Wear them out to events where you'll be seen to spark the interest. Seriously Lacey, there are new designers snapping at the heels of everyone, you need to show this collection to the world because these clothes need to be seen now!"

"Really?"

"Yes really!" Henry is behind me taking photos of the collection, occasionally taking shots of Lacey and I.

"Have you made anything recently?" She asks inhaling deeply.

"Yes, a red dress but I've been sketching a bit. I wish I had more time to design."

"You should do it full time Freya you have such a talent, more than I do, more than most people actually"

"Thank you Lacey that's a really encouraging thing to hear. I would if I could, I'd run away to the seaside and come back with a complete collection. The ideas are in my head I just don't have the time to bring them to life!"

"Can't you make the time?"

"I can't afford to give up work and that's the only way I'd have the time to design and sew properly."

"Bummer."

"I couldn't have put it better myself!"

We have a long interview. I want to ask her about Connor, who is he and why he's so secretive but despite a million scenarios I cannot think of one reason why I would want to know. Lacey and I talk fashion, men and pop culture with Henry occasionally chipping in. Interviews with young designers like Lacey, who brim with enthusiasm and a youthful confidence is a pleasure. Unlike most of the fashion houses I spend time with there is no side to her. She loves what she does and she is very, very good at it. Lacey has captured the young professional market with her futuristic designs and beautiful tailoring but has also captured their imagination, proving that young women can do whatever they put their minds too. I wonder, briefly, if I have it in me to do the same. My designs are good, different to what I see around me. Could I take the risk?

My phone beeps with a message from Lexi.

Can you meet me for a drink?

I frown. It's not like Lexi to send such a cryptic message. I reply.

Yes would be great. It's been ages!!

Meet me at Barneys at 3?

Perfect.

See you later.

I will speak to Lexi about Connor. She will make sense.

"Did you enjoy the London Fashion party?" I ask Lacey as we're packing up.

"Yes, it was fab!" She flushes, "I even copped off with Seamus!"

"Seamus as in lead singer Seamus?" I gasp.

"Yeah, but it didn't come to anything. More fish in the sea hey?"

"So they say!" *So they say.*

***

"Hello stranger." I smile as I join Lexi at the bar. We embrace awkwardly and I sit heavily in the chair confused by the inexplicable unease that has crept its way into my stomach. Lexi looks different, her hair is softer, framing her face with curls that ordinarily she straightens and her make-up, usually dramatic, is more neutral. It's like looking at a totally different person.

"Hi." Lexi says. "You look well."

"Do I?" I question. "I thought I may have dumped on my forehead?" A smile forms on my mouth, "or do I look like a woman with a secret?"

"Secret?" Lexi asks "That sounds exciting but no it's not that. I don't know what it is, you seem more upright…"

"Upright?" I interrupt. "What do you mean? Do I have better posture or something?"

She looks me up and down. "No, it's not that either, I'm not really sure what I mean." She gives an embarrassed smile, "I suppose I'm just babbling."

"It's been so long…"

"Yeah that's my fault, I've been busy…" She trails off and begins picking at her perfectly manicured nail. "So how are you Freya?"

"Now that the shock has faded I'm doing ok. Tired, life has been pretty manic recently but I've been designing and socialising and..."

"That's good."

"Are you alright Lexi? You don't seem here." I reach to give her hand a squeeze. It's cold under my warm palm. "You're cold, you've not become a vampire have you?"

Lexi laughs. "Not yet! Although I'm pretty sure I've lost my soul, sold it to the devil..."

"What on earth are you talking about? Lexi, you're being weird!" The unease has morphed into full blown anxiety. "You're not sick are you?"

"No. Not medically anyway..."

"Now you're freaking me out." The barman interrupts to take our order. I request a glass of wine, Lexi orders a brandy.

"Have you ever made a choice that is likely to change your life forever, a choice from which there is no going back from?" She wraps her hands around the brandy glass that the barman presents to her, like she's trying to warm up.

"No..."

"I have." A solitary tear rolls down her face. She wipes it with the back of her hand then takes a long draught of her drink.

"Lex..."

I watch her slowly, carefully, put the glass back down on the bar. She doesn't look at me but whispers, "I'm so sorry Freya."

"Sorry? What are you sorry for? Alexa you are being really weird, what is the matter? If you're not ill or taking drugs or being sectioned then what is going on? This isn't like you..."

"Freya," Lexi interrupts me. "Freya I have something to tell you." She is very pale under her immaculate makeup. "It's about my boyfriend."

"Is everything ok?"

"Yes it's just..."

"Am I going to meet him at long last?" I interrupt enthusiastically. When Lexi told me that she had a new boyfriend I was ecstatic for her. She always seemed to find it hard to develop any lasting relationships which I could never understand given that she is beautiful - a glossy blonde with a stunning figure and legs that go on forever – with a sharp intellect and a kind, open heart. I met The Honourable Alexa Whitington-Shaw on our first day at St Augustine's School for Girls, a very exclusive private school in west London that I gained a place at through an art scholarship. The uniform cost my mum's wages for two months. I still feel a pang now thinking about what my parents sacrificed to send me there, the fees were paid by the scholarship but each term there was an invoice for something. I still don't know how they did it, with their low income jobs, but I will forever be grateful that they did. On that first day, I was a small, terrified little girl just off the tube who bumped, literally, into an equally terrified Lexi getting out of a Bentley. We both ended up sitting in a puddle laughing our heads off and that was it, a firm friendship that has lasted through bad boyfriends, pop star crushes, separate universities and now the demands of two successful careers, me as fashion editor of R&R Magazine, an award winning women's monthly and Lexi as a partner in a city accountants.

Lexi puts her face in her hands. "Freya..."

"What's the matter? Have you split up?"

"No. It's fine...great...better than great really it's just..." She pauses and lowers her hands. "It's just that you know him already."

"I do? Who?" I lean forward in my chair. "Who it is? Not Tom?"

"No, not Tom. Tom was a fling."

"Jack?"

"No…Freya…it's no one you'd think of."

"Is it a woman?"

Lexi smiles briefly and then surprises me by bursting into tears. "It was never supposed to happen." She sobs. "I still don't know how it did and it shouldn't feel right but it does." She looks so haunted that I reach out for her hand.

"Then it must be ok? Why are you crying?"

"Please don't hate me." She whispers looking down at her hands. "I am so sorry Freya."

William.

My best friend.

My best friend and my husband?

The frigid chill clutches at my heart, squeezing me from the inside out until I can't breathe. The numbness protects me from the agony but it can't prevent the world slowly crashing down, brick by brick. The double betrayal – my husband and my best friend – is something I cannot comprehend.

"He said there wasn't anyone else." I say to no one. "I knew there was but he said he wasn't leaving me for anyone. Why you?" I look up at Lexi and almost spit. "Why you?"

"It just happened…Freya, it was never meant to…he didn't want me to tell you, not yet, not until you were ok with him leaving. He cares…I care…I just fell in love…I didn't mean to…Not William, it was never supposed to be William…"

A tidal wave smashes over me, taking my breath, pounding me down until I can't see. I am drowning slowly under the weight of her words, the huge impact of the second life changing event. My husband and my best friend. How long? How many lies? How many times did they laugh at my naivety, that I would never have suspected them. Never thought either of them capable of hurting me so badly.

I rock in the chair with my head in my hands trying to stop the voices. "This isn't happening." Then louder, "this isn't happening. What kind of sick joke are you trying to pull Lexi…"

"It isn't a joke Freya," Lexi looks distraught. "I wouldn't joke about something like this. It's always been him, the first moment I met him that was it, I was lost. No one else has ever come close to him. I fought it, ignored it, hoped it would go away but it didn't. You two were never suited, you were too vibrant, too alive and I watched as you thought you fell in love, but you never did really, you didn't ever speak about Will like he was your one true love. And it was hard to see because I loved him so completely…"

"So that makes it ok does it?" I hiss. "It's ok for you to take my husband because you thought I didn't love him. Of course I loved him…"

"There is love and there is *love* Freya."

"What do you know about love?"

"That there are no rules, no boundaries, no sense…it's when you can't bear to be apart for even a minute because you can't feel complete unless they're there beside you, it's passion and desire and understanding…"

"And that's what you and William have is it?" I spit.

She nods mutely. "Hurting you…Freya that's the last thing I ever wanted to do."

"I can't be here…" The shock rings in my voice and I put my hands over my ears to drown her out. "I can't be near you."

Blindly I stumble from the table and run across the restaurant my heels clattering on the tiled floor. Outside I hail a taxi.

"Freya…Freya…"Lexi comes running after me. "Freya I am so sorry…"

"You…you…you….absolute bitch." I scream at her. "How could you Lexi? How could you? He is my husband…you knew everything. Everything. I told you everything Lexi and you did this? How could you? Of all the men in the world, why mine? Why William? Why?" The pedestrians on the street stop to look at us. I glance around at them longing for one of them to take me away from this nightmare, to make it all go away. I need someone to make it go away.

"Because I fell in love..." She sobs, her tears mingling with her mascara sending waves of black down her cheeks.

"Love?" I am so incensed, so broken hearted that I practically froth at the mouth, "what about me? You were my best friend..."

"I am your best friend..."

"No." I hold up my hand, "no Lexi you are not." I yank open the taxi door. "Now I wonder if you ever were. Erin was right about you. I should have listened to her. Miss Perfect House and Perfect Parents and Perfect Manners...you are the lowest of the low. Was it all a lie Lexi? Our friendship? Did you always plan to take him? You always said how hot he was, why did I never think that was strange?"

"Because..."

"Were you fucking him all along? Laughing at me? Did you both laugh at me because it would never occur to me that either of you would shit on me. What the fuck did I do to deserve this? All those times, all those nights I sat up with you, reassuring you that you would meet the great love of your life and have it all. Never once did I even think it was William you wanted...You can burn in hell, both of you..." I slide into the car and slam the door. I can't stop shaking. Despite the warm day I feel the frigid chill of shock and the cold path of the tears that roll down my face. The raw intense pain of the grief I feel is clenching my heart and squeezing with wiry fingers until I heave for breath.

"Miss?" The taxi driver kindly attracts my attention. "Where too miss?"

I give the taxi driver my home address and collapse into the plastic seat. Just as I think my life is changing for the better another bombshell lands at my feet but this time it is so much worse.

The taxi driver slowly pulls away and I glimpse Lexi's stricken face before we move out into the traffic. I concentrate on the music, light pop that sounds much the same as everything that has come before it. I want to tell the driver to turn it off, I want the sun to stop shining and I want the world to stop turning. What do I do now my best friend has betrayed me?

My best friend.

Gone.

***

The door crashes open making me jump. My head pounds, the effects of too much crying and too many questions fighting to space in my brain. I rub my face, smoothing under my eyes hoping mascara hasn't left streaks down my face to give me away, and haul myself off the sofa as Erin and Imogen noisily enter the lounge.

"Jesus Freya you look like hell!" Erin stands in front of me, hands on hips, appraising my appearance with critical eyes. "Fucking Lexi…" Erin pulls me into a hug and I give into my tears. "I can't believe she'd do this to you. Bitch!."

"Erin…" Imogen warns.

"Look Freya." Erin takes my hands. "I cannot imagine how you are feeling about all of this. I don't understand how Lexi would let this happen."

"She is my oldest friend…" I whisper. "She knows everything about me. I think my heart is broken all over again. It is one betrayal too many. William I can cope with but Lexi…she knew it all. I told her all about the problems William and I were having and about the surprise holiday to Mexico I'd booked so we could sort it all out. I feel sick."

"You still have us." Imogen says.

"I know darling friends. I know and I am so grateful for you."

"So tonight we are taking you out. It may be Sunday but there is a big wide world out there." Erin says.

I start to protest but she quietens me with a glare. "We would not be doing our duty as friends if we left you to rot in your own misery."

"I don't want to go out." I mumble.

Imogen gives me a hug, "I'm going to run you a bath.... "

"I don't want to go out." I reiterate protesting and they take one of my arms each and march me to the bedroom.

"You are going out. We are going out to have some fun. You've hardly been out and you can't fester any longer in this house." Imogen leaves me with Erin and I hear the bath running.

"I do go out."

"Going to work doesn't count." She says.

"I go other places." Except it all seems like a lifetime ago. Connor seems like a lifetime ago.

Erin pulls open my wardrobe. "I like this dress," she says taking out the red cocktail dress, "this is very sexy. How come I've not seen this one before?"

"I made it for William's partnership party..." I trail off. "I don't want to go out." I whisper.

"Freya, I'm sorry to be blunt but you are a complete mess. This is not you. There is a whole world out there that is waiting for you, with opportunities and chances and even perhaps the right man. Not a jumped up dick like William, but one who will treat you right, believe in your dreams the way he never did. You need to hold your head up high and take the step into a new life. No one will repent anything with you looking like this. You are better than them so bloody well show them that you are. William needs to see what he has lost, but not for one moment are you to consider taking him back." She looks fierce. "Never are you to even think about it. Come on Freya get in the bath. A night out will do you good and will stop us badgering you." Erin pushes me into the bathroom where Imogen is running me a scorching hot bubble bath.

"There is a face pack, hair mask and exfoliator waiting for you. Pamper yourself and then be ready for a night on the town. I'll go any get you a glass of wine…"

"I don't have any." I interrupt Imogen's instructions.

"I brought some." She points at the bath. "In!"

I admit defeat and sink into the hot water closing my eyes.

Imogen knocks on the door and comes in bringing me a large glass of wine.

"How are you doing really?" She asks sitting down on the lid of the toilet.

"I don't really know how I feel Immy. The shock of Lexi is worse than the shock of William leaving me. She and I spoke almost every day, until recently, and now I know the reason she hasn't been answering my calls. I told her everything and all the while she was sleeping with him. I feel utterly foolish." I take a long drink of my wine. "I didn't realise anything could ever make me feel so bad. It's like I've been stabbed in the gut with a serrated knife that has been wrenched back out. It's all centred around my stomach and the churning is making me feel so sick."

"Do you still want him back?" Imogen looks at me with gentle eyes, "after what he's done."

"No!" I exclaim. "No, no no. I would be happy to watch him burn in hell along with Lexi and his bloody mother. But the hurt I feel, it's so painful Immy, it's like a boiling acid melting my insides. There's no escape from it. I can't forget I know, I can't turn off the words she said, like it was somehow my fault that I got in the way. I think she wanted me to understand, to be ok with it, but I'm not because she destroyed all the years we've been friends in one sentence. She's welcome to him, they deserve each other…" I feel such anguish. "What could I have done to deserve this Immy? I try to be a good person and it hasn't made a difference."

"Have you ever considered that perhaps it happened because William wasn't good enough for you?" She asks.

"Someone with his silver spoon?"

"Yes even with that. You know Freya, I think Erin is right that there is someone else meant for you and this happened so you'd meet?"

Fleetingly I think of Connor but instead I say, "what if we just get what we deserve?"

"That's what I mean! Perhaps your Mr Right is still waiting."

"Perhaps he's been and gone…"

"William was never good enough for you. He was never really supportive of you even though you tried to mould yourself to what he expected you to be." I try to object but she stops me. "No one should have to change for another person because it should just be enough to be who you are. There is someone else for you. Someone wonderful and someone who will encourage you and have faith in you and recognise your incredible talent…"

I smile. "I'm glad you don't mince your words Imogen!"

She laughs, "it's a lot politer than Erin would say!"

"That's true!"

Imogen hands me the face pack and conditioner before topping up my glass and leaving the room. "There really is someone for you Freya, the right person. He will come along when you don't expect it and fly you off to the moon."

"In a blue suit looking like Dean Cain?"

"Yep, of course. I've always told you that!" She giggles and leaves the bathroom. I lie my head back and close my eyes. Thank God for Erin and Imogen.

The next moment the sounds of the 80s, my guilty pleasure, floods through the ceiling speakers and from various areas of the apartment I hear out of tune singing to Duran Duran as my friends dance around. I giggle to myself and for the first time since Lexi's revelations I feel ready to face the world.

***

"Freya! Freya! Over here!" Henry waves enthusiastically at us from the corner of the bar. He is sitting with a group of models surrounded by bottles of champagne. "You're out on a Sunday? Is this a new Freya?"

"We're working on it!" Erin says laughingly giving Henry a kiss. "How are you gorgeous boy?"

"All the better for seeing you, laaaaaady!" He sing-songs. "It's been ages!"

"Hi Henry," Imogen leans in for a kiss.

"So...to what does London town owe this pleasure?" Henry waves at the bar tender who comes across with three more glasses and pouring the remainder of the bottle into them hands one to each of us. Henry eyes us. "On a Sunday! Freya Wood have you been possessed?"

"We are on a cheer up Freya reconnaissance." Erin tells him and leans in to give him the events of today.

"Bitch! Fucking, fucking bitch." He shouts turning red with anger. "How the fuck dare she, the bitch!"

"Shhh Henry, you'll get us thrown out!" I say mortified.

"Don't shush me Freya, the girl needs a slap!"

"Please...I don't want to talk about it, I just want some fun. I've spent all day going over and over everything and I just want talk about anything that doesn't involve them?"

"I'm going for a ciggie then we're going somewhere infinitely nicer than this." He leans in conspiratorially. "If I can't talk about your disastrous love life I can talk about mine...apparently, according to Courtney," one of the models looks up and smiles. "The Good Time Boys are at Cullen's in Mayfair. This could be my chance."

"Your chance for what?" Erin asks. I roll my eyes and smile resignedly.

"My chance of finding true love with Fred Lynch."

"The bassist?"

"Yeah, bassist and total God." Henry mocks fainting.

"They're coming in next week, can't you wait until then?" I ask drinking the nearly flat champagne.

"No I can't. Eyes meeting across a crowded bar is far more romantic."

"Oh Henry!"

"You'd do as well to get yourself a hot young thing Freya, never mind the bullshit husband and bullshit best friend…we're better friends so fuck her. Let's go mental!"

"Mental? On a Sunday?" I grimace. "With work tomorrow."

"Phone in sick. We could tell Carrie we had a dodgy curry!" Henry says beginning to collect his effects and putting an unlit cigarette in his mouth.

"She'd never believe it! She knows you too well and knows I've lost my marbles!" I stand up. "Yeah what the hell, let's go mental. I just need the cash machine because William stupidly left his wallet and cash card behind yesterday, and it just so happens that his cash card has made its way into my purse! I think he can pay for this evening!"

"Yay, wanker William has a purpose in life!" Henry links arms with me and the crowd of us leave the bar and out into the night.

It always amazes me that London is always busy no matter what the day or time. The city is so full of energy, life, promises and stories that it never sleeps. As the world turns so the city changes, new venues, events, restaurants, all popping up with an endless enthusiasm. Sometimes it can be a cold, lonely place and if it weren't for my friends picking up the pieces it would be a very isolating town for me this evening.

"How are you doing baby girl?" Henry asks slowing down. I match his pace until the others are in front of us.

"I'm doing my best to hold it all together." I take hold of his hand. "How can it be that everything can change so quickly, that one minute it was all planned and the next I am hurtling from disaster to disaster with no idea of where I am going? William wants to sell the house and I want so much to buy it from him but there is no way I will be able to find the money, he keeps apologising but now I know about him and Lexi there is no way he ever make up for what he did. I didn't ever realise that life can be so conflicting and that how I feel can be conflicting and then there is…." I stop before I can tell him about Connor.

Henry gives me a comforting hug. "Light of my life," he says, "you will come through this but honestly if you tell me ever again that you want that lying toad back I will beat you. You are so beautiful that if I was straight I'd whisk you off to Vegas quicker than you could say Elvis. Someone will come along for you, someone wonderful who will love you with all his heart and who is infinitely more attractive than that little wanker. You need cocktails my darling girl, lots of them and Uncle Henry is going to provide them."

"I want to go home." I mumble.

"That is exactly what you are not doing." Henry says. "It's time to say 'fuck it' to the universe. He was never right for you. He always held you back, put you down and just didn't love you enough. Not nearly as much as I love you. You deserve the handsome prince in the fairy tale who will leap tall buildings and fly faster than the speed of light!"

"Superman doesn't exist."

"Perhaps not the one from Krypton but a super man is out there for you. I promise. Have faith in your fairy godmother…and the cocktails I can provide!" Henry wraps his arm around my shoulder and pulls me close.

"I wish that for you too Henry. I wish that super man would find you, you have so much love in your heart…"

"Stop it you'll make me cry and my man-scara will run!"

"Your what?" I ask incredulously.

"Man-scara, oh princess you didn't think these luscious lashes were all mine!"

Giggling we weave our way into Cullen's and I order five bottles of champagne with the cash I've taken from William's bank.

Cullen's is busy with the young, beautiful and wealthy. We find a table and the conversation that flows is lively. I am sat beside a handsome male model from Massachusetts who shares my geeky obsession with the 80s. It is a fun conversation to have and the champagne continues to flow long after my five bottles are drunk. At midnight Erin and Imogen excuse themselves.

"Are you coming with us?" Erin asks gripping tightly to Imogen as she sways. "This is going to hurt tomorrow."

"No, you go on, I live the other way so I'll get a taxi as soon as I've finished this drink."

"Bye babe." They drunkenly move in to give Henry and me a goodbye kiss and I watch them staggering, giggling like students, across the room. I grin, despite the revelations it's been a great night.

"It's cool here isn't it?" Henry comments putting his feet up on the table.

"It is very cool…but then so are we!" I giggle.

"And it's full of beautiful people which is always a bonus."

"It is?"

"Of course! It means that there are plenty of hot single straight young men here for you to have a little flutter with. A shag is exactly what you need to forget about Wanker William."

"Wanker William!" I laugh hysterically.

"He is...He was never good enough for you. So bloody uptight and self-righteous. A total arse. One day you will look back on all this and breathe a sigh of relief that you had a lucky escape."

"Will I?"

"Yes you will!" He kisses my hand. "You will find your one true love my sweet, when you least expect it."

"You are such a wonderful person Henry."

"Not so wonderful that my knight in shining armour has shown up yet." Henry looks so despondent that I give his hand a squeeze.

"He will. He just has to be special enough to deserve you...Darling Henry, I am done. Home time for me!" I announce.

"No, no no!" Henry says firmly, "it most certainly is not home time! This place is full of gorgeous straight men...Go meet someone...go drink lots...go go go! Seriously Freya, have some fun, loosen up, get laid."

I give Henry a wry smile and suddenly think of Connor. I wonder where he is.

"Not tonight Henry." I lean to hug Henry. "Thanks babe, thanks for suggesting we come here tonight. Love ya long time."

"Love ya long time too." He gives me a kiss on the mouth and when I stand up and turn away I look up straight into Connor's icy eyes. I feel a momentary delicious flicker in my stomach until he turns his eyes from mine with a look of complete distaste on his face. I remain still for a moment then taking a deep breath I walk towards him but before I can reach him he is surrounded by a gaggle of giggling twenty-somethings. Feeling drunk and rejected I turn towards the exit and walk out into the night.

It's cold and the moon is bright in the sky illuminating London. I shiver against the chill and begin to walk quickly towards Claridges in the hope of hailing a taxi. I feel sad, really sad and everything that once seemed so certain has crashed in a heap on the floor. Even the excitement of Connor has faded into nothing and I feel so desolate that I can no longer hold back my tears.

I am so wrapped up in my melancholy that I don't hear the footsteps until Connor is by my side.

"Who was he?"

"Who?" Surreptitiously I wipe my eyes.

"The man you were kissing?"

"Henry? He's my friend."

"What kind of friend?"

"A gay friend."

"Are you crying?"

"No," I lie.

"You are! Why are you crying?"

I stop still. "Because I am sad Connor, I am sad because my life is out of my control. I am sad because my best friend was having an affair with my husband and now she is gone forever. I am sad because I am about to lose my home and because I'm drunk and…oh never mind Connor, none of it matters." I shout at him. "Go back to your fancy pieces and leave me be." I storm off blindly as more tears begin to fall. He runs to me.

"Red wait! They're not my fancy pieces. I have no interest in them. Red…stop…what can I do?"

I face him, fat angry drunken tears falling down my face. "You can get the fuck out of my head."

"I am in your head?"

"Yes you're in my head! You're almost all I think about. It's a crazy, fucked up disaster…" The laugh that comes out of me is bitter, mirthless, as cold as the evening. "Even when things crash down I still think about you. You need to go away. I don't know why I met you…" I slur. "I don't know why you came into my life but it's all spinning now when it was just upside down before. I feel sick…"

"You're in my head too." He mumbles. "And it drives me insane because I don't want you there. I think about you all the time and it's not something I'm used to."

"Who are you?" I wobble and reach for him to steady myself.

"Just Connor." He pulls me into a tight embrace. "Please, for now, just Connor."

I bury my head into his firm, hard chest. "Connor?"

"Yes."

"I'm tired."

Connor asks. "Are you going to stay the night?"

"The whole night!" I smile, his chest is warm and his heart beating is like a personal symphony. I inhale deeply, the wonderful manly smell of him that recently has sent my heart beating at a million miles an hour. Now, though, it just makes me feel protected.

***

I lie wrapped in Connors arms, the light from the full moon, watching over us, floating in through the open window. Below us London is quiet, the faint hum of the occasional car or conversations from pedestrians are carried in through the window. The night is cool, cooler than of late but smells fresh and perfumed, the scents from the park opposite drift in on the occasional gust of breeze. His skin, under my cheek, is warm, soft, encasing the toned muscles with silk. I lightly drop a kiss on his chest and he stirs beside me. The arms that hold me pull me tighter into him and his mouth finds mine. The kiss is gentle, soft, delicate, sweet. It's the kiss that belongs in a fairy tale where the handsome prince wakes up the sleeping princess with true loves' kiss.

Connor strokes his hands over my skin, a tender caress that I match. His skin quivers under my touch and I feel him hardening against my hip. "You are very beautiful Red." He murmurs running his finger softly over my eyelashes. "Your eyes are the most incredible colour of green, and…"

"What?" My voice is barely audible.

"I want to make love to you Red."

I smile softly and gently kiss his lips, his jaw and around his neck, his stubble prickling my inflamed mouth, taking in deep breaths of his scent as I do.

We discover each other. Slowly, tenderly, lovingly. Gentle kisses as our bodies merge, gentle hands on soft skin. We move together, two people lost in a moment, lost in the warm touch of love making. I love his body - so muscular with the heady masculine scent - and the weight of him on me bearing down on me grounds me into the reality of us. His touch is so different to what has gone before and his mouth is gentle on my breast, licking and caressing as they rise for him. I wrap my legs around him, lifting my hips for him to enter me deeply. His hands always stimulate me as mine do him. We match each other, we fit, and slowly the heat begins to spread through me.

"I am going to come," I whisper.

He gives my orgasm his full attention and as I reach the dizzy heights so he moves quicker to find his release. As I lie wrapped in his arms the first light peeps through the window.

MONDAY

"What are you doing tonight?" The lilting Irish voice asks down the phone line. "You didn't say goodbye."

I kick the office door shut with my toe, it slams and I mouth 'sorry' to those closest to my office.

"You were sleeping! I'm going to Erin's for dinner. Why?" I ask leaning back in the chair. "Did you have something in mind?"

"When it comes to you I have a lot in mind!"

"Tell me more." I say seductively leaning back in my chair and closing my eyes. I want to hear his voice telling me descriptively what plans he has, I want to know what he wants to do with me and to me. As my heart beat increases so I have the feeling of floating. I know I will not be getting any work done today.

"I'll show you. Come by after dinner but be warned, I'm in a 'bad' mood."

The phone clicks as he hangs up and my eyes spring open. He cannot seriously have left me like this, hanging on, wondering? His words leave behind an anticipation and a thrill that runs from my toes up through every sense, every nerve in my body. I look at my to-do list but the words jumble on the page until each line reads *Connor*. He is unashamed in his sexuality, confident and in some ways arrogant, like he would challenge a woman to say no to him. He makes me feel that he wants me immediately, that I can't say no because that doesn't happen to him. So different to William who never made me feel like he wanted me there and then with an all-consuming passion. It was always planned. Always timetabled in between everything else he thought was important. How did I not notice that I was just a schedule?

How did I ever think that what William and I had was enough? I sigh.

"That's a big sigh, what's the matter?" Carrie asks walking into my office.

"Nothing, I was just thinking…"

"About anything interesting?"

Yes. "No."

"Have you finished the piece on Lacey?"

"Carrie, it's ten am! I've been in for an hour! Give me a chance!" I exclaim holding up my hands.

"I know that but I also know that you and Henry were out drinking last night…"

"And?"

"And I've just seen Henry slopping off to be sick. Again. Honestly he takes the piss…"

"Carrie," I reply trying not to laugh at her outrage, "the article will be done, on time and to your exacting standards! We are having a departmental meeting at two to organise this week and Henry is going to a meeting with St Julian's College at four. Everything will be fine. Henry won't let being sick get in the way of perving at undergraduates. Stop worrying…"

"I am worrying…I can't…Never mind." She swivels on her heels and leaves the office quickly, the scent of Stella McCartney and cigarettes hanging in the air.

I try to make sense of my haphazard notes and tapes from the interview with Lacey. She is my favourite designer, perhaps not technically, but her enthusiasm and delightful personality has rocketed her skywards. I can't help feeling envious that she has achieved such acclaim but she definitely deserves it and I predict that she will eclipse even the most well-known fashion houses. Her approach is simple – young, sexy and confident – her designs reflect a young woman's outlook, to take on the world and win. Where Lacey has succeeded lies in beautifully cut clothing that complements any shape and is priced only just high enough to be a designer label.

What would the risk be to try and reach the stars? Financial? Yes. Emotional? Yes. Professional? Yes. Is it worth the risk? *Yes.* That is the biggest question of them all. As the thoughts crowd my head a design forms on the scribble pad under my keyboard. An evening dress that gives the suggestion of flowing water, the blues, greens and indigos, colours that shouldn't go together, but somehow do, colours that I've seen in Connor's eyes.

"Are you going to make that?" Henry wakes me from my creative daydream. He looks decidedly yellow.

"Maybe. One day." I stretch. "Carrie has been in…"

"Carrie has given me the biggest bollocking." He interrupts. "She's sitting in her office chain smoking like a demon."

"She needs to give up." I eye him forcefully. "You need to give up. You do know that Fred Lynch doesn't smoke, drink or do anything particularly rock star like…"

"Has a date been set yet?"

"No…"

"Freeeeeee-yaaaaaaaaa!" Henry whines.

"Henry, I've been in work for an hour…"

"Long enough to draw a sodding picture."

"I was thinking."

"Think about me!" He sulks. "Me, your bestest gayest friend."

"Henry." I say firmly. "I have work to do. I do think about you, a lot, but right now I need to think about avoiding a bollocking from Carrie and get this article finished and you need to think about the photo shoot at the college. Can we get back to your love life once all that is done?"

"I don't have a love life." Henry looks so glum that I get out of my chair to give him a hug.

"You will and it will be wonderful." I promise him.

"If I don't, ever, will you sit on the shelf with me?" He asks gloomily.

"Yes!" My phone rings loudly making us both jump like scalded cats. "God that nearly gave me a heart attack." I mutter, hand on chest, the other reaching for the receiver. "Freya Wood."

"Hi Freya, this is Fred Lynch from Good Time Boys." The voice on the other end announces. I sit down heavily in my chair.

"Hi Fred, how are you?" I reply grinning inanely at Henry.

"Fred? Fred? As in Fred Lynch Fred?" He asks bouncing up and down. I wave him quiet.

"Good thanks Freya. I was hoping to see if our diaries would fit in the shoot you mentioned. I've got a little time off."

I give Henry a beaming smile and thumbs up. Trying to maintain my professionalism I say, "Thank you Fred, that would be amazing. When's good for you, we can work around your schedule." Henry is a worrying purple colour, any minute smoke will be pouring out of his ears.

"Thursday is good. Around three?"

"Perfect. I'll book the photographer," I grin wickedly at Henry who collapses in the spare chair. "Thank you for coming back to me so quickly and I really do appreciate your time, I can imagine time off is a precious commodity."

"Like you'd not believe but I've not done anything like this on my own before, it would be too much fun to pass up."

"Well Fred, we are looking forward to having you here. Can I take an email address so that we can get some details from you before Thursday, primarily for wardrobe, I promise it won't be disclosed to anyone." I scribble down the address he gives me. "Thanks, I'll also confirm location, we normally do shoots offsite so I'll get a venue booked and we'll see you there."

"Great Freya, looking forward to it."

"Likewise Fred."

"Bye Freya."

"Bye Fred."

"Oh. My. God. I need to lie down." Henry squeals. "Then I need to book a tan, and makeup and…"

"I can sort all that…"

"For me!" As quick as lightening Henry is out of the room and flying across the open plan office. I smile at his retreating back, there is so much love in me for Henry, one of life's truly good people. It feels great to be able to do this for him, particularly after everything he has done for me.

With a contented sigh I return to the article on Lacey.

***

"God what a day!" I moan to Erin as she opens the door.

"Bad?"

"Long! It took all day to write one article that should have taken five minutes to do! Carrie was stressing…urgh…I need wine, carbs and someone to make me laugh."

"Imogen is wearing yellow, will that do?"

"Yellow? With bleached hair? Eek!" I grin.

"You are a pair of bitches!" Imogen calls from the lounge. "I am going to find new friends who like my hair."

Erin and I smile at each other and cross the kitchen. I pause to put the prosecco in the fridge and hang my coat on the back of the chair. "Hello Imogen," I say greeting her with a hug and a kiss. Today she has dyed her hair a stark blonde. It suits her, bringing out the olive tones of her skin and the flecks of gold in her eyes. "I love your hair. You look like a goddess from Vesuvius."

"Really?" She runs her fingers through her hair, the blonde catching the light.

"Yes, really! Would I lie to you?" I ask her quizzically. "It is lovely, very Marilyn Monroe!"

"Did you enjoy last night?" Erin asks handing me a drink.

"Yeah I did. It turned out to be exactly what I needed but..." I say taking a sip. "I need to stop drinking...after tonight I mean!"

"We've heard you say that for fifteen years!" Imogen giggles.

"She'll be saying it for the next fifteen too!" Erin replies. "Were you drunk last night then?"

"Yeah. Totally hammered! I am a lush!"

"A lush lush!"

"Still a lush though." I pull a face! "What would my mother say?"

"Jen is cool, she wouldn't say a lot!" Imogen says opening some crisps and pouring them into a dish next to a pot of dip.

"Yes she would! She'd say, *'Freya, it's not really appropriate behaviour for a woman of your age'*. Then I'd say, *'ah but mum, my husband did dump me you know!'*"

"And then she's say, *'ah but Freya he was a total knob!'*" Erin chips in and we all laugh. "You do know he is a knob don't you."

"Oh God do I ever! I thought it was the end of the world but looking back at it all everything about us was poles apart and I think that perhaps we lasted so long because of habit and convenience. What happened to the student with dreams of taking on the world and seeing my name in lights? Where did she go?"

"You grew up!"

"Well growing up sucks and I don't want to be grown up. I've done grown up and it's slapped me in the face. I intend to be wild and frivolous and absolutely not give a fuck about trying to be perfect."

"You are perfect." Imogen smiles gently. I smile back at her.

"So you are really over Will?" Erin asks disbelievingly. "I mean really over him. Not just pretending to make us less worried or something?"

"Yes." I reply with conviction. "Definitely over him." I wonder what Connor is doing now, what he has in mind and the fluttering in my stomach returns. I feel a secret smile begin to curve the corners of my mouth.

"Freya?" Erin pulls me from my thoughts.

"Yes?"

"Are you dwelling?"

"No just thinking about something."

"What about?"

Shall I tell them? "The future." I lie. "I am going to recharge and think about my future and what I want. There is a big world out there and its time I saw it."

"Do you really mean all this?" Erin asks. "I mean really mean it? I know you too well Freya, underneath this bravado there is a little girl lost."

"I'm not lost."

"I think you are."

"I'm not lost I've just been on the wrong road."

"Wrong road means lost."

"It does not! The wrong road just means a slight detour."

"So where are you detouring to?"

"I don't know."

"Hence my question. Do you really mean what you say?" Erin tops up our drinks. "Can you honestly tell me, hand on heart, you mean it?"

"Erin you are a cow sometimes." I drink my prosecco and glare at her.

"I'm a realist. You have been with William since you were twenty. Aside from two one night stands and a crap pre-uni boyfriend it has always been William. I just worry that you are somehow hanging on for him to come begging back to you."

"I am not." I state outraged.

"I am only asking all this because I love you Freya. We have been friends for seventeen years. Granted I don't know you as well as Lexi does but not far off and I did live with you for three years so I am allowed to comment. Imogen and I are worried that you are not handling things very well and we just want to make sure that you are coping."

"I'm coping." I think about Connor. I will tell my friends one day but for now I will enjoy the secret that gives my life a sexy warmth. "Really, I am! You don't have to worry, really I am fine! I always bounce back, you know that, this cannot be the thing that defines me. I cannot just be the person that was dumped by my husband I need to be more than that. I am going to be more than that. I feel like I have come out the other side of my black hole. I am designing, I am socialising, I am having fun... and I'm counting down to my holiday which by the way, I cannot wait for. Three weeks of sun, sea and sand!"

"And sex!"

"You never know!" I smile. "You never know."

"Are you really going to go on your own?" Imogen asks. "You hate being on your own."

"The old me hated it, the new me...well let's just say I'm embracing change and liking what I see!" I laugh and take a long drink.

"Well whatever you are doing it is certainly making you glow." Erin comments filling up our glasses, "and it's good to see. I didn't think you'd ever get over William but…" She stares into my eyes, "there is a glint in there so I am proposing a toast. To Freya and her glint...you know Freya, it's the same glint you had before life got in the way!"

"To glints!" I grin.

"To glints." Imogen holds up her glass and we clink together.

"So why do you have a glint Freya?" Erin asks eyeing me suspiciously. "Is there something you're not telling us?"

I flush slightly. "No!"

"I don't believe you." She says. "Do you Immy?"

"You do look different Freya." Imogen comments, "definitely more glowy!"

"Glowy? Is that even a word?" I laugh. "I told you, life feels good and very excitingly, for Henry at least, Fred Lynch is coming for an interview."

"Oh he's so dreamy!" Imogen swoons.

"Dreamy? Dreamy? What kind of dumbass, totally incorrect word is that for him?" Erin exclaims. "Dreamy? No way! Fuckable definitely!"

"My god, I'm surrounded by hormones!" I groan. "First Henry, now you two!"

"Can we come in? Be your PA for the day?"

"By PA I presume you mean Pain in Arse?"

"Ha bloody ha ha!" Erin grins. "But seriously…can we?"

I throw a cushion at her.

***

I knock on Connor's door. "Room service," I giggle as he opens the door.

His face darkens as he looks me up and down. "You're overdressed."

"Am I? Shall I take something off?"

"Take all of it off apart from your shoes and stand by the bed." He instructs. His eyes flash, a glittering dark blue and I shiver as I step into the room. My skin tingles as I begin to take off my coat and jeans. Wriggling them down I don't take my eyes from his face. He is watching me. His cheeks begin to flush and there is a self-satisfied smile that forms across his mouth. I fix my gaze on his mouth, the plump lips that bring me so much pleasure.

Slowly I unbutton my shirt and ease it down from my shoulders and loosen my hair from the clips that holds it tight. I shake my head then holding his eye I remove my bra and then my panties. A gasp escapes Connor's mouth as I stand before him, naked except for my shoes. "Now where do you want me?" I ask huskily. "Here?" I sit on the chair beside the bed. "Or..." I move to the bed and lie upon it. "...here?"

"Here." He says beckoning me with his finger. I walk towards him, one foot in front of the other, a Marilyn Monroe type of walk, with my hips swaying as I move. His erection is straining in his jeans and I reach for him but he moves away before I can touch him. Connor walks around me appraising me and tracing his fingers lightly across my skin as he does. I shiver. I can feel his smile in the air as he stands behind me and follows the outline of my body with his warm hands stroking and caressing me until I quiver and tremble with longing, every part of me on fire.

Connor pulls me backwards to him and I feel his heart beating fast under his shirt matching the rhythm of mine, a quick, strong pulse - the same fire in me is pulsating through him. I twist my head, straining to see his face and reach my arm back to grip the thick rich hair. Connor crushes my mouth, bruising my lips as I melt backwards, his arms about me holding me still.

"Connor." I moan against his mouth.

Connor maintains his slow exploration of my body, stroking the sensitive skin on either side of my sex. "I love to touch you." He says huskily his breath sweet against my neck, "I love the feel of your skin so soft and warm." Connor strokes his finger against me then gently slips it into me. "I love how wet you are, how I can make your body respond. Can you feel how wet you are Red, for me." He slides in another finger and I cry out, leaning against him and closing my eyes as his magical fingers begin to stroke and caress. His fingers are slick with my wetness as slowly he rubs the swollen bud of my sex.

"Oh Connor," I moan, "don't stop." The sounds of pleasure fill the room as my body lights up, each nerve fizzing and sparkling until I can almost make out the colours shimmering across my skin.

With his hand wrapped in my hair Connor leads me to the bed, lying me down on the cool sheets. He lies above me kissing my mouth, sucking my earlobes then down to my neck, the grooves of my collar bone, his hands on my breasts then his mouth on my nipples. Ever where his lips touch burns my skin, the scorching white hot response to a desire so unimaginable and so primal that conscious thought is lost. I pull at his hair but he moves himself from my grasp and continues his inspection of my body. Connor's breath is cool against the fiery furnace and the drum beat in my ears deafens me as slowly, agonisingly slowly, he licks my swollen sex. Gentle, wet strokes that send me wild. "You taste amazing," he tells me. "I could do this all day." Slowly he rubs his thumb across me and I beg for him.

"Please Connor…"

Connor flips me over and raises my hips running his hands over my arse. "You look stunning like this," he says, "such a hot ass. Shall I spank it?"

"No," I whisper but my body betrays me. Connor runs a finger up my thigh.

"Are you sure?"

"Yes." I'm not asking for it. I shouldn't even want it but the very thought of him marking me in a private way is blowing my mind.

"I think you want it." Connor slides a finger into me. "I think you like it." Whispering in my ear. "I think you'd find it fucking hot."

I hear him removing his clothes. I am so dizzy with longing and so over sensitised that right now he could do anything he wanted. Slowly he touches me and a million fireworks explode. "Connor, oh my God Connor." I gasp as he spanks my arse and as my mind processes the new sensations he enters me.

"Oh yes," I pant. "yes, oh yes Connor,.." Connor removes his cock and spanks me again. My skin burns under his hand, throbbing with the pleasurable pain. I can't control the trembles as he slides back into me, my hips moving against his powerful thrusts. Connor raises me up to lean on my hands and reaches forward to cup my breasts. His touch is rough, pleasurable and the pinching of my nipples sends sparks through me. I can barely hold myself up as the sensations ripple through my shimmering body. "You like that?" He questions.

"Yes." I whisper.

He withdraws from me and spanks me again. It is not an uncomfortable pain but more a pain that excites me. I am revolted by my body's reaction by the act and I hate that I want more. He makes me feel sexy and sensual and wanted and desired.

He grasps my hips and slides into me. I move against him pushing my hips higher for him to go deeper. We cry out and moan together as the passion for each other takes over our senses. Connor's hands explore my body over and over and the desire rises feverishly within me until I come loudly, his name on my lips. I feel him shudder behind me, his body hot against my skin and as he comes he fuses us together, two hot, perspiring bodies joined in the most intimate way.

TUESDAY

I lie in bed watching Connor sleep. He looks like an immortal god as the sun streams through the window, bathing him in golden light. Very softly I kiss his full, sensual mouth and creep out of bed.

"Where do you think you are going?" he mumbles groggily.

"I'm going home Connor."

"Why?"

"I have to go to work." I grimace at the twinges of discomfort, the ache from Connor's demanding sexual display. It's a sexy ache but one that will no doubt bring intense soreness throughout the day.

"'kay. S'later."

"Bye," I whisper and leave.

***

William is in the kitchen drinking coffee. The sight of him startles me.

"Been somewhere nice?" He asks his face hard.

"Yes thanks." I reply sharply. "What are you doing here?"

"I came to see you. I was hoping we could talk."

"I have to get ready for work Will can we do it another time?"

"No."

"Now isn't convenient."

"Why? Where have you been? Someone else's bed?"

"What business is it of yours?" I hiss. "Have you not just come from Lexi's bed?"

He sighs. "I don't want to fight Freya, I just want to talk."

"What about?"

"Us."

"There is no 'us'. You ended us, remember." I snap. To avoid looking at him I noisily refill the coffee machine banging a cup onto the counter and wrenching open the cutlery drawer in search of a spoon.

"What if I made a mistake?" I barely hear him. The whisper seems to echo around the room, bouncing from wall to wall getting louder and louder the longer I stand rigid, statue like, not moving, not breathing.

Shock leaves me speechless. I hear the clock tick as the silence between us stretches on and on. Slowly I turn to him. "A mistake?" I seethe, clenching the spoon tightly in my hand.

He swallows hard. "Yes. A big mistake. A mistake for which I am truly sorry."

"You fuck up everything and then you tell me it's a mistake?"

"I thought you wanted me back?" William looks at me anxiously, his hands twisting in on each other on the table.

"Perhaps I did once but not anymore Will. I can't look at you as anyone other than a liar and cheat who not only broke our marriage but destroyed my oldest friendship. Why would I ever go back to you? I don't want to be the person I was, who tried to be somebody that you and your precious mother would approve of. So, you can take your mistake and take a running jump William because it is well and truly over between us. You have to live with the consequences. I want nothing more to do with us, it's history. You are history."

"Did you sleep with someone last night?"

"That..." I snap, "...is really none of your business. Now please go."

"I don't want to go." He says quietly. "I have been such a fool Freya, this whole mess was such a mistake, I must have taken leave of my senses to do what I did and I want to come back. I will do whatever it takes for you to trust me again. I don't love Lexi, I thought I did but I think I was just bowled over by the attention. You seemed to stop noticing me…"

"Oh so it's my fault you cheated is it?" I interrupt furiously. "I didn't notice you? I noticed everything, you shit, everything. You were my whole world. I gave up what I wanted for you and followed the path that you walked down. I wanted to design but oh no, that didn't fit in with precious William and his rise to glory did it? You liked me doing what I did so that you could boast about it. My wife, the deputy editor yet to you and your mother I have always just been little council estate Freya with her silly job…"

"I loved you…" He corrects himself. "I love you Freya."

I shake my head. "I don't think you ever did really William. Not if you're honest. We didn't fit."

"Yes I did Freya, I still do. It's only ever really been you, of course we fitted. Everyone said so. I was such a fool to blinded by Lexi's flattery that I gave into feelings that were an illusion, it's not real, you are right for me, we are right together and if it takes a lifetime to make it up to you then that's what I'll spend my life doing. I don't feel complete without you. I want my life with you and I want the children we always talked about…"

"Why are you doing this?" I whisper the pain I am feeling echoing in my voice. "You can't do what you did and expect it to all be ok. It's not ok. I've moved on, I've repaired my life since you left me. You left me." I repeat with forceful emphasis. "You ripped our marriage apart but it won't fit back together William, the pieces are too badly damaged."

"The holiday you booked is only two weeks away, we could go…"

"I'm not going with you William. The part of my life that had you in it is over. I have to believe that what you did has opened the door to my future. The one I am supposed to have. I know you think we were right but if we had been then none of this would have happened. There has to be fire and passion and the intense need for that other person to make you feel whole and I don't think we ever had that. You are not my soul mate William, you are someone who mattered deeply and someone I will always hold in my heart but you are not the one…"

"Who is the one then?"

I ignore the question. "We both have to move forward now Will. Our marriage ending is the best thing for both of us. Lexi is right for you, you have the same background and the same outlook. She will make you happy if you let her and for what it's worth, just know that you're forgiven, I can't hold on to the hate and the anger, it's been eating me up. The house can go on the market and let's end things cleanly, take out what we put in."

"Get divorced you mean?"

"I want my life, I want to be free to love again and do the things that make me happy. You can't make me happy."

William's voice breaks. "I'll get the papers drawn up and instruct the agents."

"Thank you." I show him out, walking down the path with him. The air is cold but the sun is peeping around the edges of the cloud. "It's going to be a nice day."

"I can't persuade you to change your mind?" William asks cupping my face with his hands. "Please?"

"No, Will, it's too late."

"Freya, I…"

"Will you need to go now, don't say anything else." I leave him at the gate and without looking back I go into the house and shut the door.

How dare he? How dare he come here and say all that. My hands begin to shake violently as I give into a rage so black I could chase him down and rip out his internal organs one by one. I sit on my hands to stop the tremors but it begins to hurt so I wiggle my fingers to get the circulation moving again and pace the room. Bastard! Complete and utter bastard. Just exactly what was he hoping to achieve? That I would collapse back into his arms, that I could ever, ever forget who it was he had an affair with. Forgiveness is for my benefit because I do not want them to affect the rest of my life and to hold onto it would just weigh me down too much. But to take him back…what the fuck? No Way.

My future is so uncertain yet I know, buried deep down inside, is the answer to the path I must follow, I just need to find the map.

***

"Hey beautiful lady, how's tricks?" Henry comes waltzing into my office in a haze of hairspray and aftershave.

"Good," I reply distractedly. "You?"

"Better than you I think," he replies sitting in the chair opposite my desk and crossing his legs. "My spider sense tells me something is not rosy in Freya World…care to share?"

I sigh. "No not really."

"Still all complicated and chaotic?"

"No, not really. But you'll never guess what?"

"What?" He breathes dramatically poised for a revelation.

"William came round this morning and announced he's made a mistake."

"He didn't?" Henry leans forwarded looking outraged. "After what he did? I hold you told him to fuck off?"

"I sort of did, I told him what was what. You'd have been quite proud I think! Now I just feel like a total wreck and I could cry Henry. Not because I want my marriage and Will, more because it didn't work and I have to take some of the responsibility for that. Happy people don't have affairs…"

"You didn't have an affair…"

"I thought I was happy." The tears spill. "I really did. But now you are all saying we were never right, that he was an arse and that I tried to be someone I wasn't. Why didn't anyone tell me this years ago? Why did I let go of everything I wanted for someone who wasn't right for me? I feel like so much time has been wasted, when I could have been who I was supposed to be." Henry wraps his arms around me and I lean against his slim frame, his cologne stinging my nose.

"Sweetie, should you even be here? Just tell Carrie you're ill and go home. You've been working like a Trojan since it all happened…"

"I can't go home I've got work to do." I well up again. "I don't even know if I can call it home anymore. William needs to sell…"

"So does he want you back or not?"

"I don't think he knows what he wants."

"Do you know what you want?"

"Sometimes…" I mumble, "but then the game changes again."

"Game?"

"Do you ever feel as though you are in the middle of a game and you are not in charge of your hand? Just when I think I know where I'm going I face another direction and it's making me dizzy."

"Please tell me you don't want him back, not after this?"

I look at Henry. "I told him it was over. We can't make it work after this and I just don't want to be the Freya I was when I was with him. I have to move on Henry, I can't do that if I'm with Will, except it just means that I've failed…"

"You've not failed my angel, failure is just not a word that could ever be linked with you. You are amazing, the most amazing person I know, he failed you, this is his failure not yours but you have to find a new path, you know what you should be doing Freya, you just have to do it." Henry comes around to my desk and crouches down in front of me. Taking my hands in his he says, "Sweetie, take some time off. Go home. Get some therapy. Anything that doesn't involve sending yourself crazy...Carrie will understand, she's as worried about you as I am. Sometimes, you come in and there is a light in your eye and I think I've got Freya back, then the pale, baggy eyed you comes in and I've lost you again. Freya, I worry about you. You're my girl."

I bury my head into Henry who holds me tightly as I cry. I cry for everything, the lost dreams and the lost hope. I'm teetering on the edge of a precipice and I don't know when it will collapse, sending me falling again.

"Thank you." I whisper.

"Glad to be of service but for fucks sake Freya, go home. I love you but you look like shit and now I have to change my shirt...honestly being friends with you...!" Henry winks at me and I smile back. "Go home, take a few days off and come back in refreshed. Carrie will say the same thing..."

"Yes Carrie would..." The editor walks into my office looking pale and drawn. "She would say 'get out of here'..."

"But..."

"No buts. It's an order."

"But I have work today and my holiday..."

"Quite honestly Freya you need to just not be here. Go. Before I change my mind. I need you here firing on all cylinders tomorrow so come back refreshed and able to take over..." I look at Carrie with questions in my eyes but she gives me a 'please don't ask' look and I nod. A sense of unease creeps over me, gripping my stomach tightly with icy fingers.

I flick my eyes between them. "Thank you. Both of you. I'll be back in tomorrow.

Carrie lights a cigarette. "Don't look at me like that, you're not here!" She says giving me a stern look.

"And there I thought smoking in the work place was banned!" Henry gives a cough.

"You should be banned Henry you look like a goddamn tangerine, who on earth did that tan?" Carrie snaps back.

"Never you mind!" He winks at me and blows a kiss. "See you tomorrow sweetie," and with that Henry breezes out of my office.

"He has a point Carrie, my office is going to stink."

"It won't by tomorrow. Go!"

Needing no further encouragement I grab my bag and, kissing Carrie on the cheek, I escape the confines of the office and out into busy street where the lunchtime crowds begin to assemble, walking like ants towards the wine bars and restaurants. I join them, with a slight spring in my step and decide to treat myself to lunch.

I order a glass of sparkling water which is presented to me in a long flute with crushed ice and I sit at a table at the back of the room, away from the assembling crowd of city workers, some of whom eye me in that sleazy way of very rich men who think they own the world and every woman in it. Avoiding eye contact I watch them ordering vast amounts of alcohol as they backslap and jeer their through conversations. It's the same picture as every day in the city, wealthy men flashing the cash in a vulgar way. I turn my gaze from them and focus on the menu.

I wonder what Connor is doing. There has been no discussion on time but even I know that someone can't live in The Stark Hotel indefinitely. *Work is paying,* he'd said. *I do whatever they tell me to do.* Suddenly there is the overwhelming, breath-taking urge to see him. To see his eyes dancing, the blue/green eyes that shine at me like I'm the only woman in the world, framed by the thick chestnut lashes, to see the smile, the oh so sexy smile that curves up the corners of his sensual mouth. But more than that, I want to know him, really know him, everything there is to know and more.

I find the number I need on the internet and take a deep, calming breath before dialling.

"Good afternoon, the Stark Hotel, how may I assist?"

"Suite Four please."

"One moment please."

The one moment seems to take a very long time. I wave away the waiter who has come to take my order with a quick smile.

"Yes." The lilting Irish accent sends tingles down my spine.

"It's me."

"Hello Red."

"Hi."

"Hi!"

I can hear a smile in his voice and I feel suddenly shy. "I just wondered what you were doing."

"Not much. I could tell you but then I'd have to kill you!" Laughter dances in his expressive voice.

"So secretive." I grin.

"Secrets are fun, don't you think?"

"Yes, sometimes…"

"Only sometimes?"

"My life is an open book, I don't normally have secrets."

"Then I'm honoured."

"Don't be…I am just using you, I hope you know!" I giggle.

"I know…" He chuckles.

There is a shift, subtle but it's there and I feel a gentle warmth surround me. "So, this secretive thing…is it going to take all day?"

"Perhaps."

"Oh."

"Why?"

"I was just wondering if you wanted to go and see a movie with me."

"Like a date?" He's laughing at me.

"I suppose."

"Well Red, I am surprised…"

"Are you?"

"Are you not working?"

"Nope. Free as a bird…do you want to see a movie with me or not?"

"Are you getting grouchy?"

I take a long drink. "It's a simple question that really just needs a simple answer!"

"You are getting grouchy!"

"Forget I asked." Crossly I hang up the phone and shove a handful of peanuts into my mouth. What possessed me? I scroll through some social networking sites until the waiter comes back and I order a burger and fries with all the trimmings. "Sod it," I grumble to myself fishing in my bag for a magazine. I am midway through the editorial when my phone rings.

"What?" I ask stroppily.

"Are you pissed off?"

"No."

"You sound it."

"It will take more than you to make me pissed off." I lie.

"I don't believe you."

"Whatever."

"Where are you?"

"In a bar."

"Which one?"

"Why?"

"Because I'll come and meet you."

"Why?"

"So that we can go to the movies."

"I may not want to go to the movies."

"I'll still come and meet you."

I smile. "I'm at Luca's Bar in the city."

"I'll find it." The phone goes dead.

I settle back in the seat reading the magazine until my food arrives, closely followed by Connor. He grins as he crosses the floor towards me, his head covered by a LA Lakers baseball cap and he is clothed in a Star Wars t-shirt and jeans. He looks so handsome, his jeans fitting closely to his strong thighs and tight across the groin, that I involuntarily shiver which just makes him grin widely.

"Hey."

"Hi" I reply popping a chip in my mouth.

"That looks good."

"Mmm," I say picking up my knife and fork. Connor watches me intently as I cut my burger in half then add a huge dollop of ketchup to my plate. "What's the matter? Have you never seen anyone eat before?"

"Yes of course…but…never mind!" He relaxes into his seat and watches me as I pop a ketchup covered chip into my mouth.

"Are you going to order anything?"

"I'm going to have the same as you." A waiter appears with a poised pen. "May I have a pint of lager and a burger with everything please?"

"Of course." The waiter disappears and Connor leans back against the upholstered chair.

"I'm glad you called." He says with a smile. "My day was starting to blur. So how have you managed to be off work?"

"I think my boss is of the opinion I am cracking up!" I smile wryly.

"Are you?"

Connor's blue/green eyes seem to bore right through me.

"It feels like it!"

"Life gets crazy sometimes doesn't it?"

"Life is throwing up so many unexpected balls I'm losing the ability to juggle."

"I've got some balls you could juggle with." He grins and I laugh.

"Yeah, I bet you do!" I take a big bite of my burger. It's big and juicy and so full of flavour that my taste buds explode. "This is really good." I say with my mouth full.

"I hope they hurry up, I'm starving." Connor appraises me. "You have ketchup on your chin."

I reach for a napkin but he beats me to it, gently wiping the red sauce away. "Thanks." I flush.

"No bother." There seems be an awkward pause until Connor says, "do you still want to see a movie this afternoon?"

I nod. "I don't know what is on though. I'm not really a movie goer."

"No? So you don't queue around the block to see the latest big budget film starring the hot young actor of the moment?" He asks amused.

"No." I shake my head. "I think the last film I saw at the cinema was Titanic, although I guess it did star the then hot young actor. Actually, he's just about the only actor I know!"

"You're joking?" Connor looks astounded. "I thought women these days were all about the superhero with the huge muscles…"

"Only superman for me…" I pull a face, "I am a seriously sad case aren't I?"

"Not really, I think it's kind of cool…"

"I suppose my escapism has always been drawing, when I could. Will didn't think much of what I designed but I still liked to do it."

"How did you meet your husband?" He reaches over and takes a chip. I pull a face.

"Please don't come between a woman and her chips."

"Don't change the subject!"

"I met William at university. He was the campus heart throb. Everyone knew who he was, he was so cool…at the time…most of the girls I knew wanted to sleep with him at the very least and go out with him at the most. I didn't think he'd ever notice me, not with all the skinny blondes that floated past him regularly until one day when I was crossing campus and the heavens opened. I ran like a bullet across the car park and the rain…I'd never seen anything like it. Anyway, we met at the door and got talking, had a few drinks and that was that…until recently." Floppy haired, sports mad twenty year old William comes into my mind with his sparkling eyes and beaming smile.

I must pull a face as Connor says. "Do you miss him?"

"I did…before…" *You* hangs in the air, visible and loud. For a moment we lock eyes and the pull of the magnets are so strong neither of us can look away. I hear a drum beating inside me, loudly, a pulsating rhythm that tingles my skin. I don't know how long we remain like this but eventually I break the spell. "It was a double whammy because when William left he took my best friend too. It's kind of hard to get past the hurt from that."

"Bastard."

"Bitch!"

The waiter asks if there was anything else required. "Yes, some proper drinks please." Connor requests handing me the drinks menu.

"I don't want any alcohol today!" I say eating a chip. "I've been topping up all week!" Connor waves the barman away asking for a few more minutes.

"I bet you don't drink very often!"

"I do, I just know my limits! I used to be out and about all the time, always with a glass in my hand and occasionally a cigarette and then I hit thirty and the hangovers got so much worse. I have become boring and I've totally lost sight of the person I used to be. She was so much fun." I correct myself. "I was so much fun. I had some riotous times, so much laughter and I can't picture the time that it stopped but it did.

William's mother was so disapproving of me that I think I tried to become what was expected of me. I guess I failed on all counts. I've failed on a lot of things really and the worst part, I've failed myself. I never wanted to be the one that conformed, I used to wear wild clothes and make everything from castoffs that I found in charity shops. Sometimes it worked, sometimes I looked like a bag lady, but fashion and fun and living life to the max was my whole existence. William was always more serious, particularly after we graduated and he got his job and progressed. I couldn't wear feathers in my hair anymore because suddenly I had to dress the part. I'm thirty five years old Connor, and I have no fucking idea who I am or where I am going…"

"You're not married any more you can be whomever you want to be."

"Legally I'm still married and life is extremely confusing right now!"

"Do I confuse you?"

I smile. "Yeah you do, and the reason I met you is equally confusing. I know they say everything happens for a reason but I've never behaved like this."

"I'm your booty call!"

"Yeah, and I like it!" I giggle.

"I like it too!"

An intense look passes between us. It almost touchable, a bright light of energy that flickers as our eyes meet and a delicious shiver passes down my spine. I want to reach for him, cup my hand around his cheek, hold his face in my hand, kiss his mouth, feel his arms wrapped tightly around me, shutting out the rest of the world…

"Red…?"

"Uh…yeah?" I stammer.

"What are you thinking about?"

"All this."

"All this being what?"

"Do you ever just wonder what the reasons are that something is happening to you?"

"Not really. It all seems very simple to me."

"Does it? I wish it did for me!"

"I take life as it comes. I don't tend to think about it in too great a detail I just live it."

"Perhaps if the rest of us did that there would be less bullshit."

"Is there a lot of bullshit in your life then?"

"I don't spout bullshit I just mean that perhaps things were be simpler if we just got on with life. Not wasting time chasing impossible dreams or missing what's under our noses."

"Is that what you did?"

"I missed everything that was under my nose. If I'd noticed then perhaps things would have been different."

"But if things were different we wouldn't have met."

His blue/green eyes shine like endless pools of tropical water. I cannot look away. I try to imagine never having met Connor, how life would be if he wasn't here to provide a wonderfully exciting distraction. It's more than that but I'm not ready to admit that to myself.

"No, we wouldn't."

He laughs to lighten the mood and takes a long drink of his pint. I wonder what life would be like with Connor long term, whether the spark would ultimately fade or if it would continue like this – us pulling in different directions but ultimately meeting in the middle. His face is bright and animated but he watches me with such a serious look that I wonder what he is thinking about.

"What are you thinking about?" I ask.

"You." He cocks his head to the side as though he is considering me.

"What about me?"

"I wonder what it would take to make you see what a beautiful woman you are."

Self-consciously I look from his eyes to my hands. "I'm not, not really, just normal…"

"You are far from normal…" The sincerity rings in his voice and surprisingly I believe him.

The waiter interrupts bringing Connor's food that he attacks with gusto. "God I'm starving," he said, "I was in the gym then on a conference call and breakfast passed me by!"

"Are you ever going to tell me what you do?" I ask before biting into my burger.

"Nope," he says with a mouthful of chips and coleslaw, "if I did, like I said, I'd have to kill you and the world is much nicer with you in it!"

***

We see a low budget British film at a small cinema in a Soho backstreet. The cinema has likely not been decorated since the 20s and retains all the charm from an era past. The theatre comes alive the longer I sit in the velvet seat, the ghosts of elegant women with feathers in their hair, bedecked in furs and jewels before the depression hit and the world changed. I can hear the usherettes walking past, carrying trays of chocolate and cigarettes, their hair lacquered into perfect place. Connor sits beside me holding two big tubs of popcorn and oversized soft drinks.

"What are you doing?" He asks as I scrabble in my tote for a pencil and some paper. With my eyes firmly focused on the past I draw what I see, a fringed dress with feathers and sparkles, floor length, figure hugging with a low cut bodice and a deep v at the back. "Jesus, you're good." Connor comments as I frantically draw the lines of the dress before the image fades, "you're wasted."

I look at what I've drawn. "Another for the '*I'll make one day*' pile." I say wryly.

"You should do it, design…"

"I don't have the capital to give up work. I should have done it years ago, when money didn't make the world go round like it does now." I say putting the design in my bag.

"What if you had a backer, a silent partner, would you do it?"

"Probably not. I have lost my confidence over the years and I suppose William's snide comments haven't helped much. I always wanted to design it was my big dream from as far back as I can remember. At school while my friends went loopy over ponies and boy bands and boys I poured over the old issues of Vogue that my mum got from the people she cleaned for. I went to a private school on an art scholarship then university to do fashion design and journalism. My tutors were amazing and my collection gained me a first class degree but for financial reasons, and encouragement from William, I took a route into magazines and fourteen years later here I am!"

"He sounds like a total prick! If you were my wife I'd encourage you to reach for the stars."

I stare at him, seeing him once again in a whole new light. I allow myself a brief thought of what being married to Connor would be like, the excitement and thrill of being with someone who ignites me the way he does.

"Yeah, I guess he is a prick! His parents made a lot of money and as a result his mother became an outrageous snob and very difficult to please, from what I can gather she was very different before the money but I suppose the need for approval drove William on. He's not a bad person really."

"Do you still love him?"

"He turned my life upside down Connor."

"That's not what I asked.

"No I don't love him in the same way, not anymore. He was waiting for me when I got home this morning asking to come back." Connor's face closes over. "I said no. I don't have those feelings anymore. He is not the person I thought he was but I don't wish anything bad for him, a few times I've wanted to kill him, but now I just hope he has made the right choice for him and that he will be happy."

"Has he made the right choice for you?"

I look into his eyes, beautifully blue but wary. "I've never drawn so many dresses in my life!"

"That's not what I meant."

"I know." I smile. "I was trying to lighten the mood. Yes, he has made the right decision for me. I want the unplanned future. I want to know how it all ends."

Connor leans over and gently kisses me. It's a kiss full of promise and just for a moment I dare to hope.

WEDNESDAY

"Freya Wood." I answer the phone sharply, lack of sleep and a to-do list that is increasing by the second is sending my mood spiralling to hell.

"What are you wearing?" The sexy Irish voice asks.

"You know what I'm wearing."

"Tell me…in detail"

"I'm wearing a black fitted shirt, unbuttoned to reveal my cleavage, a knee length red skirt underneath which is some delicate lace underwear and stockings…" Everything I was told to wear at seven am this morning.

"What shoes do you have on?"

"Spiky red patent shoes with killer heels…"

"Sexy."

"Mmmm." I murmur huskily.

"What do your breasts feel like?" He asks. "Touch them and tell me."

"Connor I'm at work!"

"Tell me!" The demanding tone is back.

Slowly I slide my hand into my bra. "Smooth, heavy, soft skin…my nipple has hardened..."

"Tease your nipple."

I gasp as I do what he asks.

"And the other one. Rub your thumbs across them both."

I balance the phone between my shoulder and ear as I cross my hands over and take my breasts in them. They are high, pushed up further by the intricate detailing of my bra and the sensation of my warm hands upon them is swelling them further.

"What are you doing?"

"I am stroking and holding my breasts and rolling my nipples softly between my thumb and finger."

"Harder. Do it harder."

I close my eyes and suddenly it's Connor's hands on me, it's his touch, the commanding, knee-weakening, pulse racing touch that I crave. My body comes alive for him, it sings a song that reaches the heavens and vibrates through me, my nerves alighting, buzzing and resonating with each stroke, my skin trembling under the warmth of my hands. I shift in my seat as the pulse in my centre begins its heavy, carnal beat. "Oh."

"Move your hands down Red, tell me…are you wet?"

I slide my skirt up, moving my chair further under my desk. Trailing my hands slowly up my thighs I can feel my excitement, the silken trail that personifies my desperate want for Connor. "Yes," I whisper.

"Touch yourself. Tell me what you are doing."

"I'm stroking my thighs, they're soft, open, I can feel a heartbeat, a throbbing inside me." I murmur. "I'm wet, Connor, so wet, because of you."

"Make yourself come. I want to hear you."

I stroke myself, my body burning, my breath coming in deep pants. The warmth that floods through me is like a tropical wave, washing over me, pulling me down into its hot soothing waters. "Connor, oh Connor…" I come explosively, the orgasm shaking me and I drop the phone as I fight to control my breath.

"I'm so hard." Connor says when I eventually compose myself. "Be at my hotel at seven." He hangs up the phone.

I lean back in my chair and close my eyes, a secret smile on my lips.

"Hey cupcake." Henry swooshes in, disturbing the orgasm-basking that I was revelling in. "Oh you look flushed. What's the secret, pray tell?"

"Secret?"

"Come on Freya my angel, no one looks as radiant as you without a secret. Tell me!"

"Henry, dearest Henry, there is nothing to tell."

"I know there is something you're not telling me."

I laugh, "Henry, I have nothing to say!"

"Hmmm." He looks at me through narrowed eyes. "I smell a secret and I will get it out of you.

"Will you?" I grin. Henry flops into the chair opposite my desk. "What's the matter?"

"I can't do it, angel cheeks."

"You can't do what?" I ask subtly wiping my hands with one of the wet wipes I keep in my drawer.

"I can't meet Fred Lynch."

"Why on earth not?" I ask looking up startled.

"Because it's silly and a pipe dream, an obsession…"

I lean forward. "Henry, darling Henry, it's one photo shoot, that's all, just like all the others."

"No, it's not! It's Fred Lynch."

"Yes, a person, just a person…breathe Henry." Henry has begun to go a sickly green colour.

"Freya, sweetie, imagine if you met Madonna circa 1986, how would you feel."

"A little faint but then I don't fancy her." I smile. "Henry, you need to calm down…"

"Calm down?" He shrieks, "I thought we were friends, best friends, but you don't know me at all…" and with that Henry crashes out through the door.

I flop my head in my hands. Henry has killed my orgasmic glow and sent me hurtling back to real life with a bang. He's wrong. I do know him, very well, better perhaps that he knows himself. I know this all amounts to a total fear, fear of being made to look a fool, being rejected as I've witnessed him being so many times before, watching and desperately wanting to take his pain away as he fell for the wrong man over and over again. Fred Lynch is up there with the Gods as far as Henry is concerned and I begin to pray for someone to send the right person Henry's way. He is beautiful inside and out, funny, kind, loving and quite simply one of the greatest people I have ever met. I wish the world for him, my rock during bad times, my partner-in-crime during good times and one of the people I would fight with my last breath to protect.

I spend the rest of the morning researching Fred and the Good Time Boys. Their success is astounding, from being manufactured on a TV talent show to their rapid, breathtaking ascent to superstardom that took the industry by surprise. They took the world by storm, breaking records and hearts all around the globe, five handsome, talented men took on the critics and won with their mix of rock and pop sounds reaching across musical genres to appeal to all. I listen to their latest album online and make enough notes to interview Fred for a month. I can see the finished result in my head, moody shots to capture his intensely brooding looks and realise we may just have our bestselling edition right there.

"That's a big sigh, what's the matter?" Carrie asks walking into my office.

"Nothing, I was just thinking…"

"About anything interesting?"

"Just work!"

"I need you to cover my meeting this afternoon with the board. I have somewhere I need to be and it has come up pretty quickly."

"Anywhere nice?"

"Just the hospital. Nothing serious." Fear flits across her face.

"Carrie?" I feel cold. The normally vibrant Carrie looks as though someone has switched her inner light off and it sends a chill up my spine.

"They've found a lump." Her voice breaks and she coughs to clear it. "In my breast. It's likely nothing but I am going for a biopsy. Perhaps I need to give up smoking." Carrie attempts a grin. I start to speak but she waves me down. "I will be fine. Do not say anything. I'll see you later." She says firmly.

"A lump...?" I slump in my chair utterly shocked.

"I am fine." Carrie repeats and I wonder if it's to convince herself until she screws her face up in desperation and tears begin to flow. "I've been going through hell, Freya, I've not even told Jackson. What if it's...I can't even say it. I'm forty-five, the right age, the right lifestyle...I've spent thirty years abusing my body, drinking too much, smoking too much and eating shit. I am walking talking advert for Cancer Research..."

"You don't know it's cancer Carrie." I hear a strange thudding in my ears, like an out of time kettle drum and the world is strangely swimming in front of my eyes.

"Then why would the Dr see me yesterday and the hospital ring me today?"

"They don't take chances any more Carrie, this is a good thing. It's a good thing. You'll be in and out in no time."

"I promise, if it's all ok, that I will give up smoking." She smiles tentatively. "Which is a really fucking big thing."

"Think of all the puddings you'd have instead!" I give a short giggle. "You'll have hips like mine!"

"You have a wonderful body Freya and you are beautiful. Never let anyone make you feel any different. Ever. There will be someone for you, someone wonderful, who thinks you are the most gorgeous thing to walk the earth. Not like that fuckwit husband of yours. Quite honestly Freya, Lexi did you a favour. Life is too short, live your dreams dear girl, live your dreams because you never know when something will come and bite you on the bum." Carrie turns on her heel and leaves my office.

I watch her leave. Carrie, the life and soul of R&R, the hard living, hardworking media whirlwind, who terrifies and inspires in equal measure looking scared, thin and small.

"If anyone can hear me," I whisper, "please let her be ok."

***

I do my work on autopilot. I can't get Carrie out of my head, her face, her words, her fear. Life is so short - too short - and it seems that we spend most of it trying to predict the future. I have. So much time I've wasted looking forward instead of seeing what was in the present. I missed things, important things because I looked always to what was coming, aiming for that which was just beyond my reach. In my quest for the future I lost myself, my dreams and the person I had always planned to be. Yet it seems that life just hangs in the balance, on the edge of a precipice and with one step it could all be gone.

I grab my bag and leave the office.

***

"Good evening The Stark Hotel."

"Suite Four please."

"Just one moment please."

I listen to the awful tinny hold music, grateful that it's not greensleeves and tap out an impatient beat with my pencil.

"I'm afraid there is no answer from Suite Four, would you like to leave a voicemail."

"Yes please." It's six thirty pm, where is he?

"Transferring you now."

"Hi Connor, it's Freya. I'm at home, running late. You can reach me on my home number…" I give the number. "Perhaps see you later. Bye."

I take solace in my drawing. It's an escape. It occupies the evening, keeps my thoughts focused and my sketch pad fills with design after design. Every so often there is a voice that whispers to me, a voice so convinced that this is where my future lies, but the blackness that has taken my confidence ignores the hushed words not daring to believe.

I stop drawing when my stomach makes a loud growl. It's ten pm and the day has turned to night without me noticing. Connor hasn't phoned. I should have seen him three hours ago and as much as I don't want to succumb to anxiety about it I just can't control it. Our affair may feel like it's been forever but it's been a week, just seven days since we met. It's been a roller coaster since then, so much has changed and happened, so many bombshells – Connor, Lexi, Carrie – that I don't think I've paused for breath. God I hope Carrie is alright.

I yawn loudly and stretching I get up from the table in search of food. Apart from some mouldy bread and out of date ham there is nothing that resembles anything edible in the house so I grab my coat and purse and head out into the night.

The streets are quieter now. There seems to be a lull between the end of the working day and the end of the pub hours when people are where they want to be. I want to be wrapped in Connor's arms, listening to him speak, feeling his lips on mine, his warm hands on my body. I don't know how I got to this point, to Connor being all I think about but I have and it's a frightening realisation. He is staying in a hotel, that isn't going to last forever. What then? What happens when he goes?

"Freya!" A voice calls out to me and I turn to see who is shouting my name.

"Hi Crystal!" I wave and cross over the road. Crystal is my neighbour, living in the flat above ours. She works for the biggest independent radio station in the city as a producer and regales endless stories about musicians, usually the ones she has slept with. At twenty-six she has no intention of calming down and with her sixties gamine crop and outrageous dress sense she has no shortage of admirers.

"How are you?" She asks as I reach her, giving me two loud kisses on the cheek. "You're looking amazing Freya. How are you doing without Will?"

"I'm doing great!" I reply. "You look as fabulous as ever."

"Don't you think I've got a bit fat?" She asks sticking out her tummy.

"You! Hell would freeze over first!" I laugh.

"What are you doing out so late? I thought you fashionistas got ten hours sleep a night?"

"Hunger pains drove me out the door!"

"We're going to see Pretty Pink Drinks do a set at the Happy House. Come! They do food, go on Freya come with us!" 'Us' is Crystal and her two friends Coral and Rose who I've met a couple of times at Crystal's parties. They smile and nod encouragement.

"Yeah ok!" I say, "let me get some cash and I'll meet you there."

"Fabulous." Crystal replies. "Just mention me on the door. We're running a series of programmes on them so this is a freebie, eat and drink as much as we want! That's my kind of evening!" She grins, her cheekbones sticking out just a little bit more.

"Mine too!" I leave them and walk down the street to the cash machine. The evening is warm and the sounds of Camden are ringing through the night. Where would I move to that would ever topple this borough. Home for ten years, there is nowhere else I want to go. Cash withdrawn I retrace my steps to The Happy House. It's a spit and sawdust kind of place that refused to join the realms of wine bars, retaining its own character and personality. The pub is always busy with open mike nights, comedy clubs, big bands clamour to play here alongside the unsigned musicians hoping for a big break. I give Crystal's name and the doorman lets me in.

It's heaving and hot. I find the girls at a table perusing the menu and they all look up as I join them.

"What are you going to drink Freya?" Crystal asks. "It's all on the band tonight so order what you want!"

"Should you be telling me that?"

"Nah, probably not but considering the publicity I am going to get them they can stump up for some drinks and some tapas!" She laughs.

"I'll have a lager please." I tell her. She hops down from her stool and forces her way through the crowds to the bar. I make small take with Coral and Rose and when Crystal finally comes back we start talking about the band.

"I really fancy Damon, he's the singer." She says. "So far he is impervious to my charms but I reckon I'll get to him eventually. Oh, and I've ordered some tapas, I hope no one is a veggie."

"Damon's married isn't he?" Rose asks moving out the way of the waiter who brings over a jug of lager and four glasses.

"We'd better have another of those." Crystal tells him, "just keep them coming." To us she says, "yeah he's married but that doesn't stop them."

I smile tightly. "No, marriage doesn't!"

"Oh fuck sorry Freya!" Crystal flushes. "That was thoughtless."

"But true! Shall I pour?" They nod and I pour out four glasses of frothy ale. "It's just as well I have a job I'd make a terrible barperson!" I laugh.

The lights dim and the crowd give out a collective roar. The band walk on stage gesturing for more noise. They take up their places and the music begins. The songs and melodies take me back to university and the days of brit pop. In my memory I see life as it was, fun and riotous and full of promise with no cares or concerns, just nonstop partying and frivolity. When did it all change? When did I grow up and forget that girl? Is she still inside of me?

The evening is a step back in time. I leave just as Crystal and her friends begin on the shots. I thank them for a fabulous night and leave the hot, sweaty venue. The night time air has a chill and I pull my jacket tightly around me as I walk the few streets home. I haven't allowed myself to think of Carrie or Connor since I've been out but they fight for space in my head. I haven't heard from either of them and this worries me.

I push open the gate, the creak is loud in the quiet street. It must be nearing midnight and I yawn, suddenly feeling exhausted.

"Where've you been?" Connor's voice comes from the shadow beside the door.

"Hello Connor." I say. "I've been out."

"I thought I was seeing you?"

"You weren't there."

"I was."

"No you weren't, I left a message for you."

"Where did you go?"

"To see a band with my upstairs neighbour. I only went out to get Chinese food. Where were you?"

"I had something to do."

"Something being what?"

"Work. I was late. The hotel were supposed to let you into my room but you didn't show."

"It was a bad day. I came home early...."

"Yeah I had a bad day too." He sounds really sad and I reach out for him. Connor pulls me tightly to him, his arms around me and he kisses me with such intensity that he takes my breath away. It's not his normal kiss, it's deeper, more fiery, more impassioned and I wrap my body around his, clinging to him as his kiss evokes a white hot fever in me.

He speaks against my mouth. "Tell me you want me. Please tell me you want me."

"I want you..." I gasp as his mouth crushes mine, his teeth are pulling at my lips and his tongue dominates my mouth, probing and rediscovering mine. Connor pushes me roughly against the door, the wood hard against my back. I weaken under him as his kisses become more powerful and the rush of feelings completely overwhelms me.

"Connor..." I whisper and I fumble with the door keys. The door swings open and we stumble into the hallway, kicking off our shoes then into the kitchen. He pulls me tight to him, his hands burning my back where they touch.

"Red." He groans. "Red."

I kiss his neck, inhaling deeply. I wonder if I would ever tire of the scent of him, whether my body would ever stop responding to the fragrance, his touch or the sound of his voice. Softly I run my tongue along his jaw line, his stubble rough against it. His hands grip me, pulling at my hair and his mouth crushes mine, the urgency makes me stumble backwards.

"Connor?" I question.

His mouth finds mine again. The bruising kisses rain down, his tongue pushing into my mouth. I give in to him, leaning against him unsteady now on my feet. He wants something from me, something more than sex but suddenly I'm too scared to ask what it is. He's had a bad day...what does that mean?

Connor holds me tight, his strong arms wrapped around my chest. I can feel his heart pounding against my chest as he begins to undress me. Slow movements. Stopping to kiss me as he removes items of clothing. It feels very much like he's trying to memorise my body, exploring and tasting each part of me, seeing the response my body gives back to him. He focuses on me, there in the darkness of the kitchen, it's just about me. It feels loving somehow and as he gently opens my legs I lean my head back against the cupboard and close my eyes. The sensation of his tongue on me, in the most intimate way, sets fire to my soul, sending tingles across my skin and through my veins. I grip tightly to the kitchen counter as his tongue works its magic, repeating his name over and over, loud against the silence of the house. My trembling legs tighten around his head as he continues to tantalise me. I hear him unzip his trousers before he pulls me downwards and I sit astride him, his huge erection sliding into me.

We move together, his mouth never once leaves mine as my orgasm begins to build, the delicious golden light that shines internally as I give myself to this beautiful man. I stroke his skin, kiss his neck, hold him as tightly as I can, rocking against him as we become more frantic, the desire for each other becoming more and more intense. His hands stroke me, lingering on my breasts that swell and rise for him, with hardened nipples that he sucks and nips until the assault of the sensations make me dizzy. I pull his head up to mine.

"Tell me you want me." He whispers.

"I want you…God I want you…" I moan gripping him tightly. Our movements increase, and as Connor tugs at my hair so the orgasm rises in me, my body succumbing to the powerful feelings. He shudders and moans before he too comes and fills with his hot, wet orgasm and we crumple to the floor, wrapped in each other arms.

"This is so crazy," he whispers, kissing my shoulder.

"I know." I whisper back.

THURSDAY

"Sorry about yesterday," Henry says coming into my office. "I was a complete knob, almost as knobby as wanker William."

"You weren't being a knob, not at all…"

"But I was mean to you!" Henry flops down in the chair. "And that was knobby."

"No you weren't! Anyway, enough, no need to apologise." I smile at him. "And I must say, you are look h-o-t today, the tan is better too!" Henry has toned down his usual flamboyant dress sense and is in a slim fitting black t-shirt and black jeans. It suits him and the orange tone of the fake tan has died down.

"Carrie said yesterday that I looked like an oompa loompa! Do I? Please tell me I don't?" Henry pulls a face.

"No, you definitely don't, you look lovely, handsome and tanned and toned and…if you were straight!" I wink grinning at him.

"I bet you say that to all the boys you sauce-pot. So what are we doing to Fred today…"

We discuss the outline of the shoot, the interview and wardrobe. Henry's trembling hands bely his nerves but otherwise he remains the cool, calm professional. I can only imagine the state of his internal organs under the placid exterior but I give no impression that I've noticed the trembles.

"Sorted!" He says, "I'll go on down and set up, see you there."

"See you later. Has Carrie come in yet? Have you seen her?"

"Carrie? No not yet."

My heart sinks, it's unheard of for Carrie to be late, this can't be good news.

***

I'm in the art room when Carrie comes in. She looks pale and bare faced, and unlike Carrie she is wearing a jogging suit and trainers. She looks younger than her years but worn out.

"Hi." I say standing up from my hunched position.

"Can I see you in my office Freya?"

I excuse myself from my meeting and follow Carrie to her office. Each step feels like I'm wading through tar and the pounding of my heart is deafening because I'm dreading the outcome of what she may have to tell me. We enter Carrie's office and I close the door, noticing the faint smell of tobacco that floats under the air freshener.

"I've had my results." Carrie says. "This morning, that's why I was late." She sits down. I wait, holding my breath, not daring to speak, praying over and over and over that she is ok. "I'm clear. Oh God Freya I can't begin to tell you how shit these past few days have been. I've been to hell and back, Jackson and I have done nothing but cry and reminisce and wish we'd done things differently. In the dark of night I promised God all sorts, Freya, and I must have been heard because this morning the lump has turned out to be nothing serious. They can remove it if I want but I've had enough prodding and poking for now. Life has to change, Freya, I work too hard, I don't spend enough time with my family and I abuse myself. I'm stopping smoking and I'm going to try and repair thirty years of damage."

"Oh thank God, thank God." I exclaim. "I've been so worried, Carrie and I've been praying too. Like you wouldn't believe."

"It's opened my eyes Freya. We have to live life to the maximum, take the opportunities that are presented and run with them. Whatever you have been doing recently to give yourself the glow that you have, keep doing it, and Freya, you have to reach for your dreams."

"How is this about me?"

"I've been your friend for ten years, I've watched you grow and somehow, recently, you've emerged from a shell, you have blossomed and whatever is the reason, hang on to it tightly. Life is short, this experience has made me realise just how short, and it's precious. I'm going home now, I don't want to be here today and I'm taking tomorrow off. I suggest you let everyone leave early today, the sun is shining." Carrie packs up her laptop. "See you on Monday Freya."

I watched opened mouthed as she puts her desk phone on *'do not disturb'*. "Have a nice weekend."

"You too Carrie." I smile broadly.

"I will."

The office is busy I walk across it, back to my office, to prepare for the shoot. I love the sounds of a buzzing magazine being brought to life, the shouts of my fellow workers to each other, the constant ringing of the phones and I wonder if I could walk away from this, from the passion and excitement and the stress of producing innovative magazines month after month, surrounded by similarly enthusiastic people with whom I have worked for a third of my life. *'Reach for your dreams'* Carrie told me. But my dreams are confused.

***

I've heard of love at first sight, I even experienced it in primary school when Simon Perkins turned up with a golden tan and brilliant blond hair from early years spent in India but witnessing the moment Henry meets Fred is like walking into the middle of a love story. It is immediate. Shy smiles, warm glances and the moving together of two people that have been destined to meet. I feel like an intruder on something so beautiful and personal that I rush through the interview and drag Kirsty, our makeup artist, and Jack the lighting technician away for a cocktail and lunch. If they think my behaviour is odd they don't say as I ply them with drinks and bar snacks. Henry deserves to be happy and I put my faith in the Gods that this is it for him. Surely something so visible has to be real and then I wonder where Connor is. I didn't ask last night about his bad day but I can't help thinking that it will become my bad day too.

My mobile rings loudly. "Hello Henry."

"We're done. Are you coming back?"

"Do you want me to?"

"No!" He whispers. "Fred wants to take me for a late lunch, if I go will you cover for me?"

"Of course!" I exclaim. "You don't even need to ask!"

"Freya…I…oh my God Freya he kissed me."

"Wow!"

"Wow? Is that all you can say?" He demands.

"In present company yes, that is all I can say!" I smile. "Ring me when you have the chance now go, enjoy my darling."

"Freya, this isn't real."

"Of course it is."

"Love ya long time."

"Love you too." The phone goes dead. "Right," I announce to Kirsty and Jack, "I need to go back to the office and you two may as well go home if you've nothing else on today."

"Thanks for lunch Freya." Kirsty says.

"You're welcome." I collect my items, pay the bill and leave.

Back at the office I type up the notes from my interview with Fred. It's a good piece, one of my better ones and his personality shines through. Once done I continue with the pile of work on my desk until, utterly exhausted I realise it's eight pm. I yawn loudly and jump as the phone rings.

"Are you still working?" I smile as Connor's outraged voice sounds loudly down the phone.

"Yes, no rest for the wicked!"

"That's shit!"

"It's not too shit, I'm finished now!"

"Are you coming here?"

"Do you want me too?" I ask coquettishly.

"More and more." He replies quietly. "Don't be long, I'm hungry."

"I'll leave now."

"Good."

The phone line goes dead and I pack up my bag. From within the tote my phone beeps signalling a message.

'Fancy going out tomorrow night with Imogen and me?" Erin texts.

'Yes,' I reply. *'Where?'*

'Somewhere we need to dress up for. We'll come to you for eight and go from there.'

'Ok. Xxxx'

'xxxxx'

I take the underground to Park Lane. As usual it's crowded, sweaty and uncomfortable and I exit the station feeling grimy and smelly. The evening air is smells of rain and the sky looks heavy above me. The scent with the pollen from the trees that cluster in Hyde Park, covered with their fragrant blossom, is strong in the damp air. I hurry along the road, desperate to see Connor and desperate to have a long, cool shower.

"Good evening Madam," the doorman says as he opens the door for me.

"Good evening." I reply.

"Beautiful day." He comments.

"Very." I smile at him. "Have a good evening,"

"Thank you Madam. You too."

I cross the air conditioned foyer towards the lift. The Concierge stops me. "Excuse me Madam."

"Yes?" I say stopping in my tracks.

"I've been asked to show you to Suite Four, the gentleman has had to go out briefly. May I escort you upstairs?"

"Thank you."

The ride in the lift is silent except for the soft music that filters through the speakers. The Concierge opens the door and thanking him I enter. Connor has left a note on the table.

Red,
I had to go out unexpectedly. I shouldn't be long.
There is wine, hopefully open, ready for you!!!
See you soon
C xx

I kick off my shoes and pour a glass of the wine that has been chilling in the ornate wine bucket. It's crisp, fresh and fruity and very welcome. I cross the suite to the bathroom and run a very deep bubble bath. The quiet is soothing, relaxing and I float around the bath until the door opening jolts my consciousness.

"You look peaceful." Connor says coming into the room.

"Hi!" He looks troubled. "Is something wrong?"

"Sort of." Connor shrugs. "Is there room for me?"

"Of course. What's the matter?"

He sighs. "Work stuff, that's all."

"Yeah I know that one!" I lie back. "Do you ever feel like the world is spinning slightly too fast and you can't quite keep up?"

"I feel like the world is spinning too fast and I want it to stop turning."

I lift my head up to look at him. "Connor, what is it?"

"My manager phoned today. New arrangements have been made for me and I have to leave…"

"Leave? When?"

"Wednesday."

"No, no, no it's too soon." I burst out splashing water everywhere as I sit up abruptly.

Connor doesn't meet my eyes, eyes that are already prickling with tears. "I was never going to be here long term." His voice cracks. "I just thought there would be more time."

"It's not enough time. It's not long enough. Even another few days…" I implore.

Connor shakes his head. "I can't stay…" He whispers.

The bath water, that moments ago was warm and comforting, now feels like ice cold acid against my skin. I scramble out of the bath and wrap an oversized towel around me. As hard as fight to keep the tears at bay it's a battle I readily lose. Connor says something as I leave the room but the words aren't loud enough to hear. I sit heavily on the edge of the bed. Five more days. That's it, just five days. As much as I knew this would never be long term the very idea of London without Connor is too lonely and too despairing to contemplate.

"Red?"

I look up. Connor's beautiful face holds a haunted look, his eyes sad. He stands before me, a towel wrapped around his slim hips and his hair, wet, is tousled. His body, as ever, commands my gaze, the perfect lines and contours of the muscles that are defined under his smooth tanned skin, the body that I have five days left to know. A solitary tear rolls down my cheek and I hastily wipe it away.

"I thought we'd have longer." He says huskily. "I thought I'd have longer to know you, it's not enough time."

"Then stay?"

"I can't."

"Why?"

"If I told you I didn't own myself would you understand what I meant?"

"Not really."

"I have contractual obligations I have to fulfil. I will come back for you."

"Don't make promises you can't keep." I say, pulling the towel tighter around me.

Connor crosses the room and kneeling down before me he gives me a long, deep kiss. I can feel the desperation in his kiss, it's real, almost touchable and if it had a colour it would be blood red, the colour of my heartache. He's leaving. Connor is leaving. The brief interlude in my otherwise normal existence is ending and my heart crumples at the thought. I cling to him, trying to pass across in my kiss just how painful it is, that I feel more than I should, that in a few days everything I knew has altered so much that I don't recognise my old life nor do I want it, that every waking moment Connor is on my mind.

Connor's body is warm under my fingers, his skin like velvet. I stroke my hands down his back thinking that there hasn't been enough time to explore all of him. Too many conversations not had, too much I still don't know, kisses not kissed, skin not touched. It's over too soon and, burying my hands in his hair a silent tear falls. I feel it roll down my cheek and over the bow of my mouth. Connor moves back and licks his lip, his tongue pink against the red of his mouth.

"Don't cry Red," he pleads. Gently he rubs his thumbs under my eyes catching the few drops that escape. He licks his thumbs and grins. "Now I've tasted all of you!"

I giggle sadly and take his hand in mine. It's soft and warm but his clasp is strong. I lift it to my lips and kiss his knuckles one at a time before putting it to my cheek. "Perhaps we were only meant to have the fireworks?" I whisper.

"Perhaps." He whispers back. I reach for his face. His stubble is sharp as I dust my thumbs across his jaw and over his lips. With my fingertips I draw the outline of his eyebrows and down his nose, mapping his beautiful face. I don't break eye contact as I trace down his throat over his collar bones and down his chest across the contours of his muscles. His skin quivers under my gentle touch and his chest rises deeply. His body is wonderful – defined, bronzed and strong – and very lightly I touch my lips to his skin. Delicate little kisses inhaling the scent of his body. My hand never breaks contact as I move to his back and continue my caress. I brush my cheek against him, soft skin against soft skin and hold him tight to me, my hands firm on his abdomen.

"Freya?" He whispers.

"Yes," I whisper back.

"I..." The moment is broken with the ringing of the phone.

I move to stand by the window looking out over London as Connor talks on the phone. The rain is falling bringing a miserable grey fog to the city and I know that on the streets below people are grumpier and more impolite than normal. The rain runs in rivers down the window pane and quickly the park becomes enveloped in a heavy mist until the view is all but obscured. The change in the weather is bringing further change with it, I can feel it in the air. More uncertainty is coming and I feel like a rabbit trapped in the headlights of an oncoming steam roller.

Connor comes up behind me and wraps his arms around my shoulders nuzzling into my hair. I lean against him and he pulls me tightly to him and we stand in silence looking at the rain.

"I have something for you." He says eventually and letting me go he crosses the room to his discarded jacket. I shiver now no longer enveloped in his warmth. Connor hands me a small box covered in silver silk. The box is secured with a white and silver ribbon covered in glitter that sparkles under the lights. Connor looks nervous. I look from him to the box and my mouth goes dry.

"I saw this today when I was out ..."

I busy myself opening the box, trying not to look at Connor still undressed except for his towel. Under the pale grey tissue paper is a delicate silver necklace with links so small and individually detailed that they look like a whisper. Linked in, an inch apart are dozens of blue flowers made from cornflower coloured stones. "it's beautiful." I gasp. "Really beautiful, thank you, I love it."

"They're forget-me-nots," Connor says sitting down beside me. "It seemed kind of apt."

"Yeah," I say softly, "it does. I won't, you know."

"Won't what?" Connor asks taking my hand. I look at his strong one holding mine. Too little time. So much still to know about him, so many things still to see together and the thought of going through life without seeing Connor is the worst kind of ache.

"Forget you." The tears trickle but I keep my voice from breaking. "Can you help me put it on?"

Connor doesn't comment about my tears but fastens the necklace around my neck. I move from the sofa across the room to the mirror and look at myself. The crystals glisten like tears around my neck reflecting against my throat. "It's stunning." I say watching Connor in the mirror. "I really don't think anyone has given me anything so thoughtful and so perfect."

"Not even your husband?" I find Connor's question strange.

"No, not even him. He gave me lovely gifts, don't get me wrong, but..." *But they were never really me.*

"But what? "

"He never really got it right. Everything he got me was classy and expensive but somehow they never suited me, not even my engagement ring. And that makes me sound ungrateful and I'm not it's just...this is perfect." Connor walks up behind me. "Thank you." I whisper. "Thank you for more than you could ever know."

He wraps his arms around my waist and leans his chin on my shoulder. "It's my pleasure Red."

I lean back into him and in unison our stomachs give a collective growl.

"Shall we go out for some dinner?" He asks. "Or just stay here?"

"Let's go out, I know the most amazing Italian..."

"That would be perfect." He replies.

***

I take Connor to a small, discreet Italian restaurant in Camden. It's my favourite eatery in the whole of London, located off the main high street and down a series of small alleys. Lexi and I stumbled across it by chance, lost one evening and drunk on cheap wine a month or so after William and I moved to Camden. Lexi and I ate there frequently although William was never enamoured but I love the fresh home cooked food the comfort of the cluttered room.

"Bella..." Senora Cafrolini greets me enthusiastically with a warm embrace and two loud cheek kisses. "Welcome welcome, it's been too long Freya. You've got thin. Mama needs to feed you up." Her eyes flick to Connor and I watch as the confusion floods her face then, with a smile firmly in place she says, "and who is this very handsome young man?"

"Rosa this is Connor, Connor this is Rosa."

"Delighted." She says holding out her hand. I grin when Connor drops a kiss on it.

"Pleased to meet you Rosa," he says smoothly. "Freya tells me you do the best Italian food in London."

"Only London?" Rosa mocks outrage. "I do the best Italian food in the world! Where are you doing to sit Freya, your usual table?"

"No thank you, somewhere different this time."

"Ok." Rosa leads us to the back of the restaurant, to a softly lit corner. Connor pulls out the chair for me and I sit down.

"Another table?" Connor asks.

"New memories. I came here all the time with Lexi, we always sat in the window so we could see the world. I don't want to be reminded of her."

"Do you miss her?"

"Every day. Twenty four years is a long time to let go of. I still go to ring her and it hurts all over again when I realise that I can't. Not anymore."

"It must be a hard thing to forgive." Connor picks up his menu.

"I want to but it's not Will and her that I can't forgive, it's that she broke our friendship into pieces and she lied to me." I whisper looking down at my hands. "I wish that I could still pick up the phone, tell her everything like all the other times. It's been easier to forgive Will because I no longer want the life he could offer but Lexi…friends, best friends, are supposed to be there no matter what, to hold your hand through everything life throws up and she's gone forever."

"What about your other friends, the one's you've mentioned?"

"Imogen and Erin?" I smile. "They are the craziest most wonderful people I could be blessed to know."

"How did you meet them?" Connor asks me.

"At university. They were in the rooms either side of mine. We got on from the first moment and were more or less inseparable. Erin has never liked Lexi and it turns out she was right all along."

"Have you told them about me?" Connor reaches for my hand.

"No." I hold his gaze, the blue eyes sparkling like a tropical ocean. "I haven't told anyone. I didn't want to share you."

Rosa interrupts for our order but suddenly I no longer feel hungry. This is ending, he is leaving. It's all over but even with the uncertainty of whether I'll ever see him again I can't tell him how I feel. I can't beg him to stay. I can't tell him that he has changed my life so completely, that he was the light that took the darkness away. I want to tell him that this has been more than just fireworks, that it has been something so special and so unique that nothing could ever compare. I want to hear him say the words to me that I long to say to him but they can't be uttered because this may all just be an illusion.

"Freya?" Rosa's gentle voice brings me out of my thoughts.

"Sorry Rosa, I was miles away."

She laughs. "Looking at this handsome boy I'm not surprised." Connor winks at me. "What would you like bella?"

"Seafood pasta please."

"I don't know why I asked." She smiles. "Always the same."

Except nothing is the same. "Actually Rosa, I'll leave it up to you." I say giving her my menu. "You choose. Something spicy and hot..." I grin at Connor. "...and unique, just for me."

"I'll have the same." Connor says. His eyes, soft, bore into mine and the world around us fades away. Rosa scribbles on her pad and bustles away. The restaurant, as always, smells of garlic and herbs, drifting into the room from the kitchen from which the sounds of cooking are loud above the soft jazz emitting from the speakers. Connor takes my hand

and softly rubs his thumb over my knuckles. I smile at him gently.

"I've had the best time with you Connor, the best time. It doesn't really seem real that you'll be going. I've got far too used to you being around."

Connor strokes my cheek. "I've gotten used to being around." He pauses. "Sometimes I wish things could be different, that I could stay and see where this all goes..."

"And the other times?"

"The other times the decisions are made for me". Connor pulls a face and I giggle.

"What do you do Connor?" I ask again.

"Whatever they tell me too." The same reply as last time.

"That's what you always say!" I tell him. "It can't be that bad surely?"

"Work is work. I do it then I have time off then I do it again. When I'm not working I want to live an ordinary life..." He looks at me intently, an unsaid question on his lips. I wonder what he wants to ask but the look changes and with it comes another question. "So what about you Red, what does your future hold?"

"Apart from going to Mexico I don't know." Inexplicably the question makes me feel sad. "My future is blurry at the moment."

"It will be fun to find out then? What is meant for you next?"

"Perhaps. Connor?" I lean forward. "Why don't you ever tell me anything about you? Are you married or something?"

"No, not married." He grins. "And before you ask, no not in a long term relationship with someone I am currently cheating on..."

"I didn't mean..."

"I know! I'm teasing. My life is complicated Red, as I've said, it's not really my own, and being here with you, is giving me something I wouldn't ordinarily have. If I told you everything then..."

"You'd have to kill me."

He laughs. "It would change everything and things are going to change soon enough anyway. Look," he concedes, "there is not a whole lot to tell. I grew up in Ireland, in a small town near the coast. I have an older brother who's a teacher and two younger sisters. My Mam and Dad are probably a bit like yours, they never had a lot really but gave us everything they could. I got lucky and now I travel the world but I don't really own myself, I have a lot of people to answer to. I suppose it's like any job really. I like typical lads stuff, football, fast cars, women, music...well perhaps just *a woman* now. I didn't really have aspirations growing up, my best subject was English and everyone thought I'd be a teacher or a writer. One day I'd like to write but I don't really know what the future holds. That's it."

"I thought recently that maybe people spend too much time looking forward." I say.

"Maybe we do but don't you think there is a difference between living in the future and having something to aim for?" Connor asks. "Take you, you have options for your future, you're not living it before it's already happened, but you're making a choice."

"I don't know what to choose."

"That's the fun part though, deciding which road to take. It makes life interesting..."

"And scary. What's next for you?"

"I have some salesy stuff to do, nothing interesting."

"You're not an international drug dealer or arms smuggler or anything are you?"

"Once or twice..." He winks. "It's all above board because my mam would kill me..."

We talk nonstop pausing only for mouthfuls of the steaming pasta that Rosa serves to us. Connor listens intently to my dreams for the future and never once laughs at me.

Connor spears his final piece of pasta. "That was amazing. This place is a real find, no wonder you came here all the time."

"The food is always fabulous here." I sigh loudly.

"That's a big sigh."

"Meeting you has made me see how boring I've become, how predictable. I eat at the same places, go to the same events with the same faces, nothing changes ever. For the first time in my carefully planned life there is no plan. There has to be more out there for me, surely?"

"You need to do more with your designing." Connor's eyes glisten in the light and I reach for his face. "Even I can see that you're really good."

"So they tell me…"

"So why don't you just believe them?"

I don't answer. Instead I lean over the table and cup his face in my hands. "Connor, has this been real?"

He nods very slightly and says "very real."

FRIDAY

The clock ticks endlessly. My office, usually buzzing with people in and out, is unnaturally quiet and even the magazine floor doesn't have its usual noise. The morning is dragging already and the list of work I have to do is not getting done. I don't' want to be here.

Even though I knew that my affair with Connor was unlikely to last forever, the ending is coming sooner than I was expecting. Too soon. I feel winded and even with the window wide open I cannot seem to get any air in my lungs. Nine days. That's it. So why am I so devastated?

None of it feels real. The pages of real life and fairy-tale have blurred so much I don't know where reality sits. The dreamland that Connor brought into my life has opened up Pandora's Box and the contents are slowly emptying out. There is no way to force them back in and the choices I have to make sit heavily on my shoulders. Connor is going and the future is unclear, foggy, with no map to guide me. Which of the two paths should I take?

They are all telling me to take a leap of faith but I've always been sensible, think-it-through, Freya. Since Will left and meeting Connor I have changed so much already – can I take a risk on myself?

My email pings and with a big sigh I open it.

From CR
To Freya Wood
Re: Tonight

Ravishing Red
I'll be round at 7pm…!!!
C xxx

From Freya Wood

To CR
Re Tonight

I can't tonight, I've already made plans, unless after is ok.

From CR
To Freya Wood
Re Tonight

Who with?

From Freya Wood
To CR
Re Tonight

Erin and Imogen!

From CR
To Freya Wood
Re Tonight

Well that is total shit!

From Freya Wood
To CR
Re Tonight

Yep.

"Henry has phoned in sick." Felicity, Carrie's PA, stomps in with a face like thunder. "Do you know why Henry is sick?"

"No idea." I reply crossing my fingers under the desk.

"Why do things like this happen when Carrie is off?" Felicity groans. "As if I haven't got enough to do!"

"Henry can't help being sick…"

"No, I know that it's just he was supposed to be meeting with Danielle Kington's design team this morning…"

"So send Jason…"

"Jason won't work with Carys, she dumped him at the Christmas party remember?"

"Leave it with me. I'll swap people around, it will be covered."

"Thanks Freya." She gives a small smile. "I need coffee…"

"Flick?"

"Yes?"

"Make it decaff." She laughs and leaves the room.

I call an impromptu meeting. With some careful coercion and promises of an early finish I swap diaries around and the almost-crisis is averted.

'I'm not really sick.' Henry's text pops up on my phone

'I guessed.'

'Has anyone else?"

'No! Carrie is off, you're safe, although you nearly gave Felicity a heart attack!'

'A pot plant nearly gives her a heart attack!'

'Yeah, that's true! Are you having a love-in today then?'

'It's just amazing Freya, he's amazing. I'm going to wake up I'm sure!'

'If it's just a dream you'd better stop texting, you're wasting valuable dream time!'

'Love ya long time'

'Love ya x'

I immerse myself in work, forcing myself not to think of anything but the excessive to-do list that gets longer by the second. Each minute feels like an hour, each hour like a day. How much of what I do will need to be re-done I don't even want to consider. Apart from Felicity I speak to no one all day and eventually pack up early, my enthusiasm hitting an all-time low.

When I leave the office I text Imogen and Erin suggesting we meet at my house at eight then onto town. I buy a large bouquet of flowers from the vendor on the high street, yellows and creams with scents that permeate the air as I walk home. I stop off at the local shop to buy bottles of wine that I refrigerate as soon as I get into the house and then I run the bath.

I sing along with the songs that blast out from the ceiling speakers, deliberately happy, disco songs, to lift my spirits and banish the blueness of the day. I refill the hot water until my skin wrinkles and when the tap eventually runs cold I drag myself from the bath and begin to get ready for the evening out. Knowing that I am seeing Connor at the end of the evening I put on my sexiest, most seductive underwear and rub in the ludicrously expensive lotion that I bought on a whim. It smells fabulous, musky and sensual, and I dab the matching perfume on my neck and wrists before covering myself with my robe.

I light the candles dotted around the living room and plump up the cushions. On the coffee table, gathering dust, are a pile of as yet unread magazines so I wipe them with a tissue from the box beside the sofa and resolve to clean up…eventually. The room smells fresh, the flowers I bought sitting in the huge vase beside the fire place have opened and their scent masks the sadness I feel. Once the lounge looks presentable I open the wine, pouring myself a glass and select another CD.

The doorbell rings and I glance at the clock, noticing that my friends are early. Opening the door I expect to see Imogen and Erin, instead I find Connor wearing dark glasses, a white tee-shirt and blue jeans, looking like a rock star.

"Hi!" I say surprised.

"Hello Red!"

"My friends…" I look nervously up and down the street for signs or Erin and Imogen.

"…are obviously not here yet so I have some time to stake my claim!"

"They'll be here any minute."

"I'll be quick."

"Quick?" He reaches into my robe and cups my breast. My stomach somersaults and contracts at his touch. He tugs at the belt of the robe and I stand before him, before the street, in my underwear. "Connor, please don't do that. I have neighbours and my friends will be here in a few minutes."

He caresses my breasts which spring high at his touch and he gives a satisfied grin. "Oh come on Red, you know you want me…."

"Oh I do, do I?" I close my eyes as his persistent fingers stroke down my body. "You're very sure of yourself."

He fingers the edge of my panties and I gasp. "You give yourself away." He runs his hand down my arm. "It's not cold, why do you have goose bumps if you don't want me here?"

"I'm not wearing a lot." I reply weakly. He knows I'm going to give in.

"That's bullshit Red and you know it! Now are you going to invite me in or am I going to take you on the doorstep?"

"I can't, I told you my friends will be here soon."

"And I told you I'll be quick! I've been thinking about you all day…" His fingers slip inside of my panties where my arousal gives me away. "You know you don't want to send me away..." He begins to stroke me and my resolve melts away.

"Connor...my friends..."

He pulls me towards him and wraps his hand in my hair, the other maintaining its slow caress of my clitoris. "I don't care about your friends." He murmurs in my ear, "I care about making you come."

I can feel him hard against my stomach and my desire for him takes over. "I think you'd better come in." I say huskily. He follows me into the house. I slam the front door and lead him into my bedroom. I shrug out of my robe and turn to face him.

"Time is ticking Connor, what are you standing over there for? I'm here." My voice is low, sassy and dripping with longing. He looks me over, licking his lips and turns his hooded eyes to me. They're dark, glittering with a lust for me and I shake my hair back, giving him my sexiest smile. "Well if you're not going to undress me then I shall." I reach behind me, unclasping my bra so my breasts spring free.

Connor come towards me and wraps his hands in my hair pulling my head backwards. I look up at him. There is an emotion in his eyes I've not seen before, it's a sad look, and I wonder if it mirrors what he sees in my eyes. "Kiss me." I whisper.

His mouth comes down on mine, soft lips against soft lips. The kiss says a thousand words and as it becomes more urgent so the charge in the air changes, it cracks and sparks and envelopes us in glow, a red hot glow that pulsates and ripples, it's almost touchable. Connor cups my face in his hands and kisses me over and over.

At some point Connor removes his clothes, or perhaps I do, we are completely lost in each other. Somehow we end up on my bed but I don't recall moving. Connor tears at my panties, the delicate fabric ripping as I lie above him and then I sit astride him, slowly easing him into me.

I clutch his hair as I move up and down, around and around, seeking gratification and a release. The scent of him and my desire is a heady mix and I lose myself totally in the act. The heat begins to rise and burn and I hear myself crying out as I come eventually resting my head on his shoulder gasping for breath.

"Red?" He whispers.

"Yes," I pant.

"My turn, kneel down and turn around." He commands. Hesitantly I do as he asks.

He kneels down behind me and grasps hold of my hands pulling them behind my back. As quick as a flash he has tied them together with my robe belt. Slowly he eases me up so that I am kneeling in front of the bed, my torso and head supported by my mattress. What is he going to do? I am at his mercy, trussed up like this, and I am revolted to be enjoying it. This is something that happens in a book and not something that has ever happened to me. Connor's breath is deep and the scent of his aftershave is cool and deeply sexy. I can sense his excitement, almost taste it as it infuses the room, the tiny beads of desire like droplets of water falling onto my skin.

"Beautiful," he comments from behind me. "Beautiful and...dirty."

"Dirty?" I whisper.

"Yeah Red and you know you are. I don't think there's been enough experimentation in your life, has there?" He trails his fingernails down my spine and my skin violently quivers, my already aroused body swelling further. "I think you like being tied up like this, and I think your friends due to arrive is adding to your excitement. What would they think Red, especially as you claim to be a good girl? Especially as they don't know about me!" I twist around to look at him. "You look really fucking sexy like that. Are you going to watch while I do what I want to you? Are you going to enjoy it? Are you enjoying it now?"

"Yes," I whimper. My head is spinning with lust, revulsion, desire, guilt, passion and the fear that my friends will find me like this. I know he likes the idea that they will walk in on us, like he likes the control he has over me. I like the control he has over me. It's so disgustingly erotic that I am more turned on that ever before. My body naturally gives me away and he enjoys that it does.

He leans over me, heavy on my back and takes my breasts in his hands tweaking firmly on my nipples. I cry out, the sweet pain ricocheting around my body, melting everything in its path. Connor drops little kisses over my shoulder blades and down each vertebrae of my spine until he reaches the groove where my arse meets my back. His hands caress and massage my body as slowly, he raises my hips and buries his face between my thighs, his tongue finding the sweet spot.

"Ah…" I groan. I pull against the ties that hold me and raise myself further, Connor's insistent tongue licking me painfully slowly.

"No noise Red, imagine if your friends heard…" He says his voice vibrating against my thighs.

"They're not here," I murmur.

"Not yet, but it's seven forty-five, just imagine if they were early." As he speaks Connor eases himself up, and lies above me. He resumes his caress of my breasts but gentler this time then drops tender little kisses down my back, his touch has me squirming with lust. "So sexy," he says huskily as his kiss trail reaches the base of my spin, "so sexy…I want you to feel me all night…think about me all night…no matter who talks to you…" He strokes my entrance, teasing, never moving his finger from the skin that keeps it all secret. His skin against mine is white hot and I beg over and over. "You want me?"

"Yes…"

"Only me?"

"Yes…"

And with that he enters me and I move against him as he continues his controlled, rough and welcome entry into me, in and out, hard and fast and then…

With horror I hear the front door open. "Freya, it's us." Imogen calls out. I freeze with fear. *Oh please God don't let them come in here.*

"Tell them you'll be there in a minute," Connor whispers nipping at my back. I melt against him. "Or they'll come in here!"

"I'll be right out." Connor begins to tug at my nipples and my voice wavers.

"You need to speak normally Red."

I clear my throat. "Wine is in the fridge." I call.

"Ok." Calls back Imogen, "do you want one?"

Connor slides himself in and out of me, his hands moving to my hips. "I have one here thanks," I squeak.

"You're not doing very well with this are you?" He murmurs in my ear rubbing his hand over my arse cheek.

"You are very distracting."

"Good. Do you like me fucking you Red?"

"Yes," I whisper.

I raise my hips to him as he thrusts again hard and fast. His hands burn me where he holds me. I move against him, desire sweeping through me nerve by nerve and the heat from my centre begins to spread bringing with it a powerful orgasm. I want to cry out. I want to speak his name. Connor reaches for my breasts and I lift my torso to give him access to them. As I begin to come so he squeezes my nipples and the sensation pushes me beyond consciousness and I explode, the bedding muffling my cries. I feel him shudder above me as he comes and we collapse forward satiated.

***

"I need to get dressed," I whisper to Connor who is lying beside me, his leg wrapped around mine stroking my hair.

"Go on then," he replies not moving.

"Can you please move your leg?"

With a sigh he complies and I wearily stand up. "I suppose I'd better have a quick shower once I've said hello to the girls." I comment, "I feel sticky!"

"No!" Connor says sitting up, "I don't want you to wash. I want you to spend the night feeling me."

I look at him. Suddenly he seems young and vulnerable and far from the domineering Connor of earlier. "I ache," I grin, "I will be feeling you all night." I am rewarded by a breath-taking smile. He watches as I quickly make up my face, spritzing more perfume before covering myself with my robe.

I give him a brief kiss and leave the bedroom.

***

I can't relax. Knowing Connor is lying, possibly still naked, in my bedroom makes me feel jumpy. My face feels hot, Connor's stubble has grazed me and I wonder if it's noticeable, which makes me very glad I lit the candles and left the lights off.

"What is the matter Freya?" Erin asks pouring out the final volume of wine, "you are really twitchy."

"Am I?"

"Yeah, spill…"

"Nothing to say…Don't look at me like that Erin, if I had something to tell you I'd tell you…"

"You've been acting weird for a while now - I will get it out of you! You've not done anything foolish and slept with Will have you?"

"No!" I yelp, "as if!"

"Hmmm well I still smell a secret." Erin knocks back her wine. "Come on, let's go party. Freya, I'm going to phone for a taxi so hurry up and get dressed!"

"Ok bossy boots..." I walk through to the bedroom making sure the door is firmly shut behind me. Connor is lying on my bed, legs crossed at his ankles, arms folded behind his head. I let the robe fall from my shoulders and stand before him naked, the soft lighting of the room accentuating my curves. Without speaking I slowly dress, putting on delicate lace panties and matching bra, a bra that pushed my breasts up high and then I roll up the glossy silk stockings. Connor doesn't take his eyes off me as I move quietly around the room.

"Beautiful." He whispers as I bend over to put on my shoes. I give him a sensual smile and step into the red cocktail dress motioning for him to zip me up. He moves my hair over one shoulder and kisses the other. "Can you still feel me?"

"Yes." I reply in hushed tones.

I blast my hair with the dryer and twist it up. Connor strokes my neck and down my back until he reaches the dress.

"What are you doing tonight?" I ask as I fill my clutch with lipstick, phone and money.

"I'm going out with friends."

"Oh?"

"Didn't you think I had any?"

"I suppose it didn't occur to me as you've spent every night with me." I reply leaning in to give him a kiss.

"I know lots of people..."

"Freya, come on!" Erin calls in through the door.

"Looks like I'm going. I'll see you later."

"Have fun!"

***

The taxi drops us off in Mayfair and we opt for Barnaby's. Imogen orders champagne and both Erin and I stare at her.

"What?"

"Champagne?" Erin says.

"Yes, I have news! Big news but I wanted to save it until we had some posh fizz." She grins. "And I also want you to promise to have an early dinner with me on Sunday."

"An early dinner? Why?"

"Ok, here's the big thing. Today I had a meeting with the senior partners and I got promoted to Lead Buyer which was totally unexpected but fabulous and also comes with a hefty pay rise, hence the posh fizz…"

"Wow, well done Immy," I say grinning wildly.

"Fantastic, well done." Erin claps her hands, "you bloody deserve it, all the hours you put it."

"Yeah and sadly there will be more hours to work so this may be the last you see of me!"

"Then we need to dance until dawn!" Erin bounces in her seat. "It's been too long since we partied like we had no cares!"

"Can you remember when we sat in that bar in town from breakfast until they kicked us out at lunchtime?" I ask. "I think it was the first time we skived a lecture."

"I know I was there but I try not to remember! God, it was a dingy bar wasn't it? Plastic seat covers and a sticky carpet."

"It was cheap!" Imogen laughs. "Where did we go after that?"

"The union! For the rest of the day! I've never been able to drink tequila again!" I giggle.

"Didn't you have a snog with your lecturer that afternoon?" Erin peers at me, "or did I dream it?"

"No you didn't dream it but thanks for bringing it up. What a minger! Yuck! He had the longest nose hair…I was sick after. Not one of my finest moments. He got sacked didn't he, for being caught shagging the trainee librarian in the reference section." I shudder. "Gross!"

Imogen laughs. "We all did things we'd rather not remember! I know I did. I slept with Darren that night." She screws up her face.

"Darren? Darren as in Darren from downstairs…as in *the* skankiest person in the halls? When?" Erin yelps. "When and why didn't you tell us?"

"Would you have told anyone? I can't believe I just told you now!" Imogen shudders. "He was vile!"

"Look how far we've come in life, from cheap watered down student beer and revolting men to ludicrously expensive champers and better looking men…who'd have thought it! The next bottle is on me!" Erin says.

"Well if it's on you we'll have two bottles. This is a like a blue moon…" I giggle.

"You're hilarious Freya…" Erin pokes out her tongue.

"I know!"

"So why the early dinner on Sunday?" Erin turns her attention back to Imogen.

"Well…it just so happens that after my meeting Sidney from accounts asked me out on a date!" She squeals. "I haven't come down yet."

"Sidney? As in the Sidney you've been mooning over like a love sick teenager for the past six months."

"Yep, that Sidney! Can you believe it? Finally! Grace in the post room told him I liked him, I reckon she's one of these weird kind of psychic people because I never told her…"

"You've not exactly been subtle in your love sick teenage mooning you know."

"Whatever, anyway, he asked me out and we're meeting on Sunday for a movie, hence the early dinner with you!"

"Are you using us?"

"Totally. I am far too nervous to go out for food with him, what if I spilt…"

Erin laughs. Imogen is notoriously bad at keeping food on her plate or any of it actually making her mouth without firstly sliding down her front. "Will you be bringing a change of clothes?"

"Of course!"

The banter between us continues. Back and forth until we are laughing hysterically, one of us continually filling up our glasses until the world is fuzzy.

"We just need to find Freya and me a hot man each to complete the picture," Erin says as she pours out the remaining champagne. "Someone much better than William…" She practically spits his name, "and someone along the lines of…them…" She stops and stares as a group of beautiful and very stylish men and women walk into the bar. They carry themselves with the arrogant look-at-me stance of people who know exactly how good they look. "I'll take the blond one." She whispers directing our attention to a muscular man at the front of the pack. "In fact, he could take me any which way he wanted." She drools so obviously that Imogen and I crack up into tear inducing giggles.

"Can you be any more obvious?" I ask gasping, holding onto my stomach. "Oh I think the champagne has well and truly gone to my head."

"I don't care." She pouts. "We need to make this bar our new local."

"Are you going to take out a mortgage to fund it then?" Imogen laughs. "Because my bonus will only stretch so far."

Feeling eyes on me I turn to look at the party as they sit across the room from us. I scan the faces, recognising a couple of fashion models and then take a sharp intake of disbelieving breath. Sitting there, looking more beautiful than any of the others, his eyes coolly on me, is Connor. This is a situation for which I have not been prepared, never once expecting my secret life to be sitting in the same room as my real life. I glance over a few more times and watch as the ice cool blonde sitting beside him, her body turned towards his, leans in closer, her intentions obvious. I want Connor to shrug her off, move away from her but he remains where he is, his eyes locked on mine.

"Freya?" Erin asks leaning over to place her hand over mine. "Is something the matter you look like you've seen a ghost."

I lie. "I'm fine. I think the champagne has got to me!" I drag my eyes away from Connor and look at Erin, my heart pounding in my chest.

"Are you sure?"

"Very." I give her a tight smile. "Shall we move on? Go somewhere else?"

"Yeah..." Erin replies and as she drains her drink she stops dead. "Oh my God, that's Connor Robertson over there!" She nudges me hard, spilling the champagne that I've been clutching tightly. I rub my ribcage that has begun to throb painfully with the force of Erin's elbow and follow her gaze to Connor.

"*The* Connor Robertson?" asks Imogen, leaning back in her chair to look. "Oh my God it is. He is like *the* hottest man in the universe. Did you see him in 'The Gardener'? He had his shirt off most of the way through...I went to see it twice."

They babble and stare at him. It feels like someone has sucked all the breath out of me. It's not possible. My heart thumps wildly but for all my disbelief I know Erin is right and my stupidity at not realising reddens my cheeks. Everyone in the western world knows who Connor Robertson is. He is always in magazines, on internet gossip sites and making newspaper headlines, the broodingly handsome and intensely private Irish actor who took the world by storm aged sixteen and continues to amaze with an exceptional talent that no one can match. He is Hollywood's favourite bad boy and one of the most famous men on the planet – he grew up in Galway, Ireland and following his first film he was instantly a star, his looks winning him legions of fans. By the time he was twenty-two he'd been in and out of rehab, won three Oscars and amassed a multi-million pound fortune.

He has never been photographed with the same woman twice but his reputation as a lothario just adds to his appeal. Women want to be the one to tame him. He is always being voted 'Most Sexiest Man' in women's magazines and his looks plus his undeniable talent ensures that every film he is in is a huge success. Now I am another notch on his bedpost and I feel sick to my stomach.

"Are you sure?" I ask faintly.

"Freya you need to stop reading and start watching. When was the last time you went to the cinema?" Erin asks her eyes fixed on Connor.

I hear myself answer sounding distant and quiet. "I think it was to see Titanic!" I mumble glancing across. The blonde is leaning into him whispering and he laughs loudly, his hand on her toned, bronzed thigh and instantly I feel the painful twisted clasp of jealousy in my stomach. "Are you sure it's him?"

"Do you even know who he is?"

"Of course!" I say with assertion but she raises her eyebrow at me. *No, Erin, I don't, not like you do. I know him in a very different way to you.*

I wish I didn't know. I wish that we hadn't come here. Connor looks across at me and I watch the dismay flood his face. He knows I know.

"Has he been checking you out Freya? There seemed to be some eye contact going on." Imogen turns to me.

"No!" I whisper shaking my head.

"He bloody well was Freya, you lucky cow. He is so sexy isn't he? I don't really know what it is. There is just something about him. I wonder if I should ask for his autograph."

"You can't Immy he's out with his friends." I say but they don't listen to me. Erin and Imogen are talking in a hush about Connor, filling their champagne glasses with the remainder of the bottle. They don't notice me, shrinking under Connor's unhappy gaze, picking apart the cardboard mat upon which my champagne had been placed.

"We can't go anywhere now." Erin announces as she attracts the attention of the waiter and asks for another bottle. "I have to stay sat here, breathing the same air as Connor Robertson. Do you have any idea what I dream of doing with that man?"

I know what I dream of doing to him!

He is laughing at something the blonde has said but the humour doesn't reach his eyes. They flash darkly. I know all about his reputation, the endless women - all models, actresses and singers, lithe and toned, not soft and round red headed writers like me. The waiter comes over and opens the bottle with flamboyance, filling our glasses then excuses himself. I watch the bubbles popping on the surface of the glass, bursting like my bubble just has. My secret suddenly feels like a noose around my neck and I feel suffocated.

"I'm going to the loo." I say standing up on shaking legs. I keep my eyes resolutely forward as I cross the room. I can feel his eyes on me but I don't turn back. Shit. Shit. Shit. This is not how I imagined things to turn out. I don't actually know what I was expecting. Not forever, forever doesn't exist does it? I just didn't expect…Why do I feel so shocked? I willingly leapt into bed with a man I knew nothing about, all because I wanted him and wanted to forget about real life. I laugh bitterly to myself. He is a playboy actor, a Hollywood superstar with the world at his feet and suddenly I am nothing more than a thirty-five year old groupie. Humiliated tears spring to my eyes but what did I expect would happen with a man I went to without a second thought.

"Red?" The Irish voice breaks my thoughts.

"What?"

"I wasn't expecting to see you here." He smiles.

"Clearly." I snap despite my best intentions.

"What does that mean?"

"Well…" I turn to him slowly. "My being here obviously distracted you from stroking other body parts of the woman you were sitting beside. Sorry about that."

"Were you jealous?" Laughter dances in his voice.

"No." I lie forcefully giving him my fiercest look. "Don't flatter yourself." His face hardens. I look beyond him to his entourage who are looking at us with confused interest before they leave the foyer to the shiny black cars that assemble outside. "Your friends are waiting for you."

"They're not my friends."

"What are they then, hangers on basking in the heavenly light from the world famous superstar?"

"Don't be a bitch." Connor almost stumbles from the venom in my words.

"You must think I am so stupid…" I whisper. "So stupid. Why didn't you tell me? Why did you lie?"

"I didn't lie…"

"It feels like it." I mumble. "It feels like everything has been a lie. I asked you…" I shake my head sadly. "'Just Connor' you said."

"I am just Connor."

"Not to the rest of the world you're not. Look, your friends are waiting…"

"Red…"

"Have a good evening Connor." I stalk past him and back to the bar. Connor Robertson? I wish I didn't know.

***

There is a party in full flow at Crystal's when I get home. The music, some hot, sexy music and sounds of raucous laughter fills the silence of my flat but the darkness has me in its icy grip. I switch on all the lights, anything to banish the shadows, but I still feel intense pain. I didn't think it would last forever, I'm not sure I even believe in forever anymore, but I held on tight to it at least being honest. Who am I kidding? It was a relationship built on sex, nothing more. So why does it hurt so much?

My laptop is on the kitchen table, still switched on. I log into google and pour a large glass of whiskey, a drink I don't like but the medicinal properties are desperately needed. The whoops and hollers of Crystal's party guests keep me company as I take the amber train to oblivion. Google throws up page after page of gossip about Connor, endless women, endless accolades, endless images of his beautiful face, his films…suppositions based on rumour, his glowering expression, smiles at premiers, the smiles that aren't as wide as the one's I've seen. Connor's life, in pictures, in words - a superstar who owns the world.

A superstar who owns my heart. I slam the laptop shut and shove it away from me. Nine days, I remind myself, it's only been nine days. Not enough time to justify these feelings. But it doesn't stop the hurt, the pain, the insane jealousy for those who have past and those who will come.

Stop it Freya, you are stronger than this. I never wanted to be a woman whose entire happiness depended on the value a man placed on her and I am not about to start down that path. I survived William, I will survive Connor, despite the intensity of the feelings I have for him. Realising how much I do feel is like a baseball bat around the head. Was it better when I didn't know or does knowing somehow make him leaving ok?

I want it to. I want it to be ok that he's going. Except it's not. And it never will be.

What started out as an ego boost has changed beyond all recognition. I think about him all the time. Look at me, sitting here, thinking about him even now. When will it end? When I've finally driven myself crazy?

A few more days to get through then I'll be in Mexico. A million miles away from here - a welcome respite to my life. Everything happens for a reason, so I am told, and while I realise Will left in order for me to meet Connor, I don't know what purpose it has served. I can't see beyond the gloom so rather than sit here any longer I opt for the chaos of the party upstairs and I dance until dawn.

SATURDAY

'Are you free for an hour for coffee?' I text Henry.
'Don't tell me you're hungover?'
'Nope, just in need of coffee.' In truth I feel jaded but the dawn brought with it a decision, a decision from which there is no turning back.
'Ok, meet me in the lounge at The Stark Hotel at eleven. I'm ensconced there with Fred! I can spare you five minutes!'
Does everything in my life recently have to revolve around that bloody hotel?
'Thanks babe…I'm glad you can squeeze me in ;-)'
'I can always spare a minute or two for you!'
'Wow Henry, I am honoured!'
'You should be! Tootles'.

***

I leave the house, my portfolio under my arm and join the throng on Camden High Street. It's a lovely, warm July morning and the sunlight falling on the buildings gives the town a soft glow. I enter the underground and take the train to Hyde Park Corner, doing my best to avoid tourists and shoppers as I hurry to meet Henry. I keep my head down as I walk into the hotel and hurry across the foyer and through the door into the lounge. It is almost full when I walk in but the waitress directs me to the one remaining table at the back of the room. I order a coffee and flick through a trashy magazine that I picked up from a street vendor.

The barista brings my coffee over and I thank her before turning my attention to the magazine. As usual the content covers reality TV stars, celebs on holiday, who has the better beach body and so on until I turn a page and there is Connor staring out of the paper. It takes my breath away momentarily. His cool green/blue eyes bore into mine and the faint smile curving his full lips, seems hesitant. I wonder when the picture was taken, what he was doing that day. His is the most stunning face I've ever seen, heart shaped and perfectly symmetrical. It is no wonder at all that he is one of the world's most famous men and the object of female obsession. "How is it that you've been sleeping with me?" I whisper stroking my finger across the lines of his face. "How is it possible that I didn't know it was you?" I sit staring into space, my coffee going cold as the time ticks by, never still.

"You look like you could use this," Henry comments putting another black coffee down in front of me, jolting me from my thoughts. Quickly I turn the page, moving onto an article about a Kardashian. "You're looking a little delicate this morning sweetheart, anything you wish to share?"

"I'm so tired Henry, I feel like my eyeballs have been sucked out and really you are too bright to be anywhere near me!" I squint my eyes. "I think I'm going to need shades!" Henry is wearing a cerise pink and black striped shirt with skinny black jeans. He looks wonderful as always.

"I dragged myself away from my love-in to have coffee with you, don't be mean about my clothes."

"I'm not being mean, I'm being truthful, you hurt!" I pat his hand. "Looking hot though babe!"

"That's what Fred said!"

I grin. "I bet he did!"

Henry blushes and smiles shyly. "Yeah…" he clears his throat. "Anyway, I have news!" He leans in conspiratorially. "Last night I was at a party…"

"You are always at parties Henry, that's nothing new!"

"Don't interrupt! You always interrupt me…Anyway…I was at Florence Preston's twenty-first birthday party at Montague Heights when Connor Robertson turned up. Connor Robertson! Can you believe it? What a God!" He eyes me. "I hope you know who I am talking about?"

"Yes I know who he is…"

Henry doesn't look convinced. "You could have heard a pin dropped when he walked into the room, all testosterone and glowering looks. I don't think anyone was expecting him to be there. I think Flo peed her pants. She reckons he's been in town for a week or so and has so far managed to avoid almost every social event which apparently is totally unlike him. Floss reckons he's met someone but naturally he wasn't going to confide in her. You should see him Freya, he is so dashing and so…Irish and sexy…Anyway, Lacey Lucas was there and looking sensational as always…incidentally she told me she thought you were fabulous…"

"Fabulous? I wish I felt fabulous!" I pull a face. I wish I felt more than emptiness.

"Anyway…as I was saying and will you not interrupt me…Connor arrived and Lacey, wearing a leotard that would make Madonna blush, went all sexily up to him and he just about blanked her. Gave her a cursory peck on the check and then turned away from her in front of everyone so Florence dragged her off to the powder room for a pick-me-up…although that surprised me, I though Lacey had moved on from all that…so…Connor just sat in a corner with the dashing chap who is the current Batman and I have to say, Freya, I wouldn't mind being sat in the middle of the two of them. They are both a boy's wet dream…so the Batman chap…"

"Benjamin Hughes…"

"Wow, I am impressed…" I poke out my tongue. "Yes Benjamin Hughes. Well he was a happy smiley sort of bloke but Connor Robertson just smouldered and brooded like an Irish Mr Darcy no matter which beauty happened to parade in front of him. I thought he was a demon shagger, if the reports are anything to go by but I have no scandal to report at all." He takes a sip of his coffee and grimacing opens a sugar and enters the content of the sachet into his cup.

I expect he was all shagged out with blondie I think grimly. I don't want to hear about Connor, smouldering or otherwise not when I feel really, really foolish.

"And the news is…"

"Just that! Check me partying with the stars!"

"You're the brightest star of all Henry!" I grin.

"So what did you want to see me for, all cloak and dagger?" He asks sipping his drink. "By the way, I've given up smoking, Fred doesn't like it…"

"About bloody time!" I take a deep breath. "Henry, can I trust you? Completely trust you in that you won't tell anyone anything, not even Fred."

"Of course. Always."

"Do you ever feel like there is one opportunity to take on the world and win?"

"Sometimes."

"I always thought I would. When I was at university I had so many dreams, ambitions that have somehow got lost…"

"Well you did marry William…"

"Henry," I reply sharply silencing him with a look. "Does it ever occur to you that if I hadn't met him I'd not have met you?"

"No. Wouldn't that have been shit?"

"Exactly! The last couple of weeks have been a total rollercoaster…"

"You met someone?"

"It's not that…" I pause. "I made a decision last night…this morning…at some point midway through a bottle of whiskey…

"Whiskey? Since when do you drink whiskey? Freya, do you need rehab?"

"I gate crashed Crystal's party, it was all I had to take with me! Now you're interrupting me…"

"Sorry, please continue!" Henry laughs.

"So I made a decision and I'm not sure you are going to approve…"

"Oh fuck, what?"

"I am going to leave London…"

"You're what?" He shrieks, "no no no Freya, this is not cool. Why? Why would you break my heart like this?"

"Because I need to take a chance on myself…will you look at something for me?" I ask swallowing hard. "But before you do, will you promise to tell the truth…"

"The whole truth and nothing but the truth so help me God." He grins. "I always tell you the truth…"

"I know." I reach down for my portfolio. "Will you look at these?"

"What is it?"

"My future hopefully."

"Your future?" Henry raises a perfectly arched eyebrow. "The reason you want to leave London?"

I don't look at Henry as he opens the leather case, instead nervously sipping my drink I allow myself to think about Connor. Already I miss him, my secret lover, my secret love. The warmth that surrounded me while I basked in the glow of him has gone, now I sit under a rain cloud that lacks a silver lining.

"Did you do these?" Henry asks incredulously.

I nod.

"These are sensational Freya, truly sensational. Why would you hide this unbelievable talent? Why?" He shakes his head in disbelief. "I knew you liked to make clothes but…fuck…Freya, why have you settled for second best?"

"Second best?"

"You are a brilliant, talented journalist but seriously…why the fuck are you writing about other people's designs when someone should be writing about yours?"

"Really?" Do you mean it?" A glimmer of hope flickers inside my belly.

"When have I ever lied to you?" Henry states. "Never, that's when! The House of Freya, I can see it now!"

I laugh. "The House of Freya?"

"Nah, that's a shit name! Seriously doll, you need to do something with these. Now that Wanker Will is off the scene you can do anything you want, aim for the stars because I reckon you'll reach them!"

"Do you?" I feel like a weight has lifted, that the possibilities are endless. Henry's enthusiasm is honest and truthful and makes me believe that anything is possible.

"Yes, babe, I do. You have real talent Freya, now you have to show the world...but Freya you look so sad."

"Sad?"

"A light has gone from your eyes." Henry reaches for my hands, "what is it? Talk to Aunty Henry."

I shake my head. "I'd rather hear about you! How's things with Fred...now that you've come up for air!"

There is a subtle change in my friend, a calmness that is slowly replacing the manic person that I have always known Henry to be. He has never seemed as comfortable in his own skin as he does now, since he met Fred.

"It's all happening so fast but...I feel a better person since I met him, I feel right somehow, perhaps after all the frogs I have finally found my prince!" He giggles and takes a long drink. "He really is the sexiest man alive."

"He was always my favourite..."

"He'll be here in a minute, you can tell him that!"

"You may have to mop up my dribble!"

"Freya!" Henry squeals.

"Sorry!" I giggle. "But Henry...he is seriously fit!"

Henry chuckles. "Yes, he really is." Then his face falls.

"What's the matter?" I ask.

"He's going away in a week. For six weeks. What if he meets someone else? He is gorgeous Freya and I feel complete with him, I'm so scared it will all fall down around me. I couldn't bear the thought..." The shine in Henry's eye fades and he looks so melancholy I get up out of my chair to give him a hug.

"Henry, have you spoken to Fred about this?" I ask, kissing the top of his head. "You may very well be worrying for nothing. I saw the way he looked at you, I don't think you are just a passing fancy to him."

"Six weeks though Freya, how am I going to be without him for six weeks?"

Try a lifetime.

"You have holiday to use, you can fly out and see him, surely? Henry, go and speak to him. Tell Fred how you feel and then you will be able to stop worrying. Everyone has someone they can't live without, you may be Fred's someone, but you won't know until you ask."

"But it's been two days, just two. I'm being pathetic. He's a pop star...I'm just me. A no one in the great scheme of things, someone to forget..." Henry looks so sad and forlorn that I take hold of his hand and hold it tightly between both of mine.

"Henry, there is nothing forgettable about you. You are a wonderful, gorgeous person with a great heart. Fred is lucky to have you and who cares if it's been two days, two weeks or two decades, feelings are feelings and sometimes you meet someone who changes your world, someone who you cannot even comprehend living without for just one moment. To Fred, you may be the someone he can't live without...just have faith..."

"Speaking of the devil..." Henry grins as Fred crosses the café to join us. He sits down in the vacant chair and drops a gentle kiss on Henry's cheek.

"Hello." He murmurs to Henry stroking his cheek. I suddenly feel in the way, a spare part in a very intimate moment. Time seems to tick by loudly then Fred turns to me. "Hello again Freya, how are you?"

"I'm very well, thank you Fred. I've been reading the tour reviews!" I tell him waggling the magazine. "It looks like you set the world on fire!"

"It was a great tour to be part of but I'm tired now, I could do with more than a week off!" He grins and takes hold of Henry's hand. "It would be nice to be normal for a while."

"I bet." I take a sip of my drink. "Remind me again when does the new album come out?"

"We begin promoting next week. There is no rest for the wicked!" He grins. "I wouldn't swap it but it's going to be harder to go away this time." Fred looks affectionately at Henry. Suddenly I feel in the way, an imposter in their new and exciting love and I want to go home.

"Gorgeous boys I think I am done. Home time for me!" I announce. Henry packs up the drawings and puts them neatly back in the folder. He hands them to me.

"It's your time… but please reconsider leaving London" He says.

I smile. "Maybe…and Henry, I think it's your time too." I wink and then give both him and Fred a kiss. "Enjoy the rest of your Saturday."

"What are you going to do today?" Henry asks.

"I don't know!" I smile and Henry understands the meaning behind it. "Put my faith in the Gods or something."

"Good girl." Henry replies not really listening as he and Fred get lost in each other.

I give a brief wave and leave the lounge.

I cross the foyer, feeling nervous just being here. My heels making a loud clacking on the marble, echoing around the quiet reception. The concierges welcomes me with a "good morning," that I reply to with a smile which fades as soon as I see Connor walking into the hotel, a beautiful raven haired girl on his arm. She must be about twenty, slim built wearing black hipster jeans and a skinny red shirt tucked in. She moves with the confidence of youth, comfortable in her own porcelain skin, her glossy hair bobbed around the heart shaped face. She is also not the girl from last night. They are laughing and Connor's face is lit up, his eyes sparkling with humour.

A vice grips my heart. It's icy and squeezes so tightly I think my heart will break. Two beautiful people looking happy together. It's the reality of Connor's world, a reality that doesn't include a thirty five year old screwball. I hang my head and skirt around the edge of the foyer hoping to leave unnoticed.

"Red?" I look up. Connor lets go of the raven haired goddess and crosses the foyer. "I wasn't expecting to see you."

I snap. "You don't have to worry, I'm leaving."

"Why are you here?" Connor flicks his glance between the girl and me. She stares at me through narrowed eyes so I return with a hard stare.

"I wasn't stalking you I'm here because I met a friend for a coffee. I do realise that someone like you operates on an invite only basis!"

"Someone like me…"

I gesture to the girl and shake my head sadly. "I've read all about you. I wish I didn't know…"

I stalk out into the day. The clear blue sky is at odds with the misery I feel. He's moved on. Already. Why am I surprised, with the world at his feet and women ready to hang off his every word why would I presume that it would be different with me? I wish I'd known it was him, I'd have been prepared and shut my heart away until I was no longer the chosen one. I enter the tube at a loss of somewhere to go.

***

"Do you want a cup of tea Freya?" Mum asks giving Dad an anxious look as I sit heavily at the kitchen table. Dad has been ordered out of the shed and he stands looking twitchy in the kitchen. Dad doesn't do 'Women Talk' and I can tell he's longing to escape the girly emotional stuff back to sanctuary of the garden.

"No thanks." I slump, my head in hands. "Dad, you don't have to stay here, I'm not going to be sectioned."

"Thank God!" He drops a kiss on my head and leaves the kitchen banging the door.

"Freya? What is the matter? You look dreadful." Mum sits down beside me. "You've been so evasive lately, has something happened?"

"I met someone." I mumble. "Someone who turned everything upside down. It was so unexpected and so magical that I still don't know if it was real. Then he turned out to be someone else and I feel…I feel…I feel…" I raise my stricken face to mum. "Have you ever fallen for someone with whom there is no future, just a moment in time?"

"Yes," she admits. "Once. I was a child of the sixties Freya, there were no longer any rules, love was free, the pill came along and gave women the chance to explore relationships without repercussion…and…well anything went, the boundaries blurred and yet I'm not sure we really got past the Victorian attitude that filtered through our upbringing.

"Good girls weren't supposed to have affairs or sex outside of marriage and our parents couldn't handle the sudden change. There were good times…great times…there were bad times too. We all had secrets, sometimes we shared them but mostly, honestly, we couldn't let go of the fear that our parents would find out.

"I was sixteen when I met a musician from Liverpool. He was smart and funny and so talented. He went on to become one of the most famous men in musical history but for two weeks he was my whole world. No one knew. He and his band were just on the edge of the big time, I was on holiday at my Grandma's in Liverpool, she was really forward thinking, I think she had her own secrets, sometimes she would give me just a hint. Anyway, she let me run wild and I did. I met him one night when I was out in the centre of Liverpool with my cousins, he charmed my knickers off and we were inseparable. I thought I was in love, probably it was little more than teenage infatuation but I've never forgotten him, or the experience of the first great love."

"What happened?" I ask enthralled.

"I came home, he promised to write…he did a handful of times, beautiful words and poetry…but then the fame, glory and hangers on swept him off his feet. A few years later I met your dad and he was solid and responsible…We have made a great life together but I still have the letters and sometimes I read them. It's all I have to bequeath to you but they are worth a lot of money."

"Who was he?"

Mum whispers a name and I feel my mouth fall open.

"Really?"

"Yes, I was the first in a long line of many!" She winks.

"God mum!"

"I know!"

"You could sell your story!" I laugh.

"But what would that bring other than disruption? Your grandma is ninety two, I don't want to kill her off with the shock! So who is this man?"

"It's a similar story to yours except he is already famous. Is it possible to love someone you don't really know?"

"Love is complex Freya, there are many different types – the first love, true love and the one that got away. You've experienced the first and the one that got away, maybe true love is coming for you?"

"Mum?"

"Yes?"

"Can I have a cup of tea?"

"Of course. Go and ask your dad if he wants one. He's likely to dehydrate in there."

"Mum?"

"Yes?"

"Can I stay the night?"

"Of course!"

SUNDAY

I wander aimlessly around London. I've read everything there is to read about Connor but none of it matches the man I've spent my time with. I don't recognise the Connor the media obsesses over but I still devoured every word. The gossip about his private life spans pages. If it were printed out it would reach Mars. I read and read and read wondering how much was true, wanting to turn the computer off but unable to tear my eyes away like a psycho masochistic stalker. None of them look like me. The other women, blonde, slender, beautiful – models, actresses, socialites, pop stars – all with similar looks, the perfect face, perfect clothes, perfect, perfect, perfect...Mum made me turn it off when I hit the brandy and asked dad for a roll-up.

The one thing the media agreed on has been his undeniable acting ability. With three Oscars, five golden globes, three BAFTAs and more international awards than Imelda Marcos had shoes Connor has proved himself to be a talent that appears unstoppable – which makes it more preposterous that I didn't recognise him. Would it have made a difference? Would I have still gone to him that night? Of course I would. Only I would have protected myself from all this.

I find myself standing outside the multiplex cinema in Leicester Square. Ordinarily this is one area of London I avoid – crowded with tourists and fast food outlets – but the anonymity of it today is just what I need. I'm not likely to see anyone I know, not likely to bump into Connor and yet another woman, it's just the place I need to hide away.

Except I have nowhere to hide.

From the huge billboard above the cinema Connor's face looks out across the square. Outside the cinema crowds of girls have begun queuing for tickets, babbling to their friends, all dressed in the teenage uniform of shorts, heels and large totes, their faces made up with layers and layers of makeup, badly applied but their foray into womanhood makes me smile.

I join the queue.

I sit in the auditorium beside two girls comparing pictures of Connor in the pages of their teen bibles.

"Did you hear that he was back with Delilah Jones?" One of them says to the other slurping her cola. "He is in Paris with her today."

"Delilah Jones?" The other says aghast. "This is not good news, I can't stand her."

"You only can't stand her because of Connor."

"She's not good enough for him. She's a slut."

"Yeah well, she's in this film! Look it says here that they're in Paris for the French premiere. I can't believe our parents wouldn't let us out for the premier here. I told my mum she'd ruined my life…I'll never forgive her"

I zone out of their conversation. They munch on their popcorn discussing celebrities written about in their magazines, while I sit, ashen faced, gripping onto the edge of my seat. Delilah Jones? The girl I saw him with wasn't her. I'm just one in the middle of a long list. The nausea comes in waves, violent waves and I stand to leave just as the lights go out and the film begins.

Connor's voice fills the room. The soft whispered words of regret explaining the story as the film opens with him and Delilah in bed. Tousled, sexual and the chemistry between them tortures me that I pay little attention to the film, looking for a hint of more between them. He is so perfect, so larger than life that it's only when the girl sitting next to me hands me a tissue do I realise the tears have been falling. To think that just for one moment, one brief moment in time he may have been mine and I let him slip through my fingers like sand.

The one that got away?

It's a relief when the film ends. The air is notably cooler as I leave the cinema and cross the square to the underground, taking the train back to Camden. Camden no longer feels like home, more a place to stay until the executioner comes for me. Had I not made the decision to move I would perhaps be more inclined to find a new home in the town but the era is ending and it too breaks my heart that little bit more. I've barely caught my breath these past six weeks and I feel exhausted. It would make a good story, the good girl with a secret, but the story doesn't seem to have a happy ending and Shakespeare has the monopoly on tragedy.

It would have been no less painful to have parted ways with Connor if he'd just been an everyday normal man, not the superstar he has turned out to be. I miss his voice, his kiss, his touch, my body cries out for him and supressing it is a whole new level of discomfort. There is a gaping hole in the middle of my life, a Connor sized hole and I wonder how it could ever be filled. I leave the train at Camden wishing that I could go somewhere else. The borough is buzzing as it is every day of the week but the pedestrians on the street just serve to make me feel the clasp of claustrophobia. I chuck two pounds into the resident beggar's cup as I pass. I wonder about him on the days that I see him sat in the doorway of the bank by the entrance. He looks about my age but so tired and desperate, sadness in every line on his face. What sends people to the streets? What happens to a person to make a life of doorways a better option? He looks so lost, that life has dealt a cruel blow and I return to drop another five pounds in his cup.

"God bless." He whispers.

I give him a smile and turn away. The wind has picked up and the rain has started to fall. It doesn't fit with the summer and my thin jacket gives little protection against the coldness of the rain. What was I hoping for? That I would be Connor's one true love? I laugh bitterly, wrapping my arms around myself against the cold. Connor was the light that led me towards my new future, forever to be held in my heart as the person who gave me back to myself. It doesn't stop the anguish when I picture her, the beautiful woman at his side. She is the kind of woman he is used to, young, gorgeous and not carrying the baggage I am. It doesn't make it any less easy to swallow.

I know that my decision is the right one. To leave London and escape to the seaside, reliving the childhood memories where the dream began. I still have the drawings, childish scribbles of fancy princess dresses and the letters to Santa, that mum gave me years later, asking for a sewing machine and shiny silver fabric. My friends wanted Barbie, I wanted a mannequin to dress. I've let it pass me by - the dream got picked up on a wind and danced in the breeze just out of reach. It's so close, I can almost reach it and now is the time. Time - I have plenty. Will has gone, Connor has gone, it's time for me to take the step into the big wide world and prove to myself that my flame can still burn bright.

I thank the Gods as I walk. Thank them for turning my life upside down to get me to this point. I will never regret Will and me nor will I ever forget the insane feelings I have for Connor. It is also him that I have to thank, for the beautiful illicit love, the secret that will forever glow inside me. The one who…

"Connor?" A lone figure stands from their seated position on the wall beside the front door.

"Yeah."

"What are you doing here?" I pull my coat tightly across my chest and fold my arms.

"I came to see you." He says moving towards me.

"Why?"

"You keep stomping off…it's hard to talk to empty space." He gives me a small smile.

"I didn't think there'd be anything to say." I mumble looking down at the ground. "I didn't want to interrupt…"

"Interrupt what exactly?" He asks reaching out for me. I take a step backwards.

"Two beautiful people, a deluxe hotel…it doesn't take a genius Connor."

"The woman I was with yesterday was my sister, Aiofe. She's in town for a couple of days then coming to Australia with me before she starts university. Where have you been?"

"I stayed at my parents."

"I thought…"

"You thought what?"

"I thought you'd gone back to him…He was here the first time I came up, I saw him leave your house." Connor sighs. "I thought I'd really blown it and you went back to him. I've been back and forth, I think your neighbours must think I'm a stalker." He smiles briefly.

"Why would you worry?" I ask looking down at the floor. "Why would it bother you who I was with? You weren't bothered about me on Friday…"

"Friday?"

"Blondie."

He looks faintly embarrassed. "I wanted a reaction from you."

"A what…" I shake my head. "A reaction? And you think stroking some skinny model's thigh is the way to do it? Jesus Connor you're unbelievable." I go to shove past him. "Perhaps things work differently in your world but in mine, doing that…that's just nasty and unkind. I've been through enough I don't need you to do something like that for a reaction. I know who you are now, I know what the papers say and that behaviour just makes me wonder if everything I've read is true. You wanted to be 'just Connor' so if you want that then don't behave like a spoiled rich celebrity and don't think that something like that will be tolerated. I've been cheated on, it sucks, and I will not put myself in that situation again, where someone lies to me and leaves me feeling totally crap. If you want to play games then you'll have to find a willing victim because I am not it."

"Nothing happened with her."

I can see the sincerity in his eyes as he holds me in his gaze. I believe him, not because I want to believe him but because I just know he's not lying to me. Actor or not there is no denying that he's telling me the truth.

"Then why do it?"

"You seemed so cool, so calm and together, it was like seeing me didn't matter to you."

"Perhaps I'm just a good actress. Seeing you did matter I just didn't know how to handle the situation, it was unexpected and my friends don't know and then I found out…"

Silence falls.

"I wish you didn't know."

"Why? Because now I know you lied to me?"

"I didn't lie to you. I would never lie to you…"

I interrupt him. "You didn't tell me the truth, it's the same thing." I walk past Connor to the front door and open it just as big, fat drops of rain descend from the sky. Above us a loud crash of thunder is followed by a sheet of lightning that turns the sky an eerie lilac colour. He follows me indoors and shakes the rain from his hair, running his hands through the chestnut crop until it sticks up in all directions. I switch the lights on and Connor closes the door behind me. The storm above us rages, angry and deafening, the raindrops hitting the windows sounding like rounds from a machine gun. I fill the kettle and turn it on. "Coffee?" I ask.

"Yes please." Connor sits down at the small dining room table and leans his head into his hands. "I didn't want you to know because I liked just being me. I'm always recognised but with you, it was like I was normal. Women always know who I am and I have always used that to my advantage." He looks up at me, gaging my reaction. I keep my face impartial but it takes every ounce of acting ability I have to maintain a blasé look. "They always sell their story and then my mam rings..." He falls silent.

"So why do it then? If you know they're going to the press as soon as it's over?"

Connor looks young and vulnerable as he says, "when a hot woman hands you herself on a plate it's not something you turn down. No man would. It fills a gap. It can be lonely on the road and having someone pretty to look at and guaranteed sex...It passes the time."

"Like Delilah Jones?" I ask screwing up my face and turning from him. I measure out coffee into the coffee maker and pour out the boiling water.

"Delilah? There is nothing going on with Delilah! We went to Paris for work, private jet, there, the première then back in four hours. Look Freya, I'm not going to apologise for my past. I'm twenty five, single and living a life people can only dream about. I know what my reputation is."

"Does it make you happy?"

"It used to."

"And now?"

Connor sighs. I hand him a mug full of black coffee and add sugar and milk to mine before sitting opposite him at the table.

"And now it seems I'm in an almost relationship with you and it's driving me crazy. I don't know where we can go from here. I live in LA, you're in England - it doesn't seem that there is anywhere to take this."

"Perhaps we were never meant to be anything more than an almost relationship." I say sadly.

"Perhaps." He reaches for my hand and encases it between both of his.

I try to make light of the situation. "Now I know it's you I could always sell my story and buy a handbag!"

Connor chuckles. "Yes you could, perhaps two handbags but..." he pauses to run his thumb over my mouth which falls open at his touch. "...I don't think you want handbags..." He pauses. "I will come back."

"Connor, you're a film star with all the razzmatazz that it has to offer. Don't make a promise you can't keep."

He stands up pulls me round the table and into his arms. I nestle into his strong chest. I can hear his heart beating, in time with mine, a reassuring beat inside a man who means more to me now than he should. "Look Red, I just want to spend the next few days with you. I like being with you. I wish I could predict the future and see how it all turns out but I don't think it's going in our favour."

"Then we have to make the next few days count, don't we?" I say, a lump forming in my throat.

He kisses me softly.

"Does it ever occur to you that I may just want to talk?" I murmur smiling.

"Well then it's nice to think you don't just want me for my body!" Connor laughs and I giggle.

"Not all the time...you're not all that!"

"Oh really?"

"Yes!" I squeal as Connor sweeps me off my feet. "Put me down, you'll break your back" I giggle

"Hardly, I'm as strong as the Terminator." As if to prove a point he pseudo-drops me.

"Connor." I grip onto him tightly yelping. "I think you need to put me down!" For a brief moment I bury my head into his neck, inhaling deeply the uniquely sexy scent. It sets my heart racing and brings with it the throb of desire. I drop feather like kisses along his neck and under his jaw. As always he tastes amazing, manly and masculine, a delicacy that inflames my taste buds and sends sparks around me.

"Two days just isn't enough. Red?"
"Yes?"
"I…"

The thunder crashes and takes his words. The electricity in the air seems to surround us and we kiss and touch each other like it's the final time, with an urgency to commit each other to memory, the contours of our faces, our bodies, the texture of our hair. Connor's hands are wrapped in my hair, mine are clasped around his torso, holding him so tightly that his muscles leave indentations in my skin.

Our lips don't part.

Connor keeps one of his hands entangled in my hair while the other strokes my face then down to the hollow of my neck. His fingertips dust over my skin trailing a path to the neckline of my t-shirt. I shiver under his touch, the pressure of his fingers increasing with every caress. The storm crashes above us, the air heavy and dense as I move to grip the muscles on his arms pulling him to me and then, under his shirt I stroke his body - his hard firm and desirable body - pushing myself against his bulging erection.

He kisses me deeply his body pressed up against mine. There is a weight, heavy and low in my belly, an exquisite ache inside that only he can relieve. I undo the buttons of his black shirt, easing it from his shoulders, stroking his body as I do. The scent and flavour of him is arousing, bringing forward great waves of desire until I feel like I'm drowning. My body comes alive, each sense, each nerve, each feeling tingling and burning with want, need, lust...

"Connor…" I moan, my head spinning.

The thunder bangs above us, crashing and smashing a stormy path through the sky. We sink to the kitchen floor, the tiles cold against my back. Connor lies alongside me, his mouth on mine, his hands removing my clothes one button at a time, slowly, firmly, exquisitely, teasing and stroking. I unzip his jeans, taking his huge erection in my hand. His skin, soft and silken, encases the hardness and the ache inside increases painfully.

"Connor, I..." He kisses my words away, lying above me, the tiles rigid against my back, the muscles in his chest pushing against my body. As uncomfortable as it feels to in this position on the floor, the weight of Connor upon me grounds me into the moment. It is real. He is real. He is the light at the end of the tunnel that I fearfully walked alone but beyond that the unknown beckons and I pull him closer to me.

Roughly he pulls me to my feet and scoops me up into his arms carrying me through the house to the bedroom. "You are so beautiful." He whispers against my mouth as he lays me on the bed. The fabric is cool and I lie against it allowing the soft fabric to caress my skin. Connor cast his eyes over my body and, without taking my eyes from his face, I stretch my arms above my head, taking hold of the iron headboard which lifts my breasts high. He looks at them greedily and reaches a hand out to touch. "These are amazing," he says and pinches my nipple lightly. It hardens under his touch. "You are so fucking sexy."

I pull him towards me kissing every inch of his skin. His heart beats furiously against my chest and I move to touch him, explore him, savouring the taste of his skin under my tongue. His eyes are dark, flashing with a sexual desire that I've never seen. It's erotic and the heat within me increases until I sizzle.

I can see us, in the free-standing mirror I left in the middle of the room yesterday. His body, bronzed and perfect, glistens in the light. My skin, normally pale and creamy is flushed, a glow of pink that highlights my body. Incredulously I watch us, our two forms mimicking the other, the deep breaths, the touches, the image of two people moving together. My face, alive, bright, desire beaming from me looks radiant, a look I've never seen on my features. I've always enjoyed sex but to see myself, like this, Connor's body moving above mine, his hands holding my arms above my head – It's the sexiest moment of my life. I can't take my eyes from him…from me. HIs mouth, on my nipples, nips and sucks, the waves of heat cascade down through me and his tongue follows a sensual path down my body.

    I twist my head, turning to look over my shoulder at the mirror. I can see myself, quivering, wet, open and ready, ready for anything. I glance up at Connor, his face animated and his eyes, darker still, are filled with an emotion unreadable. We move together, two bodies merged into one and as the storm continues to rage so we give into our desire for each other.

MONDAY

"I am taking you out tonight." Connor says over the phone.

"Where?" I lean back in my office chair and grin. "I'm not sure I should be seen in public, I look totally wrecked!"

"I bet you look like you've been shagged by an Irish man!"

"That's exactly how I look…"

He laughs, "and that's how you'll look again tomorrow."

"Will I?"

"Yes beautiful Red, you will and I am going to take you somewhere you have never been before. Come straight here after work." He hangs up before I can reply.

I grin to myself and lean back in my chair.

"Where the fuck were you yesterday?" I jump as Henry comes crashing in through my office door. "I rang and rang you. Why didn't you answer?"

"I went to the cinema. Why didn't you leave a message?"

"I don't do messages!"

"So why are you moaning then Henry? I would have phoned you back…"

"Blah, blah blah…"

"Henry!"

"Look Freya, I wanted to talk to you because I have been thinking about what you said on Saturday…Freya, you can't leave London. Yes leave here and definitely go for your dreams but leaving London…no no no. Everything is here, the magazines and the models and the opportunities and me. I'll die without you Freeeya." Henry pleads. "You're my girl. You can't leave me alone."

"You won't be alone…you have a million friends and now there is Fred…"

"But you're my bestie. You are the one woman I'd go straight for, you cannot leave me. You know you'd wither away without me, just like I will wither without you. We've been besties for ten years Freya, when you were making the tea and I was running errands. Ten years! You cannot go." Henry looks so forlorn that a lump in my throat begins to constrict my airway.

"Henry…"

"Doll, don't you say anything. I have man-scara on and I refuse to shed any tears over someone who is abandoning me for wherever you're going…One day though Freya, I will get to the bottom of everything…"

"Everything?"

"There is something going on with you. I know you are hiding something from me, I can smell a secret Freya. What is it?"

"I don't have anything to tell you." I'm glad Henry changed the subject, his woeful look was beginning to make my resolve crumble.

"You are shit at keeping secrets."

"Am !? I raise my eyebrow and flutter my eyelids.

Henry looks at me critically. "I reckon you've got a man. In fact I am convinced of it. Moving from London wouldn't give you the satisfied smile I keep catching you with. Who is it? He's not the future King is he?"

"No, just Superman."

"Superman…Jesus Freya your geekness is painful!" And with that Henry sails out of my office.

***

I don't recognise myself. The clothes are mine, a fitted black cocktail dress with strappy silver sandals and a silver but my hair is covered with a blonde wig and I am wearing black rimmed sexy-secretary glasses. I've opted for dramatic makeup and matt red lips and underneath it all it's me but I can't stop looking at myself.

"I look weird." I tell Connor.

"I prefer the red hair. The blonde bob looks hookerish!"

"Thanks!" I splutter. "You chose it!"

Connor laughs and kisses me. "So I look like me?" He does a twirl.

"Not at all! You look like a geeky student." Connor is also wearing a blond wig, a darker shade to mine, some little John Lennon glasses and is dressed like Prince William during his St Andrews years.

"So if I look so geeky why are you looking at me like you want to meet me behind the bike sheds?"

I run my hand across his groin and feel him stir. "Maybe I do."

"Oh Miss are you going to give me detention!" He reaches for my arse and I slap his hand away.

"I may." I sashay to the door, "if this evening doesn't please me!"

No one is looking at us as we leave the hotel and walk to the end of Park Lane to find a taxi. The night is cool and there is an orange glow across the city as the streets light up.

"Do you like living in London?" Connor asks.

"I did. I've grown up here and when I moved to Camden it was really exciting but recently it has lost its shine, I don't want to be here anymore." I sigh heavily.

"That's a big sigh." Connor comments.

"Everything has changed. I don't recognise my life now and I want to do something different, to be somewhere different." I clasp his hand. "Tell me about LA. The real LA, the bits where you go."

"LA is everything you've probably ever heard or read about it. The sun always shines and where I live is coastal and a complete escape from the smog bowl that is the city. It's very different to here and to home. At home no one is allowed to get too big for their boots, over there it's a whole different story. The Next Big Thing is flattered and fawned over, invited to every party, event and premier but the minute there is a sniff of scandal or homosexuality or if one critic doesn't like a film they're dropped and can't even secure a bit part in a made-for-TV movie."

"You've done well though."

"I've been lucky. Bloody lucky. There are not many people who have a resume like mine. I count my blessings, my mother would clip me around the ear if I got complacent about it, but I'm still waiting for the axe to fall."

"It may never fall. Look at Tom Cruise and Tom Hanks and George Clooney…" I fan my face.

"You like George?" Connor narrows his eyes.

"Show me one woman who doesn't!" I smile.

"And there I was thinking you liked the younger man…" Connor feigns upset.

"Only one younger man…" I murmur nestling in.

"Enough to say no to George?" He asks in a low tone slowly stroking my thigh.

"I'll give that some thought!" I reply playfully.

"Perhaps I won't introduce you!" He grins. "LA will never be home. I've made a life there and I have people I suppose I can call friends because I've had to but it's not the same as Ireland. I miss the rain and the mist and the history. I miss roast potatoes and mass on a Sunday. I'm not massively religious but going to church is a big thing in our village then everyone used to go to the pub!"

"The pub?"

"Yeah swapping one lot of holy water for Dublin's finest holy water!"

"But you left Ireland at sixteen!"

"It's a village pub…!"

"Oh!"

Connor flags down a taxi and gives the address of a restaurant in Marylebone. The taxi driver does a fast U-turn and speeds up the road.

"You must enjoy LA though, to still be there. I'd have thought you could just fly in and out and live anywhere you wanted." I ask. "From what I read some actors live in the middle of nowhere."

"I love my house. It's the calm within the centre of the storm and despite what you may think there is always the fear that I'll be passed over for roles I really want because I wouldn't be immediately available."

"I bet your house has seen a lot of action over the years."

"Never." He fingers the edge of my dress. "This is a nice dress did you make it?"

"Not this one. I would have embellished it a bit more. It's actually one Lacey made..."

"It fits you very well." He murmurs approvingly stroking the skin in the centre of my cleavage.

"Connor..." I say in hushed voice nodding towards the driver. "Don't."

He gives me a wicked smile and moves his hand to my thigh walking his fingers up the inside of my legs, softly brushing my skin. I open them a little more allowing him the merest touch of my groin. "No panties?" He murmurs approvingly.

"It's a warm evening." Connor nudges open my legs further and begins a soft caress. I bite my lip to keep from moaning as his fingers stroke and tickle. Connor increases the pressure of his touch and I grip the seats as the fire begins to rage in my belly. "Connor...stop." I whisper, my voice cracking.

"I don't think you mean that..." He says nibbling my ear. "I don't think you want me to stop at all." His cheeks flush and his blue eyes darken as he looks lustfully at me while continuing to stroke my sensitive bud.

"Stop..." I croak weakly. "The taxi driver..."

"...doesn't care." Connor says kissing my neck. I close my eyes and lean my head back against the seat. I feel heavy, full up and the tingles within me explode as I give into the heat as it begins to rise. As Connor's fingers stroke me to orgasm I bite my lip to keep from crying out.

"I love touching you." Connor murmurs against my mouth, kissing me softly.

***

We are shown to a table in the back corner of the restaurant. No one looks up at us. Connor gives a smile. "Being incognito is so nice." He sits down in his chair after pulling out mine. "Sometimes I wander around Venice or Malibu in a disguise just to feel normal. I tried going out in sunglasses and a baseball cap a couple of times but I ended up being rescued by the LAPD. That was scary."

I stare at him.

"What?" He asks. "Has my wig slipped?"

"No, it's just…how do you cope? With the lack of privacy and overzealous fans?"

"I've got used to it. It used to drive me crazy but now I have big gates and better disguises. It won't last forever and then I can have a normal life."

"Doesn't it worry you that you'll leave it too late for a normal life? How do you go to normal after everything you've achieved?"

"It's no different than you changing your life. How do you go from what you're doing to something new?"

The waitress interrupts us bringing menus over. We order our drinks and the menus are left on the table untouched. "I don't know. I have always had a life plan, always knew where I was headed even if it wasn't exactly how I envisaged things to be but now, there is no plan but all of a sudden it doesn't matter. William had very strong ideas of how we should be, the jobs we did and I went along with it. I don't know if I ever wanted to do what I am doing but I was so desperate to fit in with his world – his parents, well his mother in particular, never really approved of me - that I think I let go of what was important to me. I let him convince me that my dreams weren't realistic but now I wonder if it was really a lack of confidence on my part to even try."

"What were your dreams?"

"I wanted to design. I went to a private school on an art scholarship then university to do fashion design and journalism. My tutors were amazing and my collection gained me a first class degree but for financial reasons, and encouragement from William, I took a route into magazines and fourteen years later here I am!"

"He sounds like a total prick, he must be a total prick to let you go! If you were my wife I'd encourage you to reach for the stars." I feel my face redden. Connor grins and strokes my cheek, cupping my face. "You should believe in yourself, I believe in you."

"You do?"

"Yeah, your husband is just a dick."

I laugh. "Yeah, I guess he has proved that!"

"Do you still love him?"

"I don't know if I ever really did. I never felt *in love* with Will. Since we split up my friends are saying that they never thought we were right together and actually I think they're spot on. We were so different. Too different. He and Lexi are right for each other, they are on the same page, I was always in a different book! I care for him but any love that was there, well that's long gone. He is not the person I thought he was but I don't wish anything bad for him, I hope he has made the right choice for him and that he will be happy."

"Has he made the right choice for you?"

I look into his eyes, beautifully blue and shining behind the glasses. "I've never drawn so many dresses in my life!"

"That's not what I meant."

"It didn't seem so at the time but yes, the choice was right for me."

"So what now?"

"Will is sorting the house sale and once it's sold I am going to move from London, start again, draw and design and see where that goes. I don't want any more regrets about it, I want to be able to say that at least I tried, regardless of whether it all goes wrong."

"So where will I find you?"

"Are you coming back?" I don't want to sound hopeful but it creeps into my voice.

"I hope so." His eyes sparkle like blue/green pools of ocean. "I've gotten used to my life in London, sometimes, recently I've been wondering what would happen if things were different, if I could stay and see where this all goes with you..."

"And the other times?"

"The other times I want to see what more I can achieve in my career."

"There is more to achieve than winning an Oscar?"

"Yeah plenty." He laughs. "Being an actor isn't just award ceremonies and premiers you know."

"No? "

"No! There are parties and parties and..." Connor looks serious. "I won't always be pulling in the big bucks for the studios, there will be new, handsome, talented young actors to take my place, they're already snapping at my heels and eventually they'll knock me out of the way..."

"You're twenty five!"

"It doesn't last forever, Red, this career is fickle, Hollywood is fickle. There is no loyalty, it comes down to what you're worth, as soon as your stock drops it's someone else's turn..."

"It sounds very cutthroat."

"It's business - actors are a product that the studios can sell. Oh I'm not complaining I've made a lot of money and I'm having a great time but long term, well, I have other ambitions."

"Such as?"

"I've been working on a screenplay, it's a work in progress because time is so limited but eventually I'd like it to be good enough to make into a movie."

"What's it about?"

The waitress interrupts for our order but suddenly I no longer feel hungry. This is ending, he is leaving. It's all over. A day is all that is left and I can't tell him how I feel. I can't beg him to stay. I can't tell him that he has changed my life so completely, that he was the golden light that took the darkness away. I want to tell him that this has been more than just fireworks, that it has been something so special and so unique that nothing could ever compare. I want to hear him say the words to me that I long to say to him but they can't be uttered because this may all just be an illusion and very soon he'll meet someone else and I will be confined to history with all the others.

We talk and talk, pausing only to take bites of food. Connor has so much drive and ambition, so much talent that it's no wonder he lights the world. His face is bright and animated as he talks about his plans for the future, about investing in young Irish talent and putting the country on the map as "more than U2, Guinness and the long standing feuds. Some Americans still believe there are leprechauns!"

"You mean there aren't?"

Connor pulls a face and I giggle. "What about you Red, where are you going to be? Where will I find you?"

"I don't know." Inexplicably the question makes me feel sad. "Drawing somewhere colourful, with lots to inspire." I smile gently. "I am drawn to the sea and somewhere I can see the stars for a change."

"There is always LA, lots of stars!" Connor laughs and looks intently at me. "I mean it, there is always LA."

"LA? I'm not sure it's the place for someone like me! Maybe I'll travel the world…"

"Well in that case just make sure you stop by to say hi on your travels." Connor's eyes glisten in the light and I reach for his face.

***

The imposing doormen stand aside when Connor flashes a black patent card at them.

"Good evening Sir, Madam." One of them says opening the black doors for us.

"Good evening," Connor replies.

"You have a card?" I whisper loudly.

"Red, I'm twenty-five and rich! Of course I have a card!" He grins. "Come on, let's go have us some fun!"

The club is lit by soft wall lights and lamps on each of the circular tables. Each table has a high backed semi-circular bench facing the stage. The benches are upholstered in rose pink suede that matches the colour scheme on the walls. It's a rich looking décor with polished floors a hardwood bar and the most glamorous waiting staff I've ever seen. In my line of work I've been to parties with models and celebrities but none of them have the sexy self-possession of the staff here. They know they are beautiful and they know the effect they have on the clientele here. The boys have hard, muscular bodies and little shorts that fit closely to their perfect posteriors. The girls have high, round breasts and high round bottoms that scream youthful ripeness covered with tiny scraps of material masquerading as lingerie.

A waitress comes to our table and Connor orders champagne and whiskey. I watch as he smoothly puts a £20 bill in the rim of her panties and she sways off to get our order.

"Do you come to these kinds of places a lot?" I ask bemused.

"I'm a red blooded male Red, it goes with the gender!" Connor laughs.

I look around. So many faces – men and women – all here for the same purpose of gratification. Legal porn. Exquisite and untouchable nameless people to please and arouse. There is a scent of sexual excitement and promise in the air and as I drink my champagne I realise that the intrigue is arousing me.

"It's a Monday night, does no one have jobs?" I ask.

"With the fear of sounding crass if you can afford to come here you have people running companies for you." Connor looks faintly embarrassed.

"Connor?"

"Yes?"

"I'm feeling a little rude."

"Rude?"

"Yes, it's the anticipation and the perfume in the air and you sitting there looking all preppy. It's sexy."

"Really?" Connor nuzzles my neck and sends luscious goose bumps down my spine. "Are you moist?" He winks with a grin.

"Yes," I murmur, "and you doing that is going to make me moister. Then I will need to be very rude."

"I can't wait!" Connor pulls on my ear lobe with his teeth.

The surrounding lights fade to nearly black and the music increases. The spots on the stage light up the shimmering floor and I feel my stomach clench with the thrill. I watch as two stunning girls dance their way out onto the stage. Their movements slow and precise, erotic and so sexy in their sparkling panties and high heels. It's mesmerising and is making me feel horny.

"Connor…"

"Yes."

"It's dark in here."

"Yes."

"I want you to touch me."

I feel his hand slide up my thigh and I part my legs. I watch the girls swirl and sway while Connor strokes my burning centre. It feels delicious, dirty, erotic, horny and everything in between. "Sit on my lap," he breathes into my ear. I rise off the seat and across onto his lap. Connor eases me down onto his erection and I begin to slowly move, his hand moves to my breast the other on my waist. I feel so sexy. The girls are swinging around poles their glorious bodies gliding with ease, glistening in the light. I am dancing with them, the rhythm of my hips matching theirs. I feel indecent and sexually unrestrained. I am in a crowded club. It is beyond provocative and seductive and I am on fire. I am in control and it's an aphrodisiac. The heat rises through me and with it my body trembles until I come and I feel Connor explode inside me.

The lights go up and I excuse myself to the ladies room. A wild woman looks back at me. Beautifully presented in an expensive dress and perfect makeup but underneath the façade is a deviant. Through my veins lava flows. I want to push my boundaries. I don't even know where they end anymore. I thought the spanking was my limit but now I'm in a public place and I have just fucked Connor. Who am I?

TUESDAY

"Hey you," Connor says rising from his seat in the bar at The Stark Hotel to greet me with a kiss. "You got in ok then?"

"Thankfully the doorman recognised me. Is this because they've found out you're here?" I gesture across the foyer to the crowds of press outside.

"Yes, it didn't take long for someone to blow the whistle on my whereabouts. I thought I'd got away with just saying I was in London. Apparently my alter ego wasn't enough!"

I shrug off my jacket and sit down. "Should I be here?"

"They can't come in. Security is making everyone show room keys to enter the hotel."

"But it's madness." The crowds of press and teenage girls outside the hotel are being held back by flimsy barriers. The girls, screaming Connor's name, makes me think of the days I followed Take That around the country, standing outside their front doors in hope they'd appear. Battling through the mass of people was claustrophobic and frightening. "Is this what life is like for you?"

"Sometimes. It's worse outside of LA because there, famous people are ten-a-penny so the public become quite blasé, not the tourists, they are still crazy, just the LALA Landers. Do you want a drink?"

"Can they see us here?"

"Are you worried about being caught?" Something flashes across his face.

"It would give me a lot of explaining to do!" I laugh. "So what are we doing tonight?"

"We are having dinner with Aoife, is that ok? She wants to meet you, meet the gorgeous woman I've told her about but be warned she has my back so expect a grilling." I pale. "We watch out for each other, she'll mean no harm from it, just wants to make sure you're everything I told her you were."

"Shit, how to scare me before I've even had a drink! Should I ring the girls, have someone on my side?"

"I'm on your side!" He grins. "and on your front...She won't be here until eight, we've plenty of time for some sexy fun!"

"Sexy fun?" I ask coquettishly as my insides begin to melt.

"Oh yes," he says, "lots of sexy fun."

***

Aiofe is quite simply beautiful with creamy skin, raven hair and eyes shaped like Connor's but a deep shade of green. She moves like water, fluid and shimmery and I watch as male eyes follow her lustfully across the bar. The women cannot mask their envy, looking at her through narrowed eyes but she appears not to notice any of it.

"Freya, this is my sister Aoife." Connor says taking her by the hand.

"Hi Aoife." I say smiling. She gives me a big grin and leans in to give me a kiss on the cheek.

"I've heard a lot about you Freya." She says. "It's good to meet you. I'm sorry there was a misunderstanding the other night."

I blush. "It was all my misunderstanding!"

Aoife says, "Connor tells me you're going to Mexico. Lucky you! I went once for a day, when I was staying in LA with him. Mam went nuts and I got packed off back to Ireland." She pulls a face. "I think she thinks I'm going to be the bad apple, so I wind her up...a lot!"

"Connor says you want to be a doctor?"

"Yeah, I have a place at Cambridge and Trinity but I really want to go to UCLA and stay with Connor for a while but the fees are too high..."

"I told you that I would sort that for you…" Connor interrupts.

"The fees are too high…" Aoife ignores his comment. "… and Mam would have a fit if I lived with Connor. She trusts me less than she trusts him and that isn't saying a lot!"

"Why?"

"She's never forgotten that I got drunk on cider at Mara Lloyds sixteenth birthday, which was three years ago! She thinks I could have been compromised as she put it, which is not how a good catholic girl should behave! I told her everyone was drinking cider, which just made it worse so now I have to ask to be able to breathe! I blame Connor. He was going through his 'phase' at the same time so of course being at home I took the brunt of her wrath! As a result she is being funny about me moving away and since there was something in the news about drunken behaviour at Cambridge suddenly my passport has gone missing!" Aiofe giggles, a tinkly, tuneful laugh and I smile at her.

"My parents were quite strict with me too. I am an only child and I think they tried a lot to have another one, so I became their whole focus and occasionally it was suffocating. But actually, now, looking back, I can see what they were trying to do, just keep me on the right path so that I would make something of my opportunities."

"Which you have!" Connor interjects.

"Yeah I've done ok but I had to go away to uni to find myself. So I know how you feel Aoife, my parents wanted me to study in London and live at home. So I did the total opposite. Cambridge…wow that's an amazing achievement to be given a place there."

"It is but it still rains in England and I want to follow the sun. And keep my eye on Connor's shenanigans!"

"I am shenanigan free!" Connor laughs.

"For now but you know what you're like! It won't be long before another pretty… " Aiofe stops abruptly her face paling. "Oh shite sorry! Me and my big mouth."

I want to tell her that its ok, the comment was a throwaway one but it's not. How can it be? Connor will go back to the life he knew before me and I've read all there is to know about that. I smile tightly. "Don't worry Aoife."

I can feel Connor's eyes boring into the side of my face but I can't look at him for fear he'll see the desolation in my eyes. They sting with unshed tears. "So, what are we going to eat?" I ask. "I was going to suggest a place in Camden but I'm not sure we'll get out of here alive!" Even to me my voice sounds high and false. Out of the corner of my eye I see Connor begin to reach for my hand until Aoife calls over the waiter for some drinks.

"Connor says you're a clothes designer?" Aoife turns her attention back to me.

"Not at the moment but that's the plan after Mexico."

"Really?"

"Yes, finally!"

"You were married Connor said."

I nod. "Eight years."

"So is Connor just rebound then?" She pops a handful of nuts in her mouth and daps the corners of her red lips with a napkin.

"Aoife!" Connor says outraged.

"It's ok Connor. No, he's not a rebound." To an outsider it must be how things look, something I'd not considered before. Connor happened so fast after Will that my feet barely touched the ground of single life before I was swept up in this secret world.

"So what is he then?" She asks sharply, "because it seems to me that it's not going anywhere. Are you going to sell him out too?"

"That's enough Aoife," Connor says not disguising his fury.

"No Aoife I'm not." I reply firmly. "Perhaps it's not going anywhere but that isn't for you to comment on, that is for Connor and I to decide."

"How can it, he's going back to LA..."

"The future isn't set in stone Aoife." Connor says to her, his face hard.

"So you'd give up your dreams to move here would you?" Aoife asks reaching for more nuts. "I'm starving."

Connor hesitates before replying. "No one can predict the future Aoife."

"Look I don't want to be a downer on this love affair you two have going on but does Freya realise what being with you entails? I suppose she must, to have gotten involved with you in the first place..."

"I didn't know who he was..." I say softly.

"That's not possible everyone knows who he is..." Aoife interrupts.

"Admittedly I'm in the minority but..." I sigh. "Look Aoife, I understand why you are giving me this grilling of course you want to look out for your brother but I have no intention of selling him out to anyone. You're just going to have to trust me on that."

"Trust you? I don't know you."

"No, you don't know me but if you carry on like this you won't get the chance. It may be easier if I go if this is how the evening is going to continue. That decision rests with you Aoife. We have a nice evening where you get to know me and realise I'm not like the rest or I leave..."

"Freya you're not leaving..." Connor interjects, his eyes flashing angrily, the flush on his cheeks deepening. "That's enough now Aoife."

"Aoife?" I probe.

"Stay." She says. "I'm sorry Freya but having met some of the brain dead fuck wits that Connor has been with makes me question everyone. Connor said you were different, I suppose I just had to know for myself." She hangs her head. "Sorry."

I reach across to squeeze her hand. "It's ok Aoife, no harm done!" I grin. "Can we decide on food before I waste away?"

An eruption of loud, chattering, raucous voices cuts through the relative quiet of the lounge bar. Heels clatter on the marble foyer floor as a group of about fifteen designer-clad twenty somethings cross the reception and come into the lounge.

"Oh fuck." Connor mutters. I give him a quizzical look which he ignores and reaches, instead, for the whiskey that the waiter has just placed before him and slides down into his seat.

Aoife looks round at the crowd. "Is that Paris?" She asks.

"Yeah." Connor grunts.

"I thought she was in rehab."

"Obviously not."

My heart beats out an uncomfortable rhythm. Connor's face has closed up and I get the feeling that this evening won't turn out as I'd hoped. Aoife is whispering something to Connor who grips his glass that little bit tighter but I can't hear what is said. I watch the crowd moving as one, slowly towards us, their laughter clearly buoyed by excess alcohol. I recognise a few of the women, models I've seen on shoots and on runways, all endless legs and long hair.

"Connor." The one they called Paris shrieks, "Connor you gorgeous bad boy where the fuck have you been recently? Why've you not returned my calls? How the fuck are you? You look divine as always. Have you missed me?" Her cut glass tones are shrill as she sashays towards us. Connor's face whitens and I can't help thinking that this is someone I just don't want to know.

I try to catch Connor's eye but he doesn't look at me, instead looking at a point across the room. It's obvious something happened between them, recently I'd guess and perhaps may have continued had I not come along. She looks like Connor's type, stunning, cool but her attempt at joviality is falling flat. Her companions form a semi-circle all giving greetings to Connor, the men amongst them moving chairs and tables until we are a cramped mass of bodies. They all talk loudly over each other but it's Paris that I can't take my eyes from. She folds her slim body onto the arm of Connor's chair unaware of the tense, rigid body language emanating from him.

Aiofe is speaking animatedly to a dark skinned man, his wild afro dyed a deep purple. He looks familiar but I don't know if he is a model, actor or singer, my lack of celebrity knowledge has never been more pronounced. Someone calls over the waiter and almost immediately the table is littered with glasses of whiskey, bottles of champagne and shot glasses filled with luminous liquid. Paris is slowly easing herself closer to Connor, rather like a cat looking for a lap upon which to lie. She whispers in his ear and casually runs a scarlet painted nail along his jaw line. Connor makes no move to shrug her off nor any move to reciprocate her flirtation. I hope his actions and ignoring of me is to keep our…whatever…anonymous but I am increasingly more uncomfortable and as I brood so Paris slinks her way onto Connor's lap, wrapping herself around him like a ribbon on an present. She is literally presenting herself to him on a silver platter, her intentions in every coquettish giggle and seductive touch.

I want to hit her.

Instead I accept a glass of champagne handed to me by the blond male to my right. He introduces himself as Ethan, a musician from Manchester in London to record his new album with his band. We engage in light conversation and he is charming and sweet. "Most people think if you're in a band from Manchester you're either a Gallagher wannabe or the next boy band." He says. "We're neither."

"So what kind of music do you do?" I ask.

"It's a kind of mix between rock and pop. Generic I suppose but we write our own songs and play our own instruments. It would be nice to be as cool as Oasis but we seem to be the kind of band that everyone likes."

"That's a good thing though?"

"It's not very sexy!"

I laugh. "Being in a band that has a record deal is sexy."

"Yeah?"

"Of course." I grin. "You may not be the next Oasis but you are the first you! Let others want to be you!"

"I didn't think of it that way!"

We continue to talk. All the while I am conscious of Connor who is glowering as Paris drapes herself even further across him. I don't know what to do. Leave? Stay? There is no clear outcome to either option and so I sit, making small talk with Ethan and his band mate Dex.

Suddenly Paris squeals. Connor sloshes his drink and swears loudly blotting his leg with napkins. "Oh. My. God! Cassius is in town. He's throwing a party at Carmichaels. We so have to go." The buzz begins again, excited gabbling as the women begin to repaint their faces and more champagne is ordered. I watch Paris, trying to keep my face from betraying my real feelings.

"Who is she?" I ask Ethan nodding towards Paris. "She looks familiar."

"Paris Tiffany-Jones, socialite and all round crazy kid." Ethan looks across at her. "She and Connor have an 'in London' thing, I think she is really holding out for an all the time thing but Connor won't commit. I can't blame him really, she is totally nuts and he had a hard time giving up the drugs so she would be the worst person for him…but then I expect you know all that anyway."

"I do?"

"Aren't you his new PA?" Ethan looks surprised.

"PA? Something like that." I feel cold and my hands are shaking around my glass. I am painfully sober but Connor seems to be heading further and further down a bottle of whiskey as Paris writhes on his lap doing all she can to claim his attention. Aoife has moved on to another of Paris' lapdogs and her pale skin is flushed with the alcohol as she flirts outrageously with a very sexy blond man. It's no wonder her mother wants to keep her on a short lead. The noise swarms around me, chaotic and muddled, raucous voices filled with excitement. Cassius must be a big deal but for me the high hopes I had for this evening have been extinguished like a neglected flame. Connor isn't even looking at me, his eyes resolutely on the bottle of whiskey in front of him. Paris is whispering sweet nothings in his ear and I feel such an acute sense of loneliness that it makes my head hurt.

I want to stand up, push Paris from Connor's lap and take him by the hand to lead him away from this false pretension and back to our final hours of togetherness. Time is ticking, loudly, shrilly in my ear and I long to fist my hands against my ears to drown it out. For all my bravado at leaving for a new life, a life without Connor is a wilderness.

Yet I am seeing his life clearly.

This is his life.

I can't sit here any longer, looking at Connor, not looking at Connor. I can't make any more small talk, smile any more fake smiles, nor drink any more champagne that is curdling in my stomach. I need air. I need to leave.

"Ethan it was good to meet you." I say reaching behind me for my jacket. "Good luck with the album."

"Thanks Freya! I don't envy you picking up Connor's pieces in the morning." He says nodding towards Connor who, gloweringly, pours more whiskey into his glass. "I guess you PA's are used to it aren't you."

"I guess we are." I smile through the bitterness. "Enjoy the rest of the evening."

No one notices that I stand and leave. I cross the foyer dejectedly but my path is blocked by the Concierge.

"Madam, allow us to call you a car, the crowd out there is getting impatient and for your safety I'd rather we got you where you need to go. Mr Robertson and his friends' whereabouts is all over social media."

"Thank you." I reply walking with him to the desk.

While he calls me a car I browse my phone. Twitter is alive with Connor, Paris and the others and all over the social sphere arrangements between friends and cyber friends to track them down are made. Hash tag Connor. The chants from outside, unheard from the midst of the group I've just been sat with, are like the call of the wild, the press desperate for that mega buck photo, the teenagers desperate for one glance of their idols.

The car is quickly parked out the front of the hotel and desperately tired I sink into the seat letting it take me home.

***

It's just after midnight when a drunk and scowling Connor knocks on the door. I knew he'd come.

"Baby," he slurs, "I'm so sorry it all got fucking fucked up."

"It's ok." I reply. "You didn't know this was going to happen." He sways against the door and I pull out a chair for him. "Sit down I'll get you coffee."

"It was so boring," he says stumbling into the chair and sitting with a thud. "Ow." Connor massages the elbow that he has banged on the table. "Paris was worse than a fly around shit and everyone else just…" He looks up at me, his usual blue/green eyes red rimmed and blurry. "It was bullshit. Paris wouldn't leave me alone, Cassius was being a dick…he is always a dick but was worse tonight. Why do I even know these people?"

"Did anything happen?" I ask closing my eyes waiting for an answer.

"Nah. Paris eventually went off with a racing car driver who was so stoned….shit like this, I don't want it anymore."

The kettle boils loudly and I begin making a coffee. Connor is silent, his breathing shallow, the alcohol fumes permeating the air. Although he looks crumpled and inebriated his face has taken on a look so raw and young that my heart skips a beat. I place the coffee down in front of me and he reaches for my hand, gripping it tightly. "It has all become bullshit since I met you."

"Oh?" I say as nonchalantly as I can manage. Connor doesn't seem to notice the higher pitched tone of my voice. I watch him close his eyes, his hand hot against mine.

"Yeah, it's all different now."

"Different how?"

"Red?"

"Yes?"

"Can I stay?"

"Of course."

"I'm tired and drunk. Are you drunk? I'm drunk."

"I'm not drunk."

"Can we go to bed?" I pull him up and leading him by the hand I take him to bed.

WEDNESDAY

I'm already up and drawing in the kitchen when Connor stumbles through squinting against the light.

"Good morning!" I grin. "How's the head?"

"I feel awful," he pulls a face. "All I can taste is whiskey and I bet I smell of it too?"

"You smell more bar dweller than movie god at the moment," I admit to him, "but you look quite cute so I'll let you off just this once."

Connor groans. "It was just so pretentious and boring that I drank to take the pain of it all away. All I could wonder was if you were ok and if you realised that I was ignoring you to keep you out of the firing line. Paris has been used to…uh…my attention and she has a bitchy side. You probably don't want to know that…I suppose I just want to explain. Until I met you Paris was a sure thing in London but since you, well, there's only been you. She doesn't like losing anything to anyone even if that thing isn't hers to lose. Paris is spoilt and used to her own way. Had I made any attempt to introduce you then 'somehow' the press would have found out and endless made up crap would have appeared in the papers. I just wanted to protect you from all the artificial shit that is in my life."

"Yes I did realise." I stand and walk to him wrapping my arms around him. "It can't be all artificial shit though Connor, there must be so much to enjoy about your life."

He sighs and holds me tight. "Not as much as I once thought. I've paid a high price for what I have achieved. It's only when I go home and now, with you, that I can breathe. I don't think it's just your life that will change after this. I think you've changed my life too."

"I have?" I whisper against his chest, nestling into the tight muscles and closing my eyes.

"Yeah," he whispers back. "Things won't be the same again."

"So where do we go from here?" I ask pulling back to look up at him. Sadness flits across his face and my heart sinks.

"At the moment…I'm not sure there is anywhere to go."

Hopelessness hangs heavy in the air.

***

I walk into Barneys. Imogen and Erin are already seated at the side of the restaurant and I feel a pang of guilt that I would rather be with Connor than here with them. He is at a final business meeting but I can feel his fingers on my skin and the scent of him light on my flesh. Connor was not impaired by his hangover and after the conversations in the kitchen came a lovemaking so raw and primal, a bonding of two lost souls in the most heavenly of ways.

I sit at the table with mounting nerves – today I am telling them my plans and I can already hear their response. There hasn't been a week since we met at university that we've not seen each other, through good and bad boyfriends, graduation, jobs and my marriage, endless phone conversations and even longer wine fuelled girlie gossips after work. We've been through so much and here we are still loyal and still fiercely protective. I think fleetingly of Lexi. The hole that she left behind has been filled but it doesn't stop me wondering if she's happy, if Will is giving her all that she needs. For all her status and wealthy upbringing inside is someone who lacks confidence and faith in herself. Lexi was never centre of her parent's worlds, has never known the overwhelming love that I grew up with. My parents have never had money, always scrimped and saved for everything yet for all that I never felt that I missed out on anything. Holidays were in caravans and tents in Devon and Cornwall but we had it all. I fear Lexi will always be looking for that unconditional love and with William it all has conditions.

"You look all sparkly Freya." Imogen says. Erin looks at me through narrowed eyes.

"Do I?" I ask reaching for my menu.

"Yes. There is something going on. You're never in, never around…spill."

"Imogen I've told you before!"

"Yes but I think you're lying." Erin pipes up. "No one who has been dumped looks as good as you."

"I thought I wasn't allowed to dwell?"

"You are also not allowed to keep secrets."

"Secrets?"

"Spill."

I take a deep breath. "I'm leaving London."

"What?" Erin screeches. "That's not a secret, that's just shit."

"Leaving London?" Imogen repeats shocked. "Leaving London for where? And when?"

"I'm thinking of Cornwall when I get back from Mexico…"

"Cornwall?" Erin shrieks in the same way as if I'd said Mars.

"Yes, somewhere quiet and quaint and peaceful for six months or so, to design and make and just see if I can make the cut so to speak. If it doesn't work out then I'll come back and find another magazine job. I have to try. Before it's too late to do what I should have done right at the start."

"But London is your home."

"I know. I just need some space from it, be away from the craziness and the constant worry I'm going to bump into Lexi. What would I say to her? It would be awful. I avoid everywhere now, never going to the places she and I used to just in case. I know I'm being a coward but it's just easier. If I go to Cornwall there is no one there to tell me I can't do it."

"But there'll be no one there to tell you that you can either. What about us?" Imogen asks.

"There's skype, email, phone…cyber cocktails." I reply with a small smile. "I know it's not the same but eventually it will seem normal. I have to move on now. Be Freya. Just me and know that it's good enough."

"It's always been good enough." Erin says to me, reaching for my hand. "To us it has."

"My friends," I say with tears prickling behind my eyes, "it would have been unbearable without you." We sit holding hands, unsaid words hanging in the air. "So," I say attempting to lighten the mood. "What are we drinking?"

"Nothing for me I have a raging hangover." Erin replies.

"Why?"

"I had a works thing last night. I drank far too many cocktails and ended up sleeping with Chris Parks…" Erin looks immensely proud of herself.

"Chris Parks? As in the reality star? What show is he in? Bristol Boys Go Large or something?" Imogen asks her mouth hanging in a perfect O.

"Yep."

"God, it puts my bonus and my date with Sidney to shame. Freya moving and Erin being a ho-bag. Oh well, I guess lunch in on me for having nothing to say!" Imogen announces. We voice our objections but she quietens us with a wave of her hand. "I insist. My bonus was unexpected and massive so I want to spend it here today before we end up drinking over the internet. So yes, cocktails, lots and lots and lots."

"Imogen! I like this reckless you! It goes with the hair!" I giggle.

Subconsciously she reaches for her blonde locks. "Do you hate my hair?"

"No! I was just teasing."

"So does anyone want to know about my night of passion with Chris Parks." Erin asks grumpily. "It's not every day a girl goes to bed with a sort of star."

"He wasn't a star! He's in a crap reality show that no one watches!" Imogen laughs.

"He's more of a star than Sidney the post boy." Erin retorts reaching for breadstick.

"He's not a post boy, he's a partner. Anyway, I don't know why you're being grumpy with me Erin, you're forever teasing me."

"I'm beginning to wish I'd stayed home! You two are worse than sisters." I grin.

It's comfortable banter. These girls have stayed by my side through thick and thin from frightened teens away from home for the first time, to walking behind me on my wedding day. They have always been here, unconditionally, never questioning, always supporting. I listen intently as Erin gives me a detailed account on her one night with Chris Parks. Her face lights up, as she describes his attentive loving.

"Of course he didn't phone." She says. "I knew he wouldn't but I did hope just a little and I did sort of imagine what I'd wear to the soap awards if he asked me to go!"

We laugh. "A pink tutu with feathers in your hair?" Imogen giggles.

"Nope, hot pants and nipple tassels!"

"Classy!" I say grinning.

"Are you really going to leave all this?" Erin asks. "Leave behind long boozy lunches and the chaos of London? Really?"

"Yes really. I need some quiet. I can't move on here with everything so familiar. I don't want to run the risk of bumping into Will and Lexi because even though I don't want him back and I want to be free of him now, divorce, house sale all that kind of thing, I don't want my face to be rubbed into what they have done. If anything, she did me a favour. I didn't realise how stifled I was by trying to be another person, I like being me. The past few weeks have opened my eyes to what I have to offer the world and I am going for it. I will come back though." I look between them. "I'm not going forever."

"But Cornwall? You'll end up meeting a fisherman and designing wet weather gear."

"Hardly!"

"But Freya…" Erin wails and then stops abruptly her mouth wide open mid word. I turn around to see Connor stood behind me, smart black trousers and a burgundy open necked shirt. His hair is styled to look like he's just gotten out of bed and the shirt accentuates the blue/green of his eyes and the thick chestnut lashes. Inadvertently I lick my lips and he gives me a faint wink.

"Hello ladies." Imogen and Erin are staring at him, mouths open, like stunned goldfish. He gives them his full megawatt smile and they visibly melt. "I thought I recognised you from Cullen's the other night. It was you wasn't it?"

"Yes" squeaks Imogen. Erin is looking like she may faint.

Connor says. "Are you here for lunch?"

"Yes." Erin says dribbling just a little. "We're celebrating and commiserating."

"Celebrating?"

"Imogen has received a promotion." I say calmly suppressing a grin. Erin is incapable of speech merely staring at Connor like he's a god from the heavens.

"Congratulations Imogen." He says smiling at her. I watch as she looks for something to say but instead she nods like an imbecile.

"And the commiserations?" he asks.

Erin recovers her composer just long enough to reply. "Freya," she nods in my direction, "has just announced she's moving to Cornwall."

"Two very good reasons for a nice lunch." Connor says narrowing his eyes at me. He stops a waiter, "champagne for the ladies please. Charge to my account."

"Yes sir," the waiter replies and scurries off.

"Would you like to join us?" Imogen asks breathlessly but looking ever hopeful. She turns slightly purple as she holds her breath in anticipation. I can see the speech bubbles above her head '*please say yes, please say yes…*' and I stifle a grin. I wonder how I should act. My friends would know Connor is an actor who I am unfamiliar with but I know what they both think about him and it's all a little weird.

"Yes thank you, I'd be very pleased to." He sits down between Imogen and me, his back to the room.

It's surreal. Connor makes polite conversation with Imogen and Erin, questioning them on their lives. They are animated, flushed and preening like peahens looking for a mate. It's funny and sweet and I have a slight pang of guilt that I've kept such a mammoth secret from them. The waiter comes over with menus that we accept with thanks and as I am on the outside of the conversation I peruse it. Connor excuses himself to make a phone call and with a subtle stroke of my hand he leaves the table.

"Oh. My. God." Imogen finally breathes. "I think I've died and gone to heaven."

"To think I thought Chris Parks was a star when there are people like him. He's even better looking than I'd imagined. The things I could do to him…"

"He's just a person!" I say laughing but I know he's more than that to me.

"Just a person? Freya, are you out of your mind? It's Connor Robertson! The sexiest man alive!" Imogen gasps.

"I thought Sidney was the sexiest?"

"He's the sexiest real person, Connor Robertson well…" She stops. "Do you think he'll come back or was he making an excuse?"

"I expect he'll come back!" I reply. "Now what are you going to have?"

"What? Freya seriously..."

"I'm going to the loo. If the waiter comes back I'll have the burger with fries and salad." I put my menu down on the table and stand up. Erin and Imogen begin gabbling to each other – Connor this and Connor that. I shake my head as I look between them, an affectionate grin on my face. "Imogen you may want to wipe up the drool, it's not a good look."

"Piss off Freya!" She says with humour. I cross the restaurant and walk out into the quiet foyer.

Washing my hands in the sink I give myself a critical look. There is a difference. Subtle but it's there. It's hope, I think. I am hopeful. My dreams are in reaching distance, touchable, so nearly able to reach the stars that for so long have been out of my grasp and that for now me being me is enough for Connor. Perhaps not forever, Cornwall and LA are so far apart, his world is a fairy tale in comparison to mine but he took risks to get where he has and despite his youth it's a lesson he's taught me. I twist my hair out of my eyes. Just a few hours remain then life moves on without Connor in it. How will that compare to the excitement and uncertainty? I screw up my face tightly as the grief threatens to overwhelm me. I'm trying so hard. So hard to pretend that everything is fine but it's not. It's not fine. I am not fine with Connor leaving. My feelings for him are so strong that they consume me and I lean to grip the sink. The porcelain is cold, hard against my hands that turn white the longer I grip.

Despite my eyes being closed so tightly I can see spots, droplets of water still pool in the corners, slowly sliding down my cheeks.

"Red?" Connor's voice is behind me, soft and gentle.

"Yes?" I say, my voice breaking.

"Don't cry." He walks up behind me, wrapping his arms around my waist and leaning his head on my shoulder. The scent of his skin mixes with the lavender and bleach smell of the ladies room. I rest my head against his.

"Sorry."

"Sorry?" He asks quietly. "Sorry for what?"

"For this."

Slowly Connor releases my hands from the sink, rubbing them carefully until the flesh returns to its normal colour. He links his fingers with mine and I open my stinging eyes, meeting his in the mirror. "Sorry for being so wet."

"What is this about? Me?" He asks.

I nod sadly. "Everything is changing again isn't it? Life is changing. Sometimes it just evolves and the path you take just happens and it's only when you look back that you see where the change came. This is different. I can see it before its happened, and I want to dig in my heels and stop time. Just for a bit longer. I saw your life yesterday, what you will be going back to, beautiful people…women…and I just want to stop it, press pause, for a moment longer."

Connor kisses my cheek and whispers against my skin. "I will come back for you. I will find you. Cornwall or wherever you may be. My life has changed too I told you that, I don't want the life I had before."

He holds me tightly to him. So tight I can barely breathe but I clasp my hands around his shoulders and rest my head against his chest.

"Red?" He whispers.

"Yes,"

"You need to get back to your friends." He says wrapping his arms around me.

"In a minute." I reply. He kisses me on the cheek and leaves the room. I sit down on the chair opposite the vanity mirror and cry.

Connor is at the table when I return. He gives me a brief but warm smile as I re-join the party.

"Are you alright Freya?" Imogen asks, "you look upset and flushed."

"Menopause." I reply sitting down. "I'm fine. Did you order?"

"Yes, except…sorry Connor we didn't know to order for you." Erin looks embarrested.

"I'm not staying I have something to prepare for this afternoon but it has been a pleasure to meet you again."

"Can you not even stay just for one drink?"

"Yes of course, I can." He replies casually running his hand subtly up my thigh.

I jump and spill my drink. "Shit." I grumble.

"What's the matter Freya?" Erin asks.

"Nothing, I've just spilt." I tell her dabbing my leg with my napkin.

"I will be licking Cristal off you later." He whispers.

I turn to look at him. He has a glint in his eyes and gives me the briefest smile.

"What are you two whispering about?" Imogen asks inquisitively.

"Freya has just asked if I was in Westlife. Why does everyone think anyone from Ireland is in Westlife?" He laughs.

"I did not! I know full well that you're not in Westlife…" I say outraged.

"Westlife? Westlife broke up ages ago. Seriously Freya…you need to get out of the eighties and into the now!" Imogen looks astounded.

"I am going to make you pay for this you shit." I hiss through a smile.

"I look forward to it."

"Yes, Imogen, I do need to get out of the eighties, you are right and as I am well aware that Mr Robertson is an actor I will endeavour to watch every film that he has been in and write a detailed critique of each one. In fact, I will put it in next month's magazine…How is that?"

"Do you even have a DVD player?" She asks laughing.

"No, William took it. But I didn't know how to use it so it's not big problem. I will buy a new one."

"I am honoured." Connor laughs.

"Please don't be." I snap.

***

We sit in the park, the afternoon sun warm on our faces sipping iced cappuccinos and sharing a packet of minstrels.

"I bet no one eats chocolate in LA." I say cracking the delicious chocolate shell between my back teeth. "Can you imagine anything worse?""No one eats! Unless it's liquidised green shit." Connor says popping a handful into his mouth.

"That's no life! I like food. Proper chewable food." As if to prove my point I lean my head back and drop in three chocolates. "That's why I'll never be thin."

"I wouldn't like you thin. You are gorgeous the way you are, all curves and big boobs!" Connor flicks my hair over my shoulder. "Real boobs! In LA a person could forget what real boobs feel like."

I pull my top out and look down at my breasts. "They are very definitely real and sadly not as perky as they were in my twenties."

"I'd like your boobs if they were tucked into your sock." Connor says leaning over to have a look. "In fact I like all of you." He kisses my neck and I lean against him. "I thought leaving would be easier." He says wrapping his arm around me. "I thought it would be one night and that would be it and yet here we are, two weeks later, and I don't know what to do next. I feel sad Red. Really sad."

I lean my head back and look up at him. His blue/green eyes shine as he gazes down at me. The sunlight on his face turns his stubble an auburn colour and I reach up to caress my hand across the fuzz. He leans into my hand and closes his eyes. "I had planned a full on pervy ending to all this." He whispers, "but I don't want that now."

If there was ever a moment for time to stop, for the world to sit still on its axis now is it. A lump forms painfully in my throat and I swallow hard to try and shift it. Connor pulls me tightly into his arms and there, in the middle of Hyde Park he kisses me like we're the only people in the world.

"Get a room!" Someone yells.

I feel Connor gesture in the general direction never moving his lips from mine. I could kiss him forever, feel the stubble grazing my face, his hands warm on my back. From under my closed eyes hot tears begin a slow trickle down my cheeks, mingling with the kiss. Connor starts briefly but just pulls me tighter to him and I wrap my hands in his hair.

Eventually we pull away and I nestle into his chest watching the toy boats being raced across the lake, children's squeals of delight being carried across on the soft summer breeze.

"I will see you again." He whispers. "I promise."

"Don't make promises Connor."

"Why?"

"In case you can't keep them."

"I will keep it."

We finish our drinks and discard the cups and chocolate wrapper in the bin. "What do you want to do for the rest of the day?" Connor asks.

"Just be with you."

Connor takes my hand and we walk a loop of the park. It's like being in an alternative universe, I can see life passing by, kids running, friends sitting under trees with bottles and picnics but I am contained in a bubble, a bubble of something so magical and so unbelievable that it may well have been created in the pages of a book. I steal a glance at Connor, he looks straight ahead deep in thought. I wonder what he is thinking, this God amongst men, he looks pained and instinctively I grip his hand tighter. He doesn't look down on me, lost in his own thoughts and it's bittersweet that he is being pulled apart by this too.

We complete the loop in silence. A silence that is almost peaceful, the sounds of the park filling the gaps. I want forever.

We arrive back at the entrance and pass through the gate to the main road. With our life in our hands we run across Park Lane and into the revolving doors of the hotel. I can hear the clock ticking, time not letting up for even a moment. There are a few hours left, insignificant in the endless infinite passing of time. Two crazy weeks have come to this, a blink of an eye and it will have passed by, remaining a memory as I move through my life. A story for my grandchildren, a story about a handsome man and the briefest love affair. It would make a good book or a film for rom-com lovers everywhere, except it's not funny, it's real and touchable and there isn't a happy ending.

We cross the foyer, Connor's hand wrapped tightly around mine. The heat of our skin touching is burning me and I want to hold so tight that we can never let go. I wonder if Connor feels the same way but I don't dare to hope. The double doors to the conference suite bang open and I stop still with shock as Lexi walks out. There is nowhere to hide as she comes towards me with guilt and despair flashing across her face. I want to be sick. Lexi and I stare at each other, eyes fused, hers are full of fear and sadness and mine filled with hurt and anger. She seems to reach for me before her hand falls to her side. She looks tired, drawn and the light that forever beamed from her has faded. I want to ask her if she is unhappy. I would have before. I've seen her look like this once, when Aaron left her, and I know that she has lost something just as I have lost something. We've lost each other and the heartbreak is deep and desperate.

"Freya," she whispers.

I shake my head. "Don't Lexi, don't say anything." My hand is cold and I realise that Connor is no longer holding it.

"Freya, please…please let's talk. I miss you. I…"

"I don't want to talk to you. There is nothing else to say. You said it all."

"I miss you…"

"Miss me? How can you? You made a choice Lexi, a choice between Will and me. You chose him. What else is there to talk about? Can I forgive you? No, no I can't but not because of Will, because you destroyed our friendship and that is the worst feeling of all…although," I pause, "you actually did me a favour. It took me a while to see it, but life has changed for the better since Will left. So I suppose I could thank you but…I won't."

"Freya…"

"I hope you're happy Lexi, I hope Will gives you everything you need and the choice you made was the right one for you. As far as talking, no, I don't want to talk to you. Have a nice life Alexa." I turn from her and walk towards the lifts.

"I'm sorry," I hear her whisper. I shake my head and enter the lift.

***

"Can you come to mine this evening?" I ask Connor as he opens the door. "I can't be in this hotel. Seeing Lexi…anyway, do you mind?"

"No of course not. Are you alright?" He asks pulling me into his arms.

"Yeah, I was just a bit shocked and I was probably a lot meaner that I needed to be."

"I think what she did was worse."

"Perhaps but in the long run it was the best thing for me."

"I'll finish packing and get a hotel car up. Don't be wearing a lot!"

"I won't!" I giggle.

***

I buy more flowers from the street vendor on Camden high street. This time reds, purples and pinks, bright happy colours with a summery scent. I walk down my street, thinking that there will not be many more times I can call Camden home. I'll miss the Borough - the buzz and noise and smells and the uniqueness of a village in the middle of the city.

"Will?" Sitting on the wall outside our building is William looking dishevelled and puffy faced.

"Hello Freya." He glances up at me, his eyes looking bleary and uncoordinated.

"Are you drunk?" William is swaying violently where he sits. He reaches out for the lamp post to steady himself, taking two attempts to grasp it.

"Veeer likeeeeely." He singsongs and then laughs without mirth. "Itssss aaaaaall suuuuuuuch shit."

"William." I say. "Let me call you cab."

"I don't want a cab." He hauls himself to his feet. "I just want you."

"Me?" I ask astounded. "Go home Will."

"I am home." He staggers towards me and pulls me into his arms. I try to push him away but he's too strong and his grip tightens.

"William. Let. Me. Go." I seethe. "Get off me and go home."

"It's only ever been you Freya." He's not listening to me and his arms are painfully tight around me. His breath smells of stale liquor and I am suddenly fearful.

"Please get off me." I struggle against his grip. I see a black car screech past our house and continue along the road, red brake lights coming on sharply at the junction that leads onto the high street. *You're going too fast* I think absurdly.

William wrenches my head back and kisses me. It's revolting. His lips are fleshy, unappealing and the stench of his breath turns my stomach. He sucks at my mouth like a guppy, trying to force his tongue in between my teeth. "No." I plead from between clenched teeth. "No Will."

"You know you want me." He breathes forcing his lips back onto mine.

I try to turn my head but he has me in a steely grip. The fear is indescribable. What is he going to do? Attack me further in the front garden? I want to vomit but instead terrified tears spring to my eyes and my body flops. I can't fight him, he's too strong. I keep my mouth clenched shut and stop struggling.

He appears to take my lack of fight as permission to continue so loosens his grip on me. At that moment I manage to free an arm and hit him squarely in the genitals. He doubles up and looks up at me, fury in his eyes and pain on his face. "You bitch." I swing for him, catching him on the side of his mouth and pain ricochets through my hand and up my arm. Will staggers backwards and lands on the ground. I look down at him seeing nothing of the man I married.

My heart is pounding with horror and a revulsion that I never realised I could feel. I wipe my mouth on the sleeve of my coat and hold the flowers to me like a shield of armour. "Go home William before I phone the police." My hands shake violently and I struggle to get my keys out of my bag. "Go home." I scream at him.

He struggles to his feet and gives me a loose armed, uncoordinated wave as he meanders down the road to the high street.

As soon as he is out of sight my legs give way and I crumple to the pavement.

***

I can't stay at the house. My heart doesn't slow from its relentless pounding and my entire body trembles with the fear that William will come back and the situation will get further out of hand. I scrub my face and clean my teeth until my gums bleed then ringing Connor's suite I leave a message and another with the front desk to stop him from coming here. Across the room the photo of Will and I, on the mantelpiece, mocks me and I fling it to the floor watching the pieces of glass shatter into tiny pieces. Then I cry.

***

There are still crowds of girls outside the hotel, scantily clad and screaming hysterically for Connor. The doorman lets me in and I cross the foyer to the bar. Connor isn't there so I take the lift to his floor. I knock on the door but I hear no sounds from inside the room. *Where is he?* I retrace my steps back down and search the hotel, shaking with the fear of bumping into Lexi or, god forbid, Will. Panic begins to creep through my bones when Connor is nowhere to be found. I ask at the Concierge desk but as kind as he has been he won't divulge any information so I walk from the hotel to Cullen's Bar to see if he's there. The bar is filled with socialites and businessmen but not one person resembles Connor. Confused I walk back to the hotel to see Aoife climbing into a car with blacked out windows. I begin to run, calling her name, but it's only after the car pulls away do I realise the crowd of teenage girls are chanting Connor's name as they chase the car down Park Lane.

I run back into the hotel and up to the penthouses. The door to Connor's room is propped open and the housekeeper is inside stripping the beds. "Connor?" I ask, my chest heaving with the exertion of running up the stairs.

"Sir is gone." The maid replies in halting English.

"Gone?"

"Yes." Another maid comes out of the bathroom with an arm full of towels.

"Oh my god." I whisper in disbelief gripping tightly to the doorframe.

Gone.

No goodbyes.

No proper ending to a love affair that has taken over my world. Nothing. Everything I have felt for Connor over this brief time shatters in my chest stabbing and slicing me from the inside out. How could he go, just like that? Do I mean nothing to him? All the whispered words, the touches, the kisses turn to acid deep inside and as it bubbles so the pain comes. Intense pain. Touchable, visible pain. I've never known such excruciating anguish ever. Will leaving didn't even come close to this.

Connor has gone.

Grief and pain eats away at my soul as I take a taxi home. I can't shut off my mind from the endless questions, repeating the same question – why did he go?

***

THURSDAY

Sleep evades me. I lie in bed willing myself to sleep but my eyes won't close and my mind won't quieten down. Over and over I see William coming towards me and Aiofe getting into the car with its procession of girls following with mania down the road. My stomach twists and contorts while my lungs are barely able to grasp any air. I'm having a panic attack, I'm sure of it. My throat constricts, squeezing tightly until I can no longer swallow. William attacked me, Connor has left me and I've never known pain like it.

I throw the bed covers off and get up. The flat feels freezing cold and my fingers are stiff as I wrap my robe around me. I turn on the fire in the lounge, putting on the highest setting but even with the heat beating out I still feel like I've been dipped in a bath of ice water. I make a cup of tea, wrapping my hands around the mug to warm them up and sit down on the sofa, covering myself with a blanket. So this is what heartbreak really feels like. Not the angry, shocked betrayal that William left behind but the cold, desperate grief of the end. The end of something so extraordinary and so magical that it took my breath away.

The middle of the night is another world. Dark, cold and silent except for the occasional shout or car horn. The shadows tell a thousand stories, images thrown onto the walls by the moon that peeps its delicate light out from behind the sinister clouds. I turn the radio on, the over happy female presenter chattering away about who-knows-what while my insides disintegrate and the pieces of my broken heart tear at my insides like serrated glass. This isn't how it was supposed to be. I wanted to tell him…to tell him…oh what does it matter?

I wonder if I am going crazy as I open the laptop and being an obsessive web search. Already the gossip sites and tabloid papers have printed articles on him passing through Heathrow airport, all wondering who the dark haired beauty by his side is. Connor glowers from behind his aviator shades, no hint of smile, with a baseball cap covering the mop of chestnut hair. I run my finger around his lips held tight in a grimace, wishing so much I could kiss the normally full lips just one more time. Tears plop onto the keyboard and run off my hands as I look at website after website, every picture the same, every one telling the same story – Connor has gone.

I thought after William I'd survive anything, whatever life threw at me I'd come through it with a smile on my face. It doesn't matter how often I tell myself that I'm being irrational and ridiculous, overreacting to a relationship that was based on sex and lasted two weeks, I cannot move past the crushing despair. He said I'd changed his life, I wonder now if it was all a lie, that I was just someone for the short term while he was in London, and that anyone would have passed the time until he left on his glory trip.

I stand beside the window looking out at the world, not recognising anything I see. Bathed in the ghoulish half-light I could be anywhere, suffocating slowly under the weight of my misery.

Around 4 am I begin to pace. What is wrong with me? Am I such a bad person that two men up and leave just like that with no backwards glance. William found what he was looking for in the arms of Lexi and Connor, well Connor will no doubt be finding a moment in the arms of a gorgeous blonde model-type. I grip my ears trying to drown out the voices that clamour to be heard over each other. I must be going mad, sending myself on a one way ticket to the lunatic asylum. Until there is a lone voice, ringing clearly, a voice of reason telling me that it's now or never. Now is the time to move on. There is nothing to stay here for.

Grabbing my keys I leave the house for the 24 hour shop on the high street. Camden is still. Cold and still. Nothing like the Camden I know. It's an alternative world, one I don't recognise and no longer feel a part of. I can't see the stars as I hurry along the road, the clouds and their imposing formations block the view. Ordinarily only a few stars can be seen because of the light pollution but I like to know they're there. I like to know we're not alone in the universe, that I'm not alone. There are no real sounds of life from anywhere and in all the time I've lived here I don't recall Camden ever being this quiet which adds to my feelings of isolation.

The late shop is empty. The bored overnight assistant looks up from his magazine of busty babes.

"Hi." I say.

"Alright?" He mutters back.

"I don't suppose you have any spare large cardboard boxes I can take?"

"They'll be flat."

"Flat is ok it will be easier to carry them home." I catch a sight of myself reflected in the shop window. I look like a ghost, colourless and lost.

"Out the back. On the trolley. You're lucky, they get recycled at ten. Don't steal anything, there are cameras…" He turns back to his magazine and I hesitate for a moment before crossing the shop to the store room.

It smells musty, tins of sad looking beans look out at me from under their dust. At the back of the store room is a trolley full of cardboard and I find myself clambering onto a pallet to reach the top. I remove as many as I think I can carry and stop to buy a big roll of tape and numerous newspapers. I thank the cashier gratefully but he just grunts a reply and I stagger home under the weight of the cardboard.

For the next six hours I pack and sort, throwing out paraphernalia from the past that I don't want to take into the future. My life sorted into two categories – take forward and store. I hesitate over the wedding album before leaving it for William to dispose of. I keep my favourite wedding photo and one of us at graduation. The rest I leave to memory.

Every so often a sob grips me and I have to wrap my arms around myself to keep my chest from breaking open, but I keep going until everything is packed. It's only now I give into the tears.

***

"Carrie I am resigning." I walk into Carrie's office. She looks at me with confusion spread across her face.

"Excuse me?"

"I am resigning."

"You are not!" Carrie reaches for her e-cigarette and draws on it deeply. "You can't!" Getting up from her seat she pours two whiskeys from the crystal decanters at the back of her office.

"I need to Carrie, I need to move on. I have to and if I don't do it now I probably won't and I owe it to myself."

"Move on where?"

"I am going to start designing. I have to try Carrie. Before it's too late and all I'm left with are more regrets"

"Regrets? What do you have to regret?" Carrie reaches for my hand.

"I wouldn't know how to begin telling you." I sigh. "I just don't want this life anymore Carrie. I want fresh air and no clock watching. I just want to be free for a while. Let all the dust around me settle until I can see clearly again."

"You're talking in riddles." Carrie puts the e-cigarette down. "I don't want you to leave. We will work out an alternative solution. You have worked too hard to turn your back on all this Freya."

"I need you to let me go Carrie. I need you to let me off my notice."

"You aren't serious?" She splutters.

"Very. Please." I beseech her. "Please Carrie. You said to me a few days ago I should reach for my dreams, well that is what I am going to do."

Carrie picks the device up again, twisting it through her fingers, before inhaling deeply as she looks darkly at me. "You know Freya, this is all really fucking bad news. I am not happy and you will end up sending me back on the cigarettes." She pauses glaring at me. "Alright, you can go and run away or whatever it is you are doing but you remain an employee, you can take a sabbatical, unpaid, while you sort yourself out. I want an article once a month about your life and your designs and everything that's going on. A blog almost. I want photos and comments and musings and interesting details about your life. If you agree I will pay you submission fees and give you twelve months. If it doesn't work you can have your job back. Do we have a deal?"

"Yes," I smile. "We have a deal."

"Good. Now fuck off out of my office before I change my mind or cry…"

"Carrie…"

"Go!"

I leave the room closing the door behind me.

***

"What's the matter Freya?" Imogen asks over brunch. "You look exhausted."

I want to tell her, needing to confide to someone and Imogen with her sweet, non-judgemental nature would be the right person to tell, except the words won't come. They are stuck in my throat alongside the ever increasing lump that has been strangling me since Connor went away. "I'm worried about you," she says, "you look so pale."

"I'm fine Imogen, I just didn't sleep very well. I was awake all night packing up the house. So whatever happens now at least I'm easy to ship somewhere!"

"Hmm." She says looking at me through narrowed eyes. "There's more to it than that. Is it Will?"

"No. That part is long over." It's true. I feel nothing for that part of my life, bar a sadness that my marriage didn't work and a sadness that my best friend let me down so badly.

"Then what is it?"

I feel the bubble of anguish increase in my tummy forcing its way through my pipes until it erupts from my mouth. With it comes a flood of tears, hot acidic tears of grief and despair. My eyes burn as they cascade down my face, leaving trails of lava on my cheeks.

"Freya?" Imogen jumps up from her seat and is immediately by my side, pulling me into her for an embrace that I collapse against. "Freya, what is it?"

I shake my head. "Don't ask." I stammer. "Please don't ask."

"Is it a man?" She asks ignoring my plea.

Not *A* man, *THE* man. The weight of the past two months is heavy on my shoulders so I just sit and cry. I cry until there are no tears left, just an excruciating ache in my belly. No goodbyes. Not even worthy of a goodbye.

"Sorry Immy," I say regretfully as my tears subside. "Sorry for being a lunatic!"

She smiles. "You've always been a lunatic, why change anything now?"

I laugh. "Yeah that's true, but I do also remember plenty of lunatic behaviour of yours…"

"Yeah but we're not talking about me!" She grins, "there is no need to bring up my shameful past!"

"Are we talking shameful pasts?" Erin asks sitting down. "Jesus Freya you look shit! What's the matter?"

"Mini breakdown, nothing more." I say screwing up my face. "I'm in need of my holiday now. I didn't know you were coming, I thought work had you chained to the desk!"

"Did you really think I'd let you get on the plane without witnessing your departure? I still don't believe you're going by yourself. This is not like you!"

"Nothing has been like me recently." I look at my friends and take a deep breath. "I met a man…" I hold my hands up against their barrage of questions. "Please…let me finish. I met a man and for a short while it was the most intense love affair. I know I didn't tell you and for that I am sorry but I didn't know what to say. My life has been such an open book and it was so wonderful that after a while I didn't want to tell anyone. I needed a secret to hold onto when life was tumbling down around me. I still don't want to talk about it and I won't ever tell but for a time it was the most exciting secret, something that opened my eyes to what my future could be. It was spontaneous and sexy and everything I've never been. I had no inhibitions, no questions about right and wrong and he actually believed in me. For a brief moment it was enough to just be me…"

"I told you that you'd meet someone who didn't need you to be someone else." Imogen exclaims looking delighted. "I'd like to be cross with you for keeping a monumental secret but it just sounds dreamy!"

"It was dreamy…"

"Secrets of a good girl…" Erin grins. "Well I must say this is both fabulous and disturbing…"

"Disturbing how?"

"I don't want to think of you being spontaneous and sexy, that's just weird!"

We all laugh. The waiter comes over and I order drinks. "The final drink, the final toast to friends to whom I am forever indebted. I don't intend on coming back to London unless I need to move my belongings. I told Carrie I was leaving and she's given me some freelance writing work. I am on my way to a brand new future."

"Not coming back?"

"No. Not unless I have to."

"Leaving to design waterproofs?"

"Yes! Pink and red ones!"

"Surely that would scare the fish?"

"Perhaps but far more flattering than custard yellow!"

Imogen takes hold of my hand. "You deserve a happy future Freya, you deserve the world and I hope this man, wherever he is and whoever he is realises just how lucky he was to have you."

I squeeze her hand tightly as Erin takes hold of my other. For a moment we sit in silence, reflecting on the years we've been inseparable, a friendship that will forever stand the test of time and distance. Connor or not, there are immeasurable blessings in my life.

***

I sit in the bar, facing the concourse. Thousands of faces blurring as they rush here and there, waiting to board their flights, shopping, lunching, parents chasing over excited children. Yet I only seem to pick out the couples, lovers smiling to each other, holding hands, drifting in and out of shops, or merely content to sit together. I've never felt so alone.

The young waiter comes across with my drink and makes polite small talk, asking me about my destination. I answer with as much enthusiasm as I can muster thinking how, in another life, he would be someone I'd be happy to speak to. I open my laptop as he walks away and look at Cornwall information sites on the internet. Then I find it. The perfect place for me to live, a tiny cottage on the seafront in a tiny village I've never heard of so I send an email to the letting agent.

My phone rings and I groan as the William's number flashes up. "Hello William."

"Hi Freya how are you?" He sound hesitant, nervous almost but his behaviour at the house feels like a lifetime ago.

"Stop the niceties William…"

"I am so sorry Freya, I don't know what I was thinking…I had been out all day and I never…I would never…God, I am so sorry, I behaved disgustingly…I really am sorry…please forgive me, I had leave of my senses and I…"

"William, I don't want to talk about it. I want to forget it ever happened, you've done enough and I just don't want any more to do with you. Now tell me what you want."

"The agent called. The house has been sold and it should complete within six weeks."

Just like that. The era ends. No matter what happens the world continues to turn, never slowing, never changing direction, always moving forward. The earth has a cycle, life has a cycle and we are caught up in that. It's both comforting and unnerving. As one cycle ends so the next begins.

"That's fine, I have packed everything except items for you to decide what you want to do with. I'll ask Henry to sort storage…"

"I can do that for you."

"No thanks, Henry will do it. What about the divorce Will. Have you put in the papers?"

"No."

"Why?"

"I thought you'd want to divorce me for…you know."

"I don't want a lifetime with your adultery on my paperwork. Just do it. Cite irreconcilable differences and let's end it. If I need to sign anything then it can be done through solicitors, not through you. Bye Will." I hang up the phone as my flight is called.

I don't know what the future holds for me but I am going to face it with both arms wide open. I try not to think about Connor but the more I attempt to force him out of my mind the more he holds tight. Mexico, ten hours away, can't come soon enough.

***

I can't get comfortable in my seat. Every time I move my leaden body objects, screaming at me as my heavy limbs refuse to cooperate. My tired eyes burn and I try desperately to sleep but each time I close my eyes I see Connor, smiling at me like I'm the only woman in the world. How could I have been so stupid? I know my decision to move is the right one, if I stayed in London I would only spend my life waiting for Connor and I am not that woman, never again will I be made a fool of by a man. It may be the riskiest thing I've ever done, leaving everything that I know, but it's my risk to take, no one in the background telling me I can't or I'm not good enough, only the voices of the people who love me telling me I can. *I'm* telling me I can. Right now, I long for sleep, but my body won't give in. I'm past exhaustion and have gone into the limbo of over tired hell that makes everything seem so very much worse.

It's reassuring to know I have somewhere to go, once my holiday is over. The cottage in Cornwall is financially manageable and won't make a dent in the equity I will make from the sale of the Camden apartment because of the freelance earnings from Carrie. It feels as though it's meant to be, that under the cloud of heartbreak there is glimmer of silver lining - that this is my path and my journey will take me onwards to a place where only I am responsible for my success.

I shift in the seat and the woman next to me tuts as I accidentally bang her with my elbow. "Sorry." I mumble apologetically as I adjust the angle of the back. Going back two inches makes no difference to my level of comfort but interrupts the film viewing of the man sitting behind me. He glares as I smile an apology through the gap in the seats but my smile slowly fades the longer he gives me a dirty look. I close my eyes tightly, forcing them to remain shut but once again the movie of my relationship with Connor plays and my eyes spring open bringing a fresh supply of tears that silently fall.

You are stronger than this, you are stronger than this. I repeat to myself over and over, taking deep breaths. *You're tired, you will survive. This is not the worst thing that could happen to you.* So why does it feel like it is? Why does it hurt a million percent more than William hurt me? *Because you didn't really love William* the voice in my head tells me. *Yes I did. No Freya, not like Connor.* How will I get over it? *Time.*

Time. I have endless time. Three weeks in Mexico to recharge, heal and draw. Three weeks of sunshine and scenery from which I can gain inspiration, then onto Cornwall and the solitude to create something spectacular. Time is something I have plenty of. I close my eyes again now too tired to fight the images that my mind throws at me. I understand why William chose Lexi but I will never understand why Connor just left. *Perhaps it just wasn't mean to be?*

The cabin crew come round with inedible looking slop wrapped in cellophane that turns my stomach but I make half-hearted attempts to pick at it. It tastes as it looks, watery and bland and the roll that accompanies it would make a hole in the floor should it be dropped. The woman sitting next to me grimaces and says "all the money we pay for a flight and they can't even give us decent food. Prisoners get better."

"It would go against their human rights to serve them this shit." Her male companion mutters.

"Bugger their human rights." She complains opening the miniature bottle of brandy on the tray. "At least the booze is ok."

I look at the small green bottle of wine on my tray and have the urge to vomit. Sweat begins to dampen my forehead and I wipe it away with clammy fingers. From nowhere, like blast from a rocket comes a surge of panic that swirls and swoops like a dense bleak fog, twisting my stomach and clenching at my lungs with its poisonous fingers. I can't breathe. I pull at my collar but still the air is restricted despite the great gulps I take in. What am I doing? Thirty thousand feet up in the air, in a tin can that is taking me across the world where I know no-one. I should be sectioned not sitting here looking at sludge and vinegar flavoured wine. A tremor begins in my fingertips moving slowly through my limbs until I shake violently. The woman beside me looks concerned.

"Are you alright love?"

I nod, my teeth chattering. My body is covered in beads of perspiration but I shiver with the cold. The woman reaches for the blanket under my seat and tears open the wrapping before covering me up with it. "Can I get you a hot drink? Or brandy? Brandy suits all ills."

"Tea please." I stutter through a clenched jaw.

She rings the bell and a stewardess with a false smile plastered on her ruby coated lips makes her way down the aisle. She eyes me as she draws level with our row. "Is everything alright?" She asks.

"My neighbour here is not well. Please would you get her some tea?"

"Just tea?" The stewardess asks me. "Can I get you anything to eat? A biscuit or something?"

"Yes please." I reply shivering so hard my teeth rattle.

She moves away and gestures to a colleague. They whisper between themselves and the other stewardess looks over at me with concern. She nods briefly and walks into the small kitchen area that separates economy from the first class passengers. The first lady comes back to me. "We have a doctor on board, may I offer to ask him to take a look at you? You don't look very well."

"Thank you but no, I'm just very tired. That's all." I pull the blanket closer around me feeling the beads of sweat rolling down my face. "I didn't sleep last night."

The stewardess doesn't look convinced. "I would like to move you if you don't mind, make you more comfortable. Are you able to stand?"

I nod and gingerly get to my feet. The world spins and I grip tightly to the seat in front taking a deep breath before following the stewardess down the aisle and through the curtain into first class. She stops by an empty seat and says "take this one. It pulls out into a bed. Ten hours in a seat when you feel awful isn't pleasant. My colleague will bring your tea and I will go for your bag. If you feel like eating anything then the crew in here can assist you."

"Thank you." I reply gratefully sinking into the wide seat. The other passengers look me up and down but say nothing. I recline the seat and close my eyes.

FRIDAY

I wake as the cabin crew come around with tea and find that I am ravenous - the debilitating anxiety from earlier has been swept away by the deep sleep. The sky beyond the window is clear blue and dazzling and I stare into the distance as a soft smile forms on my lips.

"How are you feeling now?" The air stewardess asks me as she refills my coffee.

"Much better thank you."

"Good." She says. "May I get you anything else?"

"No thank you." She miles at me before moving onto the next passenger.

I sip my coffee, surprisingly good for airline coffee, but then, I surmise, I am in first class. For the first time I take in my surroundings, rested eyes seeing things in a whole new light. It's so plush, decorated like a five star hotel with leather seats, duvets and smart, chic travellers. I recall the looks of economy passengers during flights past and the empty, hollow looks of people who have missed out on sleep. My look from earlier I suppose. In here everyone looks rested, immaculately made up with not a hair out of place. Across the aisle are a middle aged couple with faces I recognise but cannot place, perhaps actors, musicians or maybe just famous from another era. The cabin crew come around to clear remaining plates and cups before the captain switches on the seatbelt sign and we begin our descent into Mexico.

I clear immigration, collect my bag and meet the rep assisting with the transfer. The air outside the terminal is hot and dry making me gasp as I leave the air conditioned sanctuary of the airport. *Well*, I think, *I made it*.

I take a seat on the coach, beside the window that smells newly polished. The coach is spotless, befitting the five star holiday I've booked. The coach fills up with couples happy in their bubble made for two while I am made painfully aware of my solo status. The rep stands at the front, talking in accented English about the history of Mexico but I manage to fade him out and fall back asleep.

I awaken from a Connor related dream as the coach rolls to a standstill outside the hotel and the desolation that he isn't really here with his arms around me creeps back into my conscience. The sun is bright casting a yellow hue over the Mexican morning at odds with the black gloom I feel. I could sleep the sleep of the dead and despite the brief positive interlude earlier my brain now seems to be have woken up in meltdown, the endless questions singeing the delicate wires that keep me rational. He just left. Just like that. No reason, nothing to push him away. I've been over and over the past two weeks and can find no explanation for his actions. He left me. Regardless of the lack of promises or lack of commitment it doesn't fit with the moments before. Unless…unless…

Unless I have too much baggage? Or maybe the plans I have put in place didn't appear to include him. How did I not notice? Perhaps the possibilities for more variety led him away - the never ending supply of beautiful, sexy women to have fun with all the while the world is at his feet. Why settle for a thirty-five year old when nubile twenty year olds would sell their soul for one night with him. I fail to turn the flashing images off, the women that the internet have paraded like some sick movie montage taunting me over and over until I want to scream.

My reaction is not logical. Not logical for a brief fling. A short moment in time. I can't rationalise the idea that a fling was really all it was. Without him life feels so empty, regardless of the endless possibilities ahead of me. If it was something so unimportant in life's grand scheme then why do I want to turn off the sun and stop the world from turning? Why do I want to be in a silent, dark room not in this beautiful country? Why do I feel as though I am I falling apart?

You are strong Freya, be strong. I don't feel strong. I know there is strength inside me, strength I will find and I know that my decisions are the right ones but the awful shell shocked feeling is dominating and I have three weeks to emerge from under its control.

The passengers and I disembark the coach and are directed into the cool foyer by the porters who stand by to collect our luggage. The floor polished cream marble, overhead an intricate chandelier glistens as the sunlight streams in through the glass doors, throwing rainbows around the cream and gold room. In the centre of the room is a highly polished, circular table with a three foot high glass vase filled with brightly coloured blooms that give off a sweet fragrance.

I take my place in the queue for the receptionists. Five are on duty, beautiful Mexican women with immaculate makeup and their jet black hair entwined with flowers. I become conscious of my grimy appearance and run my fingers through my sleep-messed hair.

I check in and am shown to my room by the luggage porter. I thank him as he wheels my case into the room and places it on the luggage rack within the vast wardrobe. He leaves me in peace and I look around the room. To call it luxurious would be an understatement. Decorated in cream and crimson the room faces the beach with a window that runs the length of the room to the balcony doors on the right hand side. The wood furniture is pale with gold accessories and on the vanity table there is an ice bucket containing champagne and some chocolate dipped strawberries.

At the rear of the room behind an elaborately painted screen is the bathroom complete with a bath for two. It has been tastefully decorated with golden marble and crimson towels and on the unit above the sink is a range of expensive products. I set the bath running desperate now to rid myself of travel and airplane grime. I liberally add some bath foam and return to the bedroom to unpack. I didn't pack a lot and when it's all hung up my clothes look lost inside the walk-in wardrobe that spans the width of the room. I look at the items I have brought, chosen for a romantic break for two and yet looking at the garments none of them would have gained Will's approval. Perhaps I already knew? These are clothes for the first flush of love – beautifully cut, expensive garments to flatter and shape with tiny underwear designed to tease and excite.

I can't remember ever really believing that my marriage could be saved. Not for the first time do I consider that my meeting Connor was pre-destined to lead me down a new path. I sit down heavily on the ornate four poster bed with its red drapes and red, gold and cream bedding. It's a bed made for loving, for two people to make whispered promises and as if mocking my single status in the centre of the bed a heart has been created from rose petals that I angrily scoop up and discard in the bin. I don't need any more reminders that I'm alone.

Avoiding the bed I slide open the doors and stand out on the balcony looking out over the aquamarine ocean, sunlight glinting on the soft waves. The sand, almost white, looks as though it has been mown into the perfect flat surface, untouched by human footprints. It's another world and I marvel at the colours, the rich blues of the sky, the deep greens of the foliage against the pale sand and I know that from here there is no looking back. No more questions, no more accusatory looks within myself, in this far away land where the sun shines is the place for me to begin my life.

***

The sand is gloriously warm under my feet. For as far as the eye can see the aqua ocean sparkles under the intensity of the vivid sun and no clouds spoil the azure sky. It is heaven on earth. Peaceful, tranquil and, apart from the waves lapping at the shore and the calling of the birds in the trees, silent – the small, secluded private beach is empty and it's perfect. The forty-bedroomed boutique hotel is nestled in the hill and faces out over the Caribbean Sea. Every room, it seems, faces the sea, private balconies are drenched in sunlight and on the flat room is a terrace bar under a canopy of green. It's a romantic dream – perfect for a couple who need some together time.

Perfect for an individual looking to the future.

Perfect for reflection and healing.

Three weeks stretch out in front of me as endless as the ocean, time to draw and the quiet to plan. I need a plan. I don't function without one. I like knowing, having an aim and the more I consider my desire to follow my childhood dream the more real it feels.

I walk to the shore line. The sea comes to greet me and I hitch up my dress to walk into the warm waters. The air is salty evoking memories of childhood, when life was carefree and easy. The waves roll softly over my feet and the sea breeze drifts over me soothing and delicate bringing with it faint scents of hope. Hope that I can come out of the aftermath of my broken marriage and broken friendship stronger and wiser. Hope that I can move on from the adventure that was Connor.

Hope that I can forget that I ever loved him.

Because I do love him - deeply, passionately and all consuming. I liked the person I was with him, I respected her, she was strong and confident, nothing like the person I was with Will. In the confines of my marriage I tried too hard to be someone else, to somehow get onto a pedestal that was always out of my reach. I gave up on myself and I don't recognise that me anymore. I had buried the person I am deep down inside until I could almost pretend that she didn't exist and now I can set her free. No one to make me feel I am not good enough because finally I can recognise that I am.

I think about Connor. Of course I do, since I met him he has been the dominant thought at the forefront of my mind. At what point did I let him into my heart? The first night? The last night? The moment William said he wanted me back? The day I woke up and realised the only smile I wanted to see was Connor's? I close my eyes against the bright evening. Looking back at me is Connor engrained in my memory. His beautiful face with a smile curved on his lips. His full lips. Lips I never tired of kissing. Lips I want to spend a lifetime kissing. His eyes, deeper blue than the bluest ocean, warm and loving. I long to run my fingers through his hair, styled as if he were a rock star, the thick chestnut hair that felt so luxurious under my fingertips.

I want to swim it all away. Let the warm water cleanse me. So I strip off my summer dress and swim until I am breathless.

***

The terrace adjacent to the small lounge is empty. The sounds of frivolity and animated conversations trickle down from the roof but I have no desire to join in. I like the solitude. I watch the sun set, turning the sky a myriad of colours. The waiter brings out my cocktail, a strongly flavoured mojito and a dinner menu that I peruse to the soft Latin music that plays from the overhead speakers. This is a place where dreams can become reality. It's in the scents of the sea and the fragrance of the exotic plants. It's a place where the past no longer matters and the future is mine for the taking. Placing my meal order I begin to sketch, drawing on the sounds and perfumes that surround me, designing from the heart, a dress perfect for a new beginning. I shade the colours to match the sunset, rich crimson, orange and saffron, sweeping the design to embrace the curves of even the most slender of women. A dress that will change someone's world, bring in new love and conquer all fears.

"That is a very beautiful dress." The young waitress comments as she brings my starter.

"Thank you."

"In the market near my home you can buy fabric coloured like that." She gestures to the design. "All colours…"

"Really?"

"Yes, all made by one man. He is very clever and makes beautiful material."

"Is your village nearby?"

"It is about an hour from here. I can take you? It is a poor village, nothing like this." She sweeps open her arm. "This is the side of Mexico the government want people to see." She sounds sad and the expression on her lovely face changes. "I am off tomorrow if you would like to go." She looks almost hopeful.

"Yes please I really would but I don't expect you to come here to get me. Can I meet you there?"

"It is not that well known a village. I will be happy to come and collect you and it will be safer for you too. Not all areas of Mexico are like this. Some villages and towns…you would not like to be lost in them." She pauses. "My name is Christina."

"I'm Freya. Thank you Christina the market sounds like it could be just what I am looking for."

"It's very busy, always full of local people and some tourists who have good guides. I will be pleased to take you. Is ten am too early for you?"

"No, ten will be great."

Christina glances up as the Restaurant Manager comes into view. "I'd better serve the other guests. Enjoy your meal."

I eat slowly looking out across the beach watching the sky turns navy and the stars twinkle like fairy lights. How insignificant we are against the expanse of the universe. I wonder what else is out there. The air cools and the insects in the foliage begin their night time chorus. I pull my wrap tighter around me and pour the remaining red wine into my glass. I wonder what Connor is doing and the anguish tears at my heart, shredding what is left of my resolve to not cry.

SATURDAY

I meet Christina in the foyer of the hotel. She greets me with a wide smile but seems nervous as we walk out to her car.

"No one in my village speaks English." She says. "And they will try to make you spend as much as possible. I will help you. It is a poor village, very poor. Children don't go to school as there is not enough money to send them but the people are kind...." She tails off looking anxious. "Very different to England no?"

"It is hard to imagine poverty when I am staying somewhere so idyllic."

"It's like all of South America. The tourist areas are what they want you to see." She grins. "But everyone is happy and the sun always shines. No one wants what they don't know they haven't got."

"Your English is very good."

"Gracias. I started working in the hotel as a maid when I was twelve. I learnt slowly. When I was good enough they made me waitress. One day I want to be a manager but I have to save very hard to go to school to learn all the sums. I give most of my money to my family. We are lucky I have a job, it makes us not so poor. It's a good village though, we share what we have, no one goes hungry."

"I think that would make life a very nice place. In London, where I live, no one knows their neighbours really, no one smiles or says good morning. Everyone wants something that everyone else has. I think we have lost community."

"Community?"

"The ways things work in your village everyone looking out for each other. In London it's only ever about yourself."

"That sounds lonely."

"It is lonely."

"Do you not have friends? A man?"
"I have very good friends so I am lucky."
"Do you have a man?"
"Not anymore."

"I do. I have a man who I love but my parents don't want me to marry him because his family have no money. I think there is more than money but I cannot go against my parents. It will be different when I am a manager I think." She sighs. "I just need to work more to pay for school."

"How old are you Christina?"
"I am diece-ocho...I mean eighteen. Sorry. I speak Spanglish sometimes!" Christina laughs.
"Spanglish?"
"A mix of Spanish and English! Alberto speaks English and my parents do not. It makes things easier that way!"
"Secret conversations?"
"Lots of them. We need secrets, yes?"
"Yes we definitely do!"

The road to Christina's village takes us through shanty towns with unkempt gardens, skinny stray looking dogs roam or lie under sparse trees. Brown skinned children with mops of jet black hair play chase or kick battered looking footballs, laughing as they run around. They look so happy and it's infectious.

Christina talks quickly telling me in detail about her life. It sounds so hard, a world away from what I'm used to. Growing up, particularly during private school, we never had spare money but compared to Christina's family we lived like kings. She was taught to read by her grandmother and begged the local policeman's wife to teach her more. I recognise some of myself in her, the determination to succeed. Christina won't settle for second best, there is too much fire in her belly. I wonder what I can do to help her.

"Is school expensive?"

"I think it is about two thousand of your money a year. That is a lot. It will take me ten years to save up. But it will be worth it. Then I can marry Alberto."

"Two thousand?"

"Yes, a lot."

Such a small amount of money. Dresses I've featured in the magazine cost twice that. The difference in our worlds becomes even more apparent as we pull up to a large village, dust covering the road. Chickens peck at the earth and the dogs here too lethargic to chase them. Christina parks the car beside a small brown house.

"This is my home."

"Thank you for bringing me." I tell her and she beams.

All the houses sit in a square formation around a central area where the children play. Their screams of laughter as they rush about fill the air. Although very dry the village has trees and plants that add colour to the beige and outside some of the houses sit old women, wrinkled from the sun, smoking pipes and chatting rapidly to each other. Across the square under the shade of a cluster of trees sit four old men playing a board game and shouting, gesturing violently as each one takes their turn.

"They are always like that!" Christina says. "They have been friends for many, many years but Saturdays, well its war!"

"It looks very expressive!"

"It's just as well you don't speak Spanish." She laughs. "Follow me and I will take you to the market unless you'd like a drink first? It's a long walk"

"I'm fine for now thank you. I have water here." I tell her, pulling a bottle of water from my bag, eager to get to the market. We walk behind the houses and through a wooded area. We follow a lane for about thirty minutes, thankfully in the shade. Above us the sky is cloudless but birds soaring and swooping dot the blue. The hedgerows buzz with sound and every so often we make light conversation breaking the comfortable silence.

At the end of the lane we pass through a gate and in front of us is a huge arena, under a canopy of canvas that is awash with colour, noise and smells of cooking. People mill around the stalls, baskets brimming with produce. Tourists haggle with stall holders looking for a cheap bargain but it's the fabric stall that draws my eye. Reams of material dyed every conceivable colour, metre upon metre for the same price as a cappuccino back home. I'm like a child in a sweet shop and buy almost every sample without considering how to get it back to the car. I don't haggle and I tip the vendor. Christina gabbles to her in Spanish and then tells me she's arranged to have the material delivered to her village.

"Muchas gracias senora." I smile to the vendor.

"De nada." She replies. The woman explains that the weaver is her husband and gives me his details on a scrap piece of paper that I pocket. We move away and Christina guides me through the market. I buy unique gifts, jewellery and a beautifully bound notebook that I give to Christina.

"It's for school." I tell her.

"Gracias." She replies smiling at me. "I have to go to school now to use it."

We stop beside a food stall and I buy us a glass of horchata each, a wonderfully refreshing local drink made with spices and rice and a large portion of tamales. We sit in companionable silence while we eat. The market is more than I imagined, seemingly more of a meeting place than a place of business with an atmosphere that is charged, electric, full of joviality. The tourists continue to buy beautifully made pieces and Christina says, "the tourists keep the villages from poverty. There is never any money for school but no one goes hungry."

"The food is amazing."

"We Mexicans can make a feast from rice and beans!" She grins. "I think it must be different in England."

"It's very different although there are very poor people. But it's not the same. The state gives the poor money and there is free school and free health care so no one should be in poverty really. I think poverty at home is because of bad money choices or addiction to substances not because there is a lack of food. What school will cost you here for one year is a designer dress at home. It's an eye opener to be here."

"We also have this addiction you said. For those families there is little help. I want to get a good job, earn lots of money and help my village, for me that is a good reason to work hard."

"It's a very good reason to work hard but there is no shame in having ambition for yourself either."

"What is your ambition?"

"Just to be happy I think. I had a job…a career…that I loved but it was never really enough. Then I met someone who made me believe that I could do whatever I wanted to so I decided to follow my dreams and design clothes. So I'm changing my life, moving away from London to give myself the chance to achieve those dreams." I look at her. "Would you be interested in working with me? Earn some extra money for you to put towards going to school? The fabric here is so wonderful that perhaps you could buy and ship it for me?"

"Oh my goodness yes I would…really?"

"Yes really! I can't keep coming back to Mexico…"

"I could go to school!"

I grin. "Yes and marry your young man."

Christina looks like she's won the lottery. I feel a massive sense of worth and in some small way everything feels like it's beginning to come together, that it's somehow meant to be.

I insist on buying Christina and her family some local farmers produce for her kindness at bringing me to the market. She looks faintly embarrassed and I worry that I may have offended her.

"No you haven't." She reassures me, "it's just a lot of money to spend."

I look in the basket at the items that have cost me next to nothing. "Christina, it's a pleasure to get it for you."

She blushes. "If you are ready for the walk back I will take you back to the hotel."

"Thank you."

***

Christina drops me back at the hotel. The comparison between the villages I've seen and the hotel is so immense and being able to give some work to Christina makes me feel, in some small way, that I can make a difference. It's been a good day and as I lay my purchases out on the bed I can't help noticing that I've managed to forget everything for those few hours. I yawn. Being out in the Mexican heat has drained my energy and I look longingly at the freshly made crisp bed and decide on an indulgent afternoon nap.

***

I awake refreshed. The sky is awash with colour, vibrant and burnished. I sit out on my balcony with a chilled glass of wine from the mini bar. It's been a good day, a happy day. I deliberate between dining in my room and braving the restaurant. In the end bravery wins and after a quick shower I head downstairs.

The restaurant is humming with conversation as I am greeted by the hostess who shows me to the bar situated on the veranda. The sun, low in the sky, is still blazing, and warms my skin. I look across the garden to the beach, the white sand inviting and the sea as calm as a millpond and reflecting the colours of the evening sky. I could stare endlessly at the horizon, the thin navy line that borders the sky. The view from the restaurant across the beach to the distance looks to have been painted by one inspired by the daughters of Zeus, still and unmoving but perfect. William would have been bored already. Why I ever thought this would be a holiday for us seems implausible now. How well did I really know my husband?

I wonder what Connor is doing now. He is in LA. Not so far from here but he may as well be on the moon. I have no way of contacting him, no way of ever seeing him again and I have to screw my eyes up against the sudden attack of pain.

"Madam may I get you a drink?" The sweet faced young bar tender asks me.

"White wine please," I reply smiling up at him.

The restaurant is so full that I am seated with two couples who rearrange themselves to accommodate me. I smile my gratitude and accept a menu from the waitress.

"Hi," one of the women, a petite blonde with warm brown eyes, says in a soft American accent.

"Hi," I reply.

"I'm Beth. This is my husband Jacob and our friends Rebecca and David."

"Hello," I smile shyly, "I'm Freya." We lightly shake hands and make our acquaintance. Beth and Rebecca have the all American white smiles and the toned bodies of centrefolds. They are both stunning, petite with generous curves and glowing skin. I feel very pale and drab against them. Jacob has bronzed skin with shiny cropped black hair and deep brown eyes. His defined muscles flex as he lifts his drink and casually links his arm around Beth's shoulder. I watch her subconsciously lean into him, her hand on his thigh, showing the world he belongs to her. They move in sync, always conscious of the other. It makes me smile. David is the archetypal American jock with a firm, muscular body accentuated by the tight v-neck tee-shirt and light coloured hair highlighted by the sun. Down one arm is a detailed tattoo, a variety of patterns that all match the next. It's a work of art and I tell him so.

"When did you arrive?" Beth asks reaching across the table to the dish of olives in the centre.

"Yesterday and already I don't want to leave!" I grin. "It's too idyllic here!"

"It is isn't it?" Rebecca comments. "We're here for a week but I want to stay longer."

"What part of the US are you from?" I ask.

"Just south of San Francisco. I guess you are from England?" Rebecca replies.

"Yes, from London. I've escaped the gloom for three weeks!" I laugh.

"Who are you here with?"

"I'm here on my own. I was supposed to come with my husband but he had other ideas…" I smile. "So I decided not to waste the chance to have three weeks of luxury nor pass up the opportunity to try forty different mojitos!" I giggle. "The husband I can do without, the mojitos would be a whole other story!"

"I am three in so far. The cocktail bar on the roof is awesome. You should come with us this evening. I've turned into a star gazer! At home it's not so easy to see the stars, I forget how many there are." Beth smiles.

"It's the same with London." I comment. "Nothing to see but the haze of the orange streetlights. It's nice to think there is a big universe out there and we're part of it. Somehow everything makes more sense because of it."

"I know what you mean." Rebecca says pouring more wine into our glasses. "I also know if I drink anymore wine I'll be waking up with a bad head."

"That's what holidays are for Becs," Beth replies laughing. "A hangover isn't the same when you can recover in luxury."

"Amen to that!" She says holding up her glass. The waiter comes over for our orders and we settle into comfortable conversation.

***

"This is fabulous," I announce as I sip the first of my mojitos and lean back on the comfortable wicker sofa. The bar is on the roof of the hotel lit by lanterns and candles under a canopy of lush green foliage. Above us the black sky twinkles with a million bright stars and the occasional shooting star upon which I place a wish. Connor. That's my wish.

"If you can hear me," I whisper to the Gods, "please send him back to me." I close my eyes and imagine my wishes speeding across the sky on the star landing in their laps. I only need one to hear my prayer.

SUNDAY

The sunlight wakes me up. It beams in brazenly through the window, taunting me as I pull the covers over my head. It's there, teasing the edges of the bedding, slowly heating the room until I can't breathe. I dry retch over the side of the bed all the while a herd of overweight elephant's tap dance on my head. I lost count of the mojitos. Lost count of the tequila. Lost count of conversations. Then comes the sudden panic...what if I told them about Connor.

Gingerly I stand, the room beginning a slow spin as I walk across to the bathroom. I heave once more and climb into the shower, sinking to the floor as the warm water begins to pummel over my body. It's agony. Shards of glass rain down over me, scratching and biting but I stay there until my headache eases and the water feels less like torture and it finally begins to soothe. My stomach growls loudly and I slowly dress myself in a loose fitting dress and tying my hair back in a haphazard pony tail I make my way down to the restaurant, dark glasses hiding my bloodshot eyes from the world.

"Morning Freya," Beth groans as I join them for breakfast, "How are you feeling this morning?"

"Like I've been beaten by Rocky." I grumble sitting down, "Everything hurts from the top of my head to the tips of my toes and something has died in my mouth." I grimace. "Why, why, why did I do it to myself? Those mojitos were neat rum..."

"Don't talk about it!" Beth begs looking green. "Jacob made me a coffee this morning and I brought it back up. Has anyone else been sick?"

"Almost." I say picking up the menu. "Now I just feel hungry and empty."

"I can't face food." Rebecca announces. "I am going to find a sun lounger and stay there until I feel human again.

Jacob and David are going into the town to play golf and that gives me the perfect opportunity to read my book and recover! What are your plans today Freya?"

"I am going to the spa for a sauna and a massage. I need to sweat out the rum and for someone to help my hangover cramps!" I laugh. "I kept waking in the night with stiff legs, that's when I know I've had far too much to drink!"

"It was fun though," comments Beth. "I'm not sure how well Jacob will play today I kept him awake most of the night! I seem to get the urge when I've had a couple of drinks."

"I'm sure he won't complain," Rebecca giggles, "and David will be no good because he spent most of the night with his head in the john!"

"What a state to get in," I muse. "It's a quiet day for me and a full quota of paracetamol!"

Jacob and David join us and we eat our breakfast with a light conversation and promises to meet for dinner. "Just no mojitos for me this evening," I say as we bid our goodbyes. "Enjoy your day."

"You too Freya, see you at dinner," Beth says giving me a kiss on the cheek.

"Bye," Rebecca says and I watch them leave the restaurant before making my way to the spa.

***

I am in heaven. My hangover completely forgotten as the beautiful Mexican spa therapist massages my aches away. Her strong fingers knead my aching body and I leave the therapy room feeling as light as air. "Muchas gracias senorita," I thank her.

She bobs her head, "de nada senora. I hope to see you again."

I smile and say "you definitely will, I feel a million dollars."

"Bueno," she smiles and moves away to greet her next customer. I leave the salon and go out to the beach. The imposing heat of the day has shifted and the air is cooler. I walk down to the shore line enjoying the feel of warm sand under my feet. I wonder what Connor is doing now. Is he thinking of me? I am loathed to admit to feelings of envy when I see how Beth and Jacob and Rebecca and David look at each other. It's like an imposition to see the love passing between the couples and I long for someone to look at me in that way. Beth and Jacob always seem to be unconsciously aware of where the other is and their desire for each other crackles in the air. There seems to be no power struggle between them just a natural respect and deep friendship.

I want that for myself.

I hope that it will also happen for me, that I'm not facing a future alone.

I see a shimmering light dancing above the white-tipped waves - a heavenly light with iridescent colours that seems to leap out and touch me. It's there for a moment and then disappears but leaves me with the innate feeling that I am not alone. "Did you hear my wish?" I whisper and I know for definite that someone did.

***

It's deliciously warm lying in the shade of a wicker umbrella, the padded sun lounger encasing my body in feathery softness. The waves trickle up meeting the sand and gently call my name. It's so inviting, the delicate blue of the tropical waters, a colour so similar to Connor's eyes that I have a momentary ache until I banish the thought of him and take myself off for a swim. Below me small fish dart around, my limbs disturbing their underwater sanctuary. I swim until my body aches with the exertion of pushing against the gentle current, but my mind feels alive and refreshed. I leave the water resisting the urge to splash and stamp like a child. Grabbing my towel I wrap it about myself and cross the beach.

To the right of the hotel large lights have been set up with the back panels of white and I stop still watching the scene unfold. A familiar scene of a photo shoot being arranged, with models standing under parasols in swimwear and in front of them is a blond haired photographer barking orders at a variety of assistants.

I walk closer, taking in the action unfolding recognising the swimwear as a recently launched US designer, Zen Wong, vivid pieces only suitable for women with size 4 figures. The models, beautiful and poised, graceful like racehorses with figures like Barbie, stand smoking cigarette after cigarette while they wait their instructions. Their razor sharp cheek bones stand out further with each drag and the tell-tale signs of hunger are under their eyes and in their emaciated thighs. I resolve my clothes will only be modelled by healthy women, women with bodies that are strong and well fed, not attached to women who value themselves based on what designers will pay them but who are happy, positive, focused women, ordinary women that I see on the street every single day.

I catch the photographer's eye. He squints against the sun and he notices my proximity to his outdoor studio.

"Can I help you?" He asks walking towards me.

"Just looking." I reply shielding my eyes from the glare of the sun. "I am a fashion editor for a UK glossy…I was a fashion editor." I correct myself. "I've not been out of the industry for long enough to no longer find it interesting. I'm Freya." I hold out my hand. "I just wondered if you were a photographer I'd worked with before."

"I don't recognise you." He says in an English accent laced with slight Americanism in the vowels. "I'm Alex Cooper."

I hold out my hand. "Nice to meet you Alex Cooper." I grin. "What is the shoot for?"

"Zen Wong's website. Do you want to come and watch? Advise?" He smiles. "I never mind taking orders from a beautiful woman."

I flush. "You charmer."

He shrugs his shoulders with a smile. "English?"

"Yes, London. You?"

"Originally from Bath, took a GAP year to LA and never went home. I got a waiter job, did some modelling and funded a photography course. Now I work freelance and travel the world. It's a hard life!"

"It sounds it!"

"What about you?" He asks. "A beautiful woman like you can't possibly here alone."

"I am."

"Well if you get lonely…"

I laugh and he grins before yawning showing very white teeth and a smooth pink tongue. "Just in from Beijing." He says by way of explanation. "I had shoots for a week then an insane party last night. I could do without this…"

I look at Alex from behind the safety of my shades. He is extremely handsome with penetrating grey eyes, high cheek bones and a strong jaw framed by tousled blonde hair. I guess him to be early thirties with sex appeal that oozes from every pore. Alex waves to the waitress that is nervously making her way towards the staged shoot. "Coffee please sweetheart." He says smiling at her. I watch her melt under the full beam of his sexy smile. "I need lots and lots of coffee," he says to me, "not much sleep last night."

"Perks of the job?" I know what he's inferring to.

"Perks of having an English accent! The ladies seem to like it"

"So I've been told!" I begin to turn. "It was nice to meet you Alex."

"I'll check you later Freya." He gives me a wink and turns his attention back to the models who giggle coquettishly as he begins to position them.

I walk across the sand to the sanctuary of my sun lounger. Risking a glance back at Alex I watch as he flirts and banters with the models, clearly aware of his appeal. I imagine it makes him a very popular and successful photographer. With self-confidence that drips from him he is so different to Henry and I have such a pang of missing Henry that I open my laptop the minute I sit down to send him an email. Life without a daily dose of Henry will be weird. He is the brother I never had, the boyfriend who would never let me down and one of the loves of my life. I quickly type a brief mail to him and then send a similar one to my parents and Erin and Imogen. I can't help but smile. Here I am, all alone, on the other side of the world and I'm surviving. Is there no end to what I can achieve? I peruse the internet before closing my laptop and sit quietly watching the waves. There is one couple on the beach walking past Alex and his crew but otherwise there is nothing to see for miles. It's calming, reassuring somehow, the infiniteness of the ocean, that I send my wishes in an imaginary bottle and send it out to the gods.

***

I wake with a jolt. A shadow looms over me and for a brief hopeful moment I think it's Connor. Rubbing my sleepy eyes I focus on a smiling Alex.

"Hello sleeping beauty." He says jovially. "I came over to buy you a drink but I didn't mean to wake you."

"It's all inclusive," I say wriggling to a sitting position and checking the corners of my mouth for drool.

"Yeah, I know but the thought was there." He twinkles at me. Alex is someone that at another time in my life I would most definitely fancy. He has undeniable charm and charisma but someone I feel would be just another heartbreaker. He has obviously known more than his fair share of women and I can't prevent the immediate comparison to Connor.

"So…" He says. "About that drink."

"I'm not thirsty, but thanks for asking." I reply shading my eyes from the glare.

"Just one little drink?"

"I had enough for a week last night."

"One drink and I'll leave you alone, but you can't deny a fellow countryman a drink in a foreign land!" He laughs.

"Oh alright," I grumble getting up and reaching for my shades and laptop. "One drink!"

"Jeez Freya anyone would think I'd invited you to tap dance into hell."

"Sorry." I reply contritely. "You caught me during an anti-men week!"

"Oh?"

"Nothing I want to go into! Come on fellow English person, buy me a beer!"

"A beer? Classy!"

"I'm still swimming in rum from last night!" I giggle.

"What? A night of indulgence without me?" Alex mocks outrage.

"From what you said earlier you did your fair share of indulging last night too!"

"I'd indulge you if you wanted!" Alex winks and me and I flush slightly. "I'd get you over your anti-men week!"

"I don't think even you and your charm could manage that." I say ducking under the foliage hanging from the veranda roof. We sit at a table in the centre of the room.

Alex goes to the bar and orders two beers that get served to us by a smiling waiter.

"So what brings you to Mexico alone Freya?" Alex asks taking a long drink of his beer. "Ah hair of the dog, just what the doctor ordered." I take a tentative sip of my beer. It is smooth, refreshing and tastes sweet.

"The chance to start again."

"Sounds intriguing!"

"Not really, just something I should have done a long time ago."

Alex raises his glass. "To the future!"

I raise mine in response. "Amen!"

"So what else? What do you like doing?" He asks staring at me intently. It's enough to raise the hairs on the back of my neck.

I tell him a little about myself. "I suppose my most embarrassing indulgence is eighties music!"

"The eighties? I remember it well. Quite possibly the worst era for taste imaginable. I prefer to consider myself a child of the nineties, indie, moody bands from Manchester are more my thing!"

I laugh. "The eighties are my guilty pleasure."

"I have far more interesting guilty pleasures." He winks at the waitress who chooses that moment to come over to ask if we want more drinks. "Yes please sweetheart, same again."

When she returns her hands shake as she places the glasses on the table slopping most of Alex's on the table. "I'll sort that darlin'" he tells her and she reddens before scurrying away.

"Do you do that to all the women you come into contact with?" I ask.

"Do what?"

"Dazzle them."

"Have I dazzled you?"

"No."

"Shame." He drinks his beer, eyeing me over the rim. "You know, you are really quite stunning." He says, "I would like to take your picture."

"My picture?" I ask incredulously. "I don't think so."

"Why not?"

"Because I'm not someone who has pictures taken." I stammer flushing. Alex's eyes bore into mine and I find it really unnerving. I look away first. "I'm always behind the camera."

"You shouldn't be. You have a face that would look alive in pictures. Go on Freya, let me take your picture."

I googled Alex after I sent the emails to home. His photographs are beautiful images that appear to move, capturing the soul of the person he's photographing, and he appears to be renowned for sensual nude pictures that suggest so much but show so little. It is reported that he has such remarkable talent that fashion houses book him years in advance because no one else quite captures the colour or light or glow that he does. Private portraits cost thousands and here am I being offered the opportunity.

"Your photos are mostly naked, I wouldn't be comfortable."

"I'm betting you look sensational naked." He grins.

"That would depend on a point of view." I reply blushing. "Thank you, but no."

"Dressed photos then? Either way you have a gorgeous face and your hair would look fabulous…and no, I'm not gay!"

"I didn't think you were."

"I'm here until tomorrow evening, if you change your mind…"

"Thank you."

"Hi Freya." I look over Alex's head to see Beth and Rebecca crossing the room.

"Hi!" I smile. "How are you both now? We all had too much to drink last night," I tell Alex.

Beth looks questioningly at Alex so I make the introductions. I feel like they're watching for something to unfold but there is no story here.

"What have you two done today?" I ask.

"I slept for most of it so now I feel ready to face the mojito menu again! We're only here for a few more days and I've got a lot of mojitos to get through!" Rebecca giggles. "Who's brave enough to join me?"

"I may attempt one. Only the one you understand." I tell her grinning.

"That famous last words one?" Beth asks.

"We've all had that famous only one!" Alex chips in. "If you have enough Freya you may give in and surrender to having your photo taken!"

"That's very doubtful!" I tell him reaching for my beer.

"Are you a photographer?" Beth asks.

Alex talks Beth and Rebecca briefly through his colourful career. I can see them angling for the opportunity for a famous photographer to take their picture but he subtly ignores their hints. I must be mad, I surmise, turning down the chance for a photo shot by Alex. He's renowned for making women look amazing, his photos capturing something that is ordinarily hidden under a public façade. There is nothing apart from fear of being laughed at that is holding me back. It's not gratuitous nudity, it is the chance to look sensational which is something my fragile confidence desperately needs. I take a deep breath and say, "ok Alex, if you want to take my picture then let's do it now, before I chicken out!"

"Now? As in right now?"

"Yep as in now or never!" I stand up and drain my beer, inwardly quaking with nerves. My body, very un-model-like is a stark contrast to those bodies that Alex is used to photographing. My fear is that he will laugh and I will end up feeling foolish and humiliated or that the photos will show the lumps and bumps of a woman in her thirties. As it turns out Alex is the consummate professional. He arranges the lighting to highlight my curves and the soft roundness of my body is enveloped in shadows. Whereas I thought I would feel self-conscious and embarrassed Alex never once makes me feel that I am anything other than fabulous.

It turns out to be a lot of fun. Being directed is infinitely easier than working out the shoot and I find myself laughing continuously as Alex cajoles and charms and moves me into poses I didn't think were possible. "You don't need to worry," he says, "you won't look like a porn star!"

"I'm glad to hear it!" I grin as I drop my robe for the final time.

"Has anyone ever told you how beautiful you are?" Alex asks in a murmured voice as he repositions my hair.

"No, I'm not." I whisper as he hovers above me. I can feel his breath on my cheek and my heart skips a beat. Just one. I have a need to be wanted and in this moment to be wanted by a man as handsome as Alex could be the tonic to my heartache. What's a moment? Just a brief passing of time in the infinite turning of the earth.

"Yes," he says quietly. "You are." He leans closer, his face mere inches from mine and then he kisses me. Soft, warm lips meet mine and he pulls me up closer to him. For a moment I lose myself in his embrace until the voice in my head whispers Connor's name.

"Sorry." I say turning my head. "I can't."

I reach for the robe and cover my naked self, unshed tears stinging my eyes. I pull it around myself and tie the belt tightly. "Sorry Alex. Just too much has gone on recently for any of this. I can't, I'm so sorry."

"Perhaps my charm is broken, or has run out!" He quips making light of the uncomfortable situation.

"You are very charming I'm just not looking for anything at the moment." I stand up. "This afternoon has been the best fun and if things were different you would have charmed my knickers off. This is about me, not you. Thank you for taking my picture." I smile shamefully and leave the room. In the sanctuary of my hotel room I give into tears that wrack my body until there are none left.

***

I meet everyone in the lounge. Apart from the five of us there is only one other couple here. From the sounds coming from the roof terrace the rest of the hotel has congregated up there for pre-dinner drinks. I feel embarrassed and slightly ashamed that I was so willing to strip naked for Alex and that things progressed to the kiss. One kiss. A kiss that should have made me feel a million dollars instead it has increased the desperate ache for Connor. I miss him so much. I miss him like I'd miss my right arm. I'm permanently cold despite the Mexican heat that warms my skin, my heart is heavy and I wonder if the sadness will ever go away.

"Are you ok Freya?" Beth asks as I sit down.

"Yes I'm fine thank you."

"Was it a good photo session?" She looks at me as I pretend to be engrossed in the drinks menu.

"It was a fantastic session." Alex says behind me. I feel awkward and uncomfortable but I turn to face him. He smiles at me and proffers his laptop. "Do you want to see the pictures?"

Do I? Something that was such fun now feels empty and banal. He sits down beside me and opens the screen typing a password onto the login page. His computer screen springs to life and with a few clicks of files he opens one that is called simply 'Freya'.

I gasp and instinctively cover my mouth with my hands in disbelief. The pictures are sensational. I look glowing, the shadows carefully covering my modesty but they don't disguise the soft, womanly curves that somehow look more defined, more sensual and sexier than I ever thought could be possible. My skin glows almost looking iridescent and the redness of my hair stands out as the one splash of colour. They are the most exceptional photographs I've ever seen and I cannot believe that the woman in them is me.

"Oh my god!" I whisper. "They are incredible."

"Wow Freya, you look unbelievable." Beth says looking at me incredulously. "Not that you don't look lovely all the time but these photos…"

"I know. Alex…"

"Don't say anything. I'm glad you like them. I will email them to you and you can do what you like with them. Although they should be blown up and hung on a billboard." Alex says opening up his email. I give him my personal email address and he types it into the address line and attaches the files.

I don't know what to say. It feels very awkward and unnatural. I steal a glance at Alex who is looking at me with a somewhat cold look on his face. I wonder if he thinks that I led him on. I want to ask him, to say sorry if I did but it was never my intention and the words won't come.

"Oh what I would do to him." Beth suddenly exclaims.

"Do what to whom?" Rebecca asks glancing up from her phone.

"Connor Robertson!" Beth says gesturing to the TV screen mounted on the wall.

Slowly I turn my head. The world is suddenly moving faster than I can breathe. Connor's face fills the screen, stills from his movies, photos from premieres, snap shots from his personal life, attending parties, always with a woman…always a beautiful woman. My heart beats loudly in my ears but I feel as though I am under water, fighting against the waves that crash over my head. I want to avert my eyes, look at something else, anything else, but I cannot make my eyes move from their fixed view of Connor.

"Oh Connor Robertson," Rebecca says adoringly, "I would sell my soul to the devil for one night with him!" I want to scream at them, to tell them 'no' because he's mine. But he's not mine. He never was.

"He has to the hottest man to ever walk the earth," Beth swoons, "I've seen all his films. He is just too handsome for words. I have him at the top of my allowed list."

"Your allowed list?" I ask weakly, my tongue thick in my dry mouth.

"Yeah the list of famous people that I can sleep with if the opportunity ever arose that Jacob would not divorce me over!"

"Aha, now I understand." He would be at the top of my forever and a day list.

"Could you turn the volume up?" Rebecca asks the waiter who obliges.

The female talk show host smiles beatifically and thrusts her chest out. Fluffing her hair she announces Connor who walks across the stage with a fixed smile on his face. He looks as godlike as ever but stiff and there is something of his intense charisma missing. He looks like I feel. I remain in the bubble, the blood swooshing past my ears, blocking out the sounds. I know Beth is talking to Rebecca and I see Alex looking at me strangely but nothing is getting through. My body has shut down, protecting me from the pain that is likely to come again.

"Gorgeous isn't he?" Beth whispers, nudging me in the ribs. I nod mutely feeling like I am swimming in treacle, the sounds of life muffled against the thudding in my head.

"…the big question that every red blooded female wants to know Connor is…" the interviewer leans forward crossing her arms to maximise her cleavage "...is there a special person or are you still famously footloose and fancy free?"

Connor pauses then looking directly at the camera says in his lilting Irish brogue. "I left my heart behind in London."

The interviewer stares opened mouthed for a brief moment before realising she has media gold dust sitting in the palm of her hand. This is the most Connor has ever said about his personal life and you could hear a pin drop in the studio. I realise I am holding my breath as the thump of my heart gets louder in my ears. My hands tremble and I clasp them into my lap tightly. I don't dare breathe, waiting for a sign, any sign, that he is talking about me.

"Noooo," Beth yelps, "no no no, you are waiting for me! I reckon he was dumped and he still has a thing for whoever she is...oh my god, what if it was a he?"

Come on Connor, give me a clue.

"Sometimes you get the chance to meet someone who makes your life feel complete, even for the shortest time, when you realise you'll never quite be the same again and that you would walk across hot coals just to see her smile."

"You said you left your heart behind." The interviewer gnaws her red glossy lip, waiting like a wild cat to pounce on his next words.

"I fucked up..."

"How?"

"I didn't fight for her." Connor looks down at his hands, clenched tightly in front of him.

"In what way?"

"I let her go."

"Because of another woman?"

"The obvious assumption," he says grimly, "but no, just my own stupidity, jealousy and immaturity."

"Surely someone like you, the world in your palm doesn't get jealous?" The woman ups the flirtation, fluttering her false eyelashes and plastering a simpering smile on her face.

"Not before her."

"Who is she?"

"No one famous." He grins his heart stopping grin, "she didn't know who I was so it was nice. And she put me in my place on a few occasions."

"What happened?" The woman is leaning so far forward she is practically in his lap.

"Life happened."

"What was her name?"

He says simply "I called her Red. She had red hair but I made a terrible mistake and...well that's it." Connor's face closes over and the interview has the professional sense to stop asking questions. They run the trailer of his new film and the interview takes a less personal track.

"So you managed to tame the untameable?" Alex mutters under his breath.

"I...? What?"

"Your face said it all."

"I don't know what you mean!" I stammer trying to force some indignation into my voice.

"Oh I think you do." Alex gathers up his laptop and drains his drink. "He's a wanker you know, shits on everyone, you'd do better to stay away from him."

"You know that for a fact do you?"

"I know things about Connor that would make you sick. See you around Freya...or should I call you Red?"

I watch Alex leave the bar, his posture tight and tense. My stomach sinks to my shoes. I have a very bad feeling about this.

MONDAY

Every time I close my eyes I hear Connor. Hear his words, the sadness in his voice, the regret…It's heart breaking and yet in some way it has made me feel better, that it was real, it wasn't just me even though the fact remains – he left me.

Eventually I drift off to restless sleep but wake early, feeling drained. I drag myself out of bed, making a coffee and taking it out onto the balcony waiting for the sunrise. I thought I would feel better knowing that Connor was suffering too, but it still hasn't answered any questions and they jumble in my brain until I want to scream. On the table are the excursion itinerary hosted by the hotel so I decide to take the trip to Chichen Itza and hurry to dress. The departure time of 6am would usually have me groaning but I climb aboard the waiting coach, taking a seat beside the window.

The hotel is still. Only the chefs making their way to the kitchen to begin their day and the night porter who directs us to the coach disturb the quiet. The insects have begun their faint dawn chant, whispering amongst the foliage, conversing with each other but otherwise there are no sounds of life from anywhere else. The air has a chill, the sun not yet awake enough to warm the surroundings but it's there, peeping over the edge of the hills behind the hotel, ready to brighten the world. 'At least the world is still turning,' I think.

The driver starts the engine and we leave the hotel. After several stops the once empty coach is buzzing with people and conversations. It's not enough to distract me but it quietens the voices in my head to a murmur. I want to forget about Connor, pretend that I never knew him but his revelations have winded me more than I'd want to admit. I can't get the look on Alex's face out of my head as he realised Connor was talking about me. I don't know what he was expecting, more than I could ever give I suspect, even one night is more than I could give right now. Connor has ruined the chances of any other man for a very long time. It will take every ounce of my strength to get over him but I know I am stronger than this. I am more than the girl that everyone leaves. I am Freya and I am somebody.

***

I climb the 91 steps up to the top of El Castillo. It's exhausting and my body screams out as I haul myself up the giant steps. At the top I sit down, my chest heaving with the exertion but at least it gives me something else to think about. The views are incredible and I walk around the summit looking out over the jungle and the crowds below. It's desperately hot and I am thankful I had the foresight to bring a parasol with me. The sun beats down and the position of the monument means there is little in the way of shade. It is so much more than I was expecting and as I visit all the ancient ruins I wish I wasn't doing it alone.

Getting back onto the bus, I sink into the seat and turn up the jet of air conditioning just above my head. I feel grimy and tired but elated and promptly fall asleep as soon as the engine starts.

"Buenos tardes Senora Wood," the hotel Concierge greets me as I wearily cross the foyer. "How did you enjoy your trip?"

"It was wonderful thank you. I can understand why it's one of the Seven Wonders of the World. Not something I will forget. Thank you for the recommendation."

"You're welcome Senora."

"Hey Freya, how was your excursion?" Beth and Rebecca cross the foyer arm in arm. "You look like you've fallen into a great big pile of dirt!"

I laugh. "I've never felt so grimy but God what an experience." I wrinkle my nose. "Sorry ladies, I am in need of a shower!"

Rebecca giggles. "I was being too polite to say anything," she says, "come join us in the bar when you're done."

"Not more mojitos?" I smile, stifling a yawn.

"Yes, we've got seven to twelve to get through. You game?"

"Yeah why not. I deserve it after the number of stairs I've climbed today. My thighs will never be the same again, which is not a bad thing!" I grin. "Ok I'll go and make myself socially acceptable because I can smell myself and it's really not good! Save me a seat!"

"See you in a while." Beth comments and I leave them, walking across the foyer to the lift. I look at myself in horror as the wild eyed Neanderthal looks back at me.

"Jesus," I grumble, rubbing at a streak of grime on my face. "What a mess!" The lift pings to alert me to my floor and I hurry down the hallway to my room. The maids have already been in and there are fresh tropical flowers in the vase beside the vanity unit. The windows, open slightly, let in the scents of the ocean, and the sounds of twilight so I walk out onto the balcony and look out across the beach, down to the sea, suddenly feeling achingly and painfully alone.

***

"Hi Freya." Beth says as I join them in the bar. "You look more like you!"

"Yeah I decided the hot, sweaty, mess look wasn't really me!" I laugh. "God I'm tired, I could sleep for a week and it still wouldn't be long enough."

"How long do you have left?" Rebecca asks.

"Just over two weeks, plenty of time to recuperate. Life has been too busy and too much like a roller-coaster recently, I just need some time to chill now." I yawn widely. "Sorry! I don't think I'm long for this day. Now I've done the one excursion I wanted to I am going to spend the rest of my holiday horizontal on a sun lounger."

"I don't blame you," says Beth leaning back in her chair. "Where's your hot photographer this evening? I reckon he'd like to tuck you in!"

"Alex? I don't know. And please…" I blush. "Don't say that."

"I saw how he looked at you." Beth says. "His intentions were clear."

"Well I'm off men…"

"Never!"

"Yep, I am getting my life in order, no complications." I grin at her shock. "I don't need a man, I need space and quiet and…"

"Don't look now but there is a man staring at you. You are like some man magnet or something!" Beth comments. "Over by the bar…" She freezes mid-sentence, her cheeks flushing. "Oh my God, it's Connor Robertson. Connor Robertson is staring at you. Shit. It's really Connor Robertson! Why is he staring at you?" She asks wildly. "Unless…oh my god are you Red? " She looks at me with a crazed expression. "Are you the red he was talking about? You have red hair? Is it you? Oh my god he's even better looking in real life. Shit. What's my hair looking like? Becs, you have drool on your chin, or is it mojito. Quick wipe your mouth. Oh my God, are you going to introduce us…"

I stop listening. The world slows down and my heart thuds painfully loudly in my ears. I turn in my chair looking down at the floor, frightened of what I may see if I look up. I pray to whoever is listening that it is Connor, that someone isn't playing a sick joke on me. My twist round takes a lifetime but eventually I can turn no more and I slowly lift my head.

I hear a rush of breath. It's mine. Standing across the room in a loose white linen shirt and pale jeans is Connor. His hair messed up sticking out in all directions, his blue/green eyes surrounded by dark purple shadows. He looks pale and tired with days old stubble littering his jaw line. I stumble from my chair and with legs like wood I walk across the room.

"Connor?" I whisper. "Is it really you?"

He nods once. I can feel all eyes on us but I can't take my gaze from him. He looks worn out and white under the stubble. I go to reach for his hand but drop mine before I touch him.

"Why are you here? You left…"

"Is there somewhere we can talk?"

"Yeah." I reply, my voice distant in my ears. I feel shell shocked and awkward as I walk from the bar, Connor's footsteps light behind me. I take him to my room and close the door behind me.

"You left." I say with my back to him. "You just left." My voice cracks and I struggle to keep the tears at bay. "Why did you leave?"

"I know. I know I did."

"Why? Why would you do that?"

"I saw him, at your house, with you, his arms around you…"

"You were at my house?"

"Yeah."

"When Will was there?"

"Yeah, so I didn't stay. I assumed…"

"So you assumed what?"

"I assumed everything. It looked to me like you were having a reunion…His hands were all over you…"

"You were in the black car?"

"Yes."

"His hands were all over me..." I repeat desolately. "Yeah Connor they were because he practically forced himself on me." I whisper, closing my eyes. I can see William now, coming towards me, with his uncoordinated actions and the strength of a lion. "I had to hit him to get him off me." I shake my head. "Superman let me down...I guess Henry was right, Superman doesn't exist. So why are you here?"

"I wanted to see you with him. I wanted to have a reason to hate you so that I could go back to my life like you never existed."

"Hate me?" The air whooshes around my ears and I feel unstable on my feet. "Why do you want to hate me? I could never hate you. Never."

"It hasn't worked." He gives me a tight smile. "I was angry and jealous and wanted an excuse to be able to leave without regret. I told you before I don't do long term, commitment or any romance bullshit but it backfired on me and now that he's not here...fuck..." Connor pauses and I reach out to him but sense his defences are up. "You've got under my skin so deeply that I can't get you out of my mind and it's a crazy, fucked up experience and I can't deal with fucked up. Christ, I should not have even come here. I have to be in LA, I have two days then onto Asia and Australia for a month then I start shooting a movie in Canada...and now you tell me he did that and I want to beat him to a pulp..."

"I already did that." I smile faintly.

"I want to kill him." Connor says not looking at me. "I want to take him apart piece by piece but...fuck Freya...I don't know what to do now, there isn't the space..."

"No space for me."

"No space for anything." Connor kisses my hand and holds my palm to his cheek. "You were never supposed to be anything more than one night...

"Then go Connor because I can't let you break my heart again." I walk to the door and turn the handle. "Let yourself out." I walk out of the room and close the door behind me.

***

The moon lights up the path I tread through the sand. I can't be at the hotel facing the endless questions nor can I smile through the pain. The wondering may now be resolved, the voices silenced for now but it doesn't make anything better. Whatever the reasons that Connor left me, the fact is he left and the wound is now gushing.

The sea is black and still. The sky, normally awash with stars is covered with cloud and the tropical world feels empty. Silent tears pour down my face and I feel icy coldness all the way down to my bones. There doesn't seem to be any reason for any of this, I can't reconcile Connor's words or his actions and my heart breaks all over again.

Sitting on the sand, the night closes in. My mind churns everything over until I feel like I'm going crazy. Will – Lexi – Connor – Mexico – Alex it's like reading a tragic novel where there is no happy ending, unless I find it myself of course. I look up at the moon, the big glowing circle of white light and watch the shadows cross it, ghoulish shadows, dark shadows that block some of the light and finally some inspiration hits and I can see a dress, the shadows and the colour of the moon. Through my tears I hold the image tightly in my head and hurry back to the hotel, with my head down, to draw.

***

The lounge is empty and I sit in the corner nursing a glass, my sketch pad and colouring pencils scattered over the table. The dress is drafted, the colours blended, not perfectly but enough to work with. The design and night sky pattern looks like a lonely landscape and the dress somehow looks too melancholy to be made. The waiter brings over a bowl of olives and some nuts that I absentmindedly pick at. When will everything be simple and uncomplicated again? Why did Connor come? Why did he have to look so lost, reflecting my own feelings? He wanted to hate me. Hate me. I rest my head in my hands and resist the urge to run away. Does everyone know it's me? That I'm Red?

"Freya?" Alex comes into the room.

"Hi." I smile tentatively.

"You look lonely sitting here."

"And I suppose you have just the thing to cheer me up?" I take a long drink from my glass.

"I would but…Connor…Really? He is the world's biggest arsehole. He shits on everyone Freya, he'll shit on you before you can even say the word."

"You know that for sure do you?"

"He left you didn't he?"

"That's a low blow." I snap. "You have no idea of the circumstances. Not everything is black and white."

"So where is he then? Left again? I've seen him do this to hundreds of women. Flatter them, make them believe they're special, fuck them and leave. What makes you think you're any different?" He asks waving at the bar tender. "Beer please."

"So you're different are you? Not the fuck them and leave them kind of man, what's in it for you, this Connor slating?"

"Yes I'm different. Vastly different. I sow my seeds but I do respect women not just use them for…"

"For what Cooper?" A snarling voice cuts through our conversation. "This is like old times isn't it, you creeping around behind me." Connor's face is pure ice, set and hard, his eyes flashing almost navy blue. "So Freya..." He spits my name. "It didn't take you long did it?"

"What?" I splutter.

"To move on."

"Well she did kiss me..." Alex says leaning back in his chair hands behind, a smirk on his handsome face.

"You kissed him?" Connor's voice increases in volume.

"He kissed me." I stammer my heart sinking.

"Yeah, after I took naked photos of her." Alex sits upright. "Very sexy naked pictures of her. She has quite a body, but I guess you know that."

Connor balls his hands into fists, the skin strained white over his knuckles. "You did what?" He glares at me. "You let him do what?"

"This is ridiculous." I stand up abruptly. "You two obviously have a history, yes, he took some photos of me, gorgeous photos in which I look amazing and I needed to feel amazing. You left Connor, not one look behind, you just left. Do you have any fucking idea what that does to someone's confidence? You the big fucking movie star, the arrogance and the...the...the...why am I even explaining it to you? What the fuck do I owe you? You are no better than William.

"Goddamn it Connor, why did you even come here, to fuck me up again, to break my heart again, to make yourself feel better, let's mess with Freya's head and leave again. No, this is not happening. I have done nothing to deserve any of this, nothing to deserve this treatment...you can both just leave me alone, I have had it with everyone. I came here to find something for myself and it's all been ruined. You have ruined it." I yell.

"Why, Connor, why mess me around like this?" I fall silent for a moment. "Oh what does it matter? Just go. I don't want you here." I walk out of the bar, my shoes clinking on the marble floor. In my room I double lock the door, switch off the light and crawl into bed with a pillow over my head.

***

TUESDAY

The media has gone Connor and Red crazy. Every newspaper and internet gossip site has transcribed Connor's interview. Every red, or almost red, headed woman that Connor has been pictured with has been reprinted alongside rumours and 'sources' comments. Endless questions, endless articles all asking the same thing – who is Red?

"What will you do if they find out it's you?" Beth asks over coffee.

"I don't know, I guess I just need to pray they don't. Not that there is a story, not anymore. He's gone back to LA, I am here, it's not as though there is anything to tell. We met, we dated, we ended."

"Have you ended?"

"Yes, our lives are too different, I have too much baggage and he is Connor Robertson. You can't get any further apart than that."

Rebecca looks at me through narrowed eyes. There in her face that makes me nervous. Suddenly I don't trust her yet I cannot put my finger on why. She looks as though she'd sell her own mother it makes me very uncomfortable. "Anyway," I continue, "I am going to just enjoy the quiet, have lots and lots of massages and hopefully go home with a smaller bum!"

They laugh.

***

I sit in a beach hut, my legs tucked up under me and my sketch pad and coloured pencils out on the sun lounger. I think back to the moon, the colour of the sky and the shapes of the shadows and amend the drawing I began yesterday and start others. The designs flow and I lose hours lost in concepts and styles. Some I discard others I know are great and some I draw based around the fabrics I bought with Christina. It's only when my stomach rumbles loudly do I realise that the sun has begun to set. I pack up and wrap my sarong around my waist to walk across the sand. I am distracted by glinting coming from a motorboat moored up a short distance from the shore. I shield my eyes against the glare but the glinting keeps on. I wonder why it bothers me.

"Buenos tardes Freya," Christina smiles at me as I walk into the foyer. "Como estas?"

"Muy bien gracias!" I reply grinning. "Sorry, that's about the extent of my Spanish."

"Very good." She laughs. "Are you having a nice day?" She nods at my sketch book. "Have you been drawing?"

"Lots of drawing. Do you want to see?" A sudden disturbance in front of the doors draws our attention. Photographers clamour to get in, some blocked by the porters others manage to squeeze by. Before I know it flashes are going off in every direction, blinding me even as I shield my face with my sketch pad. The Concierge takes my arm and leads me to the safety of the lift. "Oh my god, what is happening?" I ask in shock.

"It is because of Connor Robertson." The Concierge replies. "We think that someone has told the press he was here yesterday."

"People know?" I am horrified.

"He attracts a lot of attention." The Concierge presses the button for my floor and steps out of the lift again, standing in front of the doors as they close. This isn't happening.

***

I eat in my room. The doors to the balcony are pushed open and I can hear voices above the sounds of the insects. Does everyone know? Did someone sell me out to the press?

Is it at all possible that I can continue my holiday now that my identity is likely to be splashed all over the papers? In my bikini? That thought horrifies me. What happens now?

I pick at my meal. The anxiety in my belly squirms like angry snakes, wriggling and writhing until I have the urge to vomit. The whole world will know and I will be scrutinised by nameless, faceless, unknown women who all wanted to be *The One* - the one woman who would stop Connor Robertson in his tracks. All those women, those before me, will be asking 'why her' and even I am wondering 'why me?'

A knocking at the door brings me out of my thoughts. "Freya?" Christina's voice says quietly. "Are you alright?"

I open the door and let her in. "Is it still madness out there?"

"Photographers are at the end of the drive, beyond the gates. The hotel is not letting anyone in unless they are staff or guests with keys. The hotel manager wants to keep you and the other guests safe but he is worried that the empty rooms will be filled with reporters and they won't be able to stop them without proof."

I shake my head. "This is insane."

"Insane?" I circle my finger beside my temple. "Oh yes it is." She smiles. "Do you need anything? I can take you to my village if you need to be away from here."

"That won't be necessary." Connor says walking into the room.

"What are you doing here?" I snap.

"Not letting the lions get to you." He says sharply. "I'm taking you to LA,"

"I'm not going to LA with you."

"My house is secure you'll be safer there until all this dies down."

"All this chaos that you created you mean?"

He looks at Christina. "Can you excuse us please?"

She looks from him and to me and nods giving me a brief smile as she leaves the room.

I sit down on the bed and hold my head in my hands.

"Freya?"

"How did you even know this was happening?" I ask, my voice muffled behind my hands.

"The internet. Photos of you on the beach hit LA two hours ago."

"That explains the glinting from the boat. Shit, so much for secrets. Can this get any bloody worse?"

He sits down beside me and takes my hand. "I'm sorry I hurt you. I'm sorry I did everything I said I'd never do. I'm sorry I behaved in as bad a way as your husband has and that I told the world about you. I'm sorry I've compromised your safety and mostly I'm sorry for being a total and utter arsehole." He sighs and stands up crossing the room to the mini bar where he pours out two brandies.

"The thing is that it's always been a different girl, never any romance, never any feelings just using them because I could - because I am Connor Robertson and that made it ok. That's how I know Alex, I screwed his girlfriend. He pissed me off so I paid him back. He always said that one day he would get me back and he's kissed you. I want to kill him. And the photos…why? Why did you let him? I feel sick at the thought even though I have no right to feel anything. I am so sorry for everything Freya, all of it. For walking away, for coming here like a twat and being all arrogant and for hurting you…"

"You already said that." I take the glass from him and down it in one. The amber liquid burns my throat and makes me splutter. "That never happens in the movies."

"That's because it's watered down cola." He smiles. "Look, I want to take you to LA. I'm there for two days but you can stay and I can get you a flight back to London from there. I don't want you staying here, it's not safe, the press won't let it go and I will be worrying all the time."

"You didn't worry about me when you left." I walk to the window. The sun is beginning to set and the sky is alive with vibrant colours – scorching reds, indigos, lilacs and burnt oranges. The silence between us is deafening and I search for something to say, something that isn't accusatory.

"I love you Freya." The Irish voice is soft and rings with sincerity. "I left because I couldn't handle it and I feel like a total bastard for letting the situation with William get out of hand. I've never loved anyone before and I got jealous and it was easier to walk away. I've never met someone like you, someone so strong yet so vulnerable, someone who didn't need or want anything from me. I walked away because my life is crazy but I shouldn't have done that." He sighs. "I'm just not ready to give up LA yet. I always thought I'd go home eventually, when the bright lights became too much of a glare. Five years maybe. It's very conflicting. On the one hand my selfish lifestyle still holds its appeal on the other...and now there is you and it fucks things up considerably."

"Sorry to be such a burden." I flare up. "You came here remember. You came to me. It's not me fucking up your life Connor, it's you. And perhaps you need to get your head out of your own arse and stop being a selfish prick. You either want me or you don't. If you really do love me then you have to deal with the changes that it brings. I allowed you to be in my head all the time. All the fucking time. I have spent every moment since you left me wondering what I did wrong. And to hear you say that you left because you love me is total bullshit...no it's worse than that, its cowardice.

"I have dreams too Connor. I have things I want to achieve and decisions to make about my life. There is a world outside of you, a world where the rest of us have something to aim for. The universe isn't about you and your ego, it's about each of us finding our place. If being here is messing up your life then go because I don't want any more messing up of mine.

"I am too tired for anymore shit Connor. If all I was supposed to be to you was a fling then leave it as a fling, as some fun, until I am no longer someone whose name you remember. Go back to your life and leave me to mine."

I slump, resting my head against the wall the fight leaving me. "I thought you'd gone forever," I whisper, "and I wondered what I'd say to you if I ever saw you again." A tear slides down my face. "Would I tell you the truth or would I let you walk out of my life?"

"And now?"

"I don't know. I love you Connor. I've never loved anyone like I love you. I feel whole when you're around but I don't want to be someone who fits in. I've been that once and I am not going down that path again. I am more than that and I need to feel that I am important."

"You are important. You are important to me. Come to LA. We have two days before I have to go. Please Freya, give me one chance and I promise I won't let you down again." He pleads.

"How do I know you won't? You came here wanting to hate me! How do I know that you won't suddenly disappear off to the other side of the world and then decide to hate me? I've known you for three weeks, feels like forever but that's the reality. Three weeks. We don't know each other."

"I know enough about you to know who you are. I know enough about you to know that I trust you more than I trust my own mother. Doesn't that count for something? What more do you want Freya?"

What do I want? I want a dream. I want the puzzle pieces to fit and to look at the complete picture of my life. I realise that nothing has really fitted before, the puzzle like something a young child would do, forcing pieces that don't fit into the wrong spaces and for a while they stay there until they break free and the mixed up picture falls apart. "I want the complete picture." I say. "I want to finally know things are as they should be and I want to know that I've achieved everything I have ever hoped for."

"Do I fit into any of that?" He asks sitting down on the bed. "Am I what you also hope for? Or is it just about your career?"

"You ask me that when you have made it clear over and over that I don't fit in your life."

"I want you to fit. I'll make you fit. I'll do whatever it takes."

"We want different things." I say resignedly.

"No we don't! Not really. I know that I want you."

"Really? When it took nothing to walk out of my life."

"That was a mistake…"

"How do I know you won't make that mistake again?"

"You just have to trust me."

I look up at him, his handsome face full of hope. Somehow I know he is telling me the truth that he loves me and perhaps he is just as scared as I am. There is always a fear when you let someone into your life that they will take your heart and crumple it like a thrown away drawing and the truth is, I don't want my life without Connor and I understand, in some small way, why he left, I have the same jealousy when I see the women that have been before me.

He hesitantly lifts his hand and cups my face. I lean against his soft, warm palm and close my eyes. "Please Freya," he whispers, "please give me another chance because I won't let you down again. I promise. I'll never do it again. Please forgive me."

"No more jealousy and assumption?"

"No."

"Promise?"

"I promise."

"Then yes Connor, I will give you another chance. But please, as far as William is concerned, you have to let that go. It will be over soon, I'll be divorced and free of him..."

"Freya?"

"Yes?"

"Tell me you want me." He murmurs. "Tell me you want me and I'll know then that everything is ok."

I pull backwards and look into his eyes. They are darker than normal, more navy than aqua and filled with hope. "I want you. I always want you." I say softly, intent behind my words. I do want him. Physically the ache for him hasn't diminished, not even with the days that have passed since I last saw him. My body has been made for his, it cries out for him, the throbbing in my groin begins its impatient beat the more he holds my gaze and I feel myself rise and swell as the desire begins its flow. I can forgive and I can let go because he came to find me, the Gods sent him back and I have to trust that this is how things should be.

My words hang in the air. Loud, like a clanging bell, one chime that echoes across the evening sky. Connor bangs his glass down on the table and immediately he is kneeling in front of me, his hands cupping my face, his lips – the lips I have longed for – on mine. The spark that ignites is loud in the air *crack* and my body bursts into flame burning red, orange and yellow to match the setting sun.

I pull him to me, wrapping my hands around his broad shoulders, his skin hot under my hands. He smells divine, that personal, sexy, manly scent of a man who was made for me. I bury my head into his neck, inhaling deeply, my tongue darting out to taste the skin I will never tire of. His fingernails scratch down my back and my skin responds, quivering as he strokes me. Desire is heavy in the air, the scent of it dominating the otherwise tropical scent of Mexico, it sparkles like diamonds, a stunning visual display of our deep need for one another that shines only for us. I lean my head back as his lips caress my jaw line and down to the hollow of my neck.

Connor leans me backwards onto the bed, the bed that was made for two people in love. Finally it serves its purpose, no more lonely tears but the tears of joy, the tears of a woman whose man came to find her, to make amends, to make those whispered promises for the future that she so desperately wanted to hear.

***

Connor's phone rings and he answers it while I finish getting dressed. "There will be a plane for us at eleven pm to take us to LAX." He says. "The car will be here an hour before. Are you packed?"

"Yes, it's all done." I tie my hair up. "Are you ready?"

"Yes." We leave the room to go down the restaurant. Everywhere eyes turn to stare at us, Connor and Red. I see some people reaching for their cameras but the waiting staff have a quiet word and the cameras are returned to bags.

"I just need to make a call." Connor says as we are seated. "Will you be alright for a minute?"

"Yes."

"Hi Freya." Beth and Rebecca swoop on me. "Are you alright?"

"Yes fine thank you."

"I am oozing with jealously," Beth says, "he is divine."

I smile.

"You don't have to worry," she continues, "your secret is safe."

"The secret is already out." I catch a flicker on Rebecca's face. It was her. She sold me out. "They think someone inside the hotel told the press. According to Connor stories on him can fetch up to fifty thousand dollars in the US so I guess someone will have a very small mortgage as a result."

"No!" Beth breathes. Rebecca looks uncomfortable and doesn't meet my gaze.

"Ah well, secrets don't stay secrets forever." I pick up the menu. "I just hope it was worth it for whoever it was that told." I look up at Rebecca. "Because I am in the middle of a media storm and it's not a nice feeling."

"It will all work out, I'm sure." Beth says confidently. "Look we're going to the other hotel for dinner this evening but I just wanted to wish you good luck for the future, I hope you make it with your designs, perhaps I'll see you in vogue in the near future."

"That would be good!" I grin. I watch them walk away, Rebecca glancing back briefly, guilt on her face.

***

After dinner Connor and I walk along the beach. "It's so beautiful here," I say wistfully. "Is LA beautiful?"

"Parts of it are. It's chaotic really and busy, everyone has an agenda, it's not somewhere to live if you want some peace. Let's swim."

"Swim?"

"Yeah, get naked and swim!"

"Naked? The press are lurking!"

"What's the worst that can happen?"

"My large naked arse could end up on the front cover of the papers."

"Your arse is hot!" Connor laughs. "It should be on the front cover!"

"My dad would have a heart attack!"

"Come on chicken shit, get naked!" Connor begins stripping off his clothes. His body is highlighted by the moon, toned, smooth and perfect. Quickly I take off my clothes and then pull him to me, my body fitting against his. I hold him tightly, inhaling the scent of him.

"We're like Adam and Eve," he says laughing.

"After they fell from grace perhaps," I grin, my mouth on his shoulder.

The water is cool and refreshing. I swim a few strokes before turning onto my back and gazing at the stars. "Doesn't it make you feel insignificant seeing all that above. All the potential other worlds and here we are most of the time thinking this planet is all there is."

Connor swims up beside me. "I'm not looking at the stars." He reaches a hand out and cups my breast. "I'd rather be looking at these than the sky any day!" He tweaks my nipple and I splutter under the water. Connor pulls me up laughing. "Do you need mouth to mouth? I'd be happy to oblige."

I wrap my arms and legs around him. The ocean is silent, the only sounds I can hear is the faint chatter from the hotel. The water laps around us as we embrace, enveloped by the dark of the night, only the stars above us for company. The press, the chaos, the impending storm are forgotten as we wrap ourselves in each other. Our two hot bodies are moulded together as I kiss his face, his mouth, his neck and raise myself up as high as I can to offer him my breasts. They spring up at his touch, his mouth caressing my nipples, his hands cupping me. I cry out, breaking the silence, as Connor slowly enters me and we move as one body, one soul, one mind and shrouded by the cool water that cleanses away the past, we come together.

***

The bar is quiet when we arrive back at the hotel. Connor orders a whiskey and a mojito and we sit out on the veranda. He is silent staring out across the black void. I drink my cocktail wondering if I should make conversation but Connor seems engrossed in his thoughts so I just leave him.

He finally speaks. "I should never have told Suzy Coombes about you. She'll have her minions scouring the planet for information and any dirt they can get their hands on. I've had the endless paparazzi for ten years and it's tiring. I know you are not ready for it. It was a stupid thing to do." Connor reaches for my hand. "I didn't want anyone to know about you so I'm not sure why I told."

"Are you embarrassed?"

"No, I just want to keep something to myself. My whole life is played out in front of the cameras and I just want to keep something private and I don't want anyone to think you're just another one of Connor's ladies," he does quote marks with his fingers, "because you are so much more than that. You already have a whole heap of shit to deal with without adding this to the situation, the endless rumours and character assassination. I'm sorry I said anything."

"Don't apologise, what done is done and I will just deal with whatever comes my way. It's not like I'm going to be in London and easily accessible, I'll be moving to the middle of nowhere." I reply, "Being famous actually doesn't sound so great!"

"It has plenty of advantages just a fair number of bad parts too." He reaches for my hand. "I just want to keep you to myself."

I grin. "Why?"

"Because I love you," he says simply.

WEDNESDAY

We land at LAX and a car is waiting to take us to Malibu. It's late and I try to fight the need to sleep but tiredness takes over and the next thing I know Connor is shaking me awake.

"Hey," he says. "We're home."

Groggily I clamber from the car, rubbing my eyes. 'Home' is encased in darkness save for some low level lights that guide us from the driveway. Connor wraps his arm around me and leads me into the house. Upstairs in his bedroom he gently undresses me before I give into sleep.

***

I awaken to sunlight streaming in through the windows and stretch luxuriously.

"Morning." Connor leans over me, a cup of coffee in his hand.

"Hey." I smile and rub sleep from my eyes. "What time is it?"

"Eleven!"

"I haven't slept that well in a week." I say wriggling to sit up. "God look at that view…" Connor's bedroom is immense with a glass window that looks out over the ocean. The sea twinkles under the glare of the sun and reminds me of the colour of Connor's eyes. "How would a person every tire of that view?"

"Do you want to see the rest of the house?" He asks.

"Oh my God, are those Oscars?" I leap out of bed and cross the room to the table beside the easy chair. "Wow that's heavy," I comment lifting one up then giggling I say, "I would like to thank the academy for this award, to win best song is an honour and a dream come true!"

"Best song?" Connor laughs, "you can't sing!"

"A girl can dream and I always wanted to be Madonna!"

On the bedside table is a bible, a rosary and a photo of his parents. "It keeps me real." He says coming up behind me and wrapping his arms around my waist. "I have a lot to be thankful for."

"That's true of all of us." I comment. "I have a lot to be thankful for as well."

"Do you think you will like staying here?"

"I don't think I will want to leave."

"Then don't." He says simply.

Connor's house is a sprawling beach front property built high up into the cliff. The entire front is planed glass tilted backwards giving the illusion of being part of the cliff affording exquisite views over the ocean. The living space, open plan with wooden floors, has been arranged so that the dining area and lounge area look out across the sea with windows that open so wide it feels like one is sitting on the crest of the waves. There are three double bedrooms that overlook the gardens, a gym, a study and a cinema room that can seat ten people. On the roof is a terrace and swimming pool and beyond the landscaped gardens that have been cultivated to represent the lush green of Ireland.

"Wow!" I breathe, "this is the most fabulous house I have ever seen. Look at the views and the gardens and…wow!"

"You like it?" Connor looks delighted.

"Like it? It's amazing!"

"I had it built from nothing." Connor moves around the room. "It was a pile of rubble when I bought it." He explains. "A house fire destroyed what was here so I had it cleared and worked with an architect, who had literally just graduated, but I liked him, he had vision, and this is what we ended up with. It took two years and a lot of whiskey but the result was exactly right. My grandma did the garden, she was very insistent and I wasn't going to argue. You'd like my grandma she is feisty."

I grin, "I think it is the most incredible house."

"Yeah it is. It's my home...home away from home! It's always been private, even when things were really crazy a few years ago I didn't ever invite people here. If I had parties they were in hotels, never here. I wanted to keep something to myself, even during the haze of my formative years something always held me back from saying 'come on over to my house'. The first foundation stone was from my village, from a barn in the farmyard next to our house. So I have a little piece of Ireland here too. It's modest compared to my contemporaries who live in Malibu." He laughs, "I have the same number of bathrooms as I do bedrooms, unusual for here!"

"Really?"

"Yeah people have five bedrooms and seven bathrooms or something. Wealth and prestige is determined by the number of loos! Do you want your coffee on the terrace?"

"That would be great."

The morning sun is bright and warm but there is a gentle breeze that flits across the rooftop terrace. The scenery is spectacular – endless beach to the front and imposing green mountains to the rear and I follow the view in a circle, shading my eyes from the brilliant sun. There is so much to see, so much to do that I wonder if I will have time to experience Connor's life. He comes across the terrace, bare chested and wearing shorts, looking relaxed, happy and oh so sexy.

"I burnt the toast. I'm going to take you out instead!" He laughs, "I don't list cooking as one of my skills but I know a café that does!"

I feel like I am looking at Connor for the first time. Really seeing him. Surrounded by the sunlight he looks ethereal and his feelings for me are all over his face. This man has been sent to me and I cannot let him go. He is part of me, I am part of him, the very fact he came to find me has made that never more apparent and we are meant to be together. There are no more games to play, no more withholding of feelings, we've gone beyond that and the future will be as it is meant to.

I move toward him undoing the robe as I walk, dropping it from my shoulders to my floor. The cool breeze lifts the fine downy hairs on my skin and hardens my nipples. There are tingles running through my fingers, tingles that will only ease with the feel of his skin on mine. I stand in front of him and reach out to feel the smooth skin on his chest. Softly I brush my nails down his torso and get a rush of pleasure as his mouth falls open and his skin trembles under my touch. Connor stands still, not touching me sensing that I want this to be for me. I lean to kiss his chest and the groove of his collar bone. I run my tongue of his nipples and pull at them gently with my teeth. I feel his erection uncurling against my hip which ignites my centre, warm, wet and wanting.

I sink down to my knees and take his erection in my mouth. Connor tastes divine, fresh and clean, and the act turns me on further. I can hear him mumbling my name and I increase the tempo of my mouth to bring him to climax. Connor's hands grip my hair, pulling and tugging. I like it. It sends shivers down my spine. His moans get louder and I slow suddenly desperate to feel him inside me. I rise to my feet and take his hand leading him over to the sun lounger. Connor lies down and I sit astride him guiding him into me. I gasp and moan as I move riding him with fervour and a passion that takes my mind somewhere else. I give into my senses allowing them to take me higher and higher beyond my conscious thought until I orgasm loudly and explosively enveloped in sunlight.

***

We brunch in a beach fronted café that serves the most incredible pancakes with syrup. The golden circles of fluffy loveliness come oozing with syrup, a side of berries and a frothy cappuccino. I eat them with gusto savouring every mouthful. "I'd be the size of a house if I lived here!"

"It's so nice to see a woman eat. It's sexy." He licks away a drip of syrup from the side of my mouth. "No one eats in LA."

"Can you imagine anything worse than not eating? It's no way to live. Who wants to be a size zero anyway? Those women that are just look miserable and awful. I sometimes think I am in the wrong industry to be a cake loving person." I fall silent. There is a look that flits across Connor's face, a look that tells me exactly how he feels for me and my heart skips a beat.

"Don't go to Cornwall Freya, come here to LA." He says softly. "It's the city of angels after all." Connor takes my hand. "Live with me. I want you here, I want you with me all the time. We could have endless sexy fun and you could follow your new dream. You could have the four years that I plan on staying here to build up a collection and after that we could travel the world or live in a village in Ireland by the sea."

"In four years I will be looking at forty."

"So?"

"You'd be thirty and in your prime."

"Are you really throwing up the age card or are you just scared?"

"Scared? Scared of what?"

"Being hurt, leaving your comfort zone, believing in yourself?" Connor cocks his head. "I believe in you Red. Show some balls woman! Say 'Yes Connor, I will come to LA and be with you and make my dreams come true.' Go on Red say it."

Suddenly I feel scared.

"Red?"

"Maybe."

"Maybe?"

"My head is taking me to Cornwall…"

"And your heart?"

"Is here with you."

He looks at his watch. "Shit, I'm going to be late."

"Late for what?"

He puts some steel framed glasses on.

"What's with the Clark Kent glasses? Do you have a superman suit too?"

He grins. "Superman does it for you then?"

"Superman does it for every woman…"

"What would you say if I told you I have to read for the part of Superman in two hours?"

"No!" I breathe. "Really?"

"Yes, it all comes down to their funding and my American accent not sounding like an Irish man trying to speak American!" He grins. "So that would make you Lois Lane and every boy lusted after her in her sexy power suits."

"Teri Hatcher I'm guessing!"

"Oh yes, she looked like she could teach Clark a thing or two…" He says, "You'd look hot in a little suit...now there is thought."

I laugh, "when you rip open your top is there a big S?"

"No, but when I rip open my trousers there is something big just for you…"

"You charmer!"

***

Connor is collected by a long black studio car. I wave him off and head up to the terrace with my sketch pad. The view is intoxicating. The colours are pastels and lush greens coupled with the stark whites of the houses built into the landscape but somehow too perfect, like it's been painted by an artist rather than chiselled by the power of the earth. It's so very different to London and the greyness of the British weather, but London is a city with history and culture, not one that has been invented by the studios, not like LA with its promises of dreams that for most just don't come true.

I contemplate going for a walk but I don't even know where in Malibu I am. So for a couple of hours I sit and draw but not really getting anything right. Scrapping everything into the recycling bin I leave my beach view and head back into the house to make a pot of coffee. All I can find in Connor's kitchen cupboards is toffee popcorn so I head to the cinema and from the extensive DVD collection I choose one of Connor's films and lose myself in the fantasy.

I don't hear him come in until he kisses the top of my head. "What do you think?" He asks nodding towards the final scene of the film.

"It's amazing." I tell him. "I had no idea you were so talented. I've been laughing and crying and getting rather horny…She's a very pretty girl…"

"She made you horny?" He asks incredulously. "She'd like that!"

"No!" I blush furiously. "I mean the chemistry between you and her…" I look up at him. "Was she one?"

"One what?"

"One of the infamous Connor girls?"

"We were friends…"

"Hmmmm."

He lays me back on the couch and studies my face. "You are so beautiful." He says.

"More beautiful than the perfect LA women?"

"They're not perfect."

"They look perfect."

"They all look the same. You are the most beautiful woman I've ever known, everything about you is genuine and honest and…"

"And what?" I ask running my fingers across his jaw.

"And I love you."

He gently strokes my skin, a soft caress of my face. I undo his shirt and his skin feels like velvet under my fingertips, warm and silken. I trace across his back feeling the taught toned muscles quiver under my touch. He pulls me to him and with an index finger draws the lines of my face and across my lips.

We lie together, face to face embracing, touching, and kissing. It's loving and tender. Connor's delicate touch has me shimmering. I feel radiant. I glow under the weight of his love. He loves me. I love him. Gazing into his eyes, filled with emotion, I can see his soul. His kind, gentle soul. A tired soul. I wonder if he may be tired of his life, that perhaps he wants something more. Perhaps I can give him what he needs.

Connor wraps his hands in my hair and kisses my neck. "Tell me you love me."

"I love you."

"Tell me you forgive me." He whispers.

"Forgive you? Forgive you for what?"

"For leaving."

"Yes I forgive you."

"Tell me you'll wait for me. Wait until I have finished the movie before you move on from me."

"I'm not going anywhere."

"Promise you'll wait?" He begs.

"I promise."

Connor kisses me. He is dazzling, almost godlike as his skin glitters with a faint blush surrounded by his mop of chestnut hair. He holds me tight to him as his kisses become more intense. Slowly, very slowly, we undress each other, hands on skin, touching and stroking and exploring, discovering each other again and again. Our bodies entwine, joining, meeting each other's needs as we make love, showing each other just how much we feel, how much we belong to each other and together we come, loudly, lovingly, passionately and the sensation brings forth tears that roll hotly down my cheeks as I pull Connor as close to me as he can be.

***

We walk along the sea front. The light breeze is cool and we stroll hand in hand looking like any other couple. I try not to think that in two more days this will end but I still grip Connor's hand that bit tighter. He seems to sense my feelings and pulls me into him wrapping his arm around my shoulder.

"What would you like to do while I'm here?" I ask as we sit on the sand.

"Apart from you?" He winks.

"Yes! Well?"

"I think it's more about what you want to do. Does anyone actually know you are here?"

"No. I haven't even turned on my laptop."

"So I could kidnap you and no one would know?"

"You could…"

"Now there's a thought." He grins and wraps his arm around my shoulder. "Why don't you stay?"

"You won't be here."

"I'll only be away for a few months then if I get the Superman gig I'll be filming here."

"And what would I do while you were filming for however many hours a day?" I ask looking across the ocean. "Have some botox or get my teeth done?"

"Hardly. You could draw and make and sew and write and just do all the things that you love doing."

"It would be lonely. I don't know anyone, I don't have any money or a visa…"

"Why are you making excuses?" Connor asks glaring at me. "You don't need a job, you can have one of my credit cards and you would have the space and quiet to do what you really want. Why are you being so stubborn?"

"I don't want your money. My house has been sold, I will have some cash but LA isn't my world Connor it's yours. Would you give up all this for me?" I sweep my arms around.

"I work here."

"It's just not what I had in mind." I think of my Cornish cottage, the rugged coastline and unpredictable weather, the colours and the chance to start again.

Connor drops his arm from my shoulders and we turn to walk back the way we have just come.

"Will you take me to Beverly Hills?" I ask reaching for his hand. "I've always wanted to do the Pretty Woman thing?"

"What 'Pretty Woman' thing?"

"Rodeo drive and the hotel…"

"Seriously! Can you get any sadder?" Connor laughs and the ice between us begins to thaw.

"I am sad and proud Connor!"

"Ok, your wish is my command."

***

THURSDAY

"I have interviews today." Connor tells me as we lie in bed drinking coffee and eating pastries. "It's just a load of publicity bollocks. You can either stay here or come to Hollywood with me."

"Where are you going in Hollywood?" I ask dusting the crumbs from the bed.

"One of the hotels on the boulevard. It will take around two hours I suppose then I'm all yours."

"I like the sound of that!" I grin. "I'll come with you, do the tourist thing."

"It's a dump!"

"It doesn't matter, I am living the movies."

Connor shakes his head smiling. "I thought you didn't do movies?"

"I don't after 1997! I was a teenager once you know. We all wanted Edward Lewis or Johnny Castle or Danny Zuko…in my head I am still a teenager!"

"And now?"

"Now, I just want Connor Robertson…I've heard he's very good."

"Shall I show you just how good?"

His tongue probes my mouth, soft and warm, his hands cupping my face. I give into his kisses melting against him as his touch sends white hot electricity through my veins. His breath across my neck is sweet and warm and my body begins to light up under the soft caress of his hands. His exploration of my body is painstakingly slow, the internal beat deep inside me is as loud as a bass drum, thumping in my ears. Connor strokes and caresses, his tongue following the path of his fingers until I am a writhing mass of energy, begging for more.

"Be patient," he says touching the sensitive skin either side of my centre. I open my legs wider arching my back and pushing myself into his groin. I try to turn, to kiss him, to touch him but he holds me firm. I feel faint with longing the overstimulation of my senses is making me dizzy. "I love to touch you." He says huskily, "I love the feel of your skin so soft and warm." Connor inserts a finger into me. "I love how wet you are, how I can make your body respond. Can you feel how wet you are Red, for me." He slides in another finger and I cry out. "Do you want me to make you come?"

"Yes," I beg.

Connor wraps an arm around my chest pulling me to him. I lean against him as his magical fingers begin to stroke and caress. His fingers are slick with my wetness and slide in circular motions around my clitoris causing my knees to tremble. "Oh Connor," I moan, "don't stop."

Just for a moment his mouth finds my breasts before he removes his shorts and releases his erection. I reach for it, stroking and clasping him watching the pleasure of my touch cross his face. "Harder Red," he breathes. I tighten my grip and his mouth falls open, breathing deeply with his eyes shut. "Yes," he murmurs, "yes like that."

Connor kisses my mouth, roughly, pulling at my lips with his teeth. My moans of pleasure fill the room. I give into his kisses, my body rising to meet mine. His arms pull me to him tightly and I rake my hands through his thick hair. My body is lighting up, each nerve crackling and sparkling and I can almost make out the colours shimmering across my skin. Connor kisses my mouth, sucking my earlobes then down to kiss my neck, the grooves of my collar bone, his hands on my breasts then his mouth on my nipples. I pull at his hair but he moves himself from my grasp and continues his slow inspection of my body. I can feel his breath cool against the fiery furnace that is my centre. The drum beat deafens me as slowly, agonisingly slowly, he licks my clitoris with gentle, wet strokes that increase until I am crying out with each intense touch from his tongue. "You taste amazing," he tells me. "I could do this all day." Slowly he rubs his thumb across my sex.

"Please Connor..." I moan.

"Please what?"

"Please I need you..."

"You need me to do what?"

"Fuck me." I tell him dizzy with lust.

Connor flips me over and raises my hips. "You look stunning like this," he says, "such a hot ass. Shall I spank it?"

"No," I whisper but my body betrays me. Connor runs a finger up my thigh.

"Are you sure?"

"Yes." I'm not asking for it.

"I think you want it." Connor slides a finger into me. "I think you like it." Whispering in my ear, "I think you like being bad sometimes. I think you like being bad with me. I like you being bad, it's fucking hot."

Connor rubs my clitoris and a million fireworks explode. "Connor, oh my God Connor." He removes his finger and enters me. My body trembles as he slides in and out thrusting hard. His touch, on my breasts, is rough, pleasurable and the pinching of my nipples sends delight through me. Every time he thrusts into me he squeezes my nipples, short and sharp, a sweet pain that causes me to cry out. I can barely hold myself as the sensations ripple through me. "You like that?" He questions.

"Yes." I murmur.

My desire for Connor is insatiable. "Tell me you want me," he says.

"I want you." I tell him breathlessly.

"Tell me you love me."

"I love you."

He grasps my hips and slides his long, solid cock into me. I move against him pushing my hips higher for him to go deeper. We cry out and moan together as the passion for each other takes over our senses. Connor's hands explore my body over and over and the desire rises feverishly within me until I come loudly, his name on my lips. I feel him shudder behind me, his body hot against my skin and in my ear he whispers "I love you Freya."

***

I leave Connor at the Hotel Riviera on Hollywood Boulevard and begin a slow walk down the street. The heat is stifling and the air is thick, heavy and clogging. The crowds are moving in a slow, weaving fashion but I manage to squeeze through and cross the road. I was expecting more from the area - some glitz and glamour befitting this famous street. Instead there is a n array of gift shops selling tacky merchandise and fast food restaurants whose greasy fat smells permeate the atmosphere. I wander along the pavement looking at the stars until I find Connor's name outside of the Chinese theatre. I take a picture and feel ridiculously proud of his achievements.

I continue my walk down the path of fame, name after name of actors and musicians that have set the world on fire. The surrounding area seems ill fitting for a tribute to glory with the exception of the Chinese Theatre and retracing my steps I stand in the footsteps of C3PO giggling to myself.

I think about Connor's offer as I walk around the area. A move to LA is just something I'd never considered and now he's asked me I wonder if it could be the place for me. The brief glimpse into the pandemonium that follows Connor makes it all the more a risky decision. Not only would I open myself up to scrutiny but already I've handed my heart to him on a silver platter, a carving knife by the side, not daring to really believe that he won't chop it into pieces. Connor is a player and as much as he declares, and I believe, that he loves me is it too much to hope that he has changed?

With a sigh I make my way back to the hotel and take a seat in the lounge.

"Hello Freya."

"Alex!" I say surprised to see him.

"I thought you were in Mexico?"

"I got sold out. Someone at the hotel told the press and now there are pictures all over the news. It's a nightmare. So I'm in hiding."

"In hiding? In LA? No one hides in LA."

"Well so far no one knows I'm here. Those pictures...please tell me you've deleted them?"

"Deleted them? They should be on billboards Freya! You look gorgeous in them. No, of course I've not deleted them!"

"You'll not do anything with them though, will you?"

"Freya! Relax! Can I join you?" I notice that he avoids answering my question and it bothers me. I don't want to push the issue but a slight chill grips my stomach. I hesitate for a moment then nod.

"Is Connor here with you?" I nod again. "That explains why you look like I'm the devil reincarnate."

"Sorry Alex. I realise there is no love lost between you too and I don't want to be stuck in the middle."

"We go way back Connor and me. We were friends once...actually friends is too strong a word, we were acquaintances, young, rich and wild. It was destined to go tits up."

"What happened?" I ask shifting forward until I'm on the edge of my seat.

"Too much too young. Too many women, too much whiskey, drugs, you name it, we did it. It was never going to have a happy outcome. I still think he's a twat."

"And what does he think about you?" I ask.

"Probably that I'm a twat. We'll never be friends again, he did the one thing you don't do to your mates so now I can't stand him and I reckon you must be mad to get involved with him. He has no staying power, always chasing the next best thing." He gives a wave to the waitress who acknowledges him signing one minute.

I reply sharply. "You know nothing about me or my relationship with Connor."

"I know Connor. Sorry to say but I don't think he'll ever change. We've crossed paths over the past eight years and the pattern is always repeated."

"And I suppose you are different?" I mutter.

"Not really. I love women, lots of women and never pretend otherwise. I'm in no hurry to settle down, I like sowing my seeds in a variety of gardens. Life is too short for commitment."

"It must be a lonely life." I say. "No one to come home too."

"There is always someone."

"But it's empty."

"It's fun." Alex appraises me. "I reckon you'd be fun."

I flush. "Please don't say things like that."

"Why not?" He asks, his grey eyes sparkling, "It's a compliment."

"Is it?"

"You are very defensive aren't you? What's the matter? Have I hit a nerve?"

"No!" I splutter.

"Chill Freya! I'm only being friendly."

"Are you? Everyone falls in love at some point, although I do pity the woman who captures you."

"Why?"

"She's likely to be in for a rough ride."

"I'm not really an arsehole."

"No? You could have fooled me."

"I think you quite like me really Freya and I reckon if it wasn't for Connor, you and I would be spending a pleasant evening in my bed. Go on, admit it, you are attracted to me!" He laughs taking my arm. "Lighten up, LA is not the place to be serious, it's the place to have some fun. Don't you have fun?"

"I have plenty of fun!" I retort. "Lots and lots of it, it's just that having fun with you isn't up there on my to-do list!"

"Come on, I'll buy you a pint of watered down gnats piss. The American's can't drink for toffee and I reckon you are a pint drinking girl."

"Cocktails actually."

"Not at four o'clock in the afternoon, it's the time for a pint."

Alex orders us a pint of Grand Canyon brewed ale from the blushing waitress. "It's the one thing I miss about Europe," he comments, "the beer. Over here it's just weak piss!"

"You are charming." I comment with a smile. "I'm sure they don't think their beer is piss."

"Well someone should tell them." Alex looks up as the bar tender delivers our drinks. The ale looks unappealing, pale and insipid. I wonder how long Connor is going to be "How did you meet Connor?"

"At a function. He was there with friends, I was there for work."

"And your eyes met across a crowded room?"

"Something like that." I take a drink from the glass.

"And when you're not together?"

"We do have lives outside of our relationship. It's not suffocating!" I smile. "I'm happy."

"Are you?" Alex leans back in his chair, fingers linked under his chin. "Because for all your smiles you don't seem happy."

"I am happy." I reply indignantly. "My life is full, it's inspiring. I get to see and do so much that I can find nothing to complain about."

"Really?" Alex's eyes bore into me. "You don't mind that Connor is here and you are there? You don't mind that someone like him has a short attention span? You don't mind what the press will say about you?"

"Are you really trying to piss me off?" I snap angrily. "You know nothing about me, you don't know Connor these days and you are making assumptions about things you have no idea about. You may not like Connor, you may have a history with him but you know nothing about our relationship."

"Sorry, I was out of order." He looks contrite but I would still like to slap his handsome face.

"Yes you were."

Alex reaches for my hand and before I have the chance to move mine away Connor looks above us, his face like thunder.

"What the fuck is going on?" He seethes.

"Nothing." I pull my hand away like a scalded cat.

"It doesn't look like nothing. What are you doing Alex? Finally paying me back?"

"Sorry to disappoint you Connor…" Alex spits, "but you don't feature in my life."

Connor looks between the both of us his face flushed with anger. "Fuck it." He says and spins on his heel and leaves the room. I grab my bag and follow him.

"Connor can you please slow down."

He stops and turns to me. "Is something going on with you and Alex?"

"Alex? No of course not." I put my hand on his arm but he shrugs me off. "Connor, what is the matter?"

"He is a…" The word coming out of Connor's mouth is loud enough to shock the receptionist who quickly comes across.

"Please watch your language sir." She says coldly. "And may I respectfully ask you to keep your voice down."

"Let's just go Connor, this is ridiculous. You are in a strop over nothing."

"Nothing?" He hisses venomously at me. "You think Alex sitting there stroking your hand and you doing nothing about it is nothing?"

"He was hardly stroking my hand. He stroked, I was pulling away as you arrived. He has no interest in me at all, nor I in him. Don't be a dick." I snap.

"A dick? If you knew Alex…"

"I have no interest in knowing Alex so please don't overreact like a spoilt brat."

Connor rubs his thumb over my lip, "you look hot when you're angry." He takes my hand and places it on his groin which is hardening. "And I like it."

"Take me home," I whisper the familiar throb in my centre beating out its intimate rhythm. I lean in and kiss his neck, the erotic scent of him stimulating my senses. I groan as he slides his hand into my shirt and inside my bra. "Take me home now!"

"I can't wait that long." He says taking me by the arm and leading me back across the foyer and into the cloakroom. "As I recall you liked our meeting in the previous ladies room."

He bundles me into a cubical and rips open my blouse. Immediately my bra is unclasped and his beautiful mouth is on me, my nipples rising to meet his lips. I grip his hair tightly as he suckles me, each nip by his teeth sending waves of desire right into my centre. Hot and heavy the weight of my need pulls down, and my desire spills from me, slick and silken against my skin. I bring his face up to mine and hungrily kiss him, pulling at his lips my tongue exploring his familiar mouth. As I kiss him so he raises my skirt and tears off my panties, the delicate lace disintegrating as he pulls at them.

"Oh Red!" He murmurs pleased as he follows the trail of my rapture up towards my burning core. I gasp and bury my face in his neck as his teasing fingers probe and stroke, caressing until I see stars. Nothing else exists, nothing else matters as I give myself wholly to this glorious man. The waves of pleasure wash over me and as I come so Connor kisses me before he pulls me down on him. He fills me and with trembling limbs I move above him, taking him deep within me, my hands grasping his neck, my mouth never leaving his until he begins to make the sounds of pleasure and I feel him come inside me.

***

We emerge from the cloakroom red faced and glistening, my legs like jelly. Connor holds me close to him, his arm possessively around my shoulder and we leave the hotel and out into the evening. My stomach rumbles loudly and Connor grins. "Hungry after your work out?"

"Starving! Can we go for some food?"

"What do you fancy?"

"Apart from more of the same?" I laugh. "Steak. Big juicy rare steak, chips, onion rings, peas and tomatoes."

"Your wish is my command." We stop beside Connor's car and he gives the driver the name of a restaurant. I watch the streets, so familiar yet so very different to what I imagined as the car climbs up into the hills. The houses are palatial, set back behind iron gates and patrolling security but we pass them by and drive out towards the north of the city. I am surprised that we pull up outside a neon lit café where the tables are set outside and men are playing boules. I suddenly feel that I've stepped into history, as they smoke and drink tankards of ale that the buxom waitress refills.

"Life in LA isn't all about the fancy restaurants." Connor says, "sometimes it's good to leave all that behind. It keeps me grounded, which always pleases my mam!"

I giggle. "Fancy restaurants have their place but I'd hate to upset your mum!"

"She'd like you. No frills and fuss…"

"Has she met my predecessors?" I ask quietly.

"There haven't been any worth taking home." Connor gives me a shy grin then greets the waitress. "Mona, looking good babe!"

"Ah be away with you Connor lad," she exclaims as he gives her a huge hug. Her accent, broad Irish and gravelly, explains Connor's knowledge of here. "And who's this pretty young thing?"

"This is Freya?"

"Come take a seat Freya, and let me get you a pint of my finest."

"Mona's Guinness is a little piece of home." Connor grins. "Once I told her a pint wasn't up to scratch, she tipped it over my head and sent me packing. I'm just another snotty nosed village boy to her!"

"The airs and graces get left at the door." Mona says looking affectionately at Connor. "No room for egos in my place. And…" She leans closer. "I serve the best fecking Guinness outside of Dublin." She laughs, a throaty infectious laugh that makes me giggle. "Sit yourselves down, I'll be right back."

"How did you find this place?" I ask incredulously. "It's in the middle of nowhere."

"I was lost after a particularly decadent night. It was just before I went to rehab. Mona sorted me out while I had a massive come down, she gave me food, phoned my manager, organised somewhere for me to hide until I could be collected and she kept quiet. All these years and she's never let me down. She says it's because I am a little bit of home, I think it's because she has a maternal streak the width of the Atlantic and no kids to bestow it on. I was lost, she needed to be needed and we've been friends ever since. You are the first girl I've brought here. She'll be grilling me the minute you go to the loo!"

I smile. "It's nice. Nice to be a first, I mean. With such a chequered past you likely can't remember most of your firsts."

"It's the firsts with you that count." He mumbles. Looking me squarely in the eye he says. "I want you to move here. I want you to be with me. I want it all to be out in the open." I go to interrupt but he holds up his hands. "I've lived a lot, I've nearly died twice because of my own stupidity, I'm older than my years and I don't want the shit anymore, I just want you. I love you Freya, I want everything I do to be about you. I don't want to walk into a bar and see another man…particularly Alex fucking Cooper…touching you. I want everyone to know that you're with me. Move here. Please."

I look at his face, so hopeful and so alive. "Yes." I tell him. "I will move here…" I hold up my hand to stop Connor saying anything. "Before I do I want to go to Cornwall. Do some drawing and have some quiet. You won't be in LA anyway so I'll come here when you're back."

He grins at me, the smile spreading across his face and I grin back. Finally the puzzle pieces fit.

FRIDAY

"Oh my God!" My heart plummets along with my stomach to the floor. Why oh why did I open the gossip pages on my laptop? The blood slowly drains from my body taking with it any hope I had of Mexico passing me by.

There is no denying it's me. *Connor and Red* the headline screams. Photo after photo of me in Mexico, me with Connor in the hotel and – oh no – the photos that Alex took. I curse him loudly using words that my mother would disown me for saying. I scan the article deafened by my pounding heart. This must be what it feels like to see your life flash past you at a million miles an hours. The article asks for information, who knows me, where am I from, what is my name. I begin to tremble violently. Shit, shit, shit this is the worst possible situation.

"There are press outside my gates." Connor grumbles coming into the lounge. "I was hoping they'd not know I was here."

"They're here because of us." I groan. "Look!" I twist the laptop round for him to see.

"That bastard." He yells. "Jesus Freya why did you let him take your picture…"

"Don't start that again," I snap. "What do we do now? Stay in? Go out? Shit. I didn't sign up for this."

"You think I did?" He grunts. "This has been my life for ten years."

"You chose this life. I chose you, that's the difference."

"You knew what my life was like when you found out who I was." He says sharply. "I didn't hide it from you."

"I don't want to be in the papers. What are my parents going to think when they see these pictures?" I wrap my arms around myself. "God…I'm not even divorced yet, my friends don't know anything…this is a disaster."

"But this will be your life now. You move here and they will follow us, I sell papers…"

I run up the stairs and out onto the terrace. If I stand on a chair I can see crowds of people congregating beyond the gates, TV crews, photographers and teenage girls chanting Connor's name. I can't do this. I can't be part of this circus, the mayhem and the invasion of privacy.

"Freya?" Connor calls. "Come down."

"Doesn't this scare you?" I call back.

"Not now, I have security to worry for me." He comes up the steps. "They're on their way." He takes a deep breath. "I used to have to run for my life, in the beginning. They'll…" He gestures to the crowd beyond the gate. "…move on once they have another story. There'll be another couple, another scandal, another sensation and they will chase that like a dog chasing a fox. Then your life will be back to normal."

"I don't even know what normal is anymore." I say quietly. "The lines are blurred. But this, this is crazy, I don't want this. I don't want people knowing my name. Why did you have to talk about me?"

"Because I didn't know where you were and I knew you'd read or see the interview. I had to let you know somehow that I was sorry."

"Sorry?" I mumble. "You could have just emailed."

"Let's get out of here." He says.

"How are we going to get past the crowd?" I look over at the throng. "There are so many people."

"We will go fast." Connor says taking my hand.

It doesn't take long for the extra security to arrive. Massive men built like tanks take up their places at various corners of Connor's property. We scream out of the garage and through the gates in Connor's Lamborghini sending the crowds diving for cover. In the rear view I can see them jostling each other to get to cars and vans in the vein hope of following us but Connor accelerates and we leave them far behind.

"Are you ok?" He asks.

"Yeah I guess." I reply. "So much for coming here to be incognito."

"I fed you to the wolves didn't I?" Connor sounds regretful.

"I gave them the dessert. I don't blame you Connor…"

"But?"

"I don't want this life. I don't want to be a prisoner in your home, unable to go anywhere because I'm Connor's Red. Not able to design anything because there will always be the worry that I made a successful collection because of you. I can't do this." I burst into tears. "Connor, I can't do this."

He screeches to a halt. "What are you saying?"

"I'm saying…I don't know what I'm saying…" I look unseeingly out of the window.

"Yes you do. You're ending things." His voice breaks. "Admit it, that's what you are doing."

"No…No I'm not."

"It certainly fucking sounds like it. One little hiccup and you jump ship."

"Hiccup? My face is all over the news. No one knew it was you. I didn't tell anyone, no one knew, now everyone knows, people I don't know knows, Jesus what are my parents going to say when naked pictures of me end up on their TV. This is a nightmare." I don't recognise my voice, hard and cold.

"So go home Freya, run back to the life that made you so happy." He says sneeringly.

I look at him. "Don't be a bastard."

"What do you expect? How long did you really think this would stay a secret for? Would you be staying home for parties and premieres and events that I have to attend? Would

I be still giving out the illusion of a single man, a blonde on my arm just to keep you out of the limelight? It doesn't work like that!"

"I didn't think…"

"Didn't think what? You didn't think this through?"

"I…"

"Did you think we'd stay in a cocoon forever?"

"I knew your life was crazy but…" I cover my face with my hands. "This is going to turn mine upside down."

"I thought I'd already done that." Connor tries to make a joke. "It will calm down you know. They won't be chasing our story for long."

I nod but I'm not convinced. Connor sighs and puts the car into drive and we continue towards the unknown.

***

Four hours later we are in the middle of nowhere. The sun beats down and below us sits the Pacific Ocean. The water is a deep blue, as flat as a millpond and reaches out to the navy line of the horizon. It is a scene of perfection. Connor unpacks the hamper we got from a store on the route and from it brings a blanket, a bottle of champagne, glasses and food.

I sit down on the blanket and watch as he sends the cork skyward.

Connor pours two fizzing glasses and hands me one before sitting down beside me. "Gorgeous view isn't it?" He comments.

I fleetingly wonder how many women he's brought here. "Yes, it's lovely." It seems so far away from the craziness, the noise and chaos of LA and the press determined to hunt us down.

"I came here a lot in the hazy days just to escape everything. Life was a big blur, days and nights all blended into each other, party after party, girl after girl, line after line. One day I thought my head was going to explode and I was close to being dropped from a movie that I was mid-way through shooting because I was being a total dick. Anyway I stopped here and had a massive come down and then decided to go to rehab. I've never brought anyone here, it was a little piece of something I could keep quiet about and when life went crazy I could escape here. Usually on a come down when I was feeling paranoid and insane!"

"Rehab twice?"

"Yeah, the final time was my last chance really. Thankfully it cured me and I realised how close I had come to losing everything. I got swept up in my own ego, believing everything the hangers on told me, believing when the girls told me how amazing I was and, I'm ashamed to say, believing in my own publicity. My head was in a total mess. Mona sorted me out, gave me a few kicks up the arse and even came to visit me when I was a shaking, vomiting lunatic. She's the only real friend I have here, the only person I can trust with my life. You're so lucky, to have the people in your life that will have your back whatever you do."

"Yeah I am. But you must have friends here, otherwise there'd be no reason to stay."

"My work is here and I have people I hang out with. I call them friends but they aren't in the real sense of the word. Those kind of friends are back in Ireland…"

"So why not go back and just fly in for work?"

"Because it wouldn't take long to be forgotten and I still love my work."

I lie back. The trees give us shade from the scorching sun and I close my eyes listening to the sounds of nature. Connor lies beside me and pulls me into him. I curl my body against his resting my head on his chest and marvel at how peaceful I feel being here. "Will you still move here? Regardless?" He whispers so softly I have to strain to hear.

"Yeah." I whisper back. "I just freaked a little."

Connor lifts my chin so my eyes meet his. "It won't always be like that." He kisses me lightly, brushing the hair from my face.

"What if it goes wrong?"

"Us?"

I nod.

"Then at least you can say you tried."

"Am I enough for you?" I ask quietly.

"Yes."

"Forever?"

"Yes."

"Make me believe that all this is real."

Connor kisses me, his tongue exploring my mouth. I reach for him but he raises my hands above my head and holds them to the earth, his hands clasping mine. He doesn't move focusing on the kiss as my body screams out for more. I grip his hands tightly urging my body up, wrapping my legs around him but Connor maintains his slow, steady kiss. "Please," I beg against his mouth. "Please Connor."

"What are you feeling?" He asks softly in my ear. "Tell me."

"I am feeling dizzy. My head is spinning. Please…Connor…please I need you."

"What else are you feeling?"

"What?" I don't understand his questions. Lust rages and I am blind to everything else – thought, the outside world, blind to all of it.

"You asked me to make you believe it's real. So tell me what you feel." Connor lays on me, his cheek against my cheek. "Tell me."

"I feel the grass against my back. It's soft but the earth below is crumbling and is sharp in places. I feel the air, it's warm and gentle on my skin, sometimes it feels cold but mostly warm. I feel your heart beating and the pulse in your neck against my shoulder. Your skin is so soft but your body is hard, your muscles are firm against my stomach. I feel my breasts under you, like peaks and my hips against your stomach. I feel a need for you deep inside, it's heavy and throbbing and in my head I feel a crazy, insane, frightening love for you that is beyond anything I've known before. I feel like we fit together and it scares me."

"If you can feel all that why do you need me to make you believe it's real?" Connor trails his hands down my arms and up into my hair. He looks down on me, his eyes brighter and bluer than the day. "It always has been real Red." He kisses me and I feel a tear roll down my face and dissipate under my chin. I pull him to me and kiss him back, urgently and with intensity. For now the future can wait.

***

We walk hand in hand through the forest. The trees hang overhead blocking the sun that can only peep through the breaks in the foliage. The birds sing loudly, their exquisite songs reaching out across the otherwise still wood. There is no one else here. Occasionally the undergrowth rustles but the quiet is a godsend. Here it's easy to forget the carnage we've just left behind and easy to forget what I will face when I get home.

Home.

I don't even know where that is anymore. I'm a temporary nomad, a woman with a purpose but no fixed address. Despite the blazing sun I find myself suddenly longing for the cottage that I've rented in Cornwall, away from the crowds and gossip and the famous boyfriend, somewhere to reflect and grow. Yet as much as the solitude calls to me I can't help wondering what effect the time apart will have on Connor and I. Our relationship has been for just three weeks. Such little time in the great scheme of things. He knows me better in this time than Will did in the whole fifteen years yet what I know about Connor is holding me back from fully committing to the idea of LA, despite what I said. What I saw this morning has frightened me. To become public property is not something I'd ever envisaged and while I want the world to know my name I want it to be on my merits, because I've made it, not because of who I choose to love.

"You look deep in thought." Connor comments. "Care to share."

"I was just thinking about the future. Cornwall, here, me, you…"

"And?"

I sigh. "It's all been so intense Connor, I've barely come up for breath. What happens when life keeps us apart."

"I'll be away for two months."

"Two months is a long time."

"Don't you trust me?"

"It's not about trust Connor. It's about time and distance and the craziness that follows you…"

"I'm not going to cheat."

"You may not but that mightn't stop the stories. I think I'm going to have to stay off the internet while you're away."

"You have to trust me Freya, and believe me. I don't want anyone else. Without being crude I've had more than my fair share of women and since I've met you I've realised how meaningless it all was. Yeah, it was an ego boost, to take a different woman to bed each night, but they always went to the press. Not so much fun." Connor kisses my hand. "I want to do Superman if I get the part then, maybe, I'll give it all up. Come to Cornwall with you, write my screenplay, or maybe we could move to Ireland and live by the sea. The future can be whatever we want it to be."

I nod and sit down on a fallen tree. "Yeah, I guess it can."

***

The crowds have swelled by the time we return to Connor's, even the BBC have arrived. We are news. I cover my face with oversized shades and look resolutely ahead as the security team line the drive so we can get into the property. Girls are screaming for Connor, holding banners aloft with graphic descriptions emblazoned across them, reporters holding cameras to take pictures through the car windows, the flashes blinding even with the sunglasses on. Connor's face is pale, fixed and hard as we slowly inch our way into the fortress that his home has now become.

We drive into the garage and the door closes behind us, shutting out the noise from the street. "That has to be the most surreal and scary thing I've ever experienced." I say turning to Connor. "There must be five hundred people out there."

"It's news." He says glumly. "We are news. Never mind the economic issues or the wars raging around the world or the desperate poverty, no one wants to read about that, they want the scandal and all this shit." He wrenches the door open. "If I didn't love what I do I'd be back in Ireland writing my screenplay, not living life like this. Acting is a rush, it's creating something to give someone a break from their normal life and that feels good. I like being the someone else I'm paid to be because, "he sighs and continues quietly. "Because until recently being someone else was better than being me." He gets out of the car and slams the door so loudly my ears ring in the silence of the garage. I feel shocked down to my core that he would say such a thing. That this beautiful man with the world at his feet could even think that being someone else was better. I scramble out of the car and follow the silent path up the steps and into the house.

"Connor?" I call crossing the hall to the kitchen. I find him standing by the window looking out across the ocean.

"I'm sorry." He mutters. "I am sorry that I told the world. I'm sorry that your life has been turned upside down."

"No more sorrys." I say wrapping my arms around his waist and leaning my head against his back. Tension radiates from him, his normal firm back now solid and bricklike. "It's not needed. You haven't done anything wrong. So you talked about your personal life, people do it all the time."

"I don't."

"But you have and we can deal with it. I'm going tomorrow and you're going to the other side of the world. By the time you come back it will all be back to normal. But Connor...why would you say that being someone else is better than being you? I don't understand. I thought you liked being you."

"Yeah, that's what most people think."

"Why don't you?"

"Because I've been a total shit. I've done unspeakable things, treated people in awful ways just because I could. Women have been picked up and discarded with no consideration...I've not been a very nice person."

I let my arms drop and move round to standing in front of him. I take hold of his face, a face screwed up in agony. "And what makes you any different to any other lad? So you've slept with women, made mistakes, broken friendships and perhaps have experienced attacks of guilt. Why would you think that means being someone else is better? You have had more opportunities but most men in their twenties think nothing of going out on the pull..."

"It matters now." Connor walks away from me.

"What does?" I ask.

"My past. It matters now."

"Why does it?" I ask him turning back to look at the ocean. There is nothing to see, just a still flat bed of water that glints under the fading sunlight.

"Because now there is you."

"You think your past will change how I feel?"

"When you find out about it all it will."

"Connor, I spent a whole day googling you! I've read it all. I don't care about the past, I care about the now and the future. I care that we're going to be apart when I don't want us to be, I care that my family and my friends at home are going to read me the riot act for keeping you a secret. I care that I long to be away from this madness but I want to take you with me. I care about what is going to happen when we're apart…"

"Because of my past." He says moodily.

"Because it feels too long already." I whisper.

"Come with me." He says so quietly I have to strain to hear him.

"No Connor, not yet."

"Then don't moan about the time." He snaps and stomps out of the room.

***

I leave Connor to brood and curl up on the sofa with my laptop. I can't help myself. The crowds outside the door and the chanting of Connor's name repetitively have become the itch that I can't scratch so I log onto the Daily Gossip and brace myself for the reports.

Pages are devoted to us. Entire transcripts of his recent interviews have been painstakingly typed up with detailed evaluation of what he's said. Enhanced photos of us in Mexico have been posted into a gallery and more recent ones of us leaving Connor's have been included. I shiver. My life under a microscope.

I click on the next page. *Connor's Scarlet Woman.* The headline screams.

Connor's Scarlet Woman.

Connor Robertson's mystery Red has been named as Freya Wood, Fashion Editor at R&R Magazine in London. Freya, at ten years older than the Oscar winning actor, shows all the signs of a cougar with her dangerous curves and glorious mane of auburn hair.

Freya is married to City lawyer William Walton-Willis but ever the modern woman she has retained her own name. What her husband thinks of all this is a mystery as he has so far declined to comment on the rumours surrounding his wife and the renowned womaniser. One can only imagine what it must be like for a hard working professional to see his wife cavorting so publically and so intimately with another man. What Freya would see in a multi-millionaire actor needs no explaining but what does he see in a woman ten years older who is moving past her prime....

I shut down the computer with a bang. "Total bullshit." I seethe.

"What's the matter?" Connor asks coming into the room with a contrite smile on his face.

"The assumptions." I tell him gesturing to the discarded laptop. "A cougar past my prime, or something like that."

"Growl for me baby..." Connor says kneeling down in front of me.

"You say the nicest things!"

Connor wraps his hands in my hair. Tugging my head backwards he kisses me with ferocity and I respond with equal desperation.

***

SATURDAY

The crowds of teenage girls outside are chanting Connor's name as he kisses away my tears. "Don't cry Red, don't cry. It's really just a couple of weeks."

"I know. Sorry." I cling to him and kiss his face, his mouth, his neck inhaling the musky scent of him, needing to memorise every part of him. I trace the outline of his face, the beautiful, perfect face. "I love you Connor."

"I love you too." He kisses me back. Gently. Lovingly. Our bodies fusing together – arms and legs entangled – being as close as two people can. Soft touches, tender embraces and lovemaking so heavenly that I see every speck of light dancing.

"You know something Red?" He holds me tight and kisses the top of my head.

"What?" I draw shapes on his chest with my finger.

"I can't help wondering if I'll come back to find you with William." He gives me a crooked smile. "It's not just you that worries Red. I've never worried before. I've never really cared before. I didn't like being away from you. I don't want to do it again."

"I'm never going back. Never. Life has changed, I've changed Connor and that's because of you. The confidence to chase my dreams is because of you. I am never going back to the Freya I was before you came along. I don't even know who she is!" I say fiercely.

"Why Cornwall though? Why not stay in London?"

"Because the house is sold and because I remember Cornwall as being a place of happy times, it's where we holidayed every year when I was a child. I am going to a seaside village that I've never heard of. I've rented a cottage on a short term lease. It's the right place for me to be to focus. You're away for two months, that's time for me to begin again."

"Begin again? This new beginning will include me I hope?"

"Of course including you!" The tears prickle my eyes again. "How can this have only been three weeks?"

"What's time?" Connor pulls me close to him. "It doesn't mean anything. You just have to know that all the while I'll be away I'll be waiting to come back. Come to your little cottage in Cornwall and hide…"

"Until Superman…"

"Then you'll come here and you can cook me dinner every night, be the little wifey…" Connor laughs as I reign down pillow blows onto him.

"Ow!"

"Little wifey!" I giggle as I swing the pillow around my head. "No chance!"

***

I cling to Connor. Tears flowing in a steady stream down my face. Security has arrived with the car to take me to the airport and onto a different life. Taking me away from him. He wraps his hands tightly in my hair and kisses my lips with such intensity I feel them burn. How can I be without him? There is so much uncertainty in this new future, and as much as I believe his love for me, there is also uncertainty about Connor. His past haunts me. I know it shouldn't. I know that the past should remain exactly that but as much as he worries about William so I worry about the bevy of beauties that will tempt him away. His tears mingle with mine, our kisses cover every part of the others face and the whispered declarations and promises are little rays of sunshine amongst the gloom.

"You need to go." He says.

"I need to go."

"Miss, we need to go." The burly security man says in a gruff voice.

"Ok." My voice breaks. "Ok, I'm ready."

Connor squeezes my hand as I break our embrace and wipe the tears from my face. "You've got everything?"

"Yeah I think so."

"Ticket?"

"In my bag."

"Passport?"

"With the ticket."

"And you'll call me when you get to London?"

"Yes."

"Miss?" The security guard chivvies me along.

"I'm coming." I reach up to Connor's face cupping his cheek in my hand and whisper. "I love you." His hand covers mine and just for a moment everything stops. Time freezes and we are lost in each other until a ringing phone breaks the spell.

"I'll see you in Cornwall." He says.

"I can't wait."

With one final glance I leave the house and follow the security guard to the idling car. I am grateful that they brought one with blacked out windows, now is not the time to be photographed. I sink into the leather seat and belting myself in I once again give into my tears.

The journey takes a little over an hour. I am met at first class departures by a porter who takes my luggage and escorts me through a private entrance to a personal check in desk. Once checked in I am shown through to the first class lounge which is like nothing I've seen before. The lounge is luxuriously decorated in deep purple and gold with a champagne bar and a fine dining area. My head spins as I take it all in.

"May I offer you a drink madam?" A purple suited waitress asks me. She is impeccably dressed and looks more like a model than a flight attendant. "Champagne or a cocktail?"

"Champagne please." I reply.

She gestures to one of the tables to the right of the bar. "Please take a seat and I shall bring it to you. Would you like a menu also?"

Right on cue my stomach makes a loud growl. "Yes please."

I set my laptop up on the table and switch it on, logging into the airlines Wi-Fi and opening up the internet. "Curiosity killed the cat," I remind myself as I click onto the Daily Gossip. It's not vanity driving me to see what has been reported, more interest in what is next to be considered news. I thank the waitress as she places a chilled glass of champagne and a menu beside me.

The reports delve further into my relationship with William. Photos from the first year at university have appeared along with various fashion events over the years. They've chosen the worst pictures of me with the writing of the article designed to make the reader question Connor's judgement.

I stop reading and shut the laptop with a bang and grumpily drink down my champagne. Past my prime…it's like reading all my insecurities spelt out in black and white for the world to see. It's strange to be on the receiving end of articles like this when I am guilty as the next person for devouring gossip and rumours about celebrities. Except I'm not a celebrity. The only crime I've committed is to fall in love with someone so famous that everything he does is news. I wonder what I am due to face when I get home. Will my friends understand my reasons behind my deceit or will they think so little of me that our friendship will be a tattered heap on the floor. I order another glass of champagne and an English breakfast and sit stewing until my flight is called.

***

I sleep through most of the flight home but nothing could ever prepare me for the scenes outside my house as the airline car pulls up. Hundreds of photographers jostle for space giving me no way in, aiming their cameras in through the windows, blinding me with the flashes. I cover my face with my hands and in a panicked voice I speak to the driver. "Please could you take me to Valentine Avenue in Islington?" As quick as lightening he pulls away from the crowds outside my house and speeds off towards the High Street. Mum and Dad will know what to do.

It's not much different at my parents. Photographers and journalists waiting intently for something to happen crowd the pavements. Mum has kept the curtains closed and I feel breathless with guilt that they have been subjected to this insanity.

"For fucks sake," I grumble through dry lips. "I'm so sorry please will you take me to Charlwood Terrace in Kentish Town?" *Please be home Imogen,* I beg silently.

My prayers are answered. She opens the door and I crumple into her welcoming hug.

"Is it true?" She asks incredulously.

"It depends what you have heard."

"You and Connor Robertson?"

"Yes." I burst into tears. "But he has to go to Australia Immy and now there are press outside my house and my parent's house…"

"What happened to three weeks in Mexico?"

"The press happened. One of the guests told them." I groan. "I need to ring Mum and Dad, they won't have any idea why."

"I'll get you the phone."

"Thank you." Imogen passes me the phone and I dial the number with shaking hands. "Mum?"

331

Mum's worried voice is loud down the phone line.

"Freya, Freya darling what is going on? There are people outside my house wanting to know about you and some actor. Dad has shut himself in the shed and is refusing to come out. I am supposed to be meeting Vera for coffee and I can't get out of the door! What has been happening? Are you home?"

"I got back this morning but I'm at Imogen's now. There are people outside my house too so I came to yours then to Imogen's. I have been seeing an actor, a very famous one but I thought it was a secret. Someone has told the press and this all started in Mexico but then I moved to LA for a couple of days for safety. I am so sorry that they are on your doorstep, I don't know what to do. I'm so sorry Mum…" I burst into tears.

"Well you needn't worry about your Dad and I, our concern is for you. We will go about our business and ignore the door steppers. Do you want Dad to come round and get you?"

"No, because it's mayhem at mine. I will ring Henry and see if Fred's security can come and get me."

"If they can't then you must ring Dad."

"I will."

"So is this it with William, are you over him?" Mum's voice rings with concern.

"Yes mum, even if Connor hadn't come along I would have got to this decision eventually. He is not my one forever. I just want him and Lexi to be happy and for us all to move on."

"What about this actor chap then?"

"He's the one. The one. The one who makes me feel complete."

"Are you his one?"

"He says so."

"That's good enough then. I must go darling I want to try and get to Vera's. She's made lemon drizzle cake!"

"Ok Mum. Say hi to Vera...and Mum?
"Yes?"
"Thanks."

I hang up the phone and Imogen hands me a tissue for the tears that begin to fall.

"Do you want to talk about it?" She asks kindly.

"I wouldn't know how to begin."

"I presume Connor is the mystery man you told us about? Why didn't you tell us Freya? Did you not trust us?"

"Yes. I didn't want to sell him out Im. I didn't tell anyone who it was and I hope you all can forgive me for that..."

"There's nothing to forgive." She says smiling kindly. "We're your friends and it will take a lot more than an affair with a Hollywood superstar to piss us off!"

"Thanks." I sigh. "It's been more intense, more exciting and more passionate than the whole relationship I had with William and I've never felt so strongly for anyone ever. He makes me feel complete. That I am enough and that my dreams aren't foolish but something to aim for. For someone so young he's incredibly wise. He wants me to go to LA once he's back from Asia."

"LA? Shit Freya, LA is too far. Cornwall is bad enough."

"That's the only option if I want to be with him."

"Do you love him?"

"Yes."

"Does he love you?"

"He says so and I do believe him but...all those women Immy, all those beautiful, famous women..."

"Those beautiful, famous women lasted a day..."

"That's what he said."

"Freya, I've seen the photos, it is quite obvious there is more to you two than a cheap fling. He's never talked about anyone ever and he told the whole world about you. That has to say something, surely. Freya, sweetie, you are far more beautiful than any of those plastic Barbie dolls..."

"He may not think so when he has a space in his bed in Australia. Out of sight, out of mind Imogen. "

"That's crap and you know it! You're being silly."

"Yeah." I take a deep breath. "and now I have the issue about getting into my house. I guess I ring the police…or Henry."

"Henry?"

"Friends in high places who have access to security!" My mobile rings and I answer the withheld number. "Hello?"

"Hi Red"

"Connor!"

"I wanted to make sure you got home safely."

"I got to London. I'm hiding at Imogen's, I can't get near my own door because there are crowds of people outside my house!"

"I'll get some security for you. What address are you at?"

I give him Imogen's address and he rings off without a goodbye. Imogen makes a cup of tea and sticks a packet of biscuits in the middle of the table. "Do you want to start at the beginning?" She asks. "Or wait for Erin?"

"I'd better wait for Erin, she'll only be pissed off if she thinks she's the last to know!"

My phone rings again. "Connor?"

"A security team will be round for you in about thirty minutes."

I breathe a sigh of relief. "Thank you."

"What are your plans? Are you leaving for Cornwall soon? You've only been gone a day and I miss you already."

"I'm going to go tomorrow or Monday. It depends when I can get out of the front door. I just don't want them following me…"

"And you'll send me the address?"

"Of course!"

"Keep the security for as long as you need them. They will get you where you need to go. I love you Red."

"I love you too."

He rings off and Imogen looks at me with envious eyes. "I wish he loved me too!"

I giggle. "I'm sure he will!"

"Yeah but not in the way I've fantasised!"

We both laugh and open the biscuits.

"Shall I come home with you?" Imogen asks dunking her biscuit into her tea.

"Don't mess your day up, I'll be fine. I'll have an escort and it saves you having anyone camping on your doorstep!"

"I'll come round later with food and Erin. I'm sure she'll cancel whatever for a chance to be in the paper!"

I laugh. Erin has always wanted to be famous but instead works as an agent for theatre actors. "That would be great. Can I ask for curry? I could just eat a curry!"

"Curry it is."

***

The security arrives for me - three big burly bouncers that look as though they have stepped off the World's Strongest Man competition. They say very little but their presence is enough to calm my nerves. I cover my face with large sunglasses and wear my hair loose. Somehow they manage to barge their way through the dense crowd to get me into the house. They check my apartment and advise me to lock all the doors and windows.

"A prisoner in my own home," I comment wryly.

"Something like that," one of them replies gruffly.

I close all the curtains and unpack the shopping I had the foresight to buy before I was collected. It feels eerie being home knowing cameras are poised outside of my door. I wonder what my neighbours think.

I put on my holiday clothes to wash and run a hot bath. After a ten hour flight and three hours waiting to get home it is much needed. I set music to play and sink into the hot, soapy water that seems to immediately melt away my stress. I think about Connor. I think about his smile, his eyes gazing into mine, the soft lilt of his Irish accent when he speaks. I think about the passing of time and how the next two months may as well be eternity regardless of the new adventure on my horizon. I wonder what he is doing right now and the pang of missing him hits me hard. I go over and over my decision to move to LA, questioning everything until I finally realise that it is where my happy ever after will be.

***

"So..." says Erin pouring the wine, "Connor Robertson hey? I think you'd better start at the beginning!"

I take a deep breath and let it out slowly. "It wasn't supposed to happen...well perhaps the one night but it just carried on. Snatched moments here and there. Nothing was ever really planned we just ended up seeing each other. It never felt forced more that something, or someone, kept guiding us to each other. I kept telling him it was as though we were in a game but we weren't playing it. That someone else had the dice. It was always fireworks though, we were two very different people with very different thoughts but somehow it just brought us closer. Then he came to Mexico but we were invaded by the press so I went to LA for a few days. And now I have the paparazzi camping on my door step."

"Why didn't you tell us? Did you not trust us?" Erin asks the same question as Imogen did earlier and I feel guilty when I see the hurt in her eyes.

"It wasn't like that. I suppose I just wanted to keep him a secret. He liked that I didn't know or care who he was and I liked the excitement and the intrigue. It was exciting you know," I say looking at them, "the kind of exciting you read about in books. It doesn't happen in real life…."

"It happened to you."

"Yes it did and it was too amazing to put into words."

"Do you think he's the one?" Imogen asks.

"It certainly feels like it." I tell her.

"You thought that about William," Erin said.

"I know I did. I think I just got swept along by Will and the idea of being Mrs Middle Class. I didn't ever get it right though, did I? In his family's eyes I could never rise above my station, regardless of how well I did professionally. How did I not notice that everything about Will and I was wrong? Why did you not tell me?" I grin. "With Connor…well he just doesn't care about my past or my failings or that my ambitions could go tits up, he seems to be behind me completely…"

"And he wants her to move to LA!" Imogen interrupts.

"LA?" Erin shrieks. "Can I come too? I'm sick of the rain and the London men and my life…"

"You love your life!" I laugh.

"Yeah but I think I'd rather have yours at the moment. Connor Robertson! You are the luckiest lady alive. Tell me, is he as good in bed as I imagine him to be?"

"Better!"

"Oh!" She breathes. "I don't think I can speak through jealousy. You do realise that I loved him first and therefore I stake a bigger claim!"

"I saw him before you. I took you to see *Glory Days* before you even knew who he was! Oh do you remember his bottom…filled the whole screen with its peachy yumminess. I dribbled for days after! In fact, it's still my wallpaper at work!" Imogen says excitedly.

"This is weird!" I cringe.

"I saw your boyfriend's bottom before you!" Erin sing-songs laughing. "That means I love him more than you." Her face falls. "Are you really going to LA? It's like a million miles away."

"Connor has invited me to go. He said he'd set up a studio for me and it's closer to Mexico."

"Mexico? You've just been."

"I met a waitress at the hotel who took me to a market near her village. The fabrics were one of a kind, bespoke and just amazing. She was lovely, ambitious and focused and just like us when we were eighteen. I want to help her get to college, she wants to do a hotel management course and wants to help her family improve their existence. Mexico is so poor. I was thinking that she could work for me, buy fabrics for me and I would pay her which she could use towards college. It would save me so much time sourcing material and make a difference to someone who has made a difference to me. That's if it all works out."

"It will work out. I have every faith. But I can't help wondering…"

"Wondering what?" I ask.

"I wonder what William will say when he finds out."

"I couldn't care less." I reply and I fill them in on our last meeting.

***

SUNDAY

"You've been sleeping with Connor Robertson!" William rages slamming a tabloid newspaper on the table. "You were naked in the sea with him and the pictures are all over the press! My god Freya what the fuck have you been playing at?" Without giving me a chance to answer he yells, "and now I can't even get through my own front door because of all the people outside." He is shaking and I can't help it, I start to laugh. "What the fuck is so funny Freya?"

"'You were naked in the sea with him'" I mimic. "Well William when you have sex with people generally you are naked."

"All the shit you gave me and you are just as bad…"

"I am nowhere near as bad as you. I didn't cheat on you. I didn't force myself on you, you low life shit. I think you conveniently forget all that you've done, William. I think this is convenient for you, me taking the heat of you…oh poor William, his wife ran off with an actor. I am not taking the rap for you! You did this…Have you brought the divorce papers for me to sign?"

"No…I don't want to divorce. I'm here to ask you to forgive me. I forgive you. I want us to try again…"

"What?" I shriek. "Have you not heard anything I've said? Ever? You left me Will, I've moved on. I don't want to be married to you and what on earth do you have to forgive me for you condescending arse?"

"Look Freya, I know I made a mistake and what I did recently was totally out of order but it's always been you and me. I am happy to ignore this dalliance and my name being dragged through the mud to get our marriage back on track. Lexi just isn't you…"

I turn from him. I wonder if the desire I have to punch his handsome face is rational or normal. "She never was me. You lied to me and cheated on me. Everything that has happened has made me realise how incompatible we were. Go home to Lexi, you made your bed now you have to lie in it. I don't want you, my life has changed and I want the future I can see in my head. The future that you always put down, the future that you told me I was never good enough to achieve. Well, I am good enough to achieve my dreams and now I have someone in my life that supports those dreams. It's what I deserve Will and to be honest, you don't deserve me but I have always deserved better that you and finally I have it."

"For how long?" He hisses at me, his face slowly turning a worrying shade of purple. "How long until he moves on from you? I know all about him. I've read google. What makes you think you are so special? This is your last chance to give us another go, when he dumps you I won't be around."

I explode. "What would make you think I'd even want you to be around? You are a vile, revolting cretin Will and I don't even know who you are. You make me sick. Sick! I would rather be single for the rest of my life than be with you. There is nothing about you that is remotely appealing to me. I don't even know why I stayed married to you for so long. You have been nothing but a patronising snob who just put me down. Give me the divorce papers so that I can free myself from you because now I am finally happy I can see how unhappy I was with you. Go home Will, go back to Lexi and quite frankly you can burn in hell for all I care." I storm out of the kitchen slamming the door behind me. My whole body shakes with anger, rage flowing through me like the eruption of Vesuvius, burning away what remains of the old Freya.

***

Having packed the final personal items I sit on the sofa with a chilled glass of wine mindlessly flicking through the TV channels. "A thousand channels and nothing to watch." I grumble. Storage has been arranged and the removal men are due in the morning, all thanks to Henry, my life saver. I have emailed Will, telling him to forward anything of importance to Henry who will send it on. I don't want Will to know where I am. I want nothing more to do with the man I have spent fifteen years with. For a moment I mourned a wasted life but without Will there would have been no Henry, Carrie or Connor. A life without them would be a wasted life. I finally settle on the Entertainment Network, a channel dedicated to gossip and watch a segment on the Kardashian's opening a store somewhere in the US. Theirs is a life under the microscope and I wonder how they manage the lack of privacy until it occurs to me that they have made their fortune from selling themselves.

I nearly choke when my house appears on the show.

"Scenes of chaos," the bleached, lifted and very skinny television reporter says, "from outside the home of Freya Wood rumoured girlfriend of Connor Robertson…" cue photo of Connor at the Oscars, "who has been in hiding since news of their unconfirmed romance was leaked to the press." The reporter holds up some tabloid newspapers. "Lots of photos of the couple in the papers recently looking very…um…together!" She smiles devilishly. "One can't help but feel slightly jealous. We've just seen a man we can only assume is her husband William…" a photo of us on our wedding fills the screen and I spill most of the wine in my lap.

"Shit." I leap out of the seat. "How did they get hold of that? Shit!" I wipe myself down keeping both eyes firmly on the TV.

"…leaving the house not looking very happy." The reporter continues. Footage of William, his face apoplectic, pushing his way through the hordes is relayed.

"What husband would be happy?" The brunette anchor on the red sofa asks.

"Quite! He declined to comment but one can only assume that his ego has taken a battering."

"Was Connor the reason their marriage looks to be all but over?"

"That's unconfirmed but how many women would say no to Connor?"

"Not me!" The brunette giggles flicking her hair over her shoulder.

"Nor me!" The blonde grins. "He is every woman's fantasy…"

"Any word from Connor?" The anchor woman asks from the comfort of the red studio sofa.

"None as yet. We don't know if he is aware of the furore in London. Damien in Los Angeles may know more. Damien?" The screen splits into three as Damien Gallagher joins the women.

"Connor was seen leaving his home in Malibu this morning and was driven to Lion Brothers studio in West Hollywood to, we believe, have a second reading for the part of Superman in the new production opposite the unnamed actresses lined up for Lois Lane. He hasn't yet returned to his home and his whereabouts is currently unknown. It has been suggested that he may be in one of the Beverley Hills hotels with his management waiting to fly to Australia for the Premiere of his latest movie but this is, as yet, unconfirmed."

"So what do we know about Freya, affectionately known as Red?"

"Freya works for R&R Magazine and is highly regarded in fashion circles…" cue photos of me at fashion week and society events in London looking, I am slightly mollified to see, pretty good! "She is thirty-five and many of the designers request her personally to report on their catwalk shows."

"She is very beautiful," the anchor woman says, "very stylish."

"Yes, Freya dresses her figure extremely well and has a very good eye for fashion. She may not wear current fashions but she certainly has an eye for marketing them." Up flash lots of my pages from R&R. I feel uplifted by the positive vibes I am gaining from the TV personalities.

"Any sign of her at home?"

"Not yet. The curtains have been shut since she returned from LA." The press photos of Connor and I pop up like a slide show.

The anchor woman giggles. "It looks as though they had a good time."

My cheeks burn as the moonlit swim photo is broadcast to millions of people. *Please don't let my parents be watching.*

"Every woman's fantasy," the reporter smiles.

"Any other comments from LA, Damien?"

"We will update you as soon as we have news on Connor."

"So..." the kindly faced anchor woman turns to the camera, "Hollywood Royalty meets the girl next door. I for one am very excited for Connor, I have interviewed him on a number of occasions and he is charming. If the rumours are true she is a lucky lady. Back after this short break..."

I switch the television off. I don't want to see any more gossip or hear anything else about myself or Connor. Enough is enough. I jump as the ringing phone breaks the silence.

"Hello?"

"Darling what a total nightmare, how are you holding up?"

"Hello Carrie."

"I thought you were in Mexico and then I just saw the TV. Will looked rather pissed off." Carrie laughs merrily. "It's about time he got his comeuppance the little shit."

"Yeah, we had a row earlier. He was moaning that he couldn't get in but I've been a prisoner since I got back and

I'm desperate to get out of the house. Life has been far from normal recently." I laugh.

"How do you go back to normal after Connor Robertson?" Carrie muses.

"I've no idea Carrie!"

"Well you are one very lucky lady, he's divine."

"Yeah, he is. I am lucky, very lucky."

"I hope it works out for you darling. You deserve every ounce of happiness there is. When are you going to Cornwall? Has that all moved now that you're back?"

"I want to go tomorrow. It depends if I can get out of the front door. Connor has organised security for me but there are no guarantees that the press won't follow me to Cornwall and that's the last thing I need. They're even camping outside my parent's house, it's utterly surreal."

"If you need anything at all you ring me ok? Even if it's just to bring some groceries around!"

"I will Carrie thank you."

"I expect your first article at the end of next month."

I laugh. "So this was a work call disguised as concern for my wellbeing?"

"Damn it you saw right through me." Carrie tinkles. "I mean it, if you need anything you ring me."

"I will and thank you Carrie."

She harrumphs. "I want you back at your desk in twelve months!"

"No promises."

"Bugger." She rings off and I giggle.

I can hear the press outside jostling for space. Any minute now I will wake up and I'll be in bed with William about to go to work with the suggestion of dinner in town at the close of the working day. I blink my eyes a few times and pinch my forearm. "Ow! I'm definitely awake!" Loneliness seeps in slowly. The house feels so empty and devoid of any personality, everything now packed in boxes waiting collection. Any sound I make echoes around the bare room until it begins to drive me crazy. The conversations from outside filter in and the laughter feels like nails scratching down my skin. I want to be out now, away, moving forward, not sitting here in limbo, the past not quite gone but the future not in focus.

For something to do I stand under a scorching shower as trepidation seeps out of me. If it was a colour it would be a murky swampy green covering me from tip to toe. I scrub myself vigorously perhaps subconsciously, trying to wash away my worries. Ten weeks ago William left me. How have I got to now? Press outside my door, an affair with Connor all over the media and my character assassinated? I laugh out loud. It's preposterous. This could be within the pages of a best seller, a fairy tale of sorts with some amazing sex thrown in for a zing. *Freya's Story – the secret life of me.* I giggle.

The water cools so I climb out of the shower and wrap the one remaining bath towel around me, fastening it securely. I wish I was at my parents, cocooned in their safe, warm home, Mum making me hot chocolate milk like she did when I was a child, Dad reading me a story of children who set off on wild adventures over the moors with their dog. I can't think about being with Connor. The two months I am facing without him hover over me like an executioners guillotine over my head and the silence of the house only serves to reinforce the forlornness. I need to get out here. Be away, somewhere where I can be anonymous, somewhere where no one knows my name. With inspired speed I pack up my case and quickly shove in my remaining personal items. Checking my purse contains my ID and credit cards I take a final walk around the home I have known for ten years, the home that once contained my dreams and hopes and the ambitions that it has taken me too long to put into place.

It was happy here once. When the happiness ceased I don't quite know but I suspect long before Lexi and Will, long before I even realised that something was missing from my life. I can't regret William but now I feel only pity for him. He is not a bad person just misguided and as I begin to leave my former home I wish him and Lexi a good future. I will always miss her, miss the person with the key to my history who laughed and cried alongside me, covered for me in school and supported me until her feelings for William took over. Maybe I just need to be grateful, without her I would be stuck in the rut that I failed to notice for so long. Without her there would be no Connor.

***

My hands shake violently as I unlock the door. The press outside have fallen silent in anticipation of my exit. I look the best I can…my hair is knotted in a chignon on top of my head, large sunglasses protect me and my executive costume of slim fitting white shirt, grey mid-length pencil skirt and killer red heels with matching red bag hopefully give the impression that I am confident, sassy and unfazed by their presence on my doorstep . I am terrified.

So terrified I can barely breathe. My heart is threatening to beat out of my chest and my knees are visibly knocking together. I have to keep swallowing down the acidic nausea that rises from my squirming, churning stomach. "You can do this Freya," I whisper over and over to myself. "You'll be ok. One foot in front of the other." I grip my car keys tightly, holding onto the small suitcase like it's a comfort blanket. "It's just a few feet to the road. Come on you can do this."

I open the door and step out blinded by the flashes of the press cameras. I keep my eyes down, pulling the door tightly behind me. I try to move through the crowd but they swarm me. I can't step forward. They are calling my name, shouting out questions as they close in around me. "I can't breathe," I cry out panicked. "Please step back you are scaring me." I push out with my hands but I can't make myself heard. I fight my way through but there are too many people and the lack of air makes me dizzy. I can't control the alarm I feel and I can't see beyond the flashing lights. The black terror begins to engulf me until I hear my name.

"Freya, you're safe." The male voice says.

"Bob?"

"Yes. We're here."

"Oh thank god." I cling to him gratefully.

Bob helps me up and flanked by Otis and John we move through the crowd my car.

I burst into tears.

"It's ok Freya, you're safe now." Bob says. "We saw the report and figured it would just get worse and we promised Connor we'd stay nearby."

"I am so grateful," I sob. "I have never been so scared. I thought they were going to crush me."

"Where are you going to?"

"My parents first then onto Cornwall."

"Otis will drive you in your car, John and I will be behind you."

"Thank you." I hand my keys to Otis who unlocks the car and loads my case into the boot. I keep my head down, the bright lights of the flashes are blurring my vision and I just don't want to see my house empty and dark. I send a quick text to Henry, Imogen and Erin telling them my plans as Otis drives me off. His enormous bulk makes me feel safe, no harm can come to me surrounded by this much muscle and just for a moment I allow myself to wish for Connor, that he were here and I wasn't doing this alone.

***

"I have something for you." Mum says as she leads me into the kitchen. I sit down at the table.

"Where's Dad?"

"In the shed where he has been all day. I'm not sure he's very comfortable with the images of you in the paper and on TV, you know what he's like, he still thinks you're five with pigtails and pretty pink dresses. He'd rather not know that you've been having a wonderful time with a very handsome man!"

I redden. "I was hoping he wouldn't see anything."

"It's hard to avoid, especially as the press are making no move to leave the pavement. I don't mind so much, I'm quite enjoying feeling like royalty every time I want to pop out. It is certainly making things interesting. How was Mexico?"

"It was beautiful but very short. I should still be there."

"I realise that Freya, there'll be other times." Mum switches on the kettle and busies herself making a pot of tea. She opens the cupboard beside the fridge and retrieves the biscuit tin. It's the same tin she's had since Christmas 1983 except the picture of Santa has faded but the dents tell a story of every time I took a biscuit without asking. Tea made she takes an envelope from a drawer and sits down facing me. "This is for you." Mum says handing me the envelope.

"What is it?"

"Open it and see." She gives the tea a stir then pours out two cups adding milk and sugar. I rip open the envelope finding a cheque inside. I gasp when I see the amount.

"How…?"

"Do you remember I told you about the musician in Liverpool and the letters he wrote?"

"Yes."

"Well," mum says matter-of-factly, "I sold them to a collector."

"But Dad…"

"I told him everything." She tells me taking a sip of the tea and wincing. "That's too hot! I told him the story and we decided to sell the letters, use some of the money to pay off the mortgage and you know he's always wanted to go to Graceland so we've booked that and the rest is for you."

"I can't take this. It's too much."

"Better now than when we're dead and you have to give the government half of it. It's for you to use for your dresses Freya, use it to live on so you don't have to worry about money. It's not as much as we'd like to have given you but…"

"It's more than enough but Mum…if you keep it you could both give up work."

"We don't want to. Dad likes being busy, can you imagine what a nightmare he'd be if he was here all the time, and I like my job. I know it's only a part time receptionist job but I like it, it suits me. The money is for you. We've never been able to spoil you, never been able to whisk you away to far flung destinations or buy you the things we knew you wanted but we could never afford. We are proud of you, you are our daughter, Freya. We have watched you grow into a woman I could only dream of being. You have made every little sacrifice worth it for us, you never once complained that your school friends had ponies and cars and all the material things we could never give you. So this is for all those years when you went without…"

"I don't think I did go without…" I say choked.

"Freya." Mum wraps her hand around mine pushing the cheque into my palm. "You are to take it. I don't want to hear any more about it."

"But I have money from the house…"

"That you will need for another house unless you are planning on moving in with this Connor chap. Even so, it's a good thing for a woman to have a rainy day pot, you never know when you may need it. Take the money Freya, spend it wisely, make your dresses, you have always been so talented."

"Thank you." I whisper.

"Pah! It's nothing. Now tell me, just how many of the rumours are true?"

***

It's dusk when I leave my parents, the cheque safely zipped up inside my bag. I feel a wrench leaving them, taking the money that could make so much difference to them. But I understand their pride and determination and I would not offend them by refusing. Otis, Bob and John escort me to a service station half way along the M4 and bid me good luck. I buy a coffee and change out of my smart attire in favour of loose trousers and a tee shirt. The further I travel from London the more the weight seems to lift. I start to laugh, a laugh that comes from deep within my stomach. I am free. The future is mine. I drive the whole way, stopping once for a bland tasting service station meal and arrive at the cottage in the dark of night, the stars clear and bright above me.

I retrieve the key from under the door mat and let myself in. The landlord has kindly left tea and coffee, bread, butter and jam all of which looks homemade but I climb the spiral staircase and on finding the small bedroom I fall into an exhausted sleep.

***

October

FRIDAY

Ivor, the small fishing village to which I came has welcomed me with open arms, the villagers arriving one by one over the first few days introducing themselves and bringing homemade or home grown food and local drink that I am still getting through. Their offers of help were genuine as were their invitations to any social occasions that have taken place. I've been to a wedding, a christening and three school plays. My London self laughs at the provincial life I am living but everything about it makes me feel focused and alive. It was the right move at the right time and the drama of London seems so far away. I often wonder if I dreamt so much of what has happened to me. None of it seems real until Connor rings and I am elevated to the dreamland again.

I miss him. It's a painful ache deep within my chest, an ache that scratches at my heart each time it pumps. I watch his interviews via the internet and he talks of me, of us, in such a way that there can be no doubt of his feelings towards me, but I still miss him. Despite the thousands of miles that have separated us Connor and I have remained very much a couple.

Connor.

The love of my life.

In twenty four hours he will be here with me, in my little house - the tiny one bedroomed cottage with open fires and temperamental heating and the glorious views across the water that I have come to call home. Each morning I awaken to the calls of the seagulls shouting down to the fishermen out in their boats. When the sun shines the cove is glorious but when the storms come I can spend hours watching the swirling, crashing angry waves battering the pebbles on the beach. The purple, grey sky never ceases to amaze and the dominant, angry weather always shows me the miracle of nature.

Most days I walk along the beach seeking out a colour or shape for the next design. When the tide is out it's possible to walk around the rocks, past the caves that have been carved out by the elements and onto the next village, another that time has forgotten. Since being here my mind has stilled, the grief I held onto about Lexi and Will has faded to nothing because it no longer matters. It doesn't define me, who I am now is exactly who I want to be. Free. Content. Happy. In love. Living my dream.

The sea air this morning is brisk and biting. Around me the dramatic coastline seems imposing, closing in as the weather begins to change, the blue sky being cast aside as the clouds roll in, covering the landscape with an eerie hue. Despite the ever changing climate it was good to move here. Stories of old are whispered amongst the cliffs and through the overhanging trees. Living here has inspired me and driven me on, with confidence in my ability growing more and more each day.

I turn my collar up against the chilly wind glancing up at the stormy sky that has begun to darken and I walk quickly back across the beach towards the cottage. I wave to the fishermen bringing the boats up high onto the beach and who carefully unload their catch into big blue bins. They work quickly, the waves beginning to churn as the wind picks up, screaming around the cliffs as I hurry home.

The gate squeaks as I open it, pushing is hard against the rising wind. My hands, now cold, struggle to get the key into the lock as the heavens open and the rain falls crossly to the ground. I switch on the kitchen light and shiver. The cottage is freezing. I shake off my coat and hang it over the back of the chair and pull off the bright pink wellies that I favour for beach walking. Henry would faint if he saw me in them. Giggling I take a photo of my padded raincoat and wellies, side by side, and text it to him.

I boil the kettle on the stove and crank up the heat on the thermostat. When my coffee is ready I sit in the window and look out to sea opening the biscuit tin with the farmer's wife's shortbread inside. Breaking off a piece I put my feet up on the window sill and watch the storm. Lightening flickers ice white across the sky turning the deep purple to a sinister lilac hue. The waves, white tipped and fierce, smash down onto the beach splashing the pavement and then the thunder comes. Great bangs of energy ricochet around the cove rattling the windows and seeming to incense the sky further. I shiver and wrap a blanket around my shoulders getting up from my seat to unplug my electrics before resuming my front row seat. The overhead lights flicker and die out along with all the remaining power so I remain in the eerie darkness as the storm rages.

I light some candles and move from my seat in the window back to the tiny little kitchen that overlooks the cliffs. The colours – inky blues, mulberries and flaming crimsons – are intoxicating my senses. I want to recreate the patterns I see and I feel tiny little bubbles of excitement begin to burst in my stomach. Frantically I look for my sketch pad and pencil and by the light of the flickering candles, as the storm rages on, I draw. As my designs take shape I draw inspiration from the pounding weather and create beautiful dresses. I lose track of time as I sketch, discarding some, developing others. I am like a woman possessed as the ideas flow through my pencil and onto the paper until I break from drawing and begin to mix paint colours trying to re-capture the sky.

I don't know when the storm passed or when sunshine came but in front of me are pages and pages of designs, splashed with colour and I know they are exceptional.

I unpeel myself from the chair and feeling stiff I do some quick stretches before turning on the lights. The storm has lasted hours and the beach is littered with debris thrown up by the waves. Each time the weather changes I'm ever hopeful that I'll look out to find a wreck lying on the beach, like something out of an Enid Blyton novel, full of mystery and wonder. Mostly, however, its seaweed and driftwood that lies upon the beach. I yawn then jump as the computer starts ringing.

"Hi Erin." I say loudly into the speaker.

"Hi Freya." She looks sharply at the screen. "What is going on with your hair?"

I reach up to feel the birds nest sitting on top of my head. "I've been drawing. We had a storm…"

"Another one?"

"It's the coast!"

"Are you going to come home soon?" She asks grumpily.

"Not yet." I yawn and reach for the cold coffee beside the computer. "I need to finish my designs first. And Connor is coming tomorrow…"

"But how are you managing? Do they even have shoe shops?"

"It's not a desert island Erin, it's Cornwall."

"Yes but Cornwall is all sticks of rock and King Arthur."

"No it's not Erin! Which you'd know if you came to visit, it's beautiful here and the town just along the coast has the most amazing boutiques!"

"However you try to flower it up Freya, it still sounds like hell my idea of hell."

"We do have the internet you know, I am still shopping at all my usual haunts." I grin at the camera. Erin looks so serious.

"Shopping for what? Wax jackets and a flat cap?"

"Hardly! I may have moved but I've not left my style behind."

"You tell me this while you're sitting in pyjamas?"

"It's a onesie and it's cold. I'm comfy."

Erin purses her lips. "In London we have such a thing as central heating and since when did you put comfort over style? Hasn't the novelty of the back of beyond worn off yet? We miss you. Everyone misses you."

"I miss you all too," I reply swallowing down a lump, "but it's going really well. I've been working really hard and it's all starting to take shape. I am so excited."

Erin says nothing.

"Erin? What's the matter?"

"Have you been burgled?"

"No! Why?"

"What is all that crap I can see in the background?"

"New fabric that Christina has sent over."

"You need a cleaner!"

"I clean!" I say laughing at her disgust. "Sometimes! I'm busy!"

"So am I but my house doesn't look like landfill!" Erin pokes her tongue out.

"It will be tidy by the morning." I lean back in the chair while the hyperactive butterflies in my belly start their excited dance.

"I suppose you can't let Connor think you've become a slob!"

I smile. "After a relationship on Skype for two months, during which time I looked more or less like this I think he knows what I'm like!"

"And he still wants you?"

"Apparently!"

"What is wrong with the world?" Erin laughs and I pull a stern face.

"Erin you're mean!" I huff.

"No, not mean just jealous!" She grins. "What are you doing tonight? Shaving from the neck down?"

"Nope all nicely waxed! I am going to the pub!"

"There's a pub? Will you be drinking ale out of a mug?" She asks grinning.

"No, probably gin and tonic out of a tea cup whilst dressed in my hot pink onesie."

"Classy. Come home."

"One day!"

"One day is not soon enough and then you'll be jetting off to LA to live out some Lois Lane fantasy with Connor…my life sucks." Erin grumbles and I smile gently.

"Erin, your life doesn't suck. You have the busiest life of anyone I know and you love your life. You will meet Mr Right, you just need to be in the right place at the right time."

"You think?"

"I know so. Things happen when you least expect them too."

"I guess. I'm going now Freya, I need to drown my single sorrows with Imogen and I'm going to pretend I won't know how you will be spending the weekend!"

"Erin, jealousy is a terrible emotion…"

"Jealous? It goes beyond jealous! So far beyond there isn't actually a word for it! Imogen and I are going to Cullen's tonight in the vague hope of meeting handsome, single, rich, classy men!"

I laugh. "Good luck with that! Keep me posted!"

"Love you."

"Love you." I sign off skype and look at the chaos that surrounds me. Easels hold designs, mannequins hold half made dresses and in one corner of the room lay piles of fabrics, each sourced for me by Christina. It's a work room and I love it. Wearily I take myself off to the miniscule bathroom to ready myself for the evening ahead wishing every minute would speed up to bring Connor here that much quicker.

***

I sometimes feel that I have stepped out of real life and am living in an alternative universe. I worried initially that I'd feel lonely or isolated away from the bright lights of London and the bustle of the magazine office but the serenity of the village is like being swaddled in a comfort blanket. I enjoy banter with the hard working fishermen, the farm hands who work on the farm upon which my cottage is located and I have been well looked after by the farmer and his wife. Often I open the door to find pies and stews and slabs of homemade cake on the step always with a note from Helen, the farmer's wife telling me, as ever, she's made too much. I have made friends, women I spent time with, chatting over coffee and endless cake, sharing a bowl of chips and a gossip in the pub. They are not confidants, not like Erin, Imogen or Henry, but welcome acquaintances with whom I can happily spend the evening with. Sometimes I wonder if I really do want to leave.

The temperamental water system plays ball for once and I enjoy a long, deliciously hot, bath full of scented bubbles and complimented by a cold glass of wine. The ancient CD player belts out disco tunes and I sing badly as I soap myself down, sinking under the water to rinse off. I long for Connor's touch, his soft, warm hands to stroke my skin once more. It's not just his presence I've missed, his smile, his kisses but also the demanding sexual side to him that my body is now craving. I resist the urge to touch myself, ignoring the burning, heavy ache that has increased painfully over recent days, that now needs a release. I smile to myself thinking back over the erotic skype conversations we've had, the promises and demands made and I long for tomorrow.

I wrap a towel around myself and vigorously blast my hair with the hairdryer. Once teased into loose curls I select a fitted lilac dress from the wardrobe and my favourite pair of black louboutins. I will be horribly overdressed for the local pub but there is still so much of the London girl in me that would rather go naked than wear wellies out on a Friday night. I make up my face and with a final spritz of perfume I am ready to go.

Cautiously I make my way across the farmyard and out onto the main road. I say main road loosely, it's more of a country track complete with potholes that I have fallen down too many times to count and I totter unsteadily in the dark towards the pub.

Ivor has one pub. It's cosy and warm and always full. Once a month they have a quiz and on the second Friday of each month a band comes to the village. These nights are raucous and drunken. On the two occasions I've been to band night it's taken me two days to recover. I open the door and the heat of bodies hits me.

"Hi Freya," Trudy calls to me as I walk into the pub.

"Hi Trudy, how are you?" I grin as I wipe my shoes on the muddy mat. Either side of the door are discarded wellington boots, work boots and umbrellas. I shrug out of my coat and hang it on a peg next to waterproofs and wax jackets thinking that Erin would have a fit at the clothing of choice.

"All good thank you. The monsters are in bed, Kevin is watching the football and I have a gin so no complaints from me."

"Do you want another?" I ask. Trudy nods. I put my clutch on the table and squeeze to the bar to order two gin and tonics. Trudy is the local florist, exceptionally talented with three beautiful, energetic children and a carpenter husband. She was the first person I met when I moved and she has taken me under her wing. Trudy never pries or questions and while there was a flicker of recognition when she met me she has been very protective. The villagers know who I am but having been on the receiving end of Trudy's icy glare they have never asked me about Conner for which I am grateful.

"I love your shoes." Trudy says as I sit down. "Louboutin?"

"Yes! A very muddy pair of Louboutins." I grimace.

"You must be mad walking across the farmyard in them." Trudy comments. "If they were mine they'd be on a shelf where only I could reach them, never to be worn!"

"Shoes are made for wearing," I smile, "a bit of mud can be wiped off. I can't bring myself to come to the pub in wellies."

"It's a fishing village, everyone wears wellies."

"Not me, my friend." Trudy looks longingly at my shoes and I make a mental note to ask Carrie for some sample items. "Who's playing this evening?"

Trudy consults the flyer. "By Jovi apparently."

"That could be a recipe for disaster if Taking That were anything to go by!" I laugh, "still we have gin so we can anesthetise against the pain at least!"

"Thank god for small mercies," Trudy says. She takes a long drink. "Ah I need this. The children have been little sods today and Kevin has man flu so I am glad to be out of the house, even if the ice machine is broken so the gin is warm, it's better than being at home!" She sighs. "I need a break, a total break away from all of them before you find me hanging from a light fitting."

"Ouch." I say looking at her with concern masking my features. I may have only known her for a couple of months but Trudy is an exuberant, fun loving person whose enthusiasm infuses the atmosphere around her. To hear her talking like this is disconcerting. "What has brought this on?"

She pauses and then says. "Every so often my life seems to be not my own. I'm wiping bums or clearing up, running here and there, always for someone else, picking up after Kevin who grumbles continuously that he's tired but I'm the one who has to keep it all together. I'm knackered and I want a break from it all. I want to some me time in a health spa where someone looks after me for a change. Fancy it?"

"What?"

"Coming to a health spa with me? I know you've been working hard too, wouldn't it be nice to be fed and watered and pampered…I have some money saved up for a rainy day and after today's storm I reckon I can justify using it."

"I'd love to! Once…well you know!" I can't prevent the grin spreading across my face.

"Yeah I know you will be busy for however long but promise after he goes we'll leave here for the calm serenity of somewhere where I don't have to cook or clean a thing."

"I promise!"

"Good. I'm going to hold you to that…Oh look here come the band! Blimey their trousers are tight, do you think he'll sing falsetto!"

We get the giggles as the aging band set up on the small stage. The lights dim and I sit back in my seat as the music begins.

The band is surprisingly good, uplifting and rousing. Covering all Bon Jovi's and some of Guns n Roses they have the pub singing loudly, heads nodding in time. Trudy and I have consumed enough gin to dance along unashamedly without any feelings of self-consciousness and I find myself being swung around by one of the fishermen who last had teeth in nineteen seventy.

"I'm having so much fun." Trudy pants collapsing in the chair. "Tonight has been just what I've needed."

"Thank you for suggesting it. If you hadn't arranged this I would be climbing the walls by now."

"Oh the first flush of love, it's the most wonderful feeling. You know, for all his grumbles Kevin still does it for me. I still get butterflies when he's due home, even after ten years, three kids and endless bickering. In fact, I may have to work off his man flu!"

I grin. "You go girl!"

"What time are you expecting Connor? Can you introduce me to him? I've fancied him for years." She clamps her hand over her mouth. "Oh hell, now it'll be weird."

"No it won't!" I laugh at her embarrassment. "Your secret is safe."

"I think I'm drunk."

"I know I am! Shall we go?" I ask getting wobbly to my feet. "I need to look sensational tomorrow."

"You always look sensational." Trudy says. "I look like a bag of spanners."

"Look in the mirror woman, you're gorgeous!" I take her arm and we give jovial goodbyes to the revellers as we leave. Trudy and I part at the end of the lane.

"Goodnight and thanks Trudy, I've had a lot of fun."

"Night Freya, have a great weekend. I'll see you when you come up for air." She laughs and I blow her a kiss before turning into the farmyard and towards my little cottage.

SATURDAY

I don't sleep well. Every time I fall asleep I have dreams about Conner. Dark dreams, nightmares. The kind of dreams that make a person wake in a cold sweat too scared to try and return to sleep. He is calling out to me and I can hear pain ringing in his voice and see agony deeply etched in his beautiful eyes but when I reach for him he's not there. By 4 am I am so disturbed that I get up and walk down to the beach to wait for the dawn. It's a bleak dawn. The cloud cover is so dense that the sun is barely visible. I feel so wretched that my head aches excruciatingly and my eyes burn with exhaustion.

"Freya?" I turn to see Trudy running across the beach in her dressing gown. "Freya. Oh my God I have been looking for you all over town. I tried your house and you weren't there and the news…it was all over the news…and I thought maybe you'd gone back but I saw your purse on the table so realise you must be still here. Are you alright? I can't believe it." Trudy's words are tumbling out of her mouth so fast I can hardly understand her.

"I couldn't sleep. What is the matter? You look like you've seen a ghost." I struggle to my feet.

"Have you not seen the news?"

"No. Why? Trudy you are really worrying me."

"There has been a car accident."

Conner?

"Accident?" I whisper.

"Yes in the early hours, around four I think."

Four? That's the time I finally gave up on sleep. Trudy has tears falling down her face but I feel strangely numb, like my body is shutting down to protect me from what is coming next. "What happened?" I sink woodenly to the ground, the pebbles hard and sharp under me.

"A statement has been released to say he was airlifted to a hospital in Swindon and has undergone emergency surgery.

All they are saying is that he is in a critical condition and the next few hours are crucial."

I hear a voice, mine I think, ask the question "is he going to die?" and then I give into the blackness.

***

It's a sensation rather like swimming in treacle. The heavy sticky blackness is slowly drowning me. I don't have the strength to fight with the shadows so I languish in the emptiness and stare into oblivion. There is nothing here the endless void of nothing stretches on unimaginably. The air is cold, dark and sinister but compared to the bleakness in my soul it at least has something describable.

I hear voices talking, echoing as though filtered through water. I don't want to listen to them I want the silence of my dark tomb. When I close my eyes against the murky gloom images flash like a film playing through the back of my mind. Conner. Always Conner. I see our relationship developing in fast forward – the day we met to the day we parted – in glorious high resolution colour. How beautiful he is, how I longed for him, for the excitement and the thrill, the agony of us parting each time and the euphoria of the times we came together.

What would I give for one more moment? One more smile? One kiss, one touch, one sunrise? Are we so irrevocably linked that an unseen force brought him into my dreams to call for me? The very notion that he will be taken from me makes me want to lay here in hell forever more.

I can hear the filtered sounds asking me to wake up. Then the ground begins to move in a slow, lumbering way. I am enveloped by something strong and warm but within my jumbled mind I am only aware of my pain, the deep stabbing pain of a grief I can't survive.

I want to cry out, scream, beg whoever I need to beg for Conner's life to be spared. He's twenty-five. Too young. Too much life left to live. Take me, I want to shout, take me.

There is no one listening. No one is here to come and take pain away. I hope they are with Conner keeping him safe. Oh just for one moment to tell him I love him, that I will always love him. My heart has never been opened so wide for anyone, not William or anyone else I had a passing attraction for. It has only opened for Conner. The love of my life.

The world needs him. Without Connor there is no point in the dawn or the slow turn of the earth. There is no point to dreams or hopes or the overwhelming love I have for him. There is no point in being if he's not here.

I hear whispering as I sink into softness. It's warm, comfortable and my tired, broken self gives into sleep.

***

I waken to a storm. Great rolling waves angrily throw themselves onto the beach and the wind, whipping everything in sight, is rattling my windows and whistling through the open gap. The sky is dark grey and the black clouds make sinister shadows across the landscape. It's a scene of grief, the elements livid with the gods and mirroring the agony I feel. I want to lash out, scream and cry and tell whoever is responsible for this that I condemn them to hell. Instead I rock silently feeling the tears fast flowing down my face unable to wipe them away.

My door opens and Trudy's worried face peers around. "You're awake." She looks relieved.

I cough to clear my throat. "Any news?"

"His parents have arrived from Ireland. Otherwise no."

"I want to see him." I can't stay here. I need to be near him, with him, to tell him that I love him. I have to ask him to live. To live for me, for us, for the people who put him up so high he shone like a true star.

"I don't think you'd get anywhere near him sweetie, the security is immense."

"I have to try. I'm his girlfriend"

"They don't know that." Trudy says gently.

I ignore her and force my awkward limbs to move and get out of bed. It's cold. The temperature is artic and freezes my skin. "It's so cold." I say to no one in particular.

"Freya, let me make you some food. You've been here all day. You need to eat."

"I need to go to Conner."

"Eat first. Please." Trudy looks at me imploringly.

"No thank you." I reach for her hand. "I have to go. Now!"

Trudy squeezes my hand. "I will make you something to take with you."

"You're a lovely friend, thank you."

***

I race up the motorway with no consideration of speed limits. The storm follows me, banging and waling above me as my little car reaches speeds over one hundred miles an hour. I can barely see through the windscreen as I am pelted with raindrops that fight for room on the glass. I stop once for fuel and coffee before embarking on the final leg of the journey. Arriving into the hospital at Swindon I feel exhausted and fearful.

There are press crowded in every available space outside the hospital with police preventing them from accessing the unit. Swallowing heavily I try to act confident as I push through to the entrance.

I am greeted by a security officer, a tall man with tired eyes. "Good evening Miss, are you here as a patient or visitor?"

"Visitor," I mumble.

"Who are you visiting?" He asks clicking open a computer tablet.

"Conner Robertson."

"I'm sorry miss, family only."

"I'm his girlfriend."

"I'm so sorry but you are not the first lady to tell me that this evening."

I close my eyes against the threat of tears. "I don't doubt it. My name is Freya, he calls me Red." An involuntary sob escapes me. "I have pictures of us. Would that prove who I am?" I open my eyes and stare beseechingly at him.

"I'm sorry." The security man looks like he may believe me but I turn away. Someone in the horde of press notices me and calls out "Freya! Freya over here! Anything to say? Are they not letting you in?"

"No." I shake my head. The flashes are blinding as the photographers snap away at me so I hold my hands up to my face. "Please stop," I beg calling out to them.

The security guard takes my arm and leads me into the foyer of the hospital. "Wait here," he instructs and moves away from me. I hear him talking into a mobile phone but I drift out of the conversation. I don't really hear the questions the press are calling out to me, lost as I am in my own thoughts. I just want to see Conner. Just for a moment. To hold his hand and touch his face, the beautiful face that I miss every day. I wonder how it all happened – how did he end up coming into my life. To whom do I owe my thanks for lending me him just for a brief time and to whom do I now need to beg that he will come through.

"Miss?" The security man brings me out of my thoughts.

"Yes?"

"You may go up."

I fling my arms around his neck. "Thank you." I say fiercely, "thank you."

"You're welcome," he replies unclasping my arms. "Take the lift at the end of the corridor to ICU. It's clearly sign posted. Tell the guard that McIver sent you."

"Thank you."

I hurry off to the lift.

***

The waiting room chair has seen better days. Foam is visible where the fabric has worn away and the foam itself is holey where previous sitters have picked away at it. The room is bleak with curling NHS posters peeling from the walls and a coffee machine that is only giving out hot water. The clock ticks loudly echoing around the silent room. The magazines on the coffee table are years out of date and worn. It's a sad room and the longer I sit here the more hopeless I feel.

Time just passes unending.

My phone beeps.

'*Did you arrive safely?*' It's Trudy.

'*Yes I did. I'm in the waiting room.*'

'*Good. We're all praying for him.*'

'*Thank you.*'

"Freya?" I look up to see an exhausted looking woman entering the room. She has dark hair flecked with grey and Conner's eyes.

I stand up. "Yes." I reply.

"I'm Anna, Conner's mam. They told me you were here."

"I had to come." I can't hold back the tears. "Sorry, I didn't want to cry here."

She gives me a faint smile. "We've all cried here." Anna pauses. "We wanted so much to meet you…" She falls silent and I try to stop the outpouring of tears with some very deep breathes. "We just didn't ever think it would be like this."

"How is he?" I whisper.

"He's not responding to anything. The surgery went well but he's so poorly the doctors can't make any guarantees that he will wake up." Her face crumples. "My baby," she says wringing her hands with grief in every line on her face. "He has to wake up."

I reach out for her hand. It's soft but very cold and I wrap it in both of mine. "May I see him?"

"Yes." I let go of her hand and follow her out into the corridor. The unit smells strongly of bleach which stings my nose and from everywhere comes the sounds of machines beeping. Anna leads me along the corridor to an end room outside of which is another security guard. As Anna opens the door I am suddenly fearful of what I will find on the other side of it. My legs turn to jelly and threaten to give way under me.

"Freya?"

"Yes?"

"Would you like to be alone with him?" His mother is so kind. Her soft Irish accent is warm and gentle and I feel a surge of gratitude at her compassion.

"Yes please."

"Mick come and get some coffee with me." I presume the tall man with salt and pepper hair is Conner's Dad. They look alike. He nods to me and leaves the room with Anna who says, "look after him."

I give her a brief smile then walk over to the bed. I could not have prepared for this moment. To look down on his perfect face and see deep purple bruising marring his skin. Taped to his mouth is a long clear tube attached to a beeping monitor to the side of the bed. He is perfectly still, covered in a pale blue sheet and secured in the bed by metallic sides. One arm is outside of the cover and I take his hand and hold it up to my face. "It's me," I whisper. "Can you hear me?"

I give into the tears. I cry for him, for me, for everything we have and everything we haven't yet had the chance to have. His hand becomes wet and gently I wipe it with some paper towels before wrapping it tightly between my hands.

"I miss you." I tell him in a low tone. "I have missed you every day. Please wake up Conner. The world wants you to. I want you to. Please wake up." Everything I wanted to say and now I don't remember the words. I just sit holding his hand, touching his face and gently kissing his cheek from time to time. The beeping of the machine is hypnotic and endless. After a while I begin to talk. I tell him about my life in detail describing the village, my designs and my hopes. I tell him how much I love him, I tell him how I feel. How he changed everything.

"It was so exciting Conner, the beginning and all the secrets that made me smile every day. I thrived on the thrill of you, the buzz of having something so intoxicating that no-one knew about. " I smile, "all those things we did! So sexy." I pause, "I don't know when it changed. I didn't notice that it had but suddenly I needed you. Not the secrets or the thrills just you. You became part of me and I can't be without you. Please wake up so I can tell you. Please Conner. I want to tell you that I will love you forever, that there will never be anyone else for me. You have to wake up now. Conner we all need you to wake up…" I hear my voice crack and fall silent. The machine does some high pitched beeps and a nurse rushes in. She checks the machine and pushes a red button behind the bed. Immediately an alarm sounds and in hurries medical staff. I am pushed to the back of the room as they huddle around the bed all talking in medical language I don't understand.

Someone realises I'm here and escorts me from the room shutting the door behind me. I can't breathe. In my ears I hear the pounding of my heart and the rushing of my blood. I sink onto the chair outside of Conner's room as my body begins to shake. The next minute the door crashes open and the staff run along pushing Conner's bed towards the theatre. Someone says, "we're going to lose him."

All I can do is watch them take him away.

Eleven Months Later…

I feel overwhelmed with pride as the models sashay back one by one, my dresses showcased to perfection on their curvaceous bodies. Each woman has been chosen for her attainable look and each model was someone I saw walking down the street. There are no runway models amongst them because the very ethos of *Red* is wearable clothes for all women. They all give me a warm embrace as they come off the catwalk, whispering their compliments and congratulations before they go back out to the audience for one final group walk.

The applause is deafening. I look down at my trembling hands and fail to prevent the tears of relief that begin to fall. I did it. Finally. I send a silent thank you out to the universe, a thank you that, for all the drama, dreams really do come true. Everything has been worth it. Everything makes sense now.

My name is chanted over and over, loud above the applause that is lifting the room. I take a deep breath and clasp my hands together to hide the tremors. They want me.

I step out of the shadows into the spotlight and the audience erupts further. During the dark days, sitting at the hospital, I would have traded everything, given it all up for Connor to survive. Yet no bargains were made and here I am, standing in front of the biggest names in fashion, debuting my first collection. It has been a success. All the hard work and sleepless nights, agonising over the smallest detail has culminated in this. I beam with euphoria and give a brief bow before squinting through the light for the faces I so desperately want to see. They are all here – Mum and Dad, Carrie, Henry, Erin, Imogen, Christina and Trudy – clapping wildly and wiping away their tears of pride.

The crowd erupts as a hand reaches out to clasp mine. I look up and Connor is beaming down at me, pride and love written all over his glorious face. He raises my hand to his lips and softly kisses it before he pulls me into his arms.

"I'm so proud of you, tonight has been sensational." He says quietly in my ear. "You have done it, Red, you've set the world on fire."

"I couldn't have done it without you." I say reaching my hand up to his face. "This is all because of you, because you believed in me."

"It's because of us." He corrects. "We're a force to be reckoned with aren't we?"

"Yes." I nod. "There's no stopping us now."

The audience still on their feet, still clapping and chanting my name make me feel like a superstar. I look back over to my friends, the people who stood by me and always believed in me, even when I doubted myself, the friends who picked me up each time I fell and to whom I will always be indebted. Mum is crying and Dad, pink in the face, looks beside himself with pride. How lucky I am to have had them, unconditionally, always there, always telling me to reach for the stars because they were mine for the taking.

"I don't want this night to end." I say to Connor.

"Then let's stay up until dawn," he says. "Then it won't!"

I send thanks skyward to whoever decided Connor should come into my world. Despite the hiccups and the very dark days when I didn't know if he'd live, everything has fallen into place and I cannot imagine how life could be any better. I lean into him. "Thank you Connor, thank you for believing in me."

He cups my face between his hands and says "marry me Red?"

"Yes," I squeal wrapping my arms around his neck and he kisses me, the first kiss of forever, and somewhere there is a star with our names on shooting through the sky.

X THE END X

Printed in Great Britain
by Amazon